Oar Than Friends

Lulu Moore is the creator of The New York Players Series and The Tuesday Club Series. Lulu is currently navigating her way through Romance Land one HEA at a time and trying to figure out the latest social media platform she needs to post to.

Oar Than Friends

LULU MOORE

PENGUIN BOOKS

PENGUIN BOOKS

UK | USA | Canada | Ireland | Australia
India | New Zealand | South Africa

Penguin Books is part of the Penguin Random House group of companies
whose addresses can be found at global.penguinrandomhouse.com.

First published 2024
001

Set in 12.5/14.75pt Garamond MT Std
Typeset by Jouve (UK), Milton Keynes
Printed and bound in Great Britain by Clays Ltd, Elcograf S.p.A.

The authorized representative in the EEA is Penguin Random House Ireland,
Morrison Chambers, 32 Nassau Street, Dublin D02 YH68

A CIP catalogue record for this book is available from the British Library

ISBN: 978–1–405–96582–8

www.greenpenguin.co.uk

*I'm dedicating this book to
my twenty-one-year-old self.
It's not realistic to have all the answers,
or your life mapped out, so stop trying.*

Contents

Glossary

Blue Boat – The number one boat for each of the Oxford and Cambridge University men's and women's crews

Goldie – The Cambridge number two men's boat

Blondie – The Cambridge number two women's boat

Isis – The Oxford number two men's boat

Osiris – The Oxford number two women's boat

The Cam – The river flowing through Cambridge

The Isis – The stretch of the River Thames flowing through Oxford

The Thames – The longest river in England, the main river flowing through London

The Tideway – The stretch of the River Thames in London, which is subject to tides. The Championship Course is situated on the Tideway.

The Championship Course – the Boat Race course. Four miles of the river starting at Putney Bridge and finishing at Chiswick Bridge/Mortlake

Middlesex Station – The north side of the Championship Course

Surrey Station – The south side of the Championship Course

O.U.B.C. – Oxford University Boat Club

C.U.B.C. – Cambridge University Boat Club

O.U.W.B.C. – Oxford University Women's Boat Club

C.U.W.B.C. – Cambridge University Women's Boat Club

Glossary

1. Arthur

(Auditioning for the intelligence services)

'Charlie, can you keep your bloody voice down?!' I hissed for the seventeenth time, wondering why we'd brought him along.

Then I remembered we had to, plus he was the only one who owned a collapsible ladder.

Don't ask.

'Sorry, Oz,' he whispered, leaning said ladder against the wall of the Cambridge University Boat House before turning to me.

I pressed down on the speaker in my earpiece, 'Are we all clear?'

'Clear,' replied Bitters, our five, from behind the bush where he was standing fifty metres up the River Cam to the left.

'Clear,' echoed Drake, our Canadian number four, who was in a similar spot to the right.

We were good to go.

I glanced over to Charlie, who was silently – for once – waiting for me to give the signal to begin what was considered our second most important mission for the upcoming school year; behind winning the Boat Race.

And what exactly was this mission which had eight of my Oxford crewmates and me exclusively dressed head-to-toe in black, and standing outside a place we had no business standing at any time, let alone at eleven p.m. on a Saturday night in late September?

One word, plain and simple.

Rivalry.

And before you mistake that term for a little friendly competition, stop. When it comes to this particular rivalry, I'm talking about something so deeply rooted in history it wraps itself around your bones like a boa constrictor squeezing until you're gasping for release. It's a battle of wits brought to life through generations of competitiveness flowing through our dark- and light-blue blood.

It all began nearly 200 years ago when Charles Merivale, from the University of Cambridge, challenged his old mate, Charles Wordsworth, studying three counties over at Oxford, to a race. Naturally Cambridge lost, and so began the annual rematch.

A few years after that first attempt, a wealthy parent of a winning Cambridge boy (likely down to the shock of *finally* winning) gifted the Cambridge University Boat Club a pair of golden oars. The originals, made of solid gold, were deemed too valuable – not to mention heavy – to be hanging in public and were promptly swept off to be housed somewhere safer; currently behind bullet-proof glass in the university archives like they're the *Magna Carta* or something.

In their place a pair of exceptionally less valuable, but equally important, wooden oars, painted in gold leaf, were hung above the entrance, to remind all rowers who entered the hallowed walls of the clubhouse that they would soon be part of greatness. The Cambridge crew was rightly proud of their golden oars, and word soon travelled along the meandering rowing grapevine that they existed.

There they stayed, glinting in the sunlight, until the legendary Oxford rower, Sir Henry Billingsworth – who at that point in his life was just plain old Henry – thought it would be amusing to steal them. Actually, steal is too strong a word; *'borrow for the period of one rowing season'* would be a better description. According to fable, Henry set off with eight of his crewmates on an expedition across Oxfordshire, Buckinghamshire and Bedfordshire and returned two weeks later, golden oars in tow.

In response, the Cambridge crew packed themselves up on their horse and wagon, or whatever the transport was in those days, and headed over the same roads and grassy terrain Henry had taken until they reached their destination and stole the oars right back, along with the prized Oxford University Boat Club crown. It was modelled on the crown in the Oxford University coat of arms, and kept in a case on top of the shelves of the boathouse and worn only by the president on the day he's named. Suffice to say, it was important enough to the boys that it was quite a hullabaloo to have it stolen.

Thus began the somewhat-less-famous Oxford and Cambridge University Mascot War.

Over the years, both teams became exceptionally good at making the mascot as difficult as possible to steal, just as they'd all become equally adept at out-foiling the other. In fact, if any of us decided the career direction we were heading was no longer desirable, we would all ace a job in the intelligence services.

There have only been a few years when the plans have

gone disastrously wrong, such as the great clubhouse fire of 1904; which we're still not supposed to talk about lest it bring us all bad rowing luck for the year.

Or the time the Oxford boys decided to booby trap the crown in 1973, only they didn't calculate the force of the explosives properly. It was supposed to have been akin to a loud bang, followed by the large cloud of a flour balloon popping. Instead, James Fentimen, the Cambridge number two, became disorientated by the sack full of strong white flour fogging the air around him, walked straight into a wooden column holding up the boathouse, and knocked himself out cold. He was unable to compete in races for two weeks.

At this point, both universities and the rowing federation which oversees all competition stepped in. While we would be allowed to continue with the heists, because *'it encouraged healthy competition and deepened the desire for all-round victory'*, we now had to follow a set of rules.

The rules read as follows:

1. A heist must be undertaken without any knowledge of the team being 'stolen' from. If capture takes place, mascot must remain in situ and the next race of the season is forfeited.
2. A note must be left in the empty space, so as not to be confused with a legitimate theft.
3. Any mascot not already taken back by the rightful owners must be returned no later than twenty-four hours after the Boat Race has been completed.
4. No outsiders can be involved in the heist. Rowers only, including the coxswain.

5. Only the mascot can be removed, and must be done without damage to property.
6. No booby traps.

The rules now hang in both clubhouses in full view of all rowers in the unlikely chance they might forget.

Anyway, back to the task at hand.

'Charlie, go for it.' I nodded, watching from the shadows as he shimmied up the ladder to the boathouse balcony and vaulted over the railings.

He was closely followed by Hugo Brooks, my housemate and number six, who was so tall he probably didn't need the ladder.

They each whipped out a cordless drill from their backpacks and got to work. The high-pitched screeching immediately made me wince, and I scanned the area around us for the thousandth time, searching for any sign that we were about to get caught. I moved my torch across the water, the bright yellow light bouncing back over the inky black glass, but I saw nothing except the thick bush of a fox's red tail as it darted away along the bank. The drill seemed so much louder than when we'd practised it, and I made a mental note to ask Charlie to invent a soundless one by next year. Because, rule four.

Thank God, he was a physics genius.

'Shit,' hissed Charlie, before he came in louder over the earpiece, 'Oz, they've chained the oars to the balcony railings.'

'What?'

'They've chained the oars. They're not just bolted into the plaque.'

'Hang on.' I sprinted over to the ladder, the bottom of which was being manned by Johnny Fellows and Indra Joshi, our numbers two and three respectively, and took the rungs two at a time.

Sure enough a thick black chain was wrapped around and around the spot at which the oars crossed over each other. Something Charlie wasn't happy about, given the way he was currently looking at me.

'Did we bring bolt cutters?'

Brooks nodded, 'Yeah, but what about rule five?'

'Fuck that, this is against rule six!' snapped Charlie, holding his hand up in apology before I could tell him to keep his voice down, *again*.

'I agree. They should have moved them, not chained them in place. How long will it take to cut through?'

Brooks reached behind him and pulled out a long pair of cutters, so big I wondered equally how they'd fitted in his bag, and how I hadn't noticed them already.

'A couple of minutes, I reckon.'

'Cool, go for it.' I slid back down the ladder as they got to work, and glanced at my watch. According to our practice runs, we had five minutes to go before we were out of here. We needed our getaway ready.

'Frank?' I asked down the intercom to our bow, who was more officially known as Vicomte François de Richelieu. 'Can you bring the boat around?'

'Oui, on the way now,' his response crackled down the line.

'Oz, what do you want us to do with the chain?' asked Joshi, who was trying to take it from Brooks as carefully as possible, while Fellows was now halfway up the ladder

6

with his hand out to catch the bolts holding the oars in place which Charlie was now unscrewing. Finally.

'Leave it on the floor. I don't think we can use it.'

'Okay, they're loose. Are you ready?'

'Ready.' Joshi held his hands up for Fellows to pass down the first golden oar.

He took it as carefully as he could, gently laying it into the protective oar bags we'd brought with us before taking possession of the second one.

This time when he stood up, he was holding a different set of oars; a pair of Oxford University Boat Club oars we'd had made for this moment – navy with little pink hearts scattered over them. They were passed up to Brooks and Charlie, who deftly secured them in the exact spot the golden oars had hung a minute prior. As the last bolt tightened in place I caught the soft lapping of fresh waves on the dock from the corner of my eye, and pressed down on the intercom.

'Boys, we're done. Frank's here with our ride.'

An echo of 'on the way' came over the radio.

Joshi zipped up the oar bag and carried the precious cargo over to Frank, who placed it on the floor of the large dinghy we'd brought with us, and stepped in to take his position. Bitters and Drake followed, with Fellows close behind. I waited until Brooks and Charlie were safely at the bottom of the ladder, then pulled the navy envelope addressed to Will Norris, Cambridge University Boat Club President, from my inside breast pocket.

The soft click of the ladder retracting told me it was time. I stuck the letter to the pale-blue boat club doors, and grinned into the darkness picturing Will's face when he saw it.

'Oz, hurry up.'

I jogged to the boat, turning just before I stepped inside so I could snap a picture of our victory.

'Everyone here? Bitters, Charlie, Drake, Joshi, Brooks, Fellows, Frank?' Each of the guys raised their hand as I called them. 'Right, let's go.'

We picked up the dinghy oars and powered the eight of us through the dark Cam waters. We'd rowed together so long we moved on instinct, balancing out the boat to make us as streamlined as possible, and soon we'd travelled around the bend in the river so the club house was no longer in sight. I felt the collective sigh of relief from each of us, colliding with the buzz of adrenaline still coursing through my body.

Charlie clung onto his ladder from where he was sitting behind Brooks, 'They're going to be sick we got there first. Knobheads.'

I smirked, 'Yeah. They are. But we're going for the double this year, boys.'

There were seven quiet scoffs of agreement.

The double; an additional challenge I'd set myself as this year's president.

So named, because the season was considered a double if the winning crew still maintained possession of the opposition's mascot by the Boat Race. And not that I was counting – okay, I was – but in two hundred years, it had only been achieved thirty-four times, and not since 2017 when Duke Harper, an American PhD student, led Oxford to triumph.

Additionally, after the devastating loss of last year, I was more determined than ever to bring home a win. As far as I was concerned, we would not be losing either under any circumstances, which was why I'd had the boys training for the heist all month long.

A third, slightly more selfish reason was that after experiencing the worst summer in the history of summers, I needed to get back to the normality of student life and figure out how to put off the inevitability of my future without my father murdering me in my bed.

Another minute of silent rowing and I hit the intercom for the final, most crucial element of this evening's achievements: alerting Pete Sackville-Marsh, our coxswain/getaway driver, that we were on the approach to where he was currently sitting in our plain black mini-bus, under the bridge, ready to whisk us back to Oxford. Or whisk the eight of them away.

I had other plans.

'Marshy, we're three minutes out.'

'Copy,' came his response.

I grabbed my phone and shot off a text to my best friend.

Oz: *See you for beers in twenty minutes.*

Olly: *Let yourself in, slight change of plans. Just about to enjoy some quality time with a lady I met earlier this evening. I'll be back in a couple of hours.*

I rolled my eyes, slipping my phone back into my pocket, unsure why I'd expected him to respond any differently. It was more of a surprise he'd responded at all. Oliver Greenwood was a ladies' man, through and through. He had been since the year we turned thirteen, and Eton held its first school social with Cheltenham Ladies College,

9

and fifty per cent of the girls had promptly fallen in love with him. Unfortunately for them, he'd only had eyes for Victoria Medley, a girl two years above us.

They'd spent the school year writing letters to each other and meeting up during the holidays; that was until he met someone else while visiting his eldest sister who was on a gap year travelling through Europe. And so began his journey into becoming the certified heart-breaker he is today.

Friends since boarding school, Olly is the only person in the world who knew I'd wanted to attend Cambridge to read English, instead of Oxford to read economics just like my father, and my father's father and his father's father. As it was, the only form of rebellion I could muster was shunning economics for classics, so at least I could find some refuge with the ancient Roman and Greek heroes who'd managed to topple their overbearing fathers while I still figured out how to deal with mine.

'Marshy's in place,' whispered Brooks, just as I spotted the Morse code flash of a torch in the darkness ahead of us.

The dinghy slowly bore to the left until the slight sil-houette of our coxswain solidified.

'Hello, chaps,' Pete grinned, his straight white teeth glinting in what little light there was as he waded into the shallow waters and tugged on the rope Charlie threw him. 'Fancy seeing you here.'

The eight of us jumped out, working together to pull the dinghy into shore. I grabbed the oars case and placed it in the mini-bus, then switched my wet sneakers and socks for dry ones while the others got to work rapidly deflating the dinghy with a contraption Charlie had adapted from a household vacuum cleaner. Something else he needed to make quieter by next year. It was hard enough to keep incognito with eight guys all over six foot three, without the additional noise pollution on top.

I closed the back door as softly as I could, and rubbed my hands together. 'Nice work tonight, boys. I'm feeling good about this year. Feeling very good.'

'Yeah,' Bitters nodded, ducking his head as he climbed into the bus, 'and we should be back by just after one. Might even catch last orders at the pub if we're lucky.'

I grinned, 'Make sure those oars are put away safely before you start drinking.'

'Aye-aye, Mr President.'

'Oz, you not getting in with us?'

I shook my head, 'No, I'll see you back at the house tomorrow. I'm going to catch up with Olly.'

'Cool. Tell him he still owes me a pint.'

'Arthur Osbourne-Cloud, it's been a pleasure serving under you this evening,' saluted Charlie dramatically as he jumped into the passenger seat.

I snorted as a wry smile curled up my lip, 'Get going, don't want you hanging around here with stolen property.'

I waited for the engine to start, watching until it drove off out of sight, because I half expected the Cambridge crew to lynch us as we left, but there was no one around. Not even the loud *toot-toot* of the mini-bus horn could break the grin I was currently sporting.

I turned and took off up the hill, jogging across the common until I was far away from the scene of the crime.

Win one for Oxford.

2. Kate

(Colin Firth wouldn't have spoken to me like that)

I stifled the yawn, though not well enough given the nudge I received in my ribs.

'Sorry,' I smiled sheepishly at the group of girls I was sitting with, particularly Imogen whose elbow I could still feel against my side, 'jet lag.'

I wasn't about to admit the two glasses of wine I'd drunk tonight had immediately gone to my head and were making me feel much less alert than I had when I'd sat down. Even the charm and cuteness of this movie-set-style British pub, with its thick beams and wooden bar top so shiny you could see your face in it, wasn't enough to keep me awake. But that's what happened when you were fresh over from the United States where it was still illegal for you to be consuming any alcohol at all. Not that this was the first time I'd ever drunk, it just wasn't as easily accessible without my cousins buying it for me, or a fake ID; something I had never had the inclination nor interest to make. I was not about to risk putting my scholarship in jeopardy.

I'd touched down at Heathrow two days ago, then proceeded to get incredibly lost trying to find the exit, and the Heathrow Express. The instructions I'd meticulously written down and pored over for the entirety of the week before, as well as the seven hours I'd been awake on the flight from Boston, had been for nothing. I was a some-what intelligent woman, on her way to Cambridge University to study medicine, but how anyone navigated themselves around the London Underground network without being a member of Mensa was beyond me.

By the time I'd arrived at Downing College, my home for the next six years, I was a weary, dishevelled mess. It had taken a hot shower, twelve hours of sleep, an apple I'd rescued from the bottom of my backpack, and a deep breath of fresh English air as I'd opened my window the next morning to feel somewhat human again.

Further pep had been added to my step when I made my way past the thick green striped lawns of the quad-rangle, passing by more of the ancient, butter-coloured brick university buildings and down to the Downing College boathouse, where I met with Matthew Prendergast, the coxswains' representative, a third-year student I'd been emailing with for a month.

I looked around at the small group of girls Matthew had introduced me to after we'd returned from a short session on the river. All six of them were members of the boat club and I'd soon discovered that, like me, they had spent years on the river before joining Cambridge.

Our friendship was too fresh, however, for me to ascertain what brought them to the water. For me it was the peace, the stillness and the escapism from reality. Not to mention the rowing scholarship I'd been offered on top of my medical scholarship as an added incentive to cross the Atlantic, instead of staying at my local state col-lege. There was also the vast difference in affordability between the two to consider.

Even with all the empty bottles and glasses scattered on the table in front of us, we'd only discussed what everyone was studying – English, law, medicine and physics – and who was going to try out for the Cambridge University Boat Club – all of us – because while rowing for our individual colleges was great, rowing for the university was the end game and meant we were in with a chance to compete in the Boat Race. This led on to the topic of why the Oxford team was the *'absolute worst and must be beaten on all accounts'*, but the majority of the conversation had revolved around the new *'super hot, but next level arrogant'* Oxford University President, and the fact that the Cambridge boys were currently plotting how to steal the Oxford mascot. I couldn't be certain, but I didn't think even Yale and Harvard went to these lengths.

'Did you guys hear there's more space on the crew this year because of what happened last year?' asked Imogen. 'We might all be in with a good chance of making the squad.'

'What happened last year?' I asked.

'According to my sister, two of the girls were kicked off the crew for fraternizing with the Oxford boys. Mary Heston lodged a complaint.'

'Who's that?'

'She's just been made women's president, and takes her duties very seriously. She'd probably have you kicked out of the university for so much as looking at one of the Oxford boys.'

My eyes widened. 'Seriously?'

'Don't get on her bad side,' Ivy muttered from her seat at the end of the table.

It soon became harder to keep up with the conversation flying around the table, which is when the yawning occurred.

'Ugh, poor you,' replied Imogen sympathetically, 'I hate jet lag. It's much worse when you're flying from west to east too, the overnight is a killer.'

I nodded, though I had nothing to base that nod on seeing as the first time I'd flown anywhere was two days ago.

I was unable to stifle the next yawn, 'I think I'm going to go back. I'm pretty beat, but this has been awesome. Let me know if you want to go down to the river in the morning.'

Imogen stood up and wrapped me in a warm, friendly hug, 'I'll knock on your door tomorrow. Sleep well, Kate.'

Imogen's hug was followed by Hannah's who, unlike Imogen and me, wasn't studying medicine, she was studying physics, then Sarah, the two Annas and Ivy. The hugging took almost as long as it did to order another round of drinks, which arrived just as I left. I was certain I'd never been hugged so much in my life by people I barely knew, though I could also admit that I kind of liked it. A lot.

I pushed my way out through a throng of revelling students who'd returned from their vacations glowing with rest and summer tans, into the still-warm, late-September air. Making my way up the cobbled street, lit with the kind of tall ornate lamps you saw in Charles Dickens movies, I pulled my phone out and hit speed-dial on the one person I knew would want to hear my voice, trying hard to swallow down the lump of homesickness in my throat as she answered.

'Hi, Mom.'

'Baby, hi, I was just thinking about you. How was your first day?' she sing-songed, like I wasn't 3,000 miles away and she hadn't said I could only attend Cambridge if I promised to call home a minimum of once a day.

'It was good, I met some girls from the boat club, and we went to the pub.'

'The pub? Oh, you're sounding English already. Has Mr Darcy whisked you off your feet yet?'

She didn't see my eye roll, but she heard the soft laugh I let out. 'Not yet, Mom. Don't hold your breath either. Between study and rowing, I'm not sure there's time for Mr Darcy. It's going to be busy.'

'There's always time, Katey, my girl. Romance makes time.'

I waited for a bicycle to pass by, then hurried across the road and along the passageway leading past the Business School and up toward Downing.

'How's your day? How's Dad?'

My mom paused, and I braced myself for the worst. 'He's okay, he had a rough day today. It's quieter around here now you're both gone.'

I stopped walking, waiting for the searing pain in my chest to subside as I tried to swallow down a new lump which had appeared in my throat. I shouldn't have had that second glass of wine; it wasn't helping the guilt or the control I usually had over my emotions when it came to my big brother.

'I know he can't wait to hear about how you're doing, he's so proud of you, Katey. We both are. Jake would be too. It's a wonderful thing you're doing, everyone thinks so.

I was down at the bakery yesterday and they were all talking about it.'

'Thanks, Mom.' I pinched the end of my nose, trying to hold in the sniff I desperately needed to make.

I wanted her words to make me feel better, but they didn't. Cambridge was a stupid idea. I should have stayed home, I should have gone to UConn and studied there. Travelling this far away was selfish when they needed me.

Then I remembered why I'd come here in the first place, and the pain twisted so hard it was near excruciating.

'Mom, I've got to go, but I'll call you tomorrow, okay?'

'Okay, baby. I love you.'

'I love you, too.' I managed to choke out before I hung up.

Whatever had been stuck in my throat barrelled up with the force of a freight train, culminating in a loud, rasping sob which had me doubled over and falling back against the wall I'd stopped next to.

It had been three years and I still hadn't gotten a lid on my emotions; the profound emptiness I felt whenever I thought about Jake and the unexpected heart attack which had taken him from us at nineteen years old.

Jake was why I was here in Cambridge.

Jake was why I was studying medicine.

Jake was why I spent any spare minute I had in the stern of a shell.

I stood up, wiping my sleeve under my nose, then wiped my eyes as I tried to remember the way back. Crying over Jake would not be the reason I'd get lost in a new city.

'Left, left, right, left,' I muttered as I turned the corner and found myself once more staring at the wide expanse of lawn in front of the majestic Downing College. It was a moonless night, only the stars lighting the way, and the pale stone of the building looked eerie in the faint lamps lining the gravel path.

It was still hard to believe that I was really here. That I would be . . .

'Ahhhhhhh!' My yelp echoed around the quadrangle as I jumped up from the grass I'd suddenly found myself falling almost face first onto, and spun around to see what exactly had cushioned my fall.

'Arrrrgggh . . . my . . . fucking . . . balls . . . arrrggh . . . what the fuck?!' grunted the lump rolling around by my feet, making a noise that was more reminiscent of a wounded animal than a human.

Yet, on closer inspection, it was indeed a human. A human man, in fact. A very large human man dressed entirely in black.

I forgot my shock and stared, unblinking, at the sight in front of me.

After leaning across to tap his shoulder, I stood up with clenched fists because something had stopped me before I reached out and *actually* touched him.

'Um . . . are you okay?' I asked, and rolled my eyes at my stupidity because it was clear he wasn't.

Another minute of him curling into the foetal position wheezing deeply and it was becoming a little old. Mr Darcy wouldn't have made such a fuss.

Then I remembered I was a med student and should show a little more concern and compassion.

'Excuse me, can I get you help? Is there anything I can do?'

'You've done enough, I'd say,' he grunted from the

ground where he was now on all fours, his clipped English accent adding an unnecessary bluntness to his words. 'Jesus Christ, you need to ask a man before you punch him in the balls.'

'I'm so sorry . . . it was an accident. I didn't see you.'

'Well, you should be more careful and pay attention to where you're going,' he snapped.

Two glasses of wine coupled with homesickness and the emotions I hadn't had time to bury, which were still bubbling directly under the surface of my skin, had my usual endless patience snapping like a piece of candy cane.

'What did you expect? It's not my fault you were lying in the dark, dressed entirely in black, on a lawn you're not supposed to be walking on!' I pointed aggressively to the sign-post on the path instructing exactly that.

'Then why are you walking on it if you know you're not supposed to?'

I opened my mouth to argue back, then closed it. There was a reason I hadn't taken law, and it was my inability to construct a valid argument.

'Okay, well . . . um . . . you're obviously okay. I'm going to get going.' I thumbed behind me, not that he saw as he was yet to look at me.

'That's right, debilitate me and take off.'

'What exactly do you want me to do?' I stropped.

'Did you just stamp your foot?'

It was at this point that he turned his head to face me, a curl of dark hair flopping to one side as he did, and for the first time I had a good look at him, a really *good* look, and was rendered speechless. I scowled down at my chest as it gave a little flutter.

I wasn't sure if it was due to the dim light, but his eyes – as pale turquoise as the Cambridge colours – glistened like stars in a clear night sky. His ruler-straight jaw line had unclenched slightly, but I could still see it twitching under the thick stubble coating his skin and doing nothing to disguise the rest of his face – sharp cheekbones, a full, luscious mouth, and a wide Roman nose as though he had arrived here direct from the studios of Michelangelo, chiselled by the master himself.

Woah.

I could confidently say he was easily the best-looking, scratch that, most beautiful man, nope, scratch again, the most beautiful human being I'd ever seen.

Captivating, hypnotizing and altogether entirely unsettling.

It was so unsettling that I failed to notice he was looking at me with exactly the same expression.

He cleared his throat and rolled into a sitting position, lengthening out his legs and resting back on his elbows. From the way his eyes travelled up my body, he may as well have taken a blow torch to my skin for how it was burning under his gaze.

'Tell me a story while my reproductive organs stop throbbing. What are you doing here so far away from home?'

I blinked at him, altogether confused at this sudden change in direction. His voice had gone from an irritated snap to almost a purr, coating my skin like thick molasses.

'What?'

'Your accent. American, if I'm not mistaken.'

'Oh, yes,' I frowned, 'I'm from America.'

He sat up enough to wave one arm around, 'And what, exactly, brought you to this esteemed and hallowed centre of education?'

Esteemed and hallowed centre of education? Jeez.

Did all Brits speak like him? But then I noticed the bottle of gin lying by his side. His eyes followed mine and he picked it up, unscrewing the cap before holding it in the air to me.

'Come on, Yankee Doodle. Sit down, have a drink.'

I'd never crossed my arms so quickly over my chest. 'What did you call me?'

'Yankee Doodle.' He grinned, either not noticing or not caring that I was still frowning at him. 'Now sit down, you owe me.'

'For what?'

'Rendering me infertile, for one.'

'Don't be stupid,' I scoffed with all the confidence of a first-year student who was yet to start her medical degree.

His response was to simply wave the bottle at me.

'Fine.' I snatched it and took a large gulp before I had a chance to think any further about what I was doing.

The gin burned all the way to my belly, and I sat down in front of him with a thud while he continued to stare at me with a curious smirk tipping his lip. I couldn't be certain it was the gin that had my insides flip-flopping.

'Come on then,' he said finally, pushing long fingers through his hair.

'What?'

'Why are you here? America has universities, does it not? Good ones if I recall.' He brought the bottle to his mouth and swigged it, the shadows of his dark stubble

21

highlighting the sharp line of his jaw as his neck tipped back.

'Okay. I'll tell you, if you tell me why you're lying out here dressed like you're auditioning for the CIA.'

'A question for a question.' He scratched at his beard. 'Okay, you're on.'

I took another sip of gin before I could stop myself, 'I got a scholarship to study medicine, so here I am about to start my first year. Now your turn.'

'Medicine, eh? Am I going to be able to provide children in my future?'

'Is that your question?' I raised my eyebrow, only for him to do the same, 'I think you'll be fine.'

He crossed his legs. I wasn't sure if his wince was for dramatic effect but I chose to ignore it anyway.

'What was your question again?' he asked.

I waved my hand along the length of his body. 'Why are you lying out here with a bottle of gin, dressed like a spy? Are you sure you're okay?'

His deep laugh rippled across me like a breeze over still waters. 'I'm fine, current injury notwithstanding. I'm waiting for my friend to come back. Now, I wanted to know why you came to Cambridge, instead of attending an American university, which I suspect you knew.'

I grinned back at him; he wasn't just a pretty face.

But then I hesitated, because I'd already let my emotions spill over once this evening. Even with the distraction of this current situation playing out, the call with my mom was still far too close to the surface for me to divulge 'why Cambridge?' to a stranger.

I couldn't tell if he'd noticed my unease, but he shifted

forward and loudly cracked his knuckles, 'Okay, let's start with an easy one. What's your name?'

I smiled softly, 'Kate. Kate Astley.'

'Well, Kate Astley. It's good to meet you.'

I grinned, waiting for the tell as I studied his face, expecting another quip about me ruining his chances to procreate, but nothing. 'I can't even tell if you're lying.'

He picked up the gin, holding it to his lips while he held my gaze, 'I don't lie.'

As he tipped the bottle back, I rubbed away the odd fluttering sensation taking place in my chest. Or tried to. It didn't seem to want to move.

'Now my dick doesn't feel like it's about to fall off, I can genuinely say it's good to meet you. I'm Oz.'

'Like the Wizard of?'

'Ha, maybe. I like that.' He barked out a laugh. 'Want to take a ride down my Yellow Brick Road?'

From the casual curl of his lip it was clear he was trying to get a rise out of me, but it didn't stop the heat flushing through my body, or the highly inappropriate and thoroughly distracting images of him flickering in my brain.

'No,' I scoffed, lifting the gin bottle to my lips and praying he didn't notice my shaking hand.

A cool breeze whipped across the quadrangle, rustling through the trees around us, and had me rubbing away the goosebumps along my arms. Not that it helped, especially when Oz reached behind his head to pull his sweater off, and hand it to me. I tried to look away as his t-shirt rode up, revealing a taut stretch of deeply bronzed skin and what I had no doubt was an impressive set of abs.

Suddenly I was no longer cold. Where was a bottle of water when you needed one?

I shook my head, 'No, I can't take that. I'm fine. It's just a little cool air, and I'm jet lagged and tired. I should probably head home.'

Yes, that was definitely the sensible plan. Go home. Go to bed. Not stay here in my borderline drunk state with a stranger, even if I didn't want to be anywhere else.

'It's fine, I run hot. Put it on, then you can stay until Olly gets here.'

'Who's Olly?'

'A friend.' He pointed to the sweater I was now holding. 'Put it on, Kate Astley. Do as you're told.'

I snorted, but did as ordered and my senses were immediately assaulted by the most hedonistic, earthy man scent twined with the softest cashmere brushing against my bare arms. I could wear this sweater for the rest of my life, and I'd die happy.

'Thank you,' I murmured, 'I'm sorry about hurting you.'

'I'm sorry I was lying in your path.' He grinned back, his wide mouth spreading across his face, showing off straight white teeth.

Once more I found myself thinking that he was the most beautiful person I'd ever seen.

He lay back on the grass and patted the space next to him. 'Come and join me down here.'

Suddenly the weariness I'd felt back in the bar vanished in the breeze still moving through the air, and I felt more alert than I had in a long time. Longer than I could remember. I also wasn't entirely sure what I thought I was doing.

I should be going to bed. I had work to do tomorrow. I'd arranged to meet my new friends down at the boat club. Not to mention it was past midnight. I didn't think I'd seen midnight since I was old enough to realize Santa wasn't real and didn't have to wait up for him anymore.

But for the second time in as many minutes I did as I was told.

'I'm reading classics. Third year,' he said, once I'd laid my head on the soft ground.

'You're studying classics?'

'Yes. You know, the fall of Rome and analyzing Ancient Greek literature in my spare time. *Veni, vedi, vici* and so forth.'

I frowned into the darkness. 'Huh.'

'That's all you have to say?'

I shrugged to myself; he was not what came to mind when you thought of a classics student. I lumped classics students with those studying geography and history, wearing tweed with elbow patches while swirling brandy around a glass and talking about how great they were. No classics student I'd ever imagined looked like the one lying next to me.

The one who could easily pass as a quarterback for any NFL team, having fallen directly out of a Ralph Lauren ad.

'What made you want to study classics?'

He paused, moving his hands underneath his head, his elbow brushing against my shoulder as he did. 'Have you ever felt like you're living your life to the beat of someone else's drum? Like someone else has the strings and you're just along for the ride? I guess I wanted to beat my own drum for once.'

25

I lay there in silence, absorbing his cryptic words, letting them really sink in and work their way through my body.

Since my brother had died suddenly, my life had taken itself on an unplanned trajectory – one I was only too happy to go along with at the time, because I wanted to do whatever I could to help my parents through their grief, make them proud. But recently I'd felt displaced, the equilibrium had been off, and I'd put it down to leaving home and travelling to a new country.

Except in the back of my head, I knew that hadn't been it. That it wasn't the explanation I'd been searching for.

Now this stranger next to me had summed up in thirty seconds what I'd been trying to figure out for the best part of the last few months.

It was like he was reading my mind, my heart and most likely my soul. Perhaps he knew exactly how I was feeling. Because he felt it, too.

Oz shot up like a rocket as I sniffed into the darkness. 'Hey, Kate Astley, why are you crying?'

I shook my head, unable to form the words while he reached out, and with the soft pad of his thumb brushed away an errant tear escaping down my cheek.

'My brother died a couple of years ago. He went to bed on the Wednesday and never woke up. He'd gone into cardiac arrest, and no one had been around to help him. Jake . . . that's his name . . . he's . . . he *was* so smart, the brains of the family, and the day before he died he'd been offered a full scholarship to study here. My parents were so proud of him.' I sat up, it was becoming harder to talk with the backlog of tears blocking my airways, and found myself almost face to face with Oz.

26

I took a deep breath. 'In the autopsy they discovered his heart hadn't been beating properly, and it faltered. I was sixteen, I didn't know what to do. My big brother had died, my parents were grieving, and I was starting my sophomore year of high school. I found myself changing my courses to follow what Jake was going to do. I'd planned to stay in the States and study, because I never thought I'd ever get accepted here, plus it's about ten times the cost. But I worked my butt off for three years, and somehow was awarded a scholarship, and now I'm here . . .' my voice trailed off into the dark.

I wiped my sleeve across my face, then remembered the sleeve didn't belong to me and offered an apologetic smile to Oz, who just looked sorrowful. The amused, borderline arrogant quirk of his lip which had been on permanent display since I'd met him was gone.

'I'm so sorry to hear that. I can't imagine how that must feel. Can I ask you a question?'

I chuckled quietly, 'A question for a question, right?'

'If he hadn't died would you have still come here to study medicine?'

I shook my head. 'No.'

'What would you have done instead?'

My face screwed up in an obvious cringe, 'It's dumb.'

'Nothing's dumb, but now you have to tell me.'

I looked down at the half-empty bottle of gin. I could always blame my loose tongue on that, though I knew the alcohol had nothing to do with spilling my secrets to a stranger, or maybe only a little.

'Okay, but don't judge.'

He held his palms out to me, 'I swear.'

A small grin made an appearance as I thought about it. 'I'm from the east coast, a little village up the northern Connecticut shoreline. My dad is a fisherman, he has a business fishing for oysters and lobsters. I had planned to study business, then open a restaurant in the harbour which sold them. I wanted to make the best lobster rolls in the state.'

Oz stared at me until I was almost shrinking under his scrutiny.

'I told you it was dumb.'

Then his bright blue eyes widened. 'Are you kidding! It's the best idea! I fucking love lobster, and oysters! There's a place I go with my family in Cornwall. I'll have to take you some time, I bet it's like Connecticut.'

I laughed, 'Where's Cornwall?'

He waved his hand dismissively, 'Right down at the very bottom of England. Miles away. But I'll take you.'

He sounded so determined, it was easy to believe every word which passed his perfect lips. I wanted to know more about him, where this determination and certainty came from. It wasn't arrogance, it was the confidence of knowing he could achieve whatever he set his mind to. Jake had been like that.

'Isn't it a bit early to start planning dates? Not to mention, we're both going to be very busy studying.' I glanced at my watch. 'Save for the fact we've only known each other an hour.'

'Nothing's too early when it comes to planning your dreams,' he grinned.

'What about your dream?'

'My dream?'

'Yes, the classics dream. What are you going to do with it?'

He shuffled about, uncurling his legs and stretching them back out so they were almost surrounding me. 'I've always wanted to be a teacher.'

'A teacher? Like, in a school?'

He nodded, his mouth rolling into a straight line, 'Yep.'

I frowned, that seemed simple enough. 'Why can't you?'

'Ahhh,' he took a deep breath and rubbed the back of his neck, easing whatever tension had just made a home there, 'because of the expectation of family tradition.'

I stared, my eyebrow raised until he understood that he needed to elaborate on his answer.

'I come from a long line of politicians, and I'm expected to follow.'

'And you don't want to?'

'I'd rather have my fingernails pulled out.'

I tipped my head back with a loud laugh, until I saw that he wasn't joking. Like, really wasn't joking. 'Oh no, Oz, I'm sorry. Is there nothing you can do?'

He shook his head, 'Nope. I'm planning to study for as long as I can – the longer I'm here the less opportunity to force me into politics. If I can't teach, I'll end up as Britain's best-known classicist with any luck.'

'That really sucks.' I put my hand over his, then whipped it away just as quickly.

'It does.' Oz picked my hand back up and held it firm.

This time he laughed with me, his eyes boring into mine as he did, and it became impossible to look away. Out of nowhere, the cool air became hot and sticky. Cloying.

A bead of sweat rolled down between my shoulder blades.

He glanced at his thumb brushing back and forth along mine, and when our eyes met again I swear I saw a fire blazing behind his.

'Did you know that according to Greek mythology, humans were born with two heads and four arms and legs? Zeus, sitting on his throne in Olympus, became worried that humans were going to be strong enough to overpower the Gods, and so split them down the middle. Ever since, humans have searched the earth for their other half. Their soulmate.'

I think I stopped breathing. I was absolutely certain he was much closer to me than he had been when he'd started talking about soulmates, at least his face was. His mouth was.

I definitely didn't breathe when he reached out and tucked a strand of hair behind my ear, running his thumb over my cheek as his fingers curled around the nape of my neck. The gold of the ring on his pinky cooled a tiny patch of my burning skin.

'I thought my night was good before you came along but now I realize that it was simply average, bordering on mundane.' If it was possible, his voice had dropped an octave; deep and rumbly and hitting me straight in my core.

I could barely manage a whisper.

'And now?'

'Now it's the best fucking night of my life, or it will be when I kiss you.'

'You're going to kiss me?'

'Yes, I am. So if you don't want me to, I'd say you have about a second and a half to get going.'

I didn't move a muscle. Not a single one.

He was so close to me I could almost breathe in the carbon dioxide he was expelling, and my heart was banging so hard I wondered if my ribs were still intact. Then his lips, his soft, perfect lips, the ones I'd found myself staring at for the past hour, pressed against mine.

'There you fucking are!' a voice boomed to our left. 'I've been calling you!'

The groan Oz let out was not the good type of groan, and he muttered something I didn't catch. I was so caught up in the haze of lust and the feel of Oz's lips against mine that it took me a second to realize there was someone standing over us.

I'd have scooched back further if Oz didn't still have an iron-tight grip on my hand.

'Impeccable timing as always, Oliver.'

'Sorry, am I interrupting?'

Oz got to his feet, offering me his other hand, and pulled me to standing. 'Yes.'

I looked up at our interruption. Not as tall as Oz, nor as broad; with light brown hair and a round face, but with the same, almost lazily carefree expression as he peered over at me.

'Oliver Greenwood, this is Kate Astley, my new American friend. Say hello, Oliver.'

'Hello, Oliver,' he replied with the type of grin I'd imagine got him out of a lot of trouble, or into it.

'Kate, this is Oliver. Please don't fall in love with him.'

My head snapped up to Oz, and I was about to start

laughing except he was looking at me with utmost seriousness, 'What?'

'All girls fall in love with him. I'm asking you not to.'

My brow furrowed as I glanced at this other man standing in front of me, wondering how anyone would or could possibly notice anything else when Oz was in the vicinity.

Oliver's grin widened as he looked between the two of us. 'Clearly not all girls, Osbourne.'

'I'm just saying, you interrupted our first kiss; I'd like to at least have a chance for Kate to fall in love with me before you swoop in. Though if you do, I'm afraid I'd have to break your face.'

I pointed behind me. 'Okay, while you boys make decisions for me, I'm going to bed.'

'Alone?' snorted Oliver, earning himself a punch in the shoulder.

'No, you don't have to leave.' Oz squeezed my hand, which was still in his.

'I should. I'm tired.'

'Let me walk you to your dorm.'

I shook my head, firmly. 'I'm fine, honestly. Go with your friend. You've been waiting all night for him.'

'I think, perhaps, I was waiting for someone else,' he whispered, reaching into his pocket to pull out his cell and offer it to me. 'Give me your number.'

Without hesitation I punched it in and placed the phone back on his open palm.

Oz looked over to Oliver, who had the decency to step away, then bent down and brushed his lips all too briefly over mine. 'To be continued.'

I began walking, only turning once to find him in the same spot I'd left him, and I knew without looking again that he stayed there until I was out of sight.

It was as I unlocked my door that I realized I was still wearing his sweater, and I took that deep breath I'd held off earlier.

Then another.

And when I woke up the next morning I was still holding it.

3. Arthur

(Early mornings are not a strong point for anyone)

Arthur: *Have you seen her?*
Oliver: *No.*
Arthur: *Can you find her?*
Oliver: *I'm not James Bond.*
Arthur: *Please?*
Oliver: *I thought you didn't want her falling in love with me.*
Arthur: *Twat. You're the worst best friend.*

Instead of the buzz from another message, a shrill ring sounded out because Olly had quickly gotten bored from typing.

'Mate, just text her!'

I groaned in response, mostly because I'd run out of words to use. My brain had been working overtime recently.

'Why are your knickers twisting over her?'

'They're not . . . it's just . . . on top of everything else.'

'Arthur, you deserve some fun. You've had a bullshit few months, except the time you spent with yours truly, obviously. You've got, what . . . an hour of lectures a week and seventy-five thousand hours of rowing? I'm sure you can squeeze in a couple of trips up the M40 to see a girl you haven't stopped talking about for three days. At this point it almost feels like I'm the one who wants to date her,' he grumbled.

I ignored the vicious and uncharacteristic pang of jealousy, and shoved away any unwelcome thoughts from his final point.

Three days. Jesus, it felt like a lifetime.

Technically it was less than that; fifty-six hours to be precise.

Fifty-six hours, and I'd thought about her for every single one. Even the few hours I'd tossed and turned in fitful sleep her eyes had swum through my brain. Because there was no way I could ever forget those eyes.

Brilliant green, like the luckiest clover, and edged with delicate cobalt flecks; from the moment I'd turned to see her standing over me I hadn't been able to look away. For that brief second, the pain searing through my body after she'd trampled on me had been forgotten, like she was the antidote to all ailments.

I still hadn't figured out which had shaken me more; having my balls squashed or seeing her for the first time.

She was undoubtedly the most beautiful woman I'd laid eyes on. Almost doll-like, with a slightly upturned button nose, thick walnut-coloured hair and a deep-set dimple on her right cheek that sank further when she'd smiled at me, but with a fierceness that flashed across her features the longer I stared at her. A fierceness which told me she had no clue who I was. That she hadn't spent the summer reading about the sordid escapades of my dreadful father, or somewhat heartbroken mother, splashed across the front pages of every national newspaper, searchable with the click of a button.

That as far as she was concerned, I was just a guy she'd fallen over, and was kind of annoyed at.

She was a breath of the cool Cambridge air which had been breezing around us.

I'd always found it relatively easy to attract girls, even when Oliver Greenwood was around, but up to Saturday night and the early hours of Sunday, I'd never really felt the need for a connection outside of a bedroom; rowing had always taken priority and provided a convenient excuse to get away. I'd never been totally captivated by the way a woman's mouth moved, or how they curled their legs underneath themselves like they could have been a contortionist in a different life.

I'd never opened up.

Beyond a handful of people I'd known most of my life, and a couple of the boys on the crew I'd sworn to secrecy, I'd never shared my desire to teach. To be a teacher of minds, and impart what little wisdom I had to others.

Coming from my family it was nothing more than a frivolous pipedream. *'Change lives through politics,'* my dad would bark at me whenever I mentioned teaching. But talking to someone about it, albeit briefly to someone who didn't know about the complications of my family, yet clearly understood exactly how it felt to be setting your future aside for another's dream, was liberating.

From the moment I saw her I knew I was going to kiss her. Unfortunately for me, it had only been a nanosecond of surrounding her mouth with mine, tasting the faint juniper notes from the gin on her lips, before we were rudely interrupted by the guy who was still talking in my ear.

'Oz, I'm telling you, just text her. Stop being such a pussy.'

I groaned, because he made it sound so simple when it

was anything but, because from the point in time when I'd watched her walk away, the following twelve hours had gone swiftly south and hadn't yet stopped.

It began with me waking up at the crack of dawn and desperately needing some sustenance – more than the box of cornflakes Olly's woefully bare kitchen would provide. I'd jogged to the small supermarket on campus which opened at six a.m. only to be assaulted by a wall of Sunday papers, neatly lined up on shelves welcoming me in.

The sight wasn't welcome.

My mother's face stared at me, underneath a headline about how my father had raced around to her house in a jealous rage after he'd discovered she had a new boyfriend. While I had no doubt about my father's capacity to fly off the handle, I did doubt any story about a new boyfriend, mostly because – on closer inspection of one front page image – the new boyfriend in question looked suspiciously like one of her gardeners, who was sixty-five years old, and gay. Plus, my mother wasn't in the country.

I'd turned on my heel and walked straight out, shooting off a text message to Olly telling him what had happened, and jumped straight on the train back to Oxford.

All the story did was stoke the fires of hatred I had for my father for putting us all in this position, and serve me the sobering reminder that, outside the cold walls of the university, this was my very shameful and embarrassing life. As soon as Kate Astley saw, she would sprint off in the opposite direction.

'You're a decent guy,' Olly tried again, 'just text her and put me out of my misery. She's not going to care about your family, she's American.'

'Yeah, I know,' I muttered, grabbing the tub of protein powder and scooping a portion into my shaker.

'Oz, I have to go. I need to see my professor before term starts. Are you racing this weekend?'

'Yes, against your lot. Shame you'll lose.'

'We'll see about that. I'm placing a healthy bet that Cambridge will win this year.'

'Don't waste your money, Marshy's back,' I chuckled, suddenly feeling much cheerier than I had when I'd woken up. Nothing like a bit of friendly competition to get the blood flowing again. 'Thanks for the talk, Ol. I appreciate it.'

'Any time. Speak to you later.'

'Try not to sleep with your tutor this year,' I shot out, hearing his loud laugh just before the call went dead.

I mixed up the protein shake, drinking it while I waited for my coffee to finish dripping, along with the porridge I had cooking for my first breakfast of the day. At this point, I could almost add eating as a skill on my résumé.

I'd just spooned two portions into to-go bowls when Charlie appeared at the kitchen door, his mouth open in a wide yawn.

'Morning, sunshine.'

'Morning,' he grunted, at least I think that's what he said. 'Do you have a coffee for me, please?'

I nodded to the second cup I'd placed under the coffee machine. 'Yes, that one's for you.'

'Thank you.'

It was well known among the rowing crew, plus most of Trinity College, that Charlie shouldn't be approached in the mornings until he'd had at least one, preferably two coffees. It was beyond most of us how he'd gotten into rowing, seeing as we were usually on the river by six thirty a.m. every day in the run-up to the big race. As term was yet to begin and we were still eight months out, it was currently a much more reasonable eight a.m., but not for long.

As I'd told Olly, our first race of the year was in four days' time, where we'd be back at the scene of our weekend's exploits: Cambridge University.

Charlie grabbed the cup, sighing through his first sip. 'Much better.'

'Good.' I hoisted up my backpack, nodding to the second porridge as I walked out of the kitchen, 'That's for you too. Now, come on, we can't be late for our first meeting.'

'Do you reckon they've discovered their precious oars are no longer where they left them?' he asked as we stepped out into the cool, fresh morning air.

'There's no way they haven't; we'll find out soon enough, though. They might be waiting until after the race on Saturday to retaliate.'

'Yeah, you're right. That's what we'd do.' He took another large sip of his coffee, and looked around the house, 'Where's Brooks?'

'Already left, Marshy's car broke down so he went to collect them.'

'Great, that means I ride shotgun.' He jumped into the passenger seat of my car, and we set off for the Fleming Boathouse, our river training station, sitting on the River Thames a short drive out of Oxford.

I surged up the road while Charlie spent the next three minutes trying to decide what music he wanted to listen to. By that point I'd zoned out of whatever he was doing, my mind firmly back in its debate about whether or not to text Kate, so I didn't see him pick up my phone as it buzzed.

'Oz, your dad's calling,' he announced, quietly.

'Kill it,' I snarled.

He placed the phone back in the centre console. 'Have you spoken to him at all?'

I shook my head, 'Nope. Not since June when it all hit the fan.'

'What are you going to do?'

I took a left down towards the main road leading out of Oxford, 'Nothing, he can go fuck himself.'

'How's your mum?' he asked, opening up the porridge I'd made him and spooning in a mouthful.

I shrugged, letting out a heavy sigh, 'She's okay, beyond being embarrassed. It's not like we haven't all known he can't keep his dick in his pants, but the amount of press at the moment isn't ideal.'

'Have you seen her?'

'No, she's still in Greece, avoiding it all, which is somewhat of a blessing. But my sister's at the country house and said the paparazzi were parked at the front gates all weekend. Thankfully, my brothers are already back at Eton. I just wish they'd get bored and move on to some other politician who's screwing someone he shouldn't be.'

'Want me to see if I can find one?' he asked with utmost seriousness, and I wouldn't put it past him to do it either. Charlie was capable of many things which probably shouldn't be discussed.

I snorted. 'I'll let you know, but I appreciate the offer.'

The rest of the journey was completed in silence while Charlie finished his breakfast, then leaned his head back on the rest, and I wasn't certain he hadn't fallen back to sleep. Twenty minutes later I pulled into my usual space at the boathouse to find Joshi getting out of Brooks' car, followed by Pete and Frank.

'Morning, boys.'

'Good morning,' replied Charlie, much more buoyant now he'd been fed, watered, and further rested.

'Heard anything yet?' asked Frank, hoisting his gym bag over his shoulder.

'Nope,' I shook my head, pressing the car fob again to double check I'd locked it.

'Wonder if Coach will say anything.'

'Let's go in and find out.'

We weren't the first to arrive, but we weren't the last either which was never a good place to be. There were easily thirty guys in here already, half of last year's boat race squad of twenty-four men, along with our head coach, his two assistant coaches, our physio and the boat-house manager, while more guys filed in all hoping to be part of a crew making history.

This meeting would be a full house.

'Shit, busy this year,' muttered Brooks as we all inched along the back wall.

Out of the corner of my eye I noticed a couple of nudges and whispers. I couldn't be sure if it was about the renewed tabloid interest in my family or because the eight of us together were usually considered some kind of quasi-university celebrities, which made me cringe to my core, but I tugged the peak of my cap down lower anyway.

'Quiet, quiet!' shouted Coach Lassiter as the room filled up. 'Quiet!'

There were so many of us now that it still took a minute for his instructions to seep through, but slowly volume levels dropped to nothing.

'Good morning, boys. I hope you enjoyed your lie-in.' He grinned, and a couple of the wider administrative staff behind him let out a chuckle. 'For all you newbies who spent the summer developing your skills in the hopes of a spot this year, it will be the last lie-in you'll have.'

I glanced around, seeking out any shocked faces, but came up blank. You didn't try out for the Oxford squad if you weren't a fan of early mornings, Charlie excluded.

'We have one race to win, and six months' hard training until we do. And I mean hard. Quite possibly the hardest thing you have ever done. Four point two miles of your lungs burning, while your muscles scream at you to stop. For the final sixteen of nineteen minutes your entire body will feel like it's about to collapse, if you're not lucky enough to complete it quicker. And it will be all while trying to stop Cambridge from gaining the advantage. This race is win or lose. There are no second places. Is anyone not clear?'

The room was more silent than I'd ever known it to be, even as Coach waited for someone to make a break for the door, never to be seen again.

'Good.' He looked around the group for a double check. 'We have a few housekeeping rules, then we'll hit the water. First, I hear we are in possession of a set of golden oars.'

Brooks let out a loud cheer next to me, along with

several whoops and whistles from the other side of the room.

Coach thumbed behind him where the heist rules were carved into a wooden board and hanging on the wall.

'As you know, they need to be returned twenty-four hours after we win the Boat Race.'

Brooks cheered even louder. We all knew that meant Coach wanted – no, expected – us to win the double.

'Starting tomorrow, we will be on the water or in the gym every morning at six thirty, and every evening at five thirty. No excuses. You are expected to train outside of these times, but these two are mandatory. You are part of a team now; if you're late your team is late. One, weekends will soon be spent training on the Tideway. Two, everything you do reflects on your team. Remember that. And three,' Coach Lassiter looked over to me, 'let's welcome our new president, Arthur Osbourne-Cloud.'

The cheer which bounced off the walls was louder than the first two had been and blew away the black cloud I'd been living under since Sunday morning. I grinned sheepishly around the room, pulling my cap down further when Joshi and Frank joined in with Brooks' whistling and Charlie set everyone off in chanting my name.

'Mate, stop blushing,' hissed Fellows. 'It's not presidential.'

Coach gave everyone a good thirty seconds before he called time, 'All right, all right, that is enough. Oz, come up here.'

I groaned but pushed off the wall, and made my way through the group until I could see every set of eyes on me.

'This morning's training will begin with some light racing along the river. As President, Oz gets to pick his eight, though no guesses who will be on it, so we'll be switching out after they've won the first sprint.'

I grinned back at him, looked around the room for my crew, and gestured them forward, 'Come on, boys. Let's show them how it's done.'

Ten minutes later we'd all changed into our full-body racing skins and lightweight bodywarmers; it wasn't the warmest clothing we had, but it was only September and two hours of intense cardio would have us sweating enough that we wouldn't need it. Pete, as our coxswain, however, was wrapped up like Ranulph Fiennes about to set off on an expedition to the Arctic.

We picked up Blue Boat from the boathouse, and the eight of us hoisted it up on our shoulders to Pete's command as he guided our steps to the water's edge. Laying the shell carefully in the water, we held it steady while Pete got into his seat, and one by one the rest of us kicked off our shoes and stood with one foot inside the boat, the other on the dock until we were set to take Pete's command.

'Shove.'

We pushed off in sync, balancing ourselves while we all sat down and secured our feet into the shoes already locked in place for us.

'Nice to be back, fellas,' Pete grinned, as he fitted his headset ready to guide us through the session.

My fingers gripped around my oar, flexing against the smooth rubber handle. Even though I'd rowed almost daily, my hands had recovered a little since the World

Championships earlier in the summer, and the thick calluses which were usually present had reduced enough that I would feel the sting later.

It felt good to be back, good for the eight of us to be rowing together again. It was unusual for the team to stay the same year after year but by a stroke of luck, none of us had graduated since we'd lost last year. Now Pete had returned from injury, we would be unbeatable.

This year we would get our victory.

'How're you feeling, Marshy?' I asked him, sitting directly in front of me, while I waited for everyone else to get settled.

I could already hear Charlie behind me psyching himself up.

'Good. How'd you want to take it this morning?'

As stroke, it was my job to set the pace of the boat. Behind me, Charlie in seat seven needed to keep my exact strokes to direct the boys whose oars were on his side for how fast we were pushing through the water. We became human metronomes, mirroring our rhythms precisely.

'Not too hard, need to ease Charlie into the early mornings.'

'I heard that,' came his voice from over my shoulder, and Pete laughed.

While the other guys were preparing their boats for the water, we drifted further into the middle of the river and I felt every ounce of stress from this morning melting off me.

As much as Oxford University was part of the blood I'd inherited from my father, being on the water came from my mother. Born into a family of shipping magnates, as a child she spent more time on her father's yacht than dry land, and her days would start with a morning sail around the small island my grandparents owned off the Greek mainland, near Athens; the Parthenon in full view.

After she met my father, she'd moved to England full time, though all school holidays were spent back in Greece because *'three months of cold and rain is all I can manage at a time'*. Greece is where my three siblings and I fell in love with the water in exactly the same way she had.

For my sixth birthday, I'd been given a rowing boat, which I proudly took out onto the small lake at our home in Oxfordshire, rowing round and round until my little fingers were blistered from the oars. Soon, my mother had taken me out in my first shell, teaching me how to set a rhythm with each stroke.

It was probably at that point my father began drilling into me the importance of my future as part of his side of the family. The political side. Something I have never given two shits about. But my father had seen something he didn't like.

I wasn't just good at rowing. I was excellent.

By my last birthday, when I turned twenty-one, I was already the proud owner of two World Championship gold medals, and one Olympic silver. Not to mention the several junior World Championship gold medals I'd also won, which were proudly hanging in my mother's dressing room at her estate on my grandparents' island.

My father hadn't been good enough at rowing to even make his college team. This year would be my third boat race representing Oxford, and I took perverse pleasure in how much it pissed him off – that I was a member of an elite club my father could never be part of, because it was the one place you couldn't buy yourself entry. Only talent guaranteed it.

'Count down,' Pete ordered, and the eight of us shouted out our numbers, declaring that we were all seated and ready to row at his command, right as the loud chug of Coach's motorboat announced its arrival on the water.

Five boats of eight crew were lined up, waiting for Coach to give each coxswain the go ahead. Our boat would go first, as the senior team, followed by Isis – the second boat – and then whichever ones Coach deemed to be next. Then we would race.

As the eight of us listened for Pete's command, I could almost feel the eagerness radiating off the rippling surface.

'At the catch.'

Our oars dropped into the water.

'Row.'

And off we went.

Two sweaty hours later we pulled back to the dock. Once again we took Pete's command to get out and lift our shell from the water, carefully placing her back onto the pipes. We were all in peak physical fitness, but even I knew that we were going to ache tomorrow when we were back here to do it all over again.

'Fuck, I'm starving,' announced Joshi, pushing his feet into his sliders. 'I think I'm going to need three breakfasts today. Or at least two lunches.'

'Me too.' Charlie slumped down on the bench next to him. 'Need to power up this week, boys, there's no way we're letting Cambridge win the first race of the year, even if it is a friendly.'

47

My heart thudded. Somewhere during the last two hours I'd forgotten we would be back in Cambridge this weekend.

That I would be breathing the same air as Kate.

Fuck it. Fuck my stupid family.

There's no way I could be at Cambridge on Saturday and not go in search of her. Before I could overthink it any longer, I pulled out my phone and shot off a message.

Arthur: *A question for a question . . . Kate Astley, when can we continue where we left off?*

Now I just needed to pray I hadn't already blown it.

4. Kate

(The hot ones always come with a catch)

I dropped my bag unceremoniously on the floor of my dorm room then flopped face first onto my bed.

Exhausted wouldn't cover it.

It was only my first week, and term hadn't even begun. The pleasure of that was happening on Monday; yet after a week of orientation, three separate tours of the medical school, the several detours I'd taken home via the classics building in the hopes of running into Oz, meetings with my professors and course mates where I'd received my class schedule and firmly concluded I would have absolutely zero life for the next twelve months, I felt like I'd been put through a fast spin wash and still come out soaking wet.

I'd give anything to bury myself under the covers I'd only left four hours ago and go to sleep, but I had approximately six minutes before I had to leave and head over to the Cambridge boathouse for the team huddle before today's meet. Beside the medical facility, the boathouse would be where I'd spend the majority of my time for the next six years, and I was okay with that.

The week might have gone by in a blur but easily my most favourite part of it had been spent on the river. While part of my scholarship here was based on my coxing skills and becoming part of the university rowing squad, I'd still had to try out with everyone else. Luckily

Imogen and Hannah had also been invited, and the three of us would be leaving shortly to go and cheer the teams on, even if we weren't competing ourselves.

Today – the first official race of the year – promised to be a big one. Today we were rowing against Oxford, so even if I hadn't spent the week listening to how our one goal was to beat them on all accounts, or watched the rage almost steaming off the C.U.B.C. president when he announced that Oxford had already stolen our precious golden oars, and even if the entire squad hadn't been mandated to attend, I wouldn't have been anywhere else.

Being back on the water during tryouts had given me the calm I had been desperately craving. The smell of the water, the sound of the oars breaking the surface, the rhythm of my crew powering themselves along the river at my command as the coaches watched, all worked to unravel the knots which had been quickly building under my shoulder blades.

I'd spent the last five years rowing with my local club back on the east coast; I'd competed in races and regattas during the season, but from the first time I guided my crew along the River Cam, I knew I'd never experienced *this* level of competitiveness and it was exactly what I needed to keep me focused. It would keep my mind clear from everything else happening around me, and remembering I was 3,000 miles away from home studying for a degree I didn't want. I might be completely out of my depth here in Cambridge, but my seat at the stern of a boat was the only place I knew exactly what I was supposed to be doing.

It was the only place I really felt like I belonged.

I shifted on my mattress and was immediately met with

the sharp pain of my phone sticking into my hip, though I seriously considered leaving it there if it meant I could have another minute with my face pressed into the pillow. Sadly, a quick buzzing only exacerbated my discomfort, and I was forced to retrieve it.

When a second ago I could sleep forever, the name flashing on the screen had me sitting up with all the energy of a six-month-old puppy.

Oz: *Good morning, Yankee Doodle. Still meeting me at the pub later? X*

Making the C.U.B.C. squad might have been my favourite part of the week, but without a doubt, Oz was my second.

When I'd finally woken up last Sunday morning, I couldn't be certain I hadn't dreamed him, but then my fingers brushed against the soft cashmere of his sweater and I was transported back to the bluest eyes I'd ever seen, stripping me bare until my soul was visible for anyone who might have walked past.

There was cathartic power in the knowledge I wasn't alone in feeling a little trapped in the life I was currently leading; that another person knew exactly what it was like to live with someone else's future mapped out for you. The tension which usually whispered its constant presence though my chest had been distant when I'd finally gotten out of bed, and I'd breezed through the rest of my day like I hadn't a care in the world.

If I hadn't been so busy, I might have been more upset it had taken him two days to message me, or that I hadn't run into him on campus no matter how hard I tried. I wasn't an authority on dating, and I hadn't expected to hear from him the second we'd parted ways, but two days seemed . . . I dunno . . . long?

He didn't seem like the type of guy who'd play hard to get, either.

But, if I was totally honest with myself, as much as my heart had pounded in my chest when I'd seen his first message, not hearing from him so soon had given me a little relief. Because how was I supposed to keep up with my course work, the rowing team, *and* date the most perfect specimen of a man I'd ever met? If the latter wasn't distraction enough, I didn't know what was.

Even looking at my schedule now, I still wasn't sure how I'd fit it all in without Oz in the picture. Monday to Friday I had to be on the six a.m. train out to Ely for water training, then back on campus for nine. After a full day in school, I was then expected down at the Goldie boat-house for late-afternoon land training in the gym.

At least at the weekends we just had one training session – for seven hours . . .

I no longer had time to go out because if I wasn't study-ing, I needed to be in bed sleeping. At nineteen, I'd long come to the conclusion that I was never going to be one of those people who could thrive on little sleep. I loved sleep. I craved sleep. It was also an important requirement of any friendships I cultivated that I had ample quantities; tired me was not someone people wanted to be around.

So when the message from Oz came through asking to pick up where we left off, I should have suggested maybe we didn't pick up, maybe we remembered it for what it was – the best almost-kiss there'd ever been. That I was scared if we picked up where we left off, and our kiss was everything I thought it would be, all I'd want to do was kiss him more and forget the rest.

But I didn't, because the second I saw that message all I could think about were his lips breezing over mine. All I could smell was the intoxicating oaky scent of vetiver and sandalwood, reminding me of New England in the fall, and sipping hot chocolate as you kicked through the leaves. All I could feel were his palms cupping my cheeks and long fingers brushing against the thumping pulse in my neck that reverberated over every inch of my body.

We hadn't messaged a lot, but it was enough for me to find out a third year studying classics doesn't need to spend the week before term starts doing anything other than lying around reading *The Iliad*. I'd also learned that he lived in a house off campus with two of his best friends, and that Olly, who I'd had the somewhat pleasure of briefly meeting last weekend wasn't one of them. Olly was in Downing like me.

In fact, I'd seen Olly nearly every day, and while on Monday he'd stared at me with a marginally confused expression, yesterday he shot a smirk my way which left me wondering if I had peanut butter on my face from the toast I'd just scarfed.

But tonight everything would change because I was meeting Oz at the pub, and because of the races, tomorrow's training session started at ten a.m., therefore my curfew could stretch a little longer.

Tonight would be my first date with Oz, and my second visit to an authentic English pub. Tonight I'd finally get to experience the kiss I'd been thinking about during the very minimal free time I'd had – the minutes before I fell asleep.

I ran my fingers over his name still lit up on my phone screen, allowing myself a little smile as I did, and typed out a response.

Kate: *Can't wait.*

With my renewed energy I managed to swing my feet around until they hit the floor and I sprang off the bed, while simultaneously shimmying out of my leggings and grabbing my jeans from the chair I'd thrown them onto yesterday. Replacing my sweater with the pale-blue hoodie with the C.U.B.C. crest I'd been handed in my first training session this week, I ran a brush through my hair, then snatched my cell back up and yanked open my dorm room door.

Imogen was on the other side of the hallway, opening her door at exactly the same time.

'Hey!'

'Hello, I was about to come and find you. I didn't dare lie down, I'm so tired after this morning I was in danger of falling asleep.' She pulled her door closed and locked it.

'Tell me about it. I'd give anything for a power nap right now.' I slipped my keys into my pocket and turned to face her, 'Where's Hannah?'

Imogen disappeared into the folds of her hoodie, which matched mine, and pulled it on over her head. 'She's meeting us there, she said she needed to get something to eat first.'

I rubbed my stomach as it rumbled, 'I should have done the same.'

'Here,' she rummaged in the enormous backpack she was holding in one hand before pulling out an energy bar, and thrust it at me, 'have this, we can get something after.'

'Thanks! Don't you need it?'

'I have plenty. My mother seems to think I'm going to starve here or something. She packed me off with so many I don't have enough space to store them.' She shook her head with a deep eye roll as we made our way down the one flight of stairs to the ground floor and out into the cool air.

I was used to the freezing east-coast winters, so I wasn't yet wearing the padded bodywarmer which Imogen had now shrugged on over her hoodie, but it wouldn't be long. Even in the space of a week, as we moved from September to October, the leaves had turned an array of orange, yellow and red, laying a patchwork blanket under our feet as we headed down the path. It wasn't anywhere near as impressive as the fall colours back home, but it did go a little way to stop me being homesick.

'Do you think we'll win?' I asked Imogen as a group of guys passed us on the path carrying C.U.B.C. flags.

She pulled her long, auburn hair free from its tie, then twisted it into a messy bun. I didn't fail to clock a couple of guys walking towards us who paid very close attention to the way she gathered up the strands and resecured it, though she was too focused on the job at hand to notice.

I'd spent enough time with her over the last week to realize that people paid attention to her wherever she went, and yet she remained completely oblivious. It was hard not to notice her, given she was nearly six feet tall, and I hadn't yet decided whether walking next to me at five feet one and a quarter made it worse, especially when I had to break into a jog to keep up with her strides.

If she hadn't been so kind to me during my first few days, I'd have probably found her intimidating, but instead she was quickly becoming a friend. We were taking the same course, we were both accepted onto the Cambridge crew, and she and Hannah were the only two people I'd consistently seen.

'Well,' she leaned in, lowering her voice once she'd finished fixing her hair, 'there's no reason we shouldn't, seeing as we totally creamed them in the Boat Race last year – it was *not* Oxford's finest hour. But I heard that the Oxford team haven't let up their training all summer. Every member of their Blue Boat has competed internationally, half of them were at the World Championships, and they had an exceptional performance at Henley. Clearly now A.O.-C. is president they're really going for it. I mean, they've already stolen the oars, it's never been done before term starts . . .'

'Who? What?' I puffed while concentrating on matching my pace to hers. At this rate I wouldn't need to hit the gym every day. Walking next to Imogen was enough cardio.

'Huh?'

'Who or what is A.O.-C.?'

She frowned and her arm thrust out to stop me walking, like a mom hitting the brake pads. 'Wait! Has no one told you about him?'

'About who?'

'A.O.-C.' she repeated slowly, enunciating each letter. 'Arthur Osbourne-Cloud. The President of Oxford Rowing.'

'Ohh, him.' I nodded, coming to the realization this was the guy I'd been hearing about since I'd arrived here. 'Yeah, I guess his name's a bit of a mouthful. But what I don't get is why he's such a big deal aside from rowing. You talk about him like he's a celebrity.'

'That's because he is. Have you *seriously* never heard of him? Arthur Osbourne-Cloud?'

I shook my head, 'Not before this week.'

'Okay, goodie for me then.' She rubbed her hands together, and let out a gleeful little squeak. 'I'm so glad I get to be the one.'

I stood there staring up at her. Imogen was better than any guidebook or course manual – she knew everything, and everyone. I'd already been given the low-down on where to go out, where not to go out, which colleges to avoid, who was sleeping with whom, where the hottest guys were, the best studying spots on campus, and short cuts to the train station allowing a precious extra five minutes in bed – and from the way her eyes were now wide with amusement, I knew she was about to deliver another bombshell of information.

'Well, A.O.-C. is . . .' she glanced away as she searched for the words and I waited silently and patiently for the rest of her sentence, 'he's . . . well . . . he's absolutely gorgeous. But . . .' she paused again for dramatic effect, while I soaked in her accent and how she pronounced it gorrr-jus, 'a total arse. Total, complete arse. Ruthless. The worst type of arrogant, he will stop at nothing to win, terrible temper. I heard last year when they lost that he smashed up his oars and made their cox cry. Only ended up back on the crew because his parents donated a bucketload of money.'

My mouth dropped open. I couldn't imagine my parents ever doing that even if they had the cash. 'What?'

At that moment a flash of blonde caught the corner of my eye before Imogen and I were swept up in a giant hug.

'Hey, girls, what are you talking about?' asked Hannah when she let us go but stayed in between us, and looped her arms through ours. We began walking again, thankfully a little slower.

'I'm filling our American friend in on A.O.-C.'

Hannah's eyes widened like Imogen's had. 'Oh! Did you see him in the paper today?'

I peered over to the two of them, now thoroughly confused. 'The paper? Like the newspaper?'

'Yes, basically his parents are going through a messy divorce, and it's been in the papers all summer.'

'Oh, that's sad. But why do the papers care?'

'I hadn't got to that bit yet,' Imogen began again, unlinking her arm from Hannah so we could fit through a narrow path between two cobbled streets we were now walking down. 'His family is very well known. His grandfather was Prime Minister, his father is a politician, and his mother is part of the Drakos shipping dynasty . . . you know, that type of thing. He's practically royalty, so naturally people are interested, especially because he's a totally gorgeous, total fuckboy, who couldn't give a shit about anything but himself.'

'Drakos?' I interrupted as a memory jogged in my brain, 'Wow. I've seen them when I've been out on my dad's boat. They've got huge container ships.'

Hannah nodded. 'Yes, they're one of the biggest. Worth billions.'

'Anyway,' Imogen continued, almost bursting at the seams to get the rest of her story out, 'his father's the worst. Corrupt politician, always in the papers for something controversial, and this summer he was caught having an affair with his parliamentary secretary – which surprised no one – but he was using an official government car to take them to a hotel or something so it made the news more than it should have done. There's an investigation, though I'm loose on the details. I haven't paid that much attention. The point is A.O.-C.'s apple hasn't fallen far from his father's tree.'

'Oh,' I replied, because there wasn't anything else to say and my head was spinning slightly from all the new information.

'In his defence, he's actually a decent rower. He's even got an Olympic medal. He was one of the youngest members on the GB team.'

'He probably wears it to bed,' Hannah snorted, so loudly it caused a passing group of girls to cackle just as loudly.

'Is he really that bad?'

'Yes, ask any of the girls. Apparently he slept with half the Cambridge crew last year, probably after he went through all the girls at Oxford,' Imogen continued.

'Really?'

'Yep. Someone said they saw him on campus last Sunday too, and we didn't even have a race then.' Hannah nodded gravely, then gasped loudly. 'Bet that's when he was stealing the oars!'

Imogen's head flicked round, clearly a piece of information she hadn't known, 'No way! Who saw him?'

'I heard two of the second years talking about it when I went to get a coffee.'

'Killed two birds with one stone. Gross.'

I was kind of glad I wasn't standing between them, it would have felt like bouncing around a pinball machine from the speed they were talking, 'Why does everyone sleep with him if he's so awful?'

Imogen nudged me with a wink, 'Wait until you see him, then you'll understand. Just remember Mary Heston will try and have you thrown out of Cambridge. She's already cracking the whip this year, she's desperate for us to win,' she added. 'I heard one of the second years had to break up with her boyfriend because Mary said he'd become a distraction. So hypocritical seeing as Mary's dating Will Norris, the men's president.'

I'd only seen Mary twice, the second time she was screaming at one of the guys on the squad, so I could imagine her cracking the whip, and I had no intention of getting on her bad side and losing my scholarship, or being screamed at.

'How do you know all this?'

'Oh! My eldest sister, Rosie, was telling me about it. One of her best friends from school graduated from Oxford last year, and he was well known around campus.'

When I first applied to Cambridge, I naively assumed it would be teeming with students walking the sacred corridors quietly nodding to each other in recognition of being part of something great, all while cheering the university teams on to victory in their respective sports. It was what had intimidated me the most, and what I'd tried not to think about as I took the path my brother couldn't.

I hadn't expected it to be like *Gossip Girl*.

'What does he look like?'

'You should google him later, search for British Rowing at the World Championships, he really fills out his rowing singlet.' Imogen grinned, 'I can't wait to see him in person today . . . all tall, dark hair, drop-dead gorgeous. Totally smoking hot, but if you look carefully you'll find a set of devil horns under his beanie.'

Hannah snorted again, 'Bet he's got a wicked forked tongue too.'

I barked out a loud laugh, unsure why I was so shocked. These two were like a walking *National Enquirer*, totally entertaining but not to be taken seriously under any circumstances. 'What was the story today?'

'Something to do with his dad, but a picture of A. O.-C. on a yacht with some friends and girls. Like father like son or something. Nothing interesting.'

I pulled my hood up my neck as a bitter wind whipped around us. 'How does he find the time to win medals and party so much?'

'God knows. He's got talent, that's for sure.' Hannah squinted at the church clock in the distance as the bells rang out striking the hour, 'Come on, we need to hurry.'

The cobbled path opened up and we turned left onto the short street leading down to the river. Students, all wearing various items of Cambridge University clothing – hoodies, bodywarmers, beanie hats – filled the streets, all ready to cheer their team on.

We made our way over the footbridge to the boathouse. When we arrived Imogen reached for the pale-blue door just as it was pushed open from the inside by none other than Mary Heston, who didn't look particularly happy. Or maybe her face always looked like that, with her beady little black pupils resembling the raisins in my morning bowl of granola; the ones I always picked out.

'You three are late,' she snapped. 'If you're expecting to be part of *my* women's crew, your timekeeping needs to greatly improve. Hurry up and get inside before anyone else notices.'

'Sorry, Mary,' Hannah mumbled as we slunk through the door, only to find the corridors filled with familiar faces from the week of tryouts and several of the wider squad milling about.

'Jeez. She needs to calm down,' added Imogen, thrusting her watch out to me when Mary was out of sight. 'We're not late, we still have ten minutes. Look. And why isn't she yelling at any of this lot?'

'Dunno. But let's get out of her way.'

'If we stand at the back we can try to sneak out and head to the starting line if the boys don't stop talking about stealing their oars back and taking the Oxford crown.'

'Good idea,' agreed Hannah.

'I just have to use the bathroom,' I said, veering off to the right. 'Save me a spot, I'll come and find you.'

I snuck down the corridor to the female changing rooms I'd used earlier in the week, and ducked into the nearest stall.

It was as I walked back out buttoning my jeans that the door to the changing rooms opened, and in walked the one person I'd been thinking about more than anything or anyone else for the past week. In the stark light of the bathroom, he was even more beautiful than I'd remembered, his cheekbones higher under the stubble which had definitely thickened, his jaw straighter, his legs longer. He stopped dead the second he saw me, and the way his eyes widened and mouth dropped open couldn't be taken as anything other than a compliment. My heart let out two hard thuds of approval, and fluttered against my ribcage.

'Holy shit! Kate Astley! I was just thinking about you. All that visualization crap must work.' He gave two exaggerated blinks. 'Wow, are you a sight for sore eyes.'

My jaw dropped as his had, but I managed to tear my gaze away to look around. Had I come into the men's bathroom? No.

'Wh . . . what are you doing in here?'

'Don't worry, you're in the ladies.' He grinned, which had my heart crashing hard against my sternum again. My memory had not held up well. 'I drank too much water on the way here and couldn't wait.'

'There's a men's bathroom.'

'I can't use that one.' I was about to ask why not but he continued talking as he walked straight into the stall I'd just left. 'Give me a second. Don't leave.'

The noise of him peeing loudly broke me out of the shock which had glued my feet to the floor, and I hurried over to the sink to wash my hands. Thirty seconds later he was standing next to me doing the same thing, then turned to me with a grin and handed me a paper towel he'd removed from the dispenser.

It took me a couple of seconds, mostly because we were standing there staring at each other, matching grins widening while we both wondered if what was happening was really happening. Or I was at least. It was hard to believe he was actually real, that this was the guy I'd been messaging all week.

Jeez, he was hot.

'It must have been so dark last week because you're even more beautiful than I remember. There's no way I'd have forgotten.'

I blushed hard, my eyes dropping at the compliment, even though I'd been thinking the exact same thing about him.

If my eyeline hadn't been closer to his chest than his face, I probably wouldn't have noticed what was emblazoned on his jacket so quickly. But I'd heard more this week about stealing *that* crown than I had about anything I was officially studying.

My gaze snapped to his, then once more to the crest over his left chest.

The crest which didn't match the one printed on my hoodie.

When I glanced up, I couldn't quite read the expression on his face. If I knew him better, I'd say it was nervousness.

'Oz, what's that?' I pointed to the navy-blue windbreaker jacket he was wearing.

'My jacket.'

'No, that.' The tip of my finger stopped just before it touched the crown sitting above crossed oars, like it would singe my fingerprints if it did.

He cleared his throat. 'It's the crest for the Oxford University Boat Club.'

The squirming in my belly increased.

I might have only been at Cambridge a week, but that was long enough to understand full well that a Cambridge student would rather die than wear that crest. Okay, maybe not *die* die, but I definitely knew the answer to my next question would be a negative.

'Please tell me you're wearing it because you're cold, and that happened to be the closest thing you could find to put on.'

He winced slightly, and his mouth stayed in a hard line. 'I can't do that.'

'You're supporting Oxford today?'

He looked away, taking a deep breath before he answered. 'Of sorts.'

My eyes travelled between his and the crest, my head spinning while simultaneously trying to ignore how broad his chest was, or how the navy blue of his jacket only made his turquoise eyes even paler, and his bronzed skin darker. Or how his thick black hair curled along the rim of his ball cap, and my fingers itched to push it off so I could twist them through the silky strands.

'You go to Oxford University?'

'I do.' He nodded and my thudding heart sank from my chest, beginning its journey to the pit of my stomach.

'But,' I blinked again, words jumbling in my mouth, 'your friend Olly . . .'

'What about him?'

'He's here at Cambridge.'

'So?' He smiled softly, then reached for my hand as I sighed, and implored me with his gaze. 'I'm sorry, Yankee Doodle. I should have told you when we met, but it honestly didn't occur to me because you completely stole my

65

focus. Forgive me, please? It really doesn't change anything. Does it? You'll still meet me later? Then we can talk about how we can make the distance work.'

Like last week, I found myself mesmerized, and completely disarmed; the anxiety that had risen a minute ago disappeared as quickly as it had arrived. My shoulders dropped and I mirrored his smile. 'Sorry, I wasn't expecting it. Yes, I'll still find you later; I need to go now, though. I have a crew meeting before the races, and I'll no doubt hear more about how your president seems to be rowing's answer to Hugh Hefner.' I smiled teasingly, but now it was his turn to frown.

'What? What does that mean?'

'Oh nothing, something the girls were telling me.' I waved my hand dismissively, 'I really have to go, I can't be late.'

He blinked once, then twice, 'For your crew meeting? You row?'

'Yes.' I nodded.

'On the Cambridge crew?'

'Yes. Part of my scholarship is based on being a member of the university squad.'

His eyes slowly left mine and travelled down to my feet and back again. It wasn't the same once-over he'd given me last week; that one had my toes curling, while this felt more assessing – and the weight it held was very different. 'You're a cox?'

I nodded. 'How did you know?'

'You look like one,' he said with a sly smile.

I opened my mouth to respond but then remembered his answer from a moment ago, when I asked if he was supporting Oxford. And something in my brain clicked into shocked place. 'Wait, what did you mean before . . . of sorts?'

'Um,' he shuffled back from me slightly, his hand resting on the edge of the sink. To his credit he held my stare, 'I'm not here as a supporter.'

I frowned so deeply a thick bolt of pain hit me between my eyes, and if I could have kicked myself, I would have.

How did I not see it before? The breadth of his chest, the power in his biceps; I'd spent long enough around rowers that I should have recognized one standing in front of me.

'You're rowing?!'

He nodded slowly, so slowly it allowed time for the truth to sink in; I was fraternizing with the enemy. It was one thing for him to be attending a rival university, it was quite another for him to be direct competition.

'You're a rower? You row for Oxford? How did you not tell me?!'

'You also didn't tell me! We've been texting for four days!'

'I wanted to tell you in person,' I hissed back.

He started to say something, but then my eyes fell to the bold black letters on his jacket.

A.O.-C.

The longer I stared the quicker it became clear that the O didn't stand for Oxford. And the C didn't stand for Club.

The O was for Osbourne.

Arthur Osbourne-Cloud.

Oz.

I stepped away from him, my head spiralling with everything I remembered Imogen telling me less than an hour ago . . . her words swimming before my eyes. She'd certainly got one thing right, he was absolutely gorgeous.

But it didn't matter.

'Oh my god. You're him.' My hand dropped from my mouth enough for him to hear me whisper.

He searched my face, looking as confused as I felt. He reached out to me again, but this time I stepped back. 'Who are you talking about? Who am I?'

When I didn't answer right away, I could see the cogs whirring in his brain as he figured out the person I was talking about was him.

'Did you just compare *me* to Hugh Hefner?'

I bit down on my cheek, 'You're the guy I've been hearing about. The President of Oxford Rowing. That's you, right?'

Oz's body tensed. It was almost imperceptible, but I caught the seam of his jacket strain slightly as the air took on a distinct chill. He peered down at me through narrowed eyes, and his lips pursed. 'Kate, the only guy I am is the one you met last Saturday night.'

'I . . . I . . .'

I stood there staring at him, but I had no words. All I could see was the boy I'd been dreaming about kissing all week, and all I could hear was Imogen.

Oz's massive arms folded across his chest, and even under the thick material of his jacket I could see his biceps flexing. 'What's going on?'

Glancing over to the door, I half expected it to open. I'd been in here long enough now that the girls would

68

wonder where I was, not to mention someone else would likely need to use the bathroom at some point, and come in to find me consorting with the enemy.

If that someone was Mary Heston, it would only lead to a whole host of trouble. I most definitely wouldn't get invited back to the crew. I'd probably get kicked out of Cambridge and sent back home, considering Oz's status. It seemed to be a fitting punishment for everything I'd been told about the rivalry this week.

'Kate!' Oz snapped, yanking me out of my spiralling panic. 'What have you been hearing?'

His eyes had hardened when I next looked into them; the glisten of excitement he'd greeted me with had vanished. The pale Cambridge blue of his eyes had darkened to a shade more suiting of Oxford. It wasn't quite a glare I was now on the receiving end of, but it was more than a frown, and it certainly wasn't friendly.

Imogen's words floated in front of me.

'That you're arrogant. Ruthless . . . slept with most of Oxford and half of Cambridge . . . womanizer. Arrogant.' I repeated.

Even as I spoke them aloud it was hard to believe they were associated with the guy I'd met. The one who'd teased me. The one who'd given me his sweater, shared a bottle of gin, and listened to me talk about Jake. The one I'd confided in about opening my lobster roll restaurant, and not wanting to study medicine. The one who understood exactly what I was feeling, because he felt it. The one now standing in front of me, his jaw clenched hard.

Even angry he was breathtakingly handsome.

Though maybe that's how he got all the girls into bed.

'I see . . .' a single thick eyebrow disappeared under the peak of his cap, 'anything else?'

I swallowed thickly while trying to stay as still as possible.

'Kate. What else have you heard? Tell me,' he asked through gritted teeth.

'Nothing. I've heard nothing. This was a mistake, and you shouldn't be here. I'm not the type of girl you're looking for.' My voice trailed off and I could feel my shoulders desperate to curl in under his piercing stare, but I held firm.

His nostrils flared as he breathed out. 'And what exactly is the type of girl I'm looking for?'

'I . . . I . . .' I stuttered, as every word I had in my vocabulary seemed to have vanished into thin air.

'Okay, well while you think on that, let me assure you that I am not rowing's answer to Hugh Hefner, and I have *not* slept with half of Cambridge university. Was there anything else I need to dispute?'

I shook my head, mutely.

'You believed it all,' he whispered, almost to himself, though I could still make out a hefty dose of hurt in his tone.

'It doesn't matter what I believe. You're the president. Of Oxford.'

He waited, looking at me just like he had last week whenever I needed to provide further information.

'You're the enemy,' I clarified.

'Are you serious?'

I didn't know what I was, and my head was so heavy I had to force myself to nod. 'I've got a medical degree to start and finish, piles of coursework, not to mention all the training. I don't have time for anything else.'

'Wow,' he replied, his stare hardening another degree. 'It seems we were both wrong, because up until ten minutes ago I thought you were exactly the type of girl I'm looking for, but alas.'

He hissed out his final word, the ice-cold tone of his accent sending goosebumps over my skin, and my mouth drew into a hard line.

His eyes narrowed just as mine did, and soon it became clear that neither one of us had any more to say. Yet neither of us seemed to be able to leave, or maybe neither of us *wanted* to leave.

Except he wasn't the one who'd get in serious trouble if we were caught, and from the way he'd waltzed into the girls' bathroom it was clear he did whatever he wanted.

He was right about one thing, I'd been wrong about him.

The only thing I knew for certain – I had to get out of here and as far away as I could from his piercing stare and the intoxicating scent which was still buried in the sweater he'd given me.

'I have to go.' I spun on my heels and wrenched open the door, sprinting down the corridor to find the girls before he could follow.

Tears prickled in my throat. I was so angry I was expecting them to burst forth any moment. Yet as my eyes began stinging, I realized they weren't angry tears.

And the dull ache in my chest was in fact a crack, widening by the second.

5. Arthur

(I don't even own a silk bathrobe)

I glanced up from my book as the door to my bedroom burst open.

Charlie was standing there, two cups of tea in his hands, having barged the door open with his foot. He placed the cups on my desk and pulled a packet of Jaffa Cakes from his pocket with all the enthusiasm of a magician conjuring a rabbit from his hat. At which point Brooks appeared from his room next door, because you could never have any kind of chocolate open if you didn't want him sniffing it down with his bloodhound-like ability.

'What's going on? Did you make one for me?' He gazed longingly at the steaming mugs.

'Yes, it's in the kitchen. I called you.'

Brooks tapped the large noise-cancelling headphones wrapped around his neck, 'Didn't hear.' He snatched up a Jaffa Cake, stuffed it in his mouth and ran downstairs to fetch his tea, only to return less than a minute later. 'Well?'

I rested my book on my chest, open at the page I'd been reading over and over because my mind was busy wandering too much to absorb the words. 'Well what?'

'What's going on?'

'You'll have to ask Charles that. I was reading in peace when he burst forth.' I shuffled up my bed to lean against the headboard, holding my hand out for the Jaffa Cakes.

'Something's wrong, and I want to know what,' Charlie shrugged in response.

'Nothing's wrong, but thanks for the concern. And this,' I reached for my mug, 'I was getting thirsty.'

Unfortunately for me, Charlie was surprisingly astute for a physics student – the reason Brooks and I let him be the unofficial mother hen of our house. Plus, he was the only one of us who could legitimately cook outside of our morning bowls of porridge, which is why we forgave him for spending the first three hours of every day as a mute. Or however long it usually took for him to properly wake up.

'Bollocks,' he pressed on. 'You've barely spoken since the race, and we won by three lengths. You powered us through it.'

I stuffed another Jaffa Cake into my mouth whole, Brooks and Charlie watching as I chewed slowly.

'Are you complaining we won?'

'Of course I'm not. We would have won anyway, not by that much, but we would have won. You, however, don't seem to have been happy about it at all. That's my first clue.'

'Your first?' My brows raised.

'Yep. Second, your Saturday night plans got cancelled, and third . . .' he nodded to the book now open on my lap, 'I've come in here to find you reading *Aeschylus,* and you always say he's far too tragic and insufferable to spend any time on even if it is part of the syllabus.'

A wry smile curled my lip. I'd have laughed if I was in the laughing mood; he wasn't wrong about *Aeschylus,* but I hadn't been in a laughing mood since Saturday, approximately one hour before we annihilated Cambridge in our first race of the season. Since then, my mood had been firmly residing in the black.

'Don't forget he nearly killed us in training this morning. In fact, I should probably check on Joshi, you might have *actually* killed him. He was wheezing for a good ten minutes after we got back to the boathouse. And I don't think Marshy was setting the pace,' added Brooks, backhanding Charlie on the arm.

I grinned at them, the grin of an evil mastermind that didn't quite reach the eyes. Training had been punishing this morning, but I wouldn't hear complaints, not when it meant we would win the race come March.

'How very Miss Marple of you both.'

'Fourth . . .'

I held my hand up. 'All right! I get it.'

'What's going on?'

My eyes flicked between the two of them; Charlie in my rocking chair and Brooks now sitting at my desk making himself comfortable, which meant unless I told them what was truly wrong they'd be here forever. And while I didn't particularly want to go back to my reading of one of the more tragic Greek playwrights in existence, my current brand of misery wasn't looking for company.

What's going on?

What *was* going on?

I couldn't easily answer that question as I wasn't entirely sure. I'd spent the past two days trying to unpick my interaction with Kate Astley because, without admitting I'd been desperately overthinking it, the entire situation had bothered me much more than I'd ever thought possible. I also knew that while it didn't have anything directly to do with my father, his fingerprints would be found somewhere under close examination.

All roads lead to Rome, and all that.

I should never have texted her in the first place, because this was exactly what I'd predicted would happen. I'd seen it the second she realized who I was; the way her jaw clenched and her body stiffened as her eyes travelled over my initials and recognition dawned.

I'd seen that look before. I knew that look.

I could definitely blame my father for that.

It was the one which came over people right after they remembered who my father was, and the reputation he'd garnered over years and years of questionable political activity, not to mention the affairs he seemed more adept at. Lately, however, they remembered how he'd spent the summer.

Then they'd remember one or other fabricated story about me, my rowing achievements and how I was just like him – a raging lothario – likely alongside a stolen picture of me next to one of my Greek cousins who'd been wrongly labelled as my latest girlfriend.

Or perhaps like the time when a photo had been cropped to look like I was groping the arse of a passing girl, when in fact I was trying to shield my sister after her dress had caught in her underwear.

Or the week this past August when I'd given myself the first break of the entire rowing season after the World Championships – Olly, Brooks and Charlie had come over to Greece to relax, and we'd been papped the one night we decided to take a boat to the mainland for dinner with my family. The ensuing images had been splashed across every European gossip page, making me out to be some kind of endless partier hopping from one girl's bed to another.

No one ever questioned how I have the time for all the socializing and drinking and women, alongside the gruelling training hours and my coursework. No one ever said, 'There's no way he can win Olympic medals and party *that* much, it can't be true.'

But I have a problem I can do very little about.

My face.

I look good.

And that's not me being arrogant, it's stating a fact. I am aesthetically handsome; it's something to do with the thick dark wavy hair, dimples, cheekbones, the Osbourne-Cloud blue eyes my siblings and I have, and the Mediterranean skin. My grandfather always jokes my mother is part Amazonian, and I've inherited my height from her. Rowing has sculpted my body and thickened my muscles.

I've turned down more modelling contracts than I can count. I'm given the attention of anyone I pass whether I want it or not, but stopping short of never leaving the house I can't hide. And why the fuck should I hide when I've done nothing to court the limelight except compete for my country, and win? Bottom line, I've been put on a pedestal I was never consulted about, and then ordered to cling on while everyone tried to shove me off. And it's not all bad, my face does afford me a few free passes when I need them – parking ticket here, late paper turned in there.

I have a tight circle of friends who know the real me, and that's all I give a shit about.

Then nine days ago I met someone who hadn't seen my face before, didn't know my name, or my bank account. She didn't know my rowing credentials, she didn't know where I lived, or where I studied. Or how I'd spent my summer. She'd never heard of my family.

For a week it was an incredible feeling. I was starting with the blank slate I'd never been afforded, I had the luxury to reveal myself at my own pace. Show what I wanted to show.

Me. The *real* me.

I'd come to the conclusion that was the reason I'd been so angry on Saturday – the reminder that my life would be an endless stream of living under the raincloud of my hideous father and family name, forever tarred with his brush.

I couldn't escape it. Kate Astley had shown me that. I'd seen it in her eyes. The reason she'd run out of there had nothing to do with me being the president of O.U.B.C. and everything to do with the false perception of how I lived my life, because of how my father lived his.

I ran my hands through my hair and let my head fall back against the headboard, 'Just my fucking father still ruining my life.'

Brooks drained his cup of tea, placing his mug on the desk, 'What happened?'

I sighed deeply, trying to flush out all the irritation I knew was building back up in my bloodstream, and looked at them.

'You remember that girl I told you I met, the American one?'

Charlie nodded through a mouthful of chocolate chip cookies he'd run to fetch when the Jaffa Cakes had finished. 'The one you were supposed to see on Saturday?'

'Yeah. Her. Kate. Kate Astley.' I had no idea why I kept repeating her name, but I kind of liked it. 'When I snuck into the boathouse for a piss on Saturday I bumped into her. She was in the changing rooms. I was wearing my Oxford kit, and she noticed.'

Brooks' mouth formed a little O shape, but he said nothing.

'She wasn't too happy, but I brought her around to the notion it wasn't a big deal. Then she let slip the reason she was in the boathouse was because she's part of the rowing squad.'

Charlie inhaled his cookie so sharply it set him off in a coughing fit until Brooks got up and smacked him on the back. He picked up a glass of water from my desk which had been there since yesterday and gulped it down.

'She rows for Cambridge?' he wheezed eventually, wiped his eyes dry and drew his arm across his mouth.

'Cox.'

'Well, shit.'

I nodded. That summed it up perfectly. Shit.

Brooks sat back down in the chair. 'And that's what she's pissed off about?'

I shook my head, 'No, I wasn't done . . . it was fine, but then she saw my name. She knew who I was, or she knew who people think I am. She'd clearly been fed a pack of lies from the Cambridge lot. She called me ruthless and arrogant.'

'That's just loser speak for someone who wins,' grinned

Charlie, which made me properly smile for the first time in days. I could live with being called ruthless.

'Yeah, but she also called me the Hugh Hefner of rowing.' If I was honest, that accusation was the one thing really bothering me, 'What the fuck does that even mean?'

Brooks stretched his arms over his head with a huffed laugh, 'Does that make this place the Playboy Mansion? We could definitely do with some bunnies here!'

'Fuck knows, but right!' I pointed at him, 'I can't even fucking remember the last time I hooked up with someone.'

Brooks raised an eyebrow, immediately transporting me to the night I'd won gold with the British team at Worlds. We'd trained our arses off the entire season, and that evening the team let loose at a party thrown by the rowing federation. I ended up leaving with Madison Fleming, the very beautiful number four seat from the Australian team, and spent the night in her hotel room. It was an epic night of fucking and in the morning we had breakfast, then went our separate ways.

I hadn't been with anyone since.

'I mean here!' I huffed.

'What exactly did she say?' Charlie bit down on another cookie, brushing the crumbs off his shirt.

'That I'd slept with half of Cambridge.'

He nodded solemnly though I could see his lip twitching, 'I'd say you don't have the time, but you are taking classics.'

'Oh fuck off,' I wailed, 'this isn't funny!'

It only made him laugh harder.

'Then what happened?' interrupted Brooks before Charlie could say anything else.

I shrugged, 'She clearly believes whatever lies she's been told, but even if she didn't, apparently as president I'm the enemy.'

Brooks' deep scoff told me exactly what he thought of that, but then his expression changed into one I couldn't read.

'What?'

'Well . . .' he grimaced slightly, 'you kind of are the enemy. Just like Cambridge is ours.'

The argument I was about to shoot back at him died on my lips, and I slumped back down on my bed with a sigh.

'Why do I have to meet a girl I really fucking like, who rows as well, and it turns out she's a fucking light blue? Anyway, whatever,' I shrugged, because my mood was darkening again, thick and cloying, 'she's just a girl. There'll be more. I'll get over it.'

Charlie stood up, brushing more cookie off his hoodie, and sat back down on my bed.

'Mate, I'm sorry, this is fucking shit. But you don't expect us to believe the "there'll be more" story, do you?' He air-quoted exaggeratedly.

'Charles, there's nothing I can do. She believes what she wants to believe, and she rows for Cambridge. I met her for an hour. Who cares?' I added, because perhaps if I convinced them I would be able to convince myself.

I'd make myself believe there hadn't been a connection and there'd been no spark. That everything I'd felt about her since our first meeting was down to my active imagination and nothing more.

Charlie looked at me, humour gone. 'You care.'

I shrugged, not meeting his eyes.

'I'll get over it.'

'Have you spoken to her?' asked Brooks, still in his chair by my desk.

'No, I was too mad.'

'What's Olly said?'

While Olly might not be an Oxford student, he was an honorary member of our house and the only person at Cambridge who was not considered one of the enemy. His brother had been in the same house as Charlie at school, and had spent enough time with him growing up that it was easy for him to slot into our group whenever he came to visit. And when he wasn't playing rugby, Olly would come and support our races, though this was more likely down to the socializing aspect than actually watching any rowing, but we appreciated it all the same.

'Nothing much.'

Brooks stood up and stretched his arms over his head. The ceiling in our little cottage was so low that he could brush his fingers across the beams.

'Do you know anything about her?'

I tried not to wince. While I'd been stewing in a filthy mood about Kate Astley, I'd also been curious. In what wasn't my proudest moment, for the first time ever I'd done a little Google research, though I'd limited it to rowing achievements only. Anything personal she'd wanted me to know she could tell me herself, just like she had before, not that it was likely I'd get the chance again.

But what I'd found surprising, and had only made me more mad, was that nothing I found could convince me she was anything less than perfect or that she didn't wholly deserve the scholarship. Why couldn't Oxford have got there first?

'She's a decent cox. She won the east-coast championships with her team last spring, her boat was four lengths ahead. She seems to have done well around the junior circuits over there, but I couldn't find anything to say she's competed internationally. Won a lot though.' I shrugged, trying to stay as nonchalant as possible, though the way Charlie and Brooks were now staring down at me trying hard not to smile, told me I'd failed.

Truth be told, I'd spent the best part of yesterday looking for anything I could find on Kate Astley, again trying and failing to convince myself I was scoping out the competition and nothing more.

'Reckon she'll get onto Blue or Blondie?'

'Dunno, doubt Blue though, she's only a first year. She could maybe be Blondie reserve but depends on who else they've got trying out.' I shrugged again, 'Who was the Blondie cox last year?'

'The girl with the red hair?'

Brooks nodded, 'Yeah, her. Name was Sophie something, I think? Also American.'

'Yes! She was third year, she went back to the States to do her Masters. To Princeton, I think.' Charlie snapped his fingers. 'Actually, might have been Stanford.'

Brooks shook his head, 'No, so maybe it'll be your American taking her place.'

'She's not my American. She's not my anything.'

'Well, we can cross that bridge when the time comes. Maybe she won't make any crew, then all this will cease to be an issue.' Charlie shoved his hands deep into the pockets of his tracksuit pants. 'But, given how much you've "researched" her, I'd bet you're already trying to figure out a way around it in case she does.'

I was about to throw out some sarcastic retort when Brooks stood up. 'I agree. Now if you'll excuse me, I have to go back to my essay on Japanese Imperialism and the response to the West. Thanks for the tea, chaps.'

His headphones were placed back on his ears as he sauntered out and into his room, leaving both mine and his doors wide open.

'What are you doing now?' I looked at Charlie who was flicking through one of my books on Roman archaeology.

'Not writing an essay on Japan, or whatever it was. I have a call with my study group, then we have training at four.' He put the book down, turning just before he reached the hallway. 'Maybe you could be in a better mood by then.'

He was right, I couldn't be in a bad mood forever, though I knew I could give it a good try. I might have a reputation for being competitive – or ruthless, as seemed to be the preferred term – and I put in the hours to win, but my nature was generally easygoing. Around people that knew me, that was.

It hadn't been the greatest chat in the world, but I did feel a little better than I had before they'd invited them-selves in. I picked up my phone, completely ignoring the voice in my head that said I needed to forget about Kate Astley, and instead scrolled back through the messages we'd exchanged during the week because I was a glutton for punishment.

I grinned at the message she'd sent teasing me about my classics degree, and my smile was just as wide as it had been when I'd read it the first time. Flirty, funny, smart. She was really fucking smart. I was also a complete sucker for a girl who could serve up a healthy dose of sarcasm.

She'd been wrong; she was *exactly* the girl I thought she was. Sweet, smart, loyal.

We had so much in common, we'd talked so openly and easily with each other, and that was before I discovered she rowed too.

Fucking hell.

She wasn't just a girl. She was *the* girl. I'd paid very little attention to what people thought of me in the past, yet for some reason her opinion mattered.

I couldn't do anything about my position at Oxford, but I could do something about the lies she'd been told.

And try to convince her otherwise.

6. Kate

(Naming a dead guy is harder than it sounds . . .)

Oz: *Question for a question. Did you know that the Boat Race was started by two friends? One was at Cambridge and the other at Oxford? No enemies in sight . . . Your turn next*

A watched pot never boils, or so the saying goes. Something like that, anyway.

But give me a cell phone you don't want to buzz, with a message from the one person you don't want to hear from, and it never goddamn stops.

If three unanswered messages in a row counts as never stops.

I slipped my phone into my backpack, trying not to wonder whether there'd be a fourth, and followed Imogen and Hannah out of the changing rooms, zipping up my puffa jacket on the way and pulling up my hood. The clouds had broken thirty minutes into practice and from the sounds of it crashing against the roof, the rain was still pouring.

'God, I'm starving,' Hannah mumbled, stuffing a protein bar into her mouth. 'If we hurry we've got time to grab a breakfast roll to have on the train back.'

'Good idea,' I replied, clutching my stomach as it rumbled louder than the thunder.

This morning's drills had been intense, and I wasn't one of the crew powering us through the water at what felt like a thousand miles an hour. I was the one huddled down in the back directing them where to go. At the end of the corridor members of the team were pushing open the entrance door, standing underneath the sign which read 'Where We Prepare to Win Boat Races' for a few seconds before they braved the downpour and ran the distance to the train station. Every time the door opened, a gust of cold air blew in, making me wish I'd worn my thermals.

'Astley, do you have a minute?'

I spun around in the corridor to find Coach Stephens, the Cambridge women's rowing chief coach, standing in the doorway of his office.

I glanced back at the girls, whose hunger appeared to have been momentarily forgotten as they stared at me with widening eyes. Beyond our initial meeting, none of us had spoken to Coach Stephens or really been in his presence; we were junior members of the wider training crew and our position was a little too far down the ladder for him to be part of our sessions. So far, our morning training had been run by the assistant coaches, while I also had a separate training session with Coach Godwin, my coxing coach.

A legend in the rowing world, and former Cambridge rowing alumnus and Olympian, Coach Stephens had led the Cambridge women's team to Boat Race victory six times in the past ten years, as well as claiming multiple wins at the Henley Regatta. With his shock of thick white hair and rounded belly he could be confused with Santa if his beard wasn't as black as coal, but I'd heard he always dressed up for Christmas to deliver presents to the local children's hospital, before returning in his costume for the Boat Club party.

'Sure, Coach. What's up?' I walked towards him.

'How are you finding the training?'

I blinked, trying hard not to show too much surprise, 'Good, thanks. It's been hard but I like a challenge. I'm glad to be back on the water though, it's been a few weeks.'

'It's always good to be on the water,' he nodded. 'How are you enjoying Cambridge?'

'I'm settling in, thanks. Haven't had time for a proper tour of the city yet, but soon hopefully.'

He looked down at the clipboard he was holding. 'You're studying medicine, right?'

'Yes, sir.'

'How are you with balancing your schedule? Medicine is a busy course, lots of work. Intense.'

'Excellent balancing skills, Coach. Great at scheduling.' I smiled, though not without confusion as to where this conversation was heading, and I had a train to catch so I could keep to said schedule. 'Coach, is there a reason why you're concerned about my schedule? I've not been late, I can do both.'

He pinned me with a stare, dark brown eyes boring through me until a chill zipped down my spine, making me hope I'd sounded more convincing than I felt.

'Yes. You've impressed me over the past week. Coach Godwin told me your skills have been excellent in steering through the currents, and seeing you out this morning I'm inclined to agree. Weather wasn't easy today.'

'No, sir. Thank you.'

'We have a race this weekend, against Durham. Becka

Jones has moved up to cox Blue Boat, so we need a strong coxswain for Blondie. I'd like to see how you go in the stern.' He pointed at me. 'It's hard work, requires a lot of dedication and hours, but I'm sure you can handle it.'

It was possible I blanked out for a nanosecond because one moment I was staring at my coach while he promoted me to leader of the number two women's boat and the next he was sitting at his desk shuffling a pile of paperwork.

I might have a scholarship, but I hadn't expected to be given such a prominent spot so soon.

'Better get back to school, Astley. See you at the boat-house this afternoon.'

'Yes, sir. Coach. Thank you.'

I'd completely forgotten the girls were still there, standing halfway down the corridor when I turned back, both their mouths hanging open, making it clear they'd heard everything. They swiftly grabbed me in a hug which lifted me off my feet.

'Holy shit, Asters. Blondie! This is huge!' Hannah squealed. 'Well fucking done!'

'Did that really just happen?' I whispered, once my feet were touching the floor again. 'He made me cox?'

'Yes! That's amazing!' Imogen squeezed my shoulder. 'Really amazing.'

As I looked over Hannah's shoulder I spied the clock on the wall, and the time. 'Shit, we're going to miss the train. Come on.'

We all pulled our hoods up and took off. The rain had slowed down to a less thumping pace but it still wasn't much fun to run in, having already been sitting in it for the past ninety minutes. You'd think after spending my last five falls and winters rowing, I'd be used to it, but I hated it. The only thing worse than rain was wind *and* rain.

From the look on Hannah's face as we made it to the station and took shelter under the platform awnings, along with every other C.U.B.C. squad member, she agreed.

'Bloody hell, why didn't I decide to go to Stanford instead? Bet Sophie Robson is loving the sunshine over there right now!'

'Who's that?' I asked, pointlessly shaking off my rain-coat, considering it would get wet again the second we stepped out from the shelter once the train arrived.

'She was the cox for Blue Boat last year, but graduated and went back to California for a PhD.'

'Oh! That's why Becka Jones has moved up.' I rubbed my hands together, attempting to get some warmth into them.

'Yeah, we swapped one Yank for another,' grinned Imogen as a raindrop dripped off her nose, then her eyes widened. 'Oh, thank fuck. The train's here.'

Aside from the lucky few who'd managed to grab a space on the bus taking students back to campus, everyone piled into the train carriage and immediately shook them-selves dry. A couple of the boys removed towels from their backpacks to rub through their hair, and I made a mental note to make sure I packed a towel for tomorrow.

We found a spare set of six seats and I plonked myself down in the seat next to Hannah with Imogen sitting opposite us by the window. 'Thank god we haven't got our first class until ten a.m., we need to dry off, and I need food.'

I groaned, 'You might want to rethink the food and keep an empty stomach, we meet our cadavers today.'

89

Hannah grimaced, and I swear her face took on a slightly green tinge, though it could have been the reflection of clouds outside. 'Ew. I don't know how you can spend the whole day with a dead person.'

Imogen shrugged. 'It's not all day, it's just the morning. After lunch we have theory.'

The train jerked forward and began its journey, just as a second shower of rain hit me in the face, only it wasn't rain and it was coming from inside the carriage. Three of the boys' crew had decided to sit in our empty seats, shaking off their wet jackets as they did.

'Norris, shove over, will you?' the tallest of the boys grumbled.

Norris, a tall guy with a mop of red curls stuffed into a beanie, sat down with a thud next to me.

'Hi ladies, how was your training session?'

'Harder in the rain,' I muttered, not noticing how Hannah had sat up a little straighter.

'Tell me about it!' he grinned wide. 'I'm Will Norris. These two are Fletcher and Tubbs.' Fletcher and Tubbs nodded, though neither seemed particularly interested in joining a conversation. To be fair to them it was eight thirty on a Monday morning and we'd all been awake three hours, something Tubbs was feeling seeing as it appeared he'd already fallen asleep.

'We know. You're seat six for the Blue Boat,' came Hannah's voice next to me, and he could have been Harry Styles for the way she sighed, just as I remembered this was the guy dating Mary Heston, the women's president. 'Congratulations on the Henley wins this summer, and on making President.'

'Thanks.'

My body twisted around for a better look at him. I'd clearly been half asleep when he'd introduced himself, though he looked completely different to when I'd seen him raging about losing the oars. Less red in the face, for one thing.

I'd missed watching the Henley Regatta this year. Once I'd been accepted to Cambridge, I spent all my free time helping my dad on his fishing boat trying to earn as much money as possible. I was smart enough to know I couldn't hold down work, training *and* a job. I'd also completely missed the World Championships. Perhaps if I hadn't, I'd have recognized Oz the second I'd seen him.

Since our interaction on Saturday I'd tried not to think about him, except not thinking about someone is hard when it's all you'd been doing for the week prior. The turn of events was far too confusing for me to be able to wrap my head around so quickly. Too quickly in fact for me to also not spend my newly wide-open Saturday evening reading up on the Oxford president it appeared I'd been fraternizing with.

His rowing credentials were impressive. More than impressive. And as I'd hidden under my comforter like a kid at camp after lights-out, and read page after page and watched video after video brought up in Google's search, my disappointment had sunk deeper and deeper. An Olympic medal, World Championship medals, Henley Regatta Cup winner, European Rowing Championships – you name it, Oz had competed in it. And won. He was a rowing prodigy.

I hadn't had many people in my life I could talk to about rowing, beyond the bare minimum. But looking through his achievements made me long to pick up my phone and ask him what the Olympics had been like, how he'd trained, how he liked the World Championship course.

Or anything about the Boat Race.

But I couldn't.

Every time I closed my eyes, all I could see was his cold, icy stare pinning me with a level of anger which made his jaw clench. It had been harder to forget the hurt I'd also seen as I repeated what Imogen had told me, because that hurt did more to set doubt in my mind than his words of denial. In fact, if I'd had a list of qualities for the Oz I'd met and placed it side-by-side with a list from the guy Imogen had described, I'd swear they were two different people.

But it didn't matter, because even if he was the guy I'd first thought, he was still Oxford President, and that was *way* worse. Therefore, my interlude with Oz or Arthur Osbourne-Cloud or A.O.-C., or whatever his name is, would stay relegated to the week before term began.

I just wish I didn't feel so confused about it.

'What are you thinking about?'

My head shot up to find Imogen staring at me. 'What?'

'Your face, it's all screwed up.'

'She's thinking about the cadaver you guys are hanging with later,' laughed Hannah.

'Are you taking medicine?' asked Fletcher, whose legs were now stretched out so they almost went underneath Imogen's seat diagonal to him.

I nodded. 'Yep, Imogen and I are both first year. What about you?'

'I'm fourth year med. Enjoy your first week! That means you have Professor Hull today. You need to pay attention to her because she'll call on you when you least expect it. Always look like you're writing something down,' he paused and snapped his finger, 'oh, and she likes you to name your cadavers. She gives a prize to the most inventive name at the end of the term.'

I laughed, 'Really?'

'Yeah.'

'What was yours called?' asked Imogen.

'Mephistopheles,' he grinned.

'The demon?' she replied with wide eyes, widening even more when he nodded in surprise. 'That's brave with a dead guy.'

'Did you win?'

'No, that honour went to Justin Finch who named his cadaver Marvellous Mary.'

I frowned, 'Why was she marvellous?'

'We're all still trying to figure that one out.' He chuckled.

The train slowed, and we pulled into the next stop. Imogen wiped her hand over the condensation on the window to see where we were, then turned back to me. 'Okay Asters, let's get brainstorming.'

I groaned, my head falling back on the seat rest. I didn't have the cells to come up with a winning cadaver name, I needed coffee before that happened.

'Asters?'

I opened one eye, the one nearest to Norris so I had to make minimal effort to turn, 'My name's Kate Astley. It got shortened to Asters at some point over the past week.'

'Asters here was just named cox for Blondie on Saturday.'

He grinned wide. 'No way! Congratulations.'

I straightened back up again, with both eyes open. 'Thanks. It's only for one race though.'

He laughed, and for a second I wondered what on earth he saw in Mary Heston. He seemed to have a permanent smile, whereas she looked like she was forever trying to plot your slow death.

'Have faith, Godwin wouldn't try you if he didn't believe you could do it. He's tough. But we have a strong team coming together, it's going to be a good year.'

'Yeah, we have a title to keep hold of.' Tubbs opened one eye.

'When are you getting the oars back?'

'When A.O.-C. is least expecting it, but it'll be soon.' He barked out a laugh and tapped the side of his nose. From the way he grinned at Norris and Fletcher it was clear they'd already decided exactly when, where and how they were going to do it.

'Are you planning on taking the crown too?' asked Hannah.

'Of course! We have the double to win; it hasn't been done in a good few years, but I have a feeling this will be the year.' He rubbed his hands together in the manner befitting an evil mastermind. 'And next time they attempt to get the oars back again, we'll be ready.'

'I thought we'd be ready this time, especially with my chain bolting them in place,' grumbled Tubbs who'd closed his eyes again. 'They broke Rule Five.'

'Rule Five?' I asked.

'Yes, mascot must be removed without damage to property. The heist has a set of rules which we've all agreed to abide by. Have you heard about them?'

I frowned slightly as a memory shot to the front of my brain. I'd seen that written in the boathouse. 'Are they hanging on the wall at Goldie?'

Norris nodded, 'Yes, and they're strict. Though to be fair, the chain we wrapped around the oars shouldn't have technically been there, so we overlooked the fact they cut through it. And really, it was amateur of us to assume it would stop them. It wouldn't have stopped us.'

'So when are you going to get them back?'

'That's top secret, I'm afraid. But very soon. Need to make up for the race last weekend.'

'I'm sorry you lost. We were watching on Saturday, cheering you on.' Hannah pulled nervously on the hood of her coat, as though she was speaking out of turn. 'They looked very strong. Not sure anyone would have beaten them.'

'Yeah, three lengths is a lot,' I agreed.

Norris nodded. 'I agree it was unfortunate. But I've been thinking about it, and it might have lulled them into a false sense of security that they're stronger than us this year.'

Imogen shrugged, 'I dunno, I saw A.O.-C. after they'd won and he didn't look happy about it. He stormed right past me. Didn't even look tired.'

'Yeah, he's going through a tough time right now,' replied Norris, but I'd already jerked around to Imogen, sitting so straight up it was like a metal rod had been pushed down my spine.

'When was that?'

'What?'

'When Oz . . . I mean . . . when A.O.-C. stormed past you? We were together the whole time. I never saw him.'

'Um . . .' her brows dropped, 'you'd gone to get some beers, I think.'

'Oh.' I looked down at my knees, crossing one over the other, and praying no one noticed the outburst I'd just had. Or that I'd used his name, or one of his names.

Come to think of it, I didn't know what to call him, so it was probably wiser to stay silent in future.

But Imogen didn't seem to have noticed because she was already quizzing Norris.

'What's he like? I heard he has an awful temper.'

Norris simply chuckled, and looked at Fletcher who grinned.

'Nah, he's a decent guy. Always gets dumped with a lot of unfair shit, but I'm on the British squad with him and he's a good crewmate.'

His reply did nothing to help my confusion, but Imogen harrumphed, making Fletcher laugh just as the train began slowing and he stood up. 'We're home. I have to dash. Good to meet you ladies. Asters, good luck Saturday.'

'We won't be seeing you this afternoon?'

Norris shook his head, the rest of us joining as he stood up. Fletcher was already by the carriage doors waiting for them to open as soon as we stopped moving. 'We don't normally train together; the men's and women's crews only train together on the weekends. But the three of us had a session out with your coach this morning.'

'Oh.' I threaded my arms through my backpack and hitched it onto my shoulders. 'See you at the weekend then. Thanks for the insight.'

The five of us joined the small group stepping off the train; and Norris and Tubbs took off in the direction

Fletcher had disappeared. Thankfully the rain had already stopped in Cambridge so we weren't subjected to another soaking, and the three of us headed back to our classes.

'Clive? No. Brad? No. Humphrey Bogart? No.'

I looked down at him. My guy. His waxy, lifeless body with a tiny red heart tattooed over his own heart. We'd been in here an hour, and my belly was still churning from the smell; the pungent mix of chemicals and rotting. Two guys had already thrown up, but the balm we'd had to wipe under our noses was stopping me from needing to vomit just yet. I glanced over to Imogen who seemed to be whispering quietly, taking me back to the beautiful February day we'd scattered Jake's ashes in the Sound.

Professor Hull, leading our anatomy and physiology module, had instructed us to absorb the room, understand death, show care and respect to each of the cadavers for we wouldn't make it through school without them. We'd get used to it, she said. If we didn't, we'd have bigger problems. By the end of the year your cadaver will be your best friend.

Wasn't quite sure I agreed on her last point.

What did I know about him already? Very little actually. The form on the clipboard said he'd died of a heart attack, late fifties. A Cambridge lifer, he'd donated his body to the university because he believed in the pursuit of knowledge and science. Apparently, I assumed anyway. Why else would you donate your body to be practised upon?

'Maybe I'll call you Galileo. Leo for short.' I placed my hand on the sheet covering him, pulling it up a little, then stopped myself. He couldn't feel the cold. 'I'll take care of you. Hopefully you're having a ball in heaven. I guess you're there, no one going to hell would have bothered donating their body.'

Leo didn't confirm or deny his afterlife status.

'I'm Kate. I'm from the United States. I'm studying medicine, obviously.' I chuckled, quietly, lest Professor Hull think I was being disrespectful. 'I've been here nearly two weeks now. Jet lag is gone, thank God. I'm on the rowing squad, and I'm coxing Blondie at the weekend, which I'm super pumped for. Now I need to work extra hard to keep my place so I can be part of history when we beat Oxford . . . did you ever row for Cambridge? I've been wondering what it's like to be part of the race.'

I stared down at Leo, unsure why, or what I was waiting for. It was strange talking to someone who couldn't talk back, it was almost a type of one-way therapy but without the feeling you were talking to yourself. Even though you were.

Thinking about it now, I realized I could tell him anything and he wouldn't tell a soul.

I could tell him about Oz. About the night I'd met him, because up to this point I'd confided in no one. The first week had been so busy that I'd never got around to telling Hannah and Imogen about him. I was about to, but that was right as Imogen started talking and I found out who he really was, making me thankful I hadn't.

Oz would be a very brief period of my life no one else need know about.

Perhaps Leo would become my new best friend seeing as he was the only person I could confide in about the three unreplied-to messages burning a hole in the bottom of my backpack and what I was supposed to do about them.

My very confused brain began throbbing again. Maybe Leo was my only hope in solving the conundrum.

I opened my mouth just as a bell rang.

'Okay, class done. See you all again on Friday. No vomiting this time. Get your cadaver names down on your clipboard, and leave it in the box by the door,' Professor Hull called out, her voice bouncing off the hard, white Metro-tiled walls.

I was writing out Leo's name when I was yanked hard to the right. 'Come on, let's get out of here. We need fresh air. Hannah was right, it's creepy in here.'

I chuckled. 'You're okay, be thankful you won't be forever known as Pukey Pukerson. Anyway, I saw you chatting away. What did you name yours?'

'Mr Peppermint,' she whispered as we dropped our clipboards in the box and walked out to the lockers we'd left our belongings in.

'What? Why?'

'Oh, I couldn't think of anything and Mr Peppermint was the name of my rabbit when I was a kid. He was small and fat, just like my cadaver. I thought it worked well,' she replied, making me laugh as she pulled on a hoodie followed by her puffa. She sniffed inside her shirt. 'Urgh, I smell like formaldehyde. Can we change before lunch?'

'Yes. Good idea.'

The cold fresh air hit us when we walked outside, and we breathed deep until our lungs were full. 'We'll get used to it.' I nudged her as I caught the expression on her face.

'I hope so.'

We hopped on our bikes and hurried past the dozens and dozens of students who'd all had classes breaking at the same time we did; some walking through the university streets and narrow passages, some cycling like us. Twenty minutes later our bikes were safely locked up in the bike racks at Downing College.

Imogen was waiting for me as I fastened the padlock on mine, 'Why's that guy staring at you like you murdered his puppy or something?'

I turned around to find Olly, Oz's friend, maybe not quite looking like I'd murdered something he loved, but he definitely wasn't as friendly as he'd been the week prior.

I quickly turned back to Imogen. 'Dunno, weird.'

I was hoping he'd walk off, so we didn't need to pass him, but instead he slowed his pace.

'Want to stare harder?' snapped Imogen, stalking past him up the steps at such a speed I was having to take them two at a time to keep up.

It only made him grin, which in turn made me scowl. If I wasn't careful, I'd be outed about something that I wanted no part of, and the weight of keeping that secret made itself known in my chest.

'Okay, two minutes to change, then I'll buy you a sandwich at this place my sister told me about.'

I stripped off the second I stepped inside my dorm room, throwing all my smelly clothes in the laundry on top of the clothes I'd worn for training. At this rate I needed to add extra time in my schedule to spend in the laundry.

I should have predicted it would happen before it did. After seeing Olly outside I knew I was on borrowed time before my phone buzzed with another message.

I reached for my phone, gingerly opening it up in case he somehow could see me.

There they were – four in a row.

> **Oz:** *Kate, please can we talk?*
>
> **Oz:** *I promise I'm not the Hugh Hefner of rowing,*
> *I look ridiculous in silk robes . . .* 😊
>
> **Oz:** *Question for a question. Did you know that the Boat*
> *Race was started by two friends? One was Cambridge*
> *and the other Oxford? No enemies in sight . . . Your turn next*
>
> **Oz:** *Olly just said you're definitely falling in love with him,*
> *please tell me it's not true*

That last message got me, and when Imogen found me two minutes later pulling on a fresh-smelling pair of leggings, I still had a smile on my face.

'What?'

'Nothing, just hungry.'

I slipped my phone in my pocket and followed her out. I should message him to stop, but for some reason I couldn't bring myself to, especially when all I was wondering about was what the next message would say.

7. Arthur

(Tenacity, *noun*.
The quality of being very determined)

Asking for a friend.

How many unanswered texts does it take until you're labelled a stalker? Or worse, a total loser.

Six? Seven?

Ten maybe?

I think I was currently sliding on the scale somewhere between 'Saddest Man on Campus' and 'I'm calling the police.' Why was I still trying?

Because one week and three messages ago I saw the bubble of dot dot dots appear. Then they stopped.

I waited. And waited.

But nothing.

Still, I figured the dots were a good sign.

Or at least *a* sign.

I told myself I'd stop at nine messages. One for each of the seats in a boat, plus the cox. Obviously, I couldn't leave the coxswain out, seeing as that was Kate's position. So nine it had been, until it became ten, then eleven . . .

You see my predicament.

'Mate, you've been staring at your phone for five minutes. Either fucking text her or don't. But can you make your mind up please because I'm sitting here like a total lemon, talking to myself. If anyone sees us it'll incorrectly appear like I'm boring. And I'm not, I have an actual problem.'

I put my phone face down on the table and looked up at Charlie, making sure I showed him my best and most winning smile. I knew it had worked when he huffed at me.

'I apologize,' I swapped my phone for my pint, and sipped it. 'What's up? And if you could repeat what you were saying, that would be appreciated. Also, where are the guys?'

No matter how intense things got during the year, we tried to keep to a regular Saturday evening social. Whoever was around would come down to our usual table at the Blue Oar on Saturday evenings and have a drink; some of the boys would bring a deck of cards, Scrabble, or occasionally in Charlie's case, a jigsaw puzzle.

It was a good way to bond, relax our bodies from training but also keep ourselves in check ahead of it all beginning again on Sunday. Drinking until three a.m. and staggering home wasn't an option when you rowed for Oxford and spent eight months of your year preparing for one race.

'Brooks and Frank are down at the Tank on patrol. Joshi, Bitters and Drake will be here soon, Marshy's on a date, and Fellows is polishing off an essay he's late to hand in but said he'd come for last orders if he finished it.'

'Sounds good, any news from patrol?'

'All quiet on the western front,' Charlie shook his head, serving up a mischievous smile as he did, 'for now at least, but it'll be soon. I can feel it.'

'I agree.'

I slowly drummed my fingers against my pint glass as I pondered. It had been three weeks since we stole Cambridge's oars, and the Oxford crew all knew that we were living on borrowed time.

Two weeks ago, we'd all sat down with a calendar Charlie had plotted out detailing the potential heist windows Cambridge could use to steal them back, along with our crown. He'd somehow managed to obtain the course schedules, expected coursework dates and training times, along with the personal diaries for each member of the Blue Boat crew, then mapped it all out.

I didn't ask how he'd discovered all this information, because knowing Charlie it wasn't legal and I'd need full deniability.

There was a finite number of dates. Last Thursday was one of them, but it came and went with no movement. Tonight was the next potential date on the calendar, and Charlie was convinced it would be now. I was inclined to agree with him based on the simple fact that Charlie was never wrong. Annoyingly.

Like our east of England rivals, Oxford University had two official boathouse/training facilities: a larger one based on a clear stretch of river, the other near to the university and used for land training, and in Oxford's case it was where our rowing tank was located. Since we'd taken possession of the Golden Oars, they'd been stored safely at the Tank which also happened to be where the Crown was currently under lock and key.

As both mascots were at the Tank, we'd set up our patrols there; because as stated in rule number one, the heist must be undertaken without anyone knowing and we were determined to catch them in the act. Charlie and I had our sleeping bags at the ready. We were heading down tonight after last orders at the pub, to switch out with Brooks and Frank at midnight. Our bed for the night would be the couch in the break rooms.

I just stopped myself from checking my phone to see if Kate had decided to reply to me when I realized Charlie was still talking.

'. . . so now she's going to be in my study group. Can you fucking believe it?!'

My eyes widened, which I knew was the reaction he was going for seeing as one could mistake him for a fire-breathing dragon for how irate he was. Any second I expected his nostrils to start smoking.

'Shit!'

'I know.' He gulped down half of his pint in one go, almost slamming it back on the table. 'Do you think if I lodge a complaint to the physics department I'll be able to get her removed?'

'Um . . . probably not. Why don't you want her again?'

He rolled his eyes so deeply I was surprised they didn't get stuck. 'Did you listen to anything I said?'

'Of course I did!' I protested as convincingly as possible, though my acting skills left a lot to be desired. 'I heard that you have a new lab partner . . .'

He sat back, crossing his arms over his chest. 'It's Evie.'

This time my mouth dropped open in genuine horror, or shock . . . empathy maybe. Disbelief.

'No!'

'Finally, I have your attention,' he drolled.

'Oh mate, what the fuck? How'd that happen?'

Charlie shrugged. The annoyance and anger he'd shown five minutes ago had been replaced with frustration, and the hurt he'd worked so hard on letting go flashed in his eyes and laced the heavy sigh he released.

To everyone apart from Charlie, the fact Evie Waters was no longer in his life was good riddance. To Charles Masterson, however, she was The One. The one he'd loved first, the one who broke his heart and the one he did everything he now could to avoid.

Charlie and Evie were *the* couple of sixth form. For two people who attended different schools, they were joined at the hip. She'd been his first love, and while everyone around him – friends, family, anyone who met her – found Evie a giant pain in the arse, they put up with it because they loved Charlie. That was until the night he'd snuck out of Eton and driven over to surprise Evie at school, only to find her otherwise preoccupied with Hector Bygraves, a recent graduate from Harrow who'd just returned from his gap year helping to build schools in Chile.

It was never entirely clear why Evie cheated, and to my knowledge it wasn't something he bothered to ask. He blocked her from his life then and there, and announced he was moving on. That summer he qualified for the British rowing team, and anger rowed his way to gold in the Under-23s World Championships.

Unfortunately, plans they'd had to both attend Oxford had been set in motion long before they broke up, and come August when exam results were in, they were both accepted. Charlie, like me, was expected to attend. Evie also decided to move forward with Oxford and was set to belong to Trinity College, like Charlie, until Charlie and I hacked the Oxford servers and moved her to Pembroke – the furthest college away from us. Predictably, because Evie is Evie, the second we arrived at Oxford she convinced Charlie to give it another go, but that had lasted the length of half a term when she hooked up with Dave Chamberlain, a second year on the Oriel college rugby team.

Shortly after that disaster, we moved to our house off campus, and he never ran into her again.

But now it appeared that was all about to change.

'She's added philosophy to her course, and I have physics and philosophy so for some reason she's in our module group.' He leaned back and banged his head a few times in quick succession on the wall. 'I don't know why she would do that!'

I had an idea; I'd heard a few weeks ago that Evie had broken up with David Chamberlain, and I wondered if she'd come sniffing back round to fuck with one or both of them, but if she thought she'd get anywhere near Charlie's heart, she could think the fuck again.

'Did you speak to her?'

He shook his head. 'No. I walked out.'

'How many people are in your module group?'

'Ten. So I can't even hide.' He sighed again, 'This module group is graded as a whole, so we have to carry each other. There can be no weak links, but I really don't want to be part of her getting a decent grade.'

'Oh fuck, mate, I'm sorry. That's really fucked up. I'd say I'd attend your classes with you, but not sure even I can pull off feigning interest in philosophy. Maybe we should get you some security guards . . .'

I stopped talking as his eyes widened, and he snapped his fingers.

'No! I need a girlfriend.'

'What?' I crooked my head, checking I'd heard right.

After Evie had dumped him the second time around, he'd sworn off girls and stuck to it, save for a couple of drunken hook-ups here and there. He'd never brought a girl back to the house, and he'd never mentioned one.

'Not a real one, obviously. I need someone to pretend to be my girlfriend, so Evie won't speak to me.' He frowned slightly, his thinking face forming with a slight purse of his lips. 'Yes, that's what I need. Has your American got any friends?'

'What?' I said again. Sometimes, keeping up with the speed at which Charlie's brain worked was an impossible feat.

'Oz. Does your American girlfriend have any friends who can be my fake girlfriend?' he repeated slowly, enunciating every word.

'I'm not remedial, Charles. I heard you the first time, I'm just processing your question. While I fully support your quest to find a fake girlfriend, there are some details you'll need to iron out, not to mention the first, I don't have an American girlfriend. Kate hasn't replied to a single one of my messages, and I'd imagine that any friends she does have are based in Cambridge like her. If you want a fake girlfriend she's going to need to be around campus, otherwise she's nothing more than a rumour and Evie will still bother you.'

'Yes. Yes, you're right.' He spun quickly, scanning the bar as though checking to see if Future Fake Girlfriend was in here now. I almost felt sorry for her, she had no idea what she'd be letting herself in for. 'Think there's anyone on the rowing squad?'

I did a mental scan. I hadn't noticed anyone new on the O.U.W.B.C. squad, not that I paid that much attention anyway, but recently my mind had been too busy focusing on other things. American things.

'I don't know.'

'Maybe I should put an ad out,' he pondered, then snapped his fingers a second time as a brainwave occurred for another likely suspect. 'Fuck, why didn't I think of it already? Brooks' sister started this year. She'll do.'

Beer dribbled down my chin as I missed my mouth with the glass, and wiped it away with my hand.

'Oh, please let me be there when you ask him.'

'Why? I'm not asking, I don't need permission. It's not an actual relationship, and I'm not looking to date her. I just need people to think we are.'

I grinned, 'Yes, I know.'

'Don't make it weird.'

'Oh, I have full faith you'll do that all by yourself.'

He scowled at me just as I caught a flash of movement, then the thud of a giant fist in my arm announced exactly who it was. 'Ow, fuck that hurt!'

Bitters plonked himself in the chair next to me and shifted forward as I tried to punch him back, but the guy could dodge a bullet, with reaction times to rival any championship boxer and the power to match. Come to think about it, if he stopped rowing he'd make a very mean heavyweight. Drake sat down on the other side of him, shaking his head in amusement. We'd all been the recipient of a Bitters dead arm.

I rubbed my throbbing arm. 'Is Joshi with you?'

'Yes, just at the bar.' He nodded in the general direction, though I couldn't see Joshi through the crowd of first years on a pub crawl – identifiable from the tartan socks and golfing caps they were all wearing – until the crowd split and Joshi walked through, somehow carrying five pints of beer and not spilling a drop. Bitters took one and downed half of it before Joshi had even taken his seat.

'Thanks, buddy.'

'You're welcome,' Joshi replied, taking his own large glug before wiping the thin moustache of foam from his lip. 'What's been going on? Have you heard from the boys?'

I used the opportunity to check my phone, but the screen was blank. Nothing from the boys.

Nothing from Kate.

'Nope.'

'It's going to be tonight. I'm telling you.' Charlie stretched out in his chair, his arms lengthening above him. 'And I'm thinking maybe we need a couple more sleeping over in the boathouse, especially if the whole crew comes like we did.'

Bitters cracked his knuckles. 'I'll stay over.'

'You can't punch anyone.'

'Why would I do that?' he asked, genuinely confused. 'If they do come tonight you'll need help.'

I rolled my eyes. 'Thank you. If we catch them, they have to leave empty handed. We all know the rules. They caught our boys three years ago and we left quietly, until the next attempt. They'll do the same.'

The noise of my phone buzzing on the table nearly had me falling out of my chair as I snatched it up, not from shock but the possibility it was Kate. Which was when I realized I may have entirely lost any cool I'd previously possessed.

It wasn't Kate.

'Oz, you need to get down here,' ordered Brooks.

'The Tank?'

'Yeah, we've got a problem.'

'On the way.' I hung up and stood, and four sets of eyes tracked my movement. 'Something's happened at the Tank.'

Charlie drained his beer and grabbed his jacket, 'I fucking told you they'd come tonight.'

'We don't know what it is yet,' mumbled Drake.

'Want to bet me a hundred quid it's not the Light Blues?' shot back Charlie.

'No.'

I had no doubt the grin he'd thrown Drake would soon be wiped off his face.

'Come on, we need to hurry.'

The five of us took off in a quick jog down to the Tank, though it probably would have been quicker if we didn't have a couple of pints sloshing around in our bellies. I was planning for the five of us to go in quietly, just in case Brooks and Frank needed us for the element of surprise, but as we turned the corner it was clear that whatever was going on wasn't happening under the cloak of darkness.

Joshi stopped running, and took a second to catch his breath. 'This doesn't look good.'

Every single light in the Tank was on, including the floodlights directed onto the running track outside.

'Shit!' Drake pointed to a black Land Rover which had clearly been stopped in a hurry, given it was diagonally across two spaces and the driver's door was still ajar. 'That's Coach's car.'

The sound of raised voices had us all turning in sync to the direction of the entrance, then all four boys looked at me.

'After you, Mr President.' Drake gestured for me to lead the way.

I stepped towards the increasing noise, the four boys keeping close behind until one voice above all else stopped the shouting dead. Coach Lassiter was not someone you wanted to argue with, even when he was having a good day.

Today was not that day.

The five of us sprinted down the corridor and pushed through the door. I'm not sure what we'd expected to find, but it definitely wasn't this.

Three of the Cambridge crew stood against the wall looking slightly dishevelled, while Frank was resting against the large oak pillar with his head tipped back, and from the blood across his shirt I could only assume it stemmed from his nose.

Brooks had positioned himself between Frank and Will Norris, looking like he'd happily dish out a second or third helping of whatever Frank had been served. In turn, Will Norris was standing over Brett Rogers, an American rower formerly of Princeton, and currently the Cambridge number four, who was slumped on the floor, his elbows resting on his knees, along with a rapidly purpling and swollen eye.

Normally, Will Norris, in what was a total contradiction to his fiery red hair, was one of the most affable guys I knew. Always cracking a joke, never in a bad mood, the perfect crewmate on my British squad; we shared a lot of laughs, along with our highly competitive spirit. But right now he was sporting an expression I'd never seen before — even when we'd lost to the Americans and had to take silver at the World Championships in a photo finish, he hadn't looked as angry as he did currently.

Through the glass of his office, I could see Coach pacing up and down, phone to his ear and, from the colour of his face, doing his best impression of a volcano about to erupt at any moment.

I was on the verge of asking who he was talking to when the yelling started up again, but seven loud voices all shouting over each other made it almost impossible to decipher exactly what they were saying. Frank lowered his head, only for the bleeding to start up again, thick scarlet globs dropping onto the concrete floor. A broken chair, which looked like it had been snapped in two, had been kicked to the side.

'Jesus,' muttered Joshi.

Seven large strides and I was between Brooks and Norris, who were now glaring at each other.

'Norris, what the fuck, mate? What happened?' I placed my hand on his rigid shoulder.

He was about to answer when a voice by his feet snarled, 'It was an accident.'

'Bullshit, you saw me, you did it on purpose.'

'No, I didn't, you French prick! But *you* hit *me* on purpose!'

113

'And I'll fucking do it again,' Frank spat back.

'ENOUGH!' Coach yelled, his voice once more cutting through the noise like nails down a chalkboard, making everyone wince. It didn't matter that every guy in the room was over six feet three inches, and two hundred pounds, when Coach spoke you listened.

I stepped back to join the boys I'd walked in with, and leaned into Drake. 'What's Coach even doing here?'

'Dunno,' he muttered.

'You're a bunch of goddamn children!' he snapped. 'God knows what would have happened if I hadn't been passing! All the fucking lights on and I walk in to find you two behaving like you're in a boxing ring and the rest about to join in. You could have been seriously hurt! You're lucky you're not concussed.'

He jabbed a thick finger at Frank and Brett Rogers; the latter I'm certain shrank back slightly. 'You're athletes, professional athletes. Start fucking acting like it. Both of you represent your countries, and more importantly your universities. We let you continue this heist in the spirit of competition, but it's getting out of hand.'

Coach looked slowly around the room, his narrowed eyes pinning each of us for a second longer than necessary. I heard Charlie mutter something under his breath, but I wasn't about to ask him to repeat it. He finally landed back on Norris.

'That was your coach. We've agreed we will report this incident to the rowing federation. They came up with the rules, they can decide what to do when they're broken.'

I saw several of the guys try to mask their horrified expressions, but no one argued otherwise.

'Norris, take your men back to Cambridge.'

'Yes, sir, and on behalf of the crew, I apologize for disturbing your evening.'

A couple of the Cambridge guys walked over and helped Brett Rogers stand up, supporting him as he hobbled out to the beat of Coach's head shaking slowly at them in disgust. Will Norris nodded a goodbye to me, his mouth set in a hard line as he followed.

We barely heard the main doors shut before Brooks and Frank started up again, their voices loud in protest, only to be silenced again by Coach raising his hands.

'Quiet. Jesus. One at a goddamn time, please! What the fuck happened?' He looked at Frank who was still attempting to stem the blood flow from his nose, something made impossible by the fact he kept removing the shirt so he could protest his innocence. 'One of you hold Frank's head back, will you? I don't need him collapsing from blood loss too.'

Joshi stepped in to assume the role, and Brooks began explaining.

'We thought they'd try to take the mascots tonight, so Frank and I came down to catch them in the act . . . you know, because of rule one.' Coach rolled his eyes but said nothing. 'We heard them come in. I was in here, Frank was in the break room, and when we turned the lights on Brett Rogers was standing over there,' Brooks pointed to the door. 'Frank startled him, said something along the lines of, "You've been caught," but then Rogers said, 'Not if I knock you out, we haven't,' and punched him in the face. Frank rightly retaliated, and you walked in a minute later.'

Frank started mumbling loudly underneath the shirt,

but couldn't do anything because Joshi was holding his head, nor could any of us understand what he was saying in the first place.

'It really wasn't us, Coach.'

Coach folded his arms across his chest. His cheeks had gone from bright red to a slightly more approachable shade of pink, but from the way his jaw was clenching it was obvious this situation was far from over.

'Yeah, well, you shouldn't have been in here in the first place. You're all as bad as each other,' he growled. 'Where are the mascots?'

Brooks winced, 'They're in your office, Coach. We put them on top of the bookshelves.'

Coach's head snapped back to his office, as though he couldn't believe he'd missed them. 'Are they now? Well, they can stay there. And whatever unlawfully copied key you have to my office better be left on my desk too.'

'Yes, Coach,' Brooks mumbled.

'Clear up this mess, and go home. And you can expect extra drills in the morning.'

We all had the sense to hold in the groans, even as Coach stormed out. It wasn't until we heard his car pull away that any of us dared speak.

'Shit, do you think Coach'll really report us to the rowing federation?' whispered Charlie.

'Yeah, he didn't look like he was in a joking mood.'

'What do you reckon they'll do?'

I shrugged, 'Dunno. Fine us, maybe? Even if we each forfeit a season race it's not going to make any difference to us overall. Come on, let's lock up and go home. Training will be hard enough.'

Five minutes later, we'd locked up, leaving Coach's office keys on his desk. At least the set Brooks had brought with him; we weren't about to hand in all the spare keys we had to his office.

The journey wasn't far back to our house, though thankfully Brooks had driven his rusty old Jeep which we could all, somehow, manage to fit into. It was as we dropped off Joshi, Frank, Bitters and Drake – who all lived a few streets down from ours – that I felt my phone buzzing with a message.

I wish I hadn't bothered checking it. Because just like that, the evening went from bad to worse.

Dad: *Why have I just received a call about a fight at the boathouse?*

8. Kate

(Twenty-four hours in a day and I need more)

'Do either of you have any idea what this meeting is about?' I twisted my fork into my plate of spaghetti, trying to get the biggest serving that would fit into my mouth in one go. 'It feels formal.'

Hannah shook her head with an indecipherable mumble because her mouth was also too full to speak.

We were shovelling down our food like it was our last meal because Coach Stephens had called a meeting. And the manner in which he'd called it made everyone raise a brow – stopping the crew as we'd left this afternoon's land training session an hour ago, and ordering us to return again at eight p.m. This gave us roughly two hours to get back to our respective colleges to shower, change and eat; hence our current mission to induce indigestion.

Unfortunately, any study time would have to wait until later. I'd planned to dig into the large pile of reading material currently stacked by the side of my bed last week, but it was amazing how many nights I'd been working until ten p.m. before finally crashing, ready for my alarm to go off again six hours later for training.

Following the race last weekend, my first time starting as coxswain for Blondie, where we'd won by two lengths, I'd been put in the running as the official coxswain, and therefore officially part of the gruelling training programme which would prepare us for the race in March.

I really needed to get better organized.

'Imo? What about you? Surely you know something?' I swallowed my mouthful and started on the next.

I couldn't tell whether she genuinely looked ashamed at not being able to provide the information we were all looking for, or was just figuring out how to deliver what she knew in the most dramatic way possible. It was the latter.

'I don't, but . . .' She forked an entire meatball into her mouth, while Hannah and I waited on tenterhooks for the Queen of Gossip to finish eating and continue with her sentence. She pushed her empty plate away and leaned forward. 'Yesterday I was walking back from the library, and happened to pass by the path leading to Pembroke, and who did I see walking down it, but Brett Rogers?'

'From the boys' crew?'

She nodded. 'Yep. And he was sporting a very impressive set of black eyes. He'd either had a nose job or someone had punched him, and his nose was not freshly sculpted.'

I was struggling to follow this line of conversation, even though Imogen was looking at us like it was crystal clear. 'What's that got to do with our meeting tonight?'

She held her finger in the air for a second, then tapped it against the side of her nose. 'I don't know, but it'll be linked. I guarantee it.'

Hannah tutted with a deep eye roll. 'There's not going to be a full crew meeting because Brett Rogers has a black eye. This is a mandatory meeting for every member of the men's and women's rowing clubs. Why would Coach Stephens care about Brett Rogers having a black eye?'

Imogen shrugged, but it was clear she was firm in her belief that this meeting had something to do with Brett Rogers and his eye.

'Well, whatever it is, we need to get there now. I want a good seat.' She pushed her seat back. 'Eat up.'

Hannah and I followed her, leaving our dirty dinner trays by the kitchen hatch, and hurried into the cold air to where our bikes were stored. The clocks had just changed and we were on the icy slope to winter; today had been the first training session conducted entirely in the dark for both morning and evening.

I got my phone out and switched on the flashlight, as even with the lampposts all blazing light along the footpaths it was still hard to immediately find a black bike among the twenty other black bikes.

The three of us sped along and cut left through the break in the hedgerows which brought us out just a little way up along the River Cam. The lights of the boathouse ahead bounced off the water, its ebony gloss rolling in gentle waves as the wind blew over the surface.

The bike rack was already full, which likely meant we wouldn't get a seat anywhere near the front.

'Why is the Oxford bus here?'

I looked over to Hannah to find her pointing towards a large bus painted navy blue, with the Oxford crest printed on the side. It hadn't been immediately obvious because it was parked in the shadows, but the second I saw it my entire Monday fell into place.

You know how sometimes you wake up and there's a

tingle in the pit of your belly? It's something, but it's also nothing. You try to ignore it, perhaps put it down to too much coffee, you pretend it doesn't exist and maybe even manage to forget it's there, but then something happens and the feeling of dread you've been carrying about all day makes sense.

It gets worse.

It's real.

This morning I woke up and I knew something was going to happen.

Just like I knew it would involve a six-foot-three rower with pale blue eyes, muscles for days, and a mouth so perfectly formed it was impossible not to stare. It was the something I hadn't stopped thinking about since the day I met him, made harder with every message he'd sent. Fourteen in total over the past month.

'Asters, why have you stopped walking? Come on!' Imogen gestured me to the door where she was standing, while I was still by my bike, my legs too heavy to move.

'Are you okay?' asked Hannah. 'You've gone really pale.'

I rubbed my nervous stomach, 'Yeah, probably ate too fast.'

I did my best to ignore the nerves using my insides as a race track, and jogged to catch up with them.

It was dumb, I was being dumb. I had nothing to be nervous about. It was no big deal the president of the Oxford Rowing Club had sent me a stream of messages which I'd left unanswered.

'Shit, this looks serious,' muttered Imogen, as we followed the low rumble of voices down the hallway and stepped into the large break room.

We were fifteen minutes early but everyone else had been earlier, clearly as desperate as we were to figure out what this meeting was for. The usually comfy looking space had been stripped of all furniture, only to be replaced by rows and rows of chairs, and everyone was squashed together. Like the first hour of a high-school dance full of awkward teenagers, the senior light blues were huddled along one wall while the senior dark blues were against the other. In the middle were all the first years who'd been relegated to sitting near their rivals.

A cold wave of panic washed over me as I imagined being squashed next to Oz, and tugged the girls toward the benches by the back wall which was as far away from Oz as we could get in this confined space.

I'd spotted him almost the second we walked in.

He wasn't the tallest, and he wasn't the broadest, but even from a distance you could see he was set apart from the rest. He pulled you in, your eyes were automatically drawn to the way each of his friends was leaning into whatever he was saying: listening, paying attention, laughing.

I wasn't the only one staring at them.

'Look at the guy next to A.O.-C.,' whispered Hannah, 'he looks like he's been in a fight. What's his name? The French one.'

'François something,' hissed back Imogen, nodding over to where the Cambridge boys were huddled against the wall. 'And look at Brett Rogers. That eye seems way worse in this light. I'm right, I'm telling you.'

My eyes were flicking between the Cambridge and Oxford men's first teams. 'Look at them all. Brett and

François aren't the only ones with black eyes. Tubbs looks pretty banged up too.'

The two of them mimicked my movements, but less subtly.

I was small enough to be able to hide behind most of the taller girls, except I hadn't banked on Lauren Hughes tripping over the leg of a bench right in front of me, having been knocked flying by someone rushing past, and subsequently falling into three second-year boys who crewed on Isis – the Oxford boys' reserve boat. The brief ensuing commotion momentarily had every single person stop what they were doing and turn in the direction the noise was coming from, including Oz.

Lava may as well have been poured down my spine, the way my entire body flushed red and searing as his gaze locked into mine. The momentary flare of his blue eyes hit me straight in my core, and when a slow, lazy smile tipped the corner of his lips it suddenly felt like the oxygen had been sucked from the room.

Either that or I was having a panic attack.

Thankfully, my sharp gasp was drowned out by a couple of the other girls from the Cambridge team joining us along the wall, as well as ripping me out of the staring contest I'd briefly become an unwilling participant in.

I stood there in silence listening to them all speculate on what the meeting was about; theories ranged from Imogen's suggested punch-up to the idea of joint training sessions by Jess Madeley, one of the senior girls, and we were almost inclined to agree with her, seeing as her seniority meant she probably knew better than we did.

I hummed and huhhed along, not really paying

attention but trying to give off the impression I was doing exactly that, especially as I was currently looking up at Hannah as though she was telling me the most fascinating story I'd ever heard.

I could have won an Oscar for my performance.

My mind was elsewhere, however, as it mentally flicked through the text messages I'd read over and over this week, wondering if another would come. Or when it would come, because even though I'd not replied to a single one, the messages kept coming. He clearly didn't take no for an answer. I tried to keep my cheeks from flaring when I remembered the message of congratulations he'd sent me after we'd won the race against Durham, my first as cox for Blondie. Or asking how my first week as a medical student had been. I tried even harder to ignore the way my belly sank every time I wondered if the latest message would be the final message.

For a second I'd forget he was the rival president, and my heart would thump hard at the thought he'd been interested enough to check up on me, and twice I'd almost lost my resolve not to reply.

But nothing good could come out of replying, and my list of why I shouldn't have anything to do with Arthur Osbourne-Cloud lengthened by the day, because the more I found myself falling for his charm the more I wondered if this is what happened with every other girl. Until I wondered if perhaps there actually *weren't* any other girls, something he had pointed out more than once, and I should probably believe him.

By my calculation I'd only thought about him for an hour and twenty-two minutes today, which was down on yesterday's two hours and five. I'd given myself to the end of the week to achieve less than fifteen minutes' thinking time, but I hadn't banked on this evening's meeting. In fact, I hadn't expected to see him again at all. I'd checked and double checked the C.U.W.B.C. scheduled races for the season and there wasn't another planned meet against Oxford until the Boat Race in March. Therefore, it was perfectly reasonable to assume that I could avoid him completely, and mostly erase him from my brain.

A shiver zipped across my skin; I didn't need to look over to the corner to know Oz's focus was now firmly trained on me. I could feel it. The power and heat of his gaze was curling around my bones, begging for me to look at him.

Thankfully, that was the moment the far double doors opened and in walked Coach Stephens, the C.U.W.B.C. coach, followed by Coach Westcott, the head coach of the men's team. The two Oxford coaches followed, but between them a short, balding, rotund man walked through and sat down in the middle of the five chairs placed to face the room. The two sets of coaches took their places on either side, flanking him in a way that caused silence to descend on the room.

You could have heard a pin drop, or Imogen stage whisper, 'Okay, I officially have no idea what this meeting is about.'

'Who's that?' I whispered as quietly as I could.

'That's the chairman of British Rowing.'

She stopped talking as Coach Lassiter cleared his throat; the entire front row all leaned forward in sync, waiting for the show to begin.

'Thank you for coming,' began the chairman, in a voice which didn't match his appearance. It wasn't jolly or deep, it was hard and a little cold. 'For those of you not already aware, or who haven't yet caught up with the rumour mill, let me cut to the chase. This meeting is about the future of the mascot heist.'

My brows knotted together, because that explanation didn't explain anything at all, especially when Imogen scoffed.

'We've been very clear about the rules surrounding the mascot heist. While we all appreciate the spirit of this tradition, and the friendly competition it fosters in order to have a great race day come March, this year has already got out of hand and we're only in October. On Saturday evening members of the Cambridge crew were caught trying to take back their mascot, and what ensued was a brawl of utterly unsportsman-like behaviour, which was only broken up because Coach Lassiter happened to pass by.'

Imogen turned to Hannah and me; while she didn't verbalize it, her raised eyebrow said, *I told you this was about the black eye.*

'I shouldn't have to remind you that rowers do not behave like this. You are serious athletes and academics, many of you represent your countries. This is not behaviour we encourage or accept. Fighting is for the ring or the pitch, and for this to occur so early in the academic year gives us no option but to cancel the heist. We cannot allow it to continue this season.'

A soft groan let out from many of the squad seated in the chairs in front of us, as the chairman paused for effect.

'Seems a bit of overkill. They could have put this in an email,' Hannah muttered.

But the chairman wasn't done.

'Due to the actions of the teams in question, it has been decided that your time will be better spent on the Tideway. You need to learn to appreciate the water your race is held on, and the privilege you have been given. For the final six weeks of this term your Saturdays will be spent cleaning up the Tideway, and serving our community as best we can.'

Once more, silence descended over the room, only this time it was thick with a heavy dose of shock as everyone tried to figure out if what they heard was what they *actually* heard. Whispers of indignation began moving through the room, growing louder and louder. Mary Heston's head whipped around to where Will Norris was standing.

'We have to spend the next six weeks of winter clearing up the River Thames?!' raged Imogen next to me. 'We didn't even have anything to do with this heist! It's the boys' stupid game. How are we going to do this, find the time to train *and* study?'

I was inclined to agree with her, while also trying to mentally calculate my calendar, because she was right. How the hell would we find the time? Medicine was one of the busiest courses. It wasn't like we could skip a class and write an essay. We had practicals; we had to learn about anatomy, and I had to dissect Leo. It wasn't like I spent most of my time reading. No, that would be down to the students studying, say, classics.

My top lip curled in a snarl. This was *his* fault. He was president of the Oxford team; therefore he along with

Will Norris should take full responsibility for this catastrophe which affected nearly 120 students. Even more so as he clearly had all the time in the world to do it; this punishment of cleaning the river in the freezing cold would most likely be a welcome break from lying on his bed. Whereas Imogen, Hannah and I now had to figure out how to possibly stretch out the day more than we already did.

The entire situation was unfair. Totally and utterly unfair.

'Both the mascots have been held for safekeeping and will be returned after this year's race. The Tideway cleaning will commence this coming weekend, your respective coaches will share the details you need, and your Saturday training time will be completed on Sundays instead. Speak to them if you have any questions.'

The chairman stood up, followed by all four coaches, and they left through the same door they'd entered. The room immediately erupted.

'What the actual fuck?'

'This is such bullshit!'

'Fucking hell.'

Or the one which was easily the most valid point made so far, 'Why are we being punished because of the stupid boys?'

I glanced over to where the Oxford and Cambridge Blue Boat teams were standing, their faces making it clear they hadn't known this punishment was coming. It didn't help to quell my anger at Oz, however. Just like almost everyone in this room, I would have happily given up an afternoon to help with a little community clean-up, but not a heavily mandated appearance for the final weeks of the semester when we also had exams to study for and papers to write.

'Come on, let's get out of here. I need to come up with a topic for my essay on applied maths,' huffed Hannah.

'Lead the way,' I grumbled. I had my own coursework, but at least it didn't involve applied math.

Due to the very small doorframe and somewhat narrow hallway and the hundred students all wanting to get out at the same time, the going was slower than expected. And with every extra minute it took to leave the building, the more the tension around us built. Tempers were short, and the blame was being placed firmly on whichever team you didn't belong to, but no one was as loud as Mary Heston, who was making her feelings very clear to Will Norris at the back of the room.

'Jeez,' muttered Hannah, voicing what everyone else was thinking. No one wanted to be on the end of Mary's wrath.

'I'll meet you by the bikes,' I called to Hannah and Imogen who'd now become stuck in a conversation with their assistant coach, no doubt about tonight's news.

It was as I unlocked my bike that a deep voice shouted my name, and I spun on instinct a split second before I wished I hadn't. Oz was walking toward me, though striding would be a better description. I narrowed my eyes, hoping it would give him the 'warning: do not approach' signal, and went back to my padlock code to add the final number.

It didn't stop him, though I'd long ago come to the conclusion that maybe nothing did.

'Kate?'

I ignored him, pulling my bike free, and slipped my leg over the frame. I was just about to add my helmet when it was stolen from the handle-bars.

'Give that back,' I snarled, holding my hands out.

'Not until you speak to me,' he replied, 'I really want to talk to you. Please.'

'I have nothing to say.'

He snatched his hand away as I reached for my helmet once more. 'Bullshit.'

'Give me my helmet! Thanks to you, I've lost a significant chunk of my remaining study time this semester, and I need to get back so I can catch up.'

His neck jerked, and he frowned, 'Thanks to me?'

In the past fifteen minutes I'd finally found a legitimate reason to be angry at Oz, and the angrier I was the less likely I'd crumble in my resolve to text him back. Yes, someone was to blame for this entire predicament, and it may as well be him.

'Yes! You! This stupid heist. You're the president, you shouldn't have let your team get us to this point. I have enough to do without cleaning the river,' I hissed quietly as a couple of my crewmates retrieved their bikes. The last thing I needed was for anyone to be asking me why I was shouting at the O.U.B.C. president.

'Kate, we're not here because of me. We're here because Brett Rogers is a cretin and can't even steal a crown properly. Your Cambridge boys were the ones who got themselves caught, yet we're all having to clean the river. I'm losing out on study time, just like you. It's only until Christmas,' he reasoned with a sigh.

'It's not the same thing! I'm studying medicine, you're studying a language no one has spoken for two thousand years!'

I couldn't decide whether the smirk he tried very hard not to show me made things worse. I was already at a level of rage and frustration which was making it increasingly impossible to hold my tongue, and from the way my knuckles had whitened on the bike handles, he could tell.

The tipping point came when his smile broke wide, making his eyes sparkle in amusement exactly as they had the first night I met him. 'At least this means we get to spend some more time together, so you can like me again.'

I gritted my teeth so hard the crunch of enamel shot goosebumps across my body. Snatching my helmet back, and without a further glance at Oz, I cycled away past Hannah and Imogen, who'd just arrived and were both staring with their mouths hanging open.

Now, on top of everything else, I was going to have to figure out a way to explain why the Oxford president was laughing so loudly at me I could still hear him a quarter of a mile away.

The real kicker though – the month apart had done nothing to quell the very real crush I had on him.

The one that still had my body tingling when I finally fell into bed.

9. Arthur

(Who knew community service could be so romantic?)

Oxford's dark-blue minibuses pulled up in front of the Westminster School Boat Club, the O.U.B.C. base for Tideway training.

This was where we'd arranged to meet the Cambridge team, whose Tideway base was the boat club next door. Though looking out of the bus windows it was clear we'd arrived before them.

'Right. Listen up,' Coach Lassiter called from the front of our bus, 'Cambridge are two minutes away, let's all try and remember why we're here and keep our conduct professional. Understood?'

Murmurs of 'Yes Coach' rumbled through the thirty of us.

'Coach?' called Joshi. 'How's this going to work exactly? What are we clearing up?'

'All will be revealed shortly. Just wait.'

'I bet we're picking up litter all day,' he grumbled, though quiet enough that only those within his close vicinity heard.

'Probably. Did you bring your headphones? Two of my textbooks are on audio, so I'll be picking up litter and working at the same time.' Drake tapped his forehead. 'Genius or what.'

I hid my grin at Joshi's annoyed expression that he'd not thought like Drake. I could probably have done the same, though I'd never bothered to find out whether any of my texts were on audio. I'd rather listen to music, or the sound of the boats moving along the water, or nails on a chalk board; anything except the classics on audio — they were made to be read. Not that it mattered today as I had other plans for spending our community service time.

'They're here,' yelled a voice from the front and everyone seated on the right-hand side ran over to the left to look out of the window like we were tourists on an open air sight-seeing bus, and passing by a monument of national importance.

'Watch it!' grouched Charlie, who'd been woken from a nap by an eager first year leaning too close, and pushed him away. 'Ugh. Let's get this over with.'

'At least it's not raining.'

'If it was raining, I'd have stayed in bed.'

We all filed out, pulling on thick beanies or caps, and zipping up our winter parkas to join the remaining Oxford crew from the second mini-bus while we waited for the entire Cambridge cohort to take their sweet time.

My eyes darted along the light blue of their buses, scanning through the slightly tinted windows until I spied Kate as she stepped down. It was almost hard to spot her between the two girls she'd been with on Monday, the taller auburn-haired one in front, who'd stared at me like a goldfish, and the blonde one behind. I kept my eye on her as the three of them joined the rest of the Cambridge crew, but as she shifted slightly to peer around her crewmates I stepped back closer to Brooks. I watched her gaze quickly travel over my Oxford mates, and I knew instinctively what she was searching for.

Me.

It was near freezing on this Saturday morning in November, but the feeling of her trying to find me warmed me like the Greek sun in August.

By the time those beautiful green eyes landed on me, I was sporting a grin you'd have spotted from Putney Bridge half a mile away, especially when her breath hitched. It dawned on me that given everything going on in my life right now, somehow Kate Astley could still make me smile by doing absolutely nothing but be herself, especially when she scowled at me and turned away with a flick of her thick ponytail, trying to pretend I didn't exist. But her body was still facing mine, and the subtle side glance she was sending my way told me different and buoyed my determination to get her liking me again. Or admitting she still liked me.

I knew it was there. I'd seen it in her eyes as she slowly glanced around the Monday meeting. I'd seen her the second she walked in; the way her lips parted the tiniest fraction as she spotted me, which was right when I looked away. And then that girl fell over and I was rewarded with five full seconds of Kate Astley's eyes on mine; I'd counted them as my heart thumped harder with each beat, and you couldn't have broken that connection with a sledge hammer.

'What are you laughing at?' asked Brooks.

I shook my head at him, though my grin didn't go anywhere. 'Nothing.'

He peered over in the direction I'd been staring. 'Which one is your American?'

I didn't bother to remind him that she wasn't my anything. It wasn't like I'd planted a flag and claimed her. Though maybe I should do with the way a couple of the junior guys were looking at her, because if I found out anyone else had made a move, the price to pay would be steep. Hole-digging steep.

'See the girl with the reddish hair?'

Brooks glanced along the Cambridge women's squad huddled together, until he spotted the one I was talking about. 'Woah! Is that her? Shit, Oz, she's hot!'

'She is, but that's not Kate. There's a shorter girl behind her with dark brown hair, talking to a tall blonde. That's her.'

There was no way Kate could hear me seeing as my voice was barely above a whisper, but she clearly sensed our eyes on her with the way her head suddenly shot round to Brooks and me with narrowed eyes.

Even from the distance between us I could see her dimple twitch as her teeth gritted. There might even have been a hint of the snarl Olly swore she'd given him when he'd bumped into her again the other day.

Brooks guffawed loudly, and clapped me on the back. 'Oh, shit mate. She does not look happy with you! Got some work cut out for you there. But I get it now . . .'

'Get what?'

'Why your knickers have been so twisted.'

I grinned, 'Tell me about it.'

'So that other one with the auburn hair, is she single?'

I shrugged. 'Dunno. I literally know nothing about any of the women's crew, except Kate. And even then, it's very minimal. Fuck knows how that rumour started.'

I was still smarting over that; half the Cambridge crew indeed . . .

'Presidents, come here please,' shouted Coach Westcott, gesturing us over to where he was standing with the other Oxford and Cambridge coaches.

Will Norris fell into stride next to me, with a smile showing he was back to his usual cheery self. 'All right, mate? Fancy seeing you here.'

I chuckled, giving up a heavy eye roll as I did. 'Bet I can pick up more rubbish than you can.'

'Yeah? What's the wager?'

'Hundred quid.'

'You're on.'

None of the coaches seemed to share in the good mood Will and I greeted them with, but as I saw it, we were here because of them. They might think they were punishing us, but they were also punishing themselves, and this episode could certainly have passed without all the unnecessary drama, and standing around in freezing temperatures.

'Right, Mr Osbourne-Cloud, Mr Norris. As presidents of the respective crews, we are leaving it up to you to lead the plans for today. It's nearly ten a.m. and we have the next six hours to make a difference before the tide comes in again.'

Norris raised his brows at me as Coach Westcott held out two identical pieces of paper to us. 'These are the stations along the Tideway where we'll be working. We'll split into pairs, and some of you will be cleaning graffiti off the walls, but most of you will be picking up the rubbish on the banks while the tide is low. We'll base ourselves near each of the bridges along the course, and the buses will transport anyone assigned to the further locations. It's up to you how we split the crews, but it would serve you well to consider that while we might be rivals on the river you all clearly need a reminder of the meaning of comradeship.'

Norris scanned the paper in his hand, then looked at Coach. 'What are we supposed to use for all this cleaning?'

Westcott nodded over to where a trestle table was being set up with disposable gloves, cleaning equipment, sponges, buckets and big black bags, all of which could work very well in my favour for the plan I'd been hatching for most of the journey here.

'We should mix the crews,' I suggested before anything else could be decided.

'What do you mean?'

'Oxford men with Cambridge women. And vice versa.'

Norris tilted his head slightly, and a couple of faint lines appeared on his forehead, 'Why?'

I shrugged as nonchalantly as possible. 'Comradeship. Why else?'

He paused for a second and studied me. 'You're up to something.'

I laughed loudly. 'I swear I'm not. Just want to get to know your team a little better.'

'You'd better not be, Cloud,' grumbled Coach Westcott, 'but as long as you all do your duty, I don't care how your teams are split up.'

'Great,' I clapped my hands together with renewed enthusiasm. 'Let's get this show on the road. Coach, you want to do the honours, and let everyone know?'

Coach frowned but he clearly wanted to get this over with as quickly as everyone else did, and the sooner we started the sooner we got to go home.

I leaned into Norris as Coach barked out his instructions to everyone standing around. 'I'll give you the hundred pounds if you put me with your new Blondie cox.'

He turned, his face filled with confusion. 'What? Why?'

'Please, mate,' I begged as quietly as I could. 'I'll explain later.'

'Okay,' he shrugged, and I tried not to jump for joy, settling instead for a smile.

'Great! You go first.'

'Fine.' He stepped forward once Coach had finished speaking. I looked around the group; it was clear most of them would rather be anywhere else. Yet as I watched Kate's name being called with mine, I didn't think there was anywhere I'd rather be.

I took my time collecting the cleaning supplies and disposable gloves from the table, and walked over to her standing by the railings, her entire body stiff with annoyance. 'Hi, cleaning buddy.'

'Did you do this too?' she hissed, trying to ensure no one else overheard her.

'Do what?'

She waved her hand between us. 'This. Working together?'

'Yes.' I smiled broadly, even more so when my admission left her momentarily speechless. It was clear from the way her shoulder jerked back slightly that she'd expected me to say no.

'You're wasting your time. We don't have anything to say to each other.'

'On the contrary, I think we have a lot to say to each other. And haven't you heard . . .' I swept my arm through the air to our fellow students all moving off to clean their designated patches of river, 'today's all about comradeship.'

Her dimple flexed as she ground her jaw, which only made me chuckle.

'Let's go then, shall we? I've managed to get us the spot by Putney Bridge, so we don't have to walk far.' I nodded over in the direction we needed to go, following a couple of other pairs who were heading the same way. 'Let's find a good dirty spot. I want to make sure we fill more rubbish sacks than anyone else. There's a wager on who can collect the most.'

Her eyes rolled, but I knew her competitiveness wouldn't let me down.

'Fine,' she huffed.

We walked in silence along the bank of the Thames; I waited for her to say something but then realized that she was too busy looking out to the water. The spot of the river at Putney Bridge was quieter than usual, given it was a Saturday. During the week the Tideway waters bustled with the Thames Clipper commuters, private passenger boats, ferries, the occasional cargo barges carrying logs or fuel, and rowers to name a few, but today it was mostly rowing shells from the local clubs and runners along the bank.

'Have you ever been to London?' I asked her quietly, and she reluctantly shook her head. 'So you've never seen the River Thames before?'

She turned to look up at me and her eyes darkened as they widened, 'No, only on television when I've watched the Boat Race, or in movies.'

'Then let me officially welcome you to the best river in the world.'

She smiled softly, even though her tone still dripped in annoyance, 'Thank you.'

We continued on until we reached the spot on the river-bank allocated to us. Fifty metres up I could see Joshi and a girl I didn't recognize, fifty metres beyond him was our Isis cox and that awful girlfriend of Will Norris, who already appeared to have filled a rubbish bag.

'This is us.' I peeled off a bag from the roll and passed it to her, along with gloves and a mechanical claw gripper thing I'd spotted on the table and snatched up before anyone else could.

'Thank you.'

'So, if you've not seen London yet, I take it your Tide-way training hasn't started?'

She glanced over to me, a heavy scowl set on her face. 'Are you trying to pump me for information? Because I'm happy to spend all day in silence.'

I shook my head, 'No. Just making conversation and trying to find that sweet American who stepped on my nuts.'

She tried so hard to stop the snort of laughter, only didn't get there quick enough and ended up in a coughing fit which had her doubled over gasping for air. I opened one of the bottles of water I'd brought and passed it to her.

'See, the Yankee Doodle I met is trying to get out.' I

smirked, though was careful not to let her see it just in case she started snarling again. I probably shouldn't admit that it kind of turned me on; it would only make things worse.

She took several gulps before replacing the lid and setting it to one side by the bucket I'd also brought along for us.

'You're going to talk all day unless I stop you, aren't you?'

'Probably.'

She rolled her eyes, shook out her black bag, reached for a rusty can with her mechanical grip, and dropped it in. 'Oz, why did you want to be in a pair with me?'

'I told you, I wanted to talk to you. And you won't reply to my messages.' I bent down and picked up an old plastic bottle, throwing it into my own bag.

'Why though? We're on opposite sides of two teams who want to do nothing but beat each other. It was literally the first thing I was told when I had my orientation: *"do not fraternize with the enemy"*,' she mimicked. 'Get good grades and beat Oxford. I'm not even sure which they put more importance on.'

'Oh, it's definitely to beat Oxford,' I chuckled.

'Then why all this? Nothing good can come of it. We both have a ton of work . . .' she peered over at me with a wry smile, 'well I do, and it's a distraction we don't need.'

I put my black bag down and turned to her. 'Because we're more than our coursework and a boat race, and because six weeks ago I met a girl I haven't been able to stop thinking about.'

I tried to hold her eyes, tried to show her how serious I

141

was, but she turned and picked up a pink sweet wrapper in silence. I watched a tugboat pass us while I waited for her to say something, until it became clear she wasn't going to.

'A question for a question?'

'I don't have any questions. And it looks like I'm the only one working here,' she added, tying off her full bag and pulling a new one from the roll.

'Okay. Then I have some.'

She let out a deep sigh. 'What?'

I moved around her and picked up a discarded shopping bag, stuffing it into the bag, 'Why haven't you replied to my text messages?'

'Told you. There's no point.'

'That's the only reason?'

'Yes, what else would there be?' she replied, but from the way she turned her body so she didn't have to look at me it was clear there was more. We both knew there was more, and it didn't have anything to do with my presidency or coursework and everything to do with the unwarranted reputation I'd steadfastly denied, especially when she changed the subject. 'The water is really low here, huh?'

'Yes, it feels lower today than usual.' I pointed over to the wall where the tell-tale sign of green moss illustrated the depths the tide usually hit.

'Oh.' She carried on in silence, then . . . 'What's it like to row on?'

'You mean compete in the Boat Race?'

She nodded, 'Yes.'

I never told her I'd competed in the Boat Race before, and hid my smile at the thought of her talking about me more than just in regards to my father, or whatever tabloid trash had been spreading lies this week; that perhaps she'd been researching my achievements just like I'd been doing for her. And hopefully she'd seen something to persuade her that I was more than tabloid column inches, because while her argument about the Oxford and Cambridge rivalry was valid, I was certain my unwarranted playboy reputation was what was really keeping her away.

'The Boat Race is the most intense twenty minutes you'll ever experience. More than the Olympics, more than the World Championships . . .' I dropped my head as I nearly added '*more than sex*'; I knew full well that was a one-way ticket to receiving the silent treatment, 'it's like nothing else. Two hundred and fifty thousand people lined along the four miles of river on both sides, half screaming for you to win, the other half screaming for you to lose, while millions more watch you on the television. I hope you're ready for it.'

'Me?' she blinked up, each blink turning the bright green greener. It almost rivalled the fresh moss clinging to the huge pebbles underneath our feet.

'Yeah, you'll be coxing for Blondie.'

'Oh . . . oh, no,' she spluttered as the realization hit her that she'd be here in little under six months. 'No. That's not been decided. I'm training with the crew, and I've won a couple of races but I'm not the only cox they're considering. And I have no experience of rowing on a tideway, so I'm sure I'll be back-up cox for Blondie at best. I doubt I'll be picked, especially as this is my first year. But I'm enjoying the challenge.'

'You've never coxed on tidal water?'

She shook her head. 'Nothing like this. A little on the Connecticut River.'

'Let me show you.' I held my hand out for her to take, only for her to dismiss it with a withering glance. 'Kate, do as you're told. Take my hand, it's slippery.'

She pursed her lips and glared at my outstretched palm, but finally took it. As she did, it was like a pressure had loosened in my chest; it was slight, but my next breath was definitely deeper.

I guided her to the edge of the river; the water was so far out that we were almost standing on the murky silt, which was more like quicksand for the way it sucked you in. As it was, the pebbles I kept us on were so slippery it provided the very real possibility of a dramatic slide and fall into a tangled heap. Not that I objected to her falling onto me in a tangled heap, as long as she avoided my dick this time – hence the hand holding.

Or not, as she'd taken her hand back the second we stood still. I moved behind her; even though the pale-blue bobble on the top of her beanie made her seem taller, she was so short she barely came up to my chest. The subtle scent of summer limes and jasmine, which had been living on the tip of my tongue since the day I'd met her, whipped in the wind around us. It took all my discipline not to bury my face in her neck, and breathe her in.

'The race begins here.' I pointed to the stretch of the river just in front of Putney Bridge, then thumbed behind me. 'You can't see it right now, but there's a granite stone up on the footpath which marks the official starting point. Each boat is held so the bow is lined up with the stone. If the weather's bad, the water can be terrible and it makes it hard to navigate. As soon as the buzzer goes it's up to the cox to steer out of the choppy water, and fight over the smooth channel in the middle.' I guided my finger along to the centre of the river where the lowest current flowed. 'Marshy's an aggressive coxswain; two years ago he nearly got us tangled up with your lot by steaming ahead and turning them too hard, but he was brought up on this river and knew exactly what he was doing. We won by two lengths.'

She nodded along, listening, then, 'Is he the cox who cried last year?'

'What?' I frowned down, only to see her look away. A faint tint of pink crested her ears, but she offered nothing more.

'I heard after your race last year you were angry and snapped your oar in two . . . and made the coxswain cry.'

'Are you serious?' I stared, waiting for her to crack a smile under the pressure of this ridiculous statement, before it became clear it was a genuine question, 'Oh Jesus, you are serious.' I laughed loudly, 'Oh, Yankee Doodle, that's definitely one of the better stories about me I've heard. Wait until I tell Pete . . .' I laughed again, especially when her features contorted with annoyance. 'He's going to love that.'

'So, it's not true?'

'No. It's not, I've never made anyone cry, that I'm aware of. And I've never snapped my oars. I'm not sure I'm even strong enough.' I grinned at her.

She crossed her arms angrily. 'How am I supposed to know what to believe?'

The smile dropped from my face, and I sighed deeply.

'I know we've only known each other six weeks, but did I ever give you the impression I'm the type of guy who snaps carbon fibre oars in half?'

After a long, *long* second she looked away, her mouth curving down at the edges, 'No, no, you haven't.'

'Tell you what, moving forward let's just assume that everything you hear about me is untrue. Unless of course it's that I'm devastatingly handsome and the best stroke ever to have walked the earth. That you *can* believe.'

She replied with a deep eye roll.

'I'm serious, Kate. I know what people say about me, and what you've no doubt heard, but you want to know something, come and ask. I will tell you everything, and I'll never lie to you.'

She held my gaze, unblinking. She stared so long I'd almost finished counting the little flecks of navy blue scattered around the edges of her green irises, but she turned back to the river before I could. We stood in silence, watching a couple of rowers enter the water from a boat club a couple of hundred metres away, and push off, 'What happened last year? Why didn't you win if your cox is so good?'

'He'd broken his leg and couldn't compete. Our reserve cox didn't know the river quite as well,' I waited for her to say something, but she stayed staring at the current, the undulating waves almost hypnotic. 'There are two big bends along the course, you have to know how to steer them. And aggression works, which Marshy has.'

'Why didn't he get disqualified for cutting in front?' she frowned.

'Rules are slightly different than the Olympics or World

Championships, you don't get fined for disruption or interference. As long as no one loses their oars then you have to use the river to your advantage.'

'Which side of the river is best?'

I shrugged. 'Depends who you ask. Marshy would say the Surrey station, which is the opposite side of the river to this one. You're closer to the bends, and once you pass under Hammersmith Bridge you can really take the lead. Eighty per cent of teams who've been in the lead at Hammersmith Bridge have gone on to win.'

'What if I asked you?'

'Is that one of your questions?' I grinned, but she simply raised one of her perfectly shaped brows at me. 'We rowed on the Surrey station last year, and lost. If Oxford wins the coin toss, I'm going with Middlesex.'

'Why are you telling me this? I'm your enemy. I could be asking these questions to pump you for information.'

I chuckled again, at the seriousness carved so earnestly into her features, as though speaking to me was akin to sharing trade secrets with the Russians. A thick strand of hair had been flapping in her face for our entire conversation, and no matter how much she tried to push it away with her forearm, it didn't budge. I pulled off one of my disposable gloves, allowing myself a moment to touch her soft skin as she stood still, her brow warm against my fingertips even in the cold early-November wind. I brushed it under the rim of her beanie. 'No, Yankee Doodle, you're not. You could never be my enemy.'

'I'm on the opposite team.' Her shoulders dropped for the first time since we'd arrived here, like she'd been fighting an internal battle she wasn't ready to surrender to.

'So?' I responded, as I had the first time she'd protested a month ago in the boathouse changing room.

She closed her eyes in frustration and let out a deep breath.

'Kate, you're on the women's crew, so we're not direct competitors. But even if we were I couldn't give a shit. I like you, I like you a lot. And I've liked you since the first night we met. I've thought about you every day after that. What's more, I know you like me.'

Deep ridges appeared between her eyebrows. 'That's mighty arrogant of you.'

'It's not arrogance if it's the truth. Tell me it's not true . . .'

I waited. And waited. But just like me she didn't lie.

'See, you like me.' I leaned in, expecting her to step back but she stayed in place, bin bag in one hand, claw grip in the other. I was so close I could smell the soap she used, clean and fresh like warm laundry. 'I want to go back to the week before you decided I was your enemy, before you thought I was someone I'm not. Please, Kate. I want us to get to know each other. I want to continue what we started.'

This time when she looked at me the anger had gone, and there was a warmth which hadn't been present before, so I tried for one more push.

'I promise, unless it's to do with rowing, anything you've heard about me is not true,' I repeated, hoping it would sink in further, 'and for the first time, maybe ever, I've met someone I can totally be myself with. Please don't let other people ruin what we found that night. If you really don't want to see where this could lead then tell me, and I'll respect that, but if you're basing your decision on lies someone's told you, then don't you owe it to yourself to find the truth?'

'Oz, we have a lot going on. I barely have time to sleep let alone date long distance. Not to mention, I'm trying to make friends with people who . . .' she looked away, trailing off.

'Hate me?'

'They don't like you,' she corrected with unnecessary diplomacy.

'Kate, I couldn't give a single fuck about what other people think. I only care about what you think. Please. Get to know me better before you decide you're not going to fall in love with me,' I added with a wink which made her eyes roll again.

It might have been hours, it might have been seconds; all I knew was that it felt like the longest stretch of silence in my life while I waited for her to respond.

'Okay,' she replied, quietly, 'we can get to know each other.'

My heart bashed against my sternum while I triple checked I'd heard what I thought I'd heard. 'Really?'

'Yes,' she nodded, her cheeks pinking slightly as her dimples made an appearance, 'but can we keep it to ourselves? I don't want to get kicked off the crew and lose my scholarship.'

'You won't get kicked off the crew, but yes we can keep it our secret. However . . .' I looked behind me to where Joshi was standing by a pile of black bags, then back at Kate, 'if we weren't in public I'd kiss you right now, just so you know.'

Her cheeks glowed pink as she bit down on her lower lip; I could see she was about to say something but stopped herself.

'What? What were you going to say?'

Her bashful smile hit me right in the chest. 'That if we weren't in public, I might let you.'

10. Kate

(London calling)

'Hands on the boat.'

The eight rowers in front of me followed my instruction.

'Up to waist. Ready . . . Up.'

The shell was hoisted out of the water in one seamless movement. Once they were settled with the weight, the eight of them followed my next order to lift it above their heads and turn in sync, walking the boat back into the Crabtree boathouse – the Cambridge base for Tideway training.

I followed behind, shouting my instructions to the crew until the boat was safely laid on its pipes ready for the next time we took it out.

'Nice work today, ladies. Thanks for taking me through my first time,' I called to them all, while packing up my coxbox and microphone headset.

Imogen grinned at me from the bench she'd collapsed down on, cheeks red from the exertion of the morning session and the cold air. 'All you, Asters. We took ten seconds off our time to Hammersmith Bridge, and we beat Blue Boat. Nice work. Even more impressive considering we spent yesterday here cleaning up.'

'Tell me about it.'

'Teamwork makes the dream work,' cried a voice from the other side of the boathouse.

'Yeah,' I pulled my beanie off and ran my fingers through my hair, gathering up all the strands and tying it up in a knot on top of my head, 'it was a good morning, although I'm almost too tired to speak.'

I hadn't mentioned it to Oz yesterday, but today marked the first day of official Tideway training. My first day coxing on the River Thames. I knew it would be different from rowing on the Cam, but even on a relatively calm day like today, the drag of the current had felt stronger than anything I'd experienced. I knew I'd had a good session; while I hated to admit it, Oz had been right about coxing along here, and without his brief instructions during our community trash picking I had a feeling I would have struggled.

Seeing as this was my first time on this stretch of the river, I was quietly confident I hadn't done too badly. Though from the way Coach Stephens had yelled down the megaphone from his motorboat I could be mistaken. The only thing I did know – it was going to be a long five months until the Boat Race if I had any hope of staying in my seat. I might be an experienced coxswain but I had my work cut out for me, because the thing about coxing – it's based on skills, instincts, practice. And I was going up against people who'd coxed on this river before, coxed in this race.

It was going to be tough, but I knew I was tougher.

'Nice work today, Kate.'

I turned to find Coach Godwin, my coxing coach, out of his motor boat and heading in my direction.

I startled a little at the compliment, especially as he wasn't known for dishing them out. He was the type of guy who grunted with a brusque nod if you'd done something good. 'Thanks, coach.'

'Is that the first time you've rowed on a tidal river?'

I shook my head, hoping he couldn't tell what little experience I'd had. 'No, but I've not spent a lot of time on tideways. Back home it's mostly freshwater rivers. I've done a little racing on the tidal stretch of the Connecticut River, which is like the Thames I guess, but also nothing like it.' I laughed, hoping my nerves didn't show through.

He nodded, slowly.

In the six weeks I'd been part of the coxswains' crew I'd learned that Coach Godwin was a man of few words. Though he couldn't be more than forty, he had the aura – not to mention the thick beard – of someone much older – considered, thoughtful with his words, and curt with his delivery. I should probably find him a little more intimidating than I did, but he also reminded me of Vinny, one of my older cousins who ran my dad's fishing crew.

More importantly, Vinny was also the guy I credited for saving my dad when Jake died. He'd carried him in those days; when he'd set aside his own grief for the guy he always called his *surrogate baby brother* and stayed with my dad while he stared out at nothing but the water after a memory had caught him so hard he'd forgotten what he'd been doing a minute before; when he couldn't focus on anything but his own grief.

It was most likely why I could hold a conversation with Godwin longer than most of the other coxswains, who found his way of speaking too abrupt, borderline rude and a massive knock to their confidence. Three of the girls who'd joined the coxswains' university crew at the beginning of term had already dropped out and gone back to cox for their respective colleges, under less pressure.

'It's impressive. I haven't seen many coxswains handle the Tideway on their first time like you did today. In my years on this river I've only seen four, maybe five hit dead centre of the Hammersmith cables and you managed without me even asking.'

'Thank you.'

'Was it a fluke?'

I shook my head, 'No, sir. I meant to do it.'

'Could you do it again?'

'Yes.'

He stared at me, and I waited for his next set of questions to be barked out, 'How're you finding the training? You weren't full time at your old club, right?'

'No, sir, it wasn't affiliated with my school. Training wasn't as intense, but I still managed four times a week.'

He hummed under his breath with a glare that had me glued into place. 'Who taught you?'

'My coach was a guy called Chad Brownings. He'd spent most of his career as coxing coach at Harvard. He really showed me how to read the water. I think that's probably what helped today,' I smiled.

I was not about to add that the president of O.U.B.C. had probably been more responsible for my performance today than anyone, or anything else. I could almost picture the smug look on Oz's face when I updated him later, as he typed out a reply something along the lines of '*I told you so*' before we resumed our question for a question game. In fact, since we'd called a truce yesterday and decided to get to know each other better our texting had resumed at a rate that made it clear we were making up for lost time, our fingers flying over our phone screens quicker than Swifties registering for tour tickets.

Oz: *Q4AQ. What's your favourite music?*

Kate: *Oh, that's a tough one. What am I doing while listening?*

Oz: *Training*

Kate: *That's easy. EDM*

Oz: *Same! See, I told you we're soulmates. What about driving the car?*

Kate: *Nope, it's my turn for a question. Don't cheat*

Oz: *Oof. Stickler for the rules! I'll remember that. Okay, what are you asking?*

Kate: *What's your favorite season?*

Oz: *Rowing season . . .*

Kate: 👀

Oz: *It's summer. I love the sunshine*

Kate: *why?*

Oz: *Oh no, Miss Rulebreaker, that's a second question. My turn . . .*

And on it had continued for the last eighteen hours. We'd only broken to sleep, and I'd woken this morning to the sun rising over the quadrangle, and a fresh question.

'Kate, are you listening?'

I jolted out of my daze to find Coach stroking his beard and frowning at me. Crap.

'Sorry, sir, could you repeat that?'

'You should tell him he did a good job.'

Oh, right. We were talking about rowing.

'I will, yes. Thanks, Coach.'

'I want you down here every weekend training, and any

spare days during the week. You need to get to know this water better than anything you've ever coxed on; I want you to be able to steer through these waters with your eyes closed. I want you hitting dead centre of the cabling, on instinct. You need to know where to turn, how to cut through the currents, where to increase stroke, where you can conserve energy. If you do that, you could win us the race come March.'

I nodded, but didn't say anything more. I wasn't really sure what there was to say. I hadn't dared hope I'd be coxing in the Boat Race my very first year, but now Coach was talking like it was a possibility, and I suddenly wanted it more than I wanted anything else.

'Have you spent time with Becka Jones?'

'Yes, we've spent some time together, she's been super helpful with advice.'

'Good. Keep talking.' He bobbed his head again, as though having some kind of conversation with himself. 'Go and get dry.'

With that he walked off, and I turned to find a couple of the girls walking through from the boathouse changing rooms.

'Nice work, Asters. That was really something getting us through the Hammersmith cables.'

I grinned up at Anna Selway, the number three seat, after Coach had disappeared from sight, 'Hey, you did the hard work.'

'Didn't seem quite so hard today.' Imogen handed me my long puffa jacket, the same one we all wore to keep our bodies and muscles warm the second we stepped back onto dry land. 'You really did an awesome job.'

'Thank you.' I grinned at her. 'It would be so awesome if we're rowing Blondie together for the race.'

'I know.' She put her arm around me, 'I think we're in for a decent chance. We've won our last three races. Stephens seems happy with the crew we have right now, he hasn't swapped us out for a few weeks. Maybe next year we'll be in Blue Boat.'

'Yeah,' I yawned, the tiredness from the early morning hitting me even though I'd been in bed by eleven thirty, but given we were here yesterday it really would have been more time efficient to have slept here too. Blue Boat seemed a long way off, especially as right now all I could imagine was my bed, but I had other things to do. 'Hey, do you want to go over the anatomy coursework together later? We have to hand it in on Wednesday.'

'Yes. Let's get lunch and we can eat it in your room while we do it. And nap on the way back.'

Three and a half hours later I was sitting on the floor of my dorm room picking at the cooling fries from the cardboard container, and dipping them into the ketchup pot while simultaneously frowning at Imogen who was dipping hers in mustard, then mayo.

I mean, each to their own, but mustard was gross.

The fish finger sandwich, however, was pretty darn good for a town that wasn't situated near an ocean. It didn't have the 'just caught' vibes of the sandwiches my mom made from the fish my dad brought home every day, or the type I'd serve from my lobster roll restaurant in my dreams, but I'd managed to finish it in approximately seven bites.

The sound of Imogen rapidly tapping her pen against her human anatomy course book returned my attention to the job in hand and we continued with the quiz we were working through, hoping we could cram as much information into our brains as possible.

I was just deciding between asking her to list the mechanisms of a disease process backwards and asking her to name every bone in size order when the door burst open, and we looked up to find Hannah, her arms laden with textbooks.

'Thought I could come and study with you.' She dropped to the floor while miraculously managing to keep all the books in her arms.

'Han, have you raided the library, or something?' asked Imogen, reaching for her bottle of water and moving it out of the way.

'I wish.' She gave a heavy sigh, 'This is for one assignment.'

I reached over and picked up the heaviest-looking textbook, and glanced at the cover – applied mathematics. 'Jeez, you could curl this alone, and you'd have a decent set of biceps.'

'Maybe that's why people take maths,' Imogen added with a snort, making Hannah groan.

'I know. I should have just taken straight physics. Not sure why I thought physics and maths was a good idea.'

'I can't help you there,' I laughed, grabbing the last handful of cold fries and throwing them in my mouth. 'I'm not sure I've ever understood the point of math outside of calculating the tip on a bill.'

'Tell me about it,' Imogen leaned back against my bed,

'and it's only going to get harder for the next six years. Makes you realize why people opt for classics or English, even history. Or art. History of art. You know, one of those degrees where all you have to do is read, then write about it. How hard can that be really?'

I tried to hide my grin, because it was exactly what I'd said to Oz more than once.

'What's that look for?' asked Hannah.

'Nothing, I just agree with you,' I laughed.

'Yeah?' She looked at me pointedly, then over to Imogen.

'What?'

'A.O.-C. is taking classics, isn't he?' They both turned to me, and my smile morphed from one of mild amusement to decidedly guilty.

I stood, picking up the empty sandwich cartons, and threw them in the trash. Then I cracked the window a little because the three of us in here, with food, and the heating, was getting ripe. Not to mention I was suddenly in need of fresh air because my cheeks were burning red hot.

'Asters?'

'Yes?' I dropped down in my desk chair, because we'd clearly reached *that* point. The one I'd been dreading for a week. The one I thought I might have gotten away with. The one I didn't know how to explain.

I'd been waiting for the subject of Oz to be broached, on tenterhooks for the week whenever the three of us were together, and it wasn't that I didn't want to tell them, I just didn't know how. The two girls in front of me had quickly become my best friends, and aside from Hannah taking different classes, we did everything together.

Back home I had my best childhood friends; the kids of my parents' friends, all of us forced to grow up together whether we wanted to or not. That's not to say I didn't love my friends from home, but they were never interested in rowing, or had the urge to run their own business, and after Jake died and I took up studying harder they took up dating, and we kind of drifted apart a little.

But here, with these two in front of me, was the first time I'd made friends on my own, who liked what I liked, and weren't kids of my parents' friends. They were part of a life separate to poor dead Jake's sister, and I hadn't wanted to fuck it up by making a stupid mistake.

'Are we going to talk about what happened last week?'

I chewed on the end of my thumbnail, trying to buy myself even the minutest amount of time so I could figure out how to word the conversation we were about to have. 'Which bit exactly?'

'Let's start at the bit where we found you shouting at A. O.-C. after the heist meeting, shouting like you knew him, and finish with yesterday when you were partnered with him for cleaning duty.'

'Okay.' I rubbed my hands along my thighs, then brought my legs up to my chest, hugging them close. 'Well . . . I do know him. Kind of.'

'What?! How?' Imogen's eyes popped wide. 'And how have you not mentioned this before?'

I sighed, my head whirring in a cyclone of confusion and guilt, 'It wasn't on purpose. I didn't know I'd met him until it was too late . . . until the first race of the season against Oxford.'

Hannah put her book down and knelt forward, her

arms resting on her knees, 'You're going to have to start from the beginning. I'm having trouble keeping up with this, my brain is obviously fried from all the maths.'

I huffed a laugh, 'What's my excuse then?'

I looked between them, both their faces mirroring the other's confusion. Ugh.

'Do you remember the first night we went to the pub? I'd just arrived the day before and we went with some of the girls from the Downing crew ... Sarah, Ivy ... remember?'

They both nodded, and I proceeded to tell them everything, starting with my walk home from the pub and the nearly kiss, and ending with me storming out of the changing room.

And now they were both staring at me with mouths wide open. I wondered how long they'd stay quiet and if I had time to pee before they started talking, but then Imogen broke.

'With Arthur Osbourne-Cloud?'

'In the girls' bathroom?' added Hannah, horrified.

I nodded. 'Yeah, in hindsight he did look like he was sneaking in, but as we were talking I realized he was who you'd been talking about.' I pointed at Imogen, who at least at the grace to look slightly guilty. 'He figured out that something had changed my mind, I alluded to some of what you'd said, and he got really mad. But I told him that we couldn't see each other, and left.'

The pair of them sat there looking at me with the exact expressions I'd expected them to have. They'd made it no secret they didn't like him, but after a minute their faces changed. Hannah looked like she'd gone back to her applied mathematics, while perfectly straight lines formed down Imogen's forehead as her brows knotted together.

'Hang on, the Oxford race was over a month ago.'

'I know. What's that got to do with anything?'

'Well . . . A.O.-C. was mad at you last week . . .' She gesticulated so wildly that she nearly knocked her water over, 'What happened since the race?'

'Oh,' my shoulders sagged, 'nothing. He'd been texting me, but I never replied, and he wanted to know why. The heist meeting was the first time I'd seen or spoken to him since that day in the bathroom.'

'Are you telling us he's been texting you since the first race of the season?'

I nodded.

Hannah's mouth opened wider, as did Imogen's.

'Arthur Osbourne-Cloud has been texting you since the Oxford race and you haven't replied,' Imogen repeated slowly, because she was clearly still struggling with this breaking news.

I nodded. 'Correct.'

'I don't know what to say.'

'What's he been texting?'

I shrugged. 'Just general stuff, you know like asking how my day was, that sort of thing.'

'Awww. That's really cute,' sighed Hannah, then, 'OMG! You were partnered with him yesterday! I was so tired when we got on the bus, I fell asleep before I asked. What happened?'

'More of the same. He swears that he's not the guy he's made out to be, and . . . I believe him. What you've told me about him is not the guy I first met. It's been driving me crazy. He's sweet and thoughtful, and kind. I like him. I know it's an issue we have to beat Oxford, but I'll have to figure that one out for myself.' I got off my chair and joined them on the floor, 'I'm so sorry I didn't tell you. The first week I barely had time to think, and then the Oxford race you spent the entire walk there telling me about how awful the president was. Then when I realized it was the guy I was supposed to go on a date with I was so embarrassed, and kind of thought I'd been taken for a sucker. So I never said anything and that's why I never replied to him. It's not like we have time to date anyway.'

Imogen sucked her cheeks in, and her head tilted the way it did when she needed to think really hard. She spent so long considering her words I was close to snapping.

'Asters, do you want to date him?'

My brow furrowed at the question I hadn't been expecting. I hadn't dated a lot in my life; I hadn't had time. After Jake died, when everyone else was dating, my time was spent studying or coxing, and I'd never thought about it. Plus, I already knew all the guys in my town, and it didn't take me long to figure out that none of them was the guy for me – not even Billy Polinksi, no matter how much our moms thought otherwise.

Oz was the first guy I'd ever met who seemed to know how to have a conversation, who I could talk to, share my thoughts with and have them understood. That fluttering you get in your chest that makes it feel like you need to go to the emergency room? He was the first guy who'd ever done that. The first guy I'd not stopped thinking about.

So while Oz and I hadn't yet discussed how we would date while living a hundred miles apart, I did know that I wanted to keep messaging, I wanted to see him and I definitely wanted that kiss.

'Yes, I think I do.'

'Then go for it. Regardless of what anyone says, it's important to have a semblance of life outside of rowing and medicine, and you have to find it where you can. But,' she held up her pointer finger, with a smile which didn't reach her eyes, 'if he turns into the person he's promising he's not, then Hannah and I will carve him up in a slow, painful death.'

'You got it. And please can we keep this our secret?'

'Oh absolutely, Mary Heston would carve you up otherwise,' said Hannah, jumping up and opening the door, 'I have to go to the bathroom.'

'It's a good time for a break anyway. I'm getting more snacks, I've got some popcorn next door.'

Imogen followed Hannah; the open door and the window behind me causing a cold blast of air to hit me as I got up to close it. For once I ignored the anxiety tickling my skin, and pushed all thoughts of Mary Heston and what I was doing away.

It was almost second nature to me now that I reached for Oz's sweater whenever I was cold, and I was pulling it over my head before it even registered. It no longer smelt like him, but the soft cashmere brushing against my cheeks took me back to that night on the quadrangle when his scent buried itself so deep under my skin that I could almost conjure it now.

Reaching for my cell I typed out a message.

Kate: *First time on the Tideway and I finally got a compliment from my coach. I had to take all the credit though*

Oz: *I'm sure I'll find a way you can make it up to me, Yankee Doodle. X*

The smile was still on my face when the girls returned five minutes later.

11. Arthur

(Tattoos and video chats)

The blades sliced through the water; my legs pushed down, driving me back in my seat as my body lengthened out, powering the oar forward.

And repeat.

It was cold enough this morning that my breath was visible in the air, a cloudy trail blowing out with every exhale I made, but I could still feel the trickle of sweat running down my ribcage and soaking my undershirt. To the left of me the sun was just peeking over the horizon, brightening the pale grass in the fields cut short for the winter.

There was something about being out on the water this early, before the sun rose, before anyone else could spoil it. We passed a barge moored to the bank, its chimney already puffing out smoke from its log burner, and the smell of fire filled my lungs, but they could take it.

We weren't pushing ourselves too hard this morning. This wasn't a session to end all sessions. This was a Monday morning session, and we were easing in our muscles for the week. Marshy was keeping us in easy time with his pace setting while huddled up in front of me. The crews had been switched out and this morning I was stroke for the new joiners; it was something Coach liked to do so he could see where the drag was, who the weak links were and how he would build two crews to race in March.

Tomorrow our Tideway training would begin; then it would start getting really hard, and I couldn't fucking wait.

Since Saturday I had a renewed energy; my body was still buzzing with a latent adrenaline which had kept me awake most of the night, and given how long it had taken Charlie to wake up this morning, plus the somewhat sluggish appearance of the rest of the boys, I'd say I was the only one.

The reason: Kate Astley.

The reverberation of Coach's megaphone echoed around the banks as he called time on our session. Even without pushing hard we'd set a decent pace, and I could see a couple of the newbies earning a spot on the crew for Isis.

As I looked to the bank, near Fleming Boathouse, I could see Charlie and Brooks standing by the dry dock, having already put their shell away. As I slowed down, Charlie waded into the water to pull my scull forward and Pete stepped out.

'Morning,' I grinned, nodding to the two steaming cups in Brooks' hands, 'one of those for me, perchance?'

'Might be.'

I unclipped my shoes to step out, ready for Pete's instructions so we all got out in unison and no-one's weight toppled the shell causing us to fall in, which happened more on a Monday than any other day. I placed my oars gently on the dock, before slapping Charlie's outstretched hand. 'Thanks, Sunshine. I appreciate your help. And I appreciate you for that coffee I'll be drinking in a minute.' I leaned in to smack a kiss on Brooks' cheek, only for him to push me away with a loud laugh.

'Oz, stop fucking around,' snapped Pete as quietly as he could, seeing as he was addressing the president in front of the junior crew, and who clearly wasn't in as good a mood as me this morning. 'You're supposed to be leading by example.'

Brooks' eyes widened, hiding a grin behind his coffee mug.

'Sorry, mate.'

He mumbled something under his breath and walked to the end of the boat, ready to bark out his orders and get us back to the boathouse as he followed behind, until the shell was safely resting on its pipes.

'Marshy, what's up, mate?' I put my arm around his shoulder, though with our nine-inch height difference it was a little lopsided.

'Nothing. Just tired. Sorry for snapping.'

'Sorry for fucking about,' I winked, expecting it to raise a smile, which it didn't. He simply walked off to the showers.

'What's up with Marshy?' I asked, relieving Brooks of my coffee.

Charlie and Brooks both shrugged with a shake of their heads, so I didn't push it, but it was definitely more than being tired. I'd been with him after forty hours of no sleep on a trip to Australia where our oars stayed in Singapore and we needed them for a race in two days' time, and his perma-smile never faltered.

'Speaking of moods, Charles here seems to have woken up.' I smacked him on the back.

'Damn right.'

Brooks pulled Charlie into a headlock, which distracted me enough that I didn't notice the buzzing at first as it started up in the pocket of my jacket, and it took me so long to grab before it rang out that I pressed green before I could think.

'Hello?'

'Arthur?' barked a voice which sent red-hot torrents of fury through every cell in my body.

I looked at my phone screen. How did I not notice the name flash up? I always looked at my screen for the simple reason that it could be any one of a huge group of people I didn't wish to speak to, therefore wouldn't answer. Unfortunately, it was the one person I didn't wish to speak to the most.

'What do you want?'

'To speak to my son,' my dad snapped back.

'You have nothing to say that I wish to hear.'

'For God's sake, Arthur. Don't be so childish. If your brothers and sister can speak to me, then so can you.'

Whatever glib reply I was about to snap out died on my lips. I was ninety-five per cent certain none of my siblings had spoken to him. I knew this because I spoke to them all at some point most days. We were also in a group chat with my mother, and any contact with him had not been mentioned, so I called bullshit. Though there was always the possibility there could be a grain of truth in it which they hadn't wanted to admit to.

'I didn't realize they were more interested in hearing your bullshit than I am, but I can assure you I'm definitely not.'

169

'No,' he snapped, 'seems you're too busy with not only fucking up your schooling, you're fucking up your rowing as well. I've heard about this childish stunt gone wrong, wasting valuable study time on cleaning up all the shit on the river, when there are already people to do it.'

'You mean like you have people to clean up your shit? Believe me I'll do a much better job, though keeping you out of the papers seems to be as near an impossible feat as you keeping your dick out of your secretary. Or whoever the last one was.'

From the silence on the line, I knew if I could see him his face would be turning a healthy shade of beetroot.

'You're an obnoxious little shit, Arthur. You will amount to nothing with this attitude. When will you grow up?'

'Problem there, Dad . . .' I spat, 'I've already amounted to far more in my twenty-one years than you have in your fifty. So fuck you. And don't call me again.'

I hit call end and turned around to find Charlie and Brooks standing close enough that I knew they'd heard every word, but far enough away to give me a little privacy while also stopping any of the guys on the crew from approaching me. Like my own personal security team.

I took a deep breath. The calm I'd felt as I'd breezed along the river this morning had vanished in the sunrise, only to be replaced by grinding teeth and a pounding heartbeat. Not the good kind.

'You okay?' Brooks squeezed my shoulder. 'Need a minute?'

'No,' I grunted, as the thick, unwelcome wedge of angry tears lodged itself firmly in my throat, 'Yes.'

Charlie moved around me, blocking me from the view

of anyone passing as I took a huge sniff, and wiped my watery eyes. I pressed my palms so hard into my eye sockets that my vision blurred for a second when I opened them.

'I think I legit hate him.'

'I know I do,' Brooks and Charlie replied in unison, making the three of us laugh and diluting the rage sitting on my chest.

'Thanks.' I pulled them both in for a hug. 'Don't know what I'd do without you.'

'Great, then perhaps you could get in the shower before you buy Brooks and me second breakfast on the way home. You stink.' Charlie wafted his hand dramatically under his nose.

I laughed but did as Mother Hen requested.

I shuffled up my bed and settled in, propping myself on my pillows, and leaned back against the headrest. The cup of herbal tea I'd made was cooling on the nightstand next to my pint of water. Running my fingers through my hair, I smoothed down the hoodie I was wearing, and cupped my hands around my mouth before I realized what I was doing.

Nope, she couldn't smell me, even though I was minty fresh.

It dawned on me I'd never put this much effort into a conversation I was about to have with any girl I was dating. Sort of dating. Definitely dating. Well, if I had any say in it at all. Not that I had ever really dated.

But Kate Astley was not just any girl. It had taken me approximately nine seconds to realize that.

I hit dial.

For a second as the screen cleared, my breath caught. I had a good memory, and every time I thought I'd committed her face to it I only realized how woefully I'd failed the next time I saw her. She really was breathtaking.

'Hey, there.' Her breathy voice as she shuffled around in her room had my body jolting out from the relaxed state I'd been in a minute ago. 'I wasn't expecting a video call.'

Her bare face, freshly washed and without a scrap of make-up, smiled back at me, making her dimple deepen and the apple of her cheeks appear pinker than usual. I tried to ignore the fact her hair was wet and she was fresh from the shower, because my dick had already been paying attention to her and was now twitching at the thought of her soaped up and running shampoo through her long, dark hair – the entire scene was too much for me to cope with before bed.

As it was I'd mentally mapped out the quickest route from Oxford to Cambridge, and at this time of night avoiding any speed cameras, I could probably get there in an hour and twenty. It would almost be worth the morning tiredness and skipping my lecture on philology and linguistics in lieu of a nap. I mean, I skipped them most weeks anyway and caught up on the coursework in my own time.

'Hello there, Yankee Doodle. Thought I'd surprise you.'

'Consider me surprised,' she replied, propping her phone on what I assumed was her desk as she pulled a sweater over her vest top, though I was willing to bet she hadn't meant to position it directly in front of her tits. It was brief but as she stretched her arms over her head the white cotton of her top pulled so taut I could very clearly see the outline of a hard nipple. It did nothing to help my dick calm down; that visual was being committed to my brain forever.

I cleared my throat to stop a groan escaping just as she came back into view and moved over to her bed. 'I figured if we're going to get to know each other long distance, that we shouldn't just rely on texting. If we were at the same uni, I'd have seen you this evening.'

'Oh yeah?'

'Yes,' the conviction in my tone only made her blush harder, and suddenly pink was my new favourite colour, 'and I'd have kissed you goodnight.'

Her bottom lip caught in her teeth as she looked straight down the camera, and I completely forgot what I was about to say. Hell, this girl could make me forget my own name.

I think she already had.

'I like the sound of that,' she smiled, 'and we'd have talked about our days. So, tell me, how yours was.'

'Definitely ending better than it started, that's for sure.' I grinned, but her face dropped a little.

'Did something happen this morning?'

I tugged on the back of my neck before tension set in as it always did when I thought of my father. But just like the first night I met Kate, I had an urge to spill more than my usual dismissive responses. Also just like the first night, Kate asked questions because she wanted to get to know me, like normal people did, and not because she was after a juicy nugget of salacious gossip. And I found I wanted to tell her, just like I had then.

'I had an argument with my dad this morning, and it normally puts me in a bad mood for the entire day.'

'I'm so sorry. What did you argue about?'

'Same as usual. He hates that I'm studying classics, thinks I've fucked up my future and wants me to grow up. Loosely translated as doing what he does.'

'He wants you to work in politics, right? Like him?'

I nodded. 'He does.'

She picked up her water bottle, and I watched her twisting the cap on and off before she spoke. 'Have you ever tried to talk to him about doing something else?'

'No. It's not a conversation that will ever take place. He wouldn't hear it. Therefore I will stay forever a student.'

'I get it, it's a hard conversation to have.'

'Yeah, just like your lobster rolls.' I sighed, and from the way her smile had now disappeared, decided to change the subject before we delved any further, which would result in bad moods all around.

'Anyway, how was your Monday? What did you learn in the world of medicine?'

She chuckled, 'I was with Leo today. I learned about compartments of a body, the muscles . . .'

But I wasn't listening. I'd only focused on one part of that sentence. In a flash, jealousy, green, thick, ugly and raw, seeped into my blood like sewage, almost winding me with its ferocity like nothing I'd ever experienced. Jealousy was for the weak.

I didn't get jealous, except clearly I did.

'Kate, who's Leo?' I tried to keep my voice as calm as possible.

'My cadaver.' She grinned, with absolutely no awareness

of the irrational turmoil I was currently experiencing at the thought of her with another man. 'We had to name them, and I called him Galileo. Leo for short.'

I blinked, the whirring in my brain stopped while her words sank in and it became clear I was jealous of a dead guy.

'Well, I thought it was funny. Or cute at least,' she added, totally misreading my silence.

'No! It's great. It's perfect. Galileo. Father of modern science.'

'Yeah?'

'I love it, couldn't think of a better cadaver name,' I added with enthusiasm so over the top it earned me a frown. 'Is it weird being with dead bodies?'

She reached out of sight again and picked up her bottle of water, drinking while she thought. 'No, I thought it would be, but it's kind of comforting. I feel like I'm taking care of Leo and helping him fulfil his purpose for the pursuit of science and knowledge.' Her voice trailed off and she dropped her head. She was silent for a few seconds. 'It sounds dumb but it makes me feel closer to Jake.'

'Your brother?'

'Yeah, he didn't donate his body, but I feel like I can visualize him afterwards, if you know what I mean . . . you know, after he died . . . and that maybe Leo would know him in heaven.'

Her head had dropped down so low I could barely see her.

'Kate, it's not dumb at all. The Ancient Greeks believed that the moment a body died, its spirit left in a small puff of air, and continued to exist forever around us. I'm sure

175

Jake and Leo are floating around the clouds together having an excellent time.'

When she looked at me, her eyes glistened. If I could, I would have reached through the screen to wipe them; as it was, her tears sat heavily on my chest. I might not have lost any siblings, but I understood grief and right then I wanted to take it all away for her.

'Yes,' she laughed softly, 'I'm sure they're causing havoc. Leo has a tattoo, so he definitely has a story to tell.'

'Yeah, I bet. What's it of?'

'A red heart on his chest.'

'He's a romantic. What about you? Any tattoos?'

She shook her head hard. 'Noooo. I can barely make it through the dentist and the buzzing of the drill; the thought of having a needle repeatedly pierce my skin,' she shivered dramatically, 'no thanks.'

I laughed at the expression on her face; gone was the heartache from a moment ago. 'Really? You seem too tough to me to be scared of a little needle.'

'Hey,' she pinned with me a stern glare, 'looks can be deceiving.'

'So what you're telling me is that you need protecting at all costs, and I'm the one man for the job?'

Her grin widened, before she burst into peals of laughter which rang in my chest and reverberated off my ribcage. It was a sound I'd play on repeat forever.

'What about you?' she asked, finally. 'Any tattoos? Or are you about to tell me you're also scared of needles?'

'Hey! I'm scared of nothing.' I crooked a grin at her, 'I do have a tattoo actually, two in fact. Wanna see them?'

She frowned, 'Depends. Where are they?'

'Nowhere x-rated.' I laughed, reaching behind my head to remove my hoodie.

My tattoo was inked along the inside of my left bicep; I could have left my t-shirt on, it would have been easy to pull up the soft cotton sleeves to show her, but instead it went the way of my hoodie, tossed to the side of the bed. Seeing the appreciative look on her face as she took me in, as her gaze moved slowly across my chest, her eyes flaring bright, made it the best decision of my life to date.

Her eyes were now focused on the way my bicep flexed, and my tattoo of the five Olympic rings I had inked there. I'd opted to keep them in black outline, that perhaps I'd have them coloured in when I won a gold, though I kind of liked them as they were.

'Where's your medal?' she asked, finally looking at me.

'My mother has it. She has all my medals, she keeps them in her bathroom.' I laughed with Kate, because maybe it was a little kooky. 'I don't know why she keeps them in there, she has all our school achievements framed or hanging. Everything from my sister winning the school fun run to those medals. They all have equal placement.'

'That's cute,' she smiled. 'How many siblings do you have?'

'Three younger ones. A sister and two brothers.'

'What are they called?'

'Alexander and Hector are my brothers. Phoebe is my sister.'

'I like their names.'

'They're all Greek, but also English enough that my dad didn't complain.'

'Is Arthur a Greek name?'

I shook my head, and began twisting the signet ring on my pinkie, 'No, it's English, but my middle name is Titus. King Arthur was a legendary warrior who defeated the Saxons when they invaded Britain. It's my grandfather's name, and as the first-born son I inherited it. But no one calls me Arthur.'

'I like it, but I like Oz too.'

'You, Kate Astley, may call me whatever you want and I will likely break into a sprint to get there as quickly as possible.'

She grinned at me, and I had to rub away the heavy thudding in my chest. I was reaching to put my hoodie back on when she stopped me, 'Oh, what's your second tattoo?'

'You only have to ask if you want me to sit here naked,' I waited for her to blush, but she merely raised an eyebrow that had me chuckling and I moved back a little, twisting in the frame of the screen so she could see me properly, and lifted my arm up.

She squinted into the lens, trying to get closer, 'What is it?'

I ran my fingers down the length of the extravagantly drawn blade printed into my left side, stretching from my third rib all the way down to the top of my pelvis, 'It's Excalibur. King Arthur's legendary sword. The story goes that it held magical powers, providing strength and protecting him from forces that would otherwise have killed him.'

'Do you need protection?' she asked quietly.

I pulled my hoodie back on, and sat back. My herbal tea was now almost cold, but I drank it anyway while I thought about her question. I could dismiss it with a head shake, or a simple 'no', but not many people ever asked what it was. Only a handful had ever seen it properly, and in those situations we'd always been too busy to stop and discuss why I had a sword tattooed down the length of my torso.

'No, not as such,' I replied, finally, and she waited for me to expand. 'I don't need physical protection. I can take care of myself, but I worry about my mother, and my siblings. I got this about eighteen months ago. The day before, I'd been at home alone, and a woman showed up at my parents' house claiming she was in love with my father and she was pregnant . . .'

Kate stayed silent; her wide eyes did all the talking. 'She wasn't, but I called my father and it was clear he knew her. She was quickly sent off to the family lawyers and paid off with a chunk of money, never to be heard from again. My parents haven't technically been married for a long time, not in the truest sense anyway, and I'm not sure he'd ever been faithful. If you ask me I still can't comprehend why they got married.' I sighed, 'Anyway, where was I? Oh yes, my mother was at home in Greece, with my siblings, and I had to call and tell her what happened. It was the first time I'd ever seen her cry over him, and I think that was the day which cemented my hatred. I couldn't do anything to protect her, but the next day I got my own Excalibur, in the hope it might protect us all. Stupid really,' I added.

Her expression of shock morphed into one of sadness, but not pity which I was glad for. I wasn't sure I could take pity right now. Or ever.

'Oh, Oz, I'm so sorry. That's awful for you to have to

experience, I can't imagine how hard that must have been for you. No wonder you don't want to go and work with him.'

I shrugged a little, thinking back to this morning and my father's vicious words. Even though I knew they weren't true, it never stopped the sting when they came. 'My father doesn't have one moral bone in his body, but he's very charming, and I sometimes wonder if he can't help himself, like he doesn't even realize. It's gross, and manipulative, and makes me all the angrier when people say I'm just like him. I'm nothing like him.'

'No, I don't think you are.' She smiled softly, then sat up straighter. 'I know I've been told things about you, but the stories I heard didn't match up to the same person I'd met. You're kind and sweet,' her collarbone dipped as she shrugged one shoulder and looked at me from under her thick, sooty lashes, 'you're kind of funny . . .'

I barked out a laugh. 'Hey! I'm funnier than you are!'

She shook her head with a grin, 'No, you're not, but that's okay, we can't be good at everything.'

'Oh! Just you wait. I'm going to have you laughing so hard, I'll need to take you to A&E to get your sides stitched back up.'

She drummed her fingers to her lips, 'Hmmmm. I don't think so, but it's cute you believe it.'

'Cute . . .' I shook my head with an exaggerated huff. 'Unbelievable. I've literally bared my chest and my soul, and all I get is a cute.'

'Hey, I'm not making your head bigger than it needs to be, Mister Olympian!'

'Ooh, Wizard of Oz and Mister Olympian. I can't decide which I like more.'

Her eyes darted to the side, then back at me. 'Well you think on it and let me know tomorrow. I need to go to sleep, in fact we both do.'

'You're right, I should stock up on beauty sleep to move from cute to devastatingly handsome.'

She rolled her eyes, her light laugh wrapped around my heart and squeezed, 'Night, Oz. Sleep tight.'

'Sleep tight, Yankee Doodle. Dream of me.'

The screen went dead before I had a chance to press end, making me laugh again. The day might not have started off so well, but it couldn't have had a better end.

And just like that, I was in my first long-distance relationship.

12. Kate

(Who knew community service could be so romantic? Part 2)

It started exactly the same as it had last Saturday, with a quick nudge to my ribs from Hannah sitting next to me, waking me up from the deep sleep I'd fallen into. I could sleep anywhere, a skill I really should add to my résumé.

'We're here,' she added, stretching her arms over her head.

Only this time I didn't groan with the irritation that I'd been ordered to spend my Saturday cleaning up the river. No, quite the opposite. This morning, I was excited, and I had been since the text message I'd received from Oz before I'd even woken up.

Oz: *Can't wait to see you later x*

I pulled up my sleeve to see if the excitement I was tingling with was visible to anyone else, but no. Just me then. Probably for the best.

I'd managed to tamp down the smile I'd been wearing all through my shower, my getting dressed and my eating breakfast, though I knew it was creeping back up.

Hannah's head peered through the seat divide. 'Do you reckon we'll be in the same pairs as we were last week?'

My head snapped up to hers, 'What? You think they'll change them?'

'Dunno.' She shrugged, not noticing my momentary panic, though Imogen did.

She leaned in. 'Don't worry, I'm sure Captain Perfect will fix it so you're together.'

I responded with a sly side-eye and a reminder, 'It's President Perfect, if you want to be correct about it. But I thought we weren't going to call him that.'

'I agreed no such thing. What I did agree to was putting him on probation, so he can prove his worthiness.'

'Hmm.'

If I'd learned anything this week, it was Oz's true worthiness. Not that I had any intention of sharing with the two girls next to me both checking their watches while simultaneously staring out of the window waiting for the Oxford crew to appear any minute. Oz would reveal his worthiness in his own time, while Imogen and Hannah would have to get used to the fact Oz and I were friends. Or more than friends, hopefully, because it had become clear to me that after the first night of our FaceTime, ninety per cent of me definitely wanted to be more than friends.

Much more.

The other ten – the ten which said I could get expelled from Cambridge if they took away my scholarship – I was trying to ignore as best I could.

It had only been five days ago, and yet it was possible we'd crammed the entire seven weeks since we'd first met into every conversation, every text, every exchange. I wasn't even sure how I'd found the time, but Imogen had been correct, I'd found it where I could. Once it dawned on me I'd never bump into him on campus, I didn't look for him. I didn't lose focus worrying about fitting him into my schedule, or seeing him every day, because I couldn't. The pressure drifted off in a little puff of fresh Cambridge air.

We were both in the same position. Both training, both studying.

And so it might have been only five days, but it proved to me that perhaps the hurdle of dating wasn't such a hurdle after all, even though we weren't officially dating. If we were, today might constitute the first date, because today we were going to see each other for the first time being on the exact same page.

The page that said we were going to kiss.

Except cleaning the river was not the most romantic of situations for that to happen.

'Okay, everyone off the bus,' called Coach Stephens as he peered in through the doors at the front. 'The dark blues have arrived.'

I jumped up, glancing out of the window to see if Oz was there, but the bus was still pulling to a stop.

'Here,' Hannah thrust a bottle of hand sanitizer at me as I stepped ahead of her and shuffled down the seat aisles. 'Use this before you put your gloves on. It was gross last week.'

I rubbed my palms together after she'd squeezed a dollop on, the cool gel sending a shudder through me. Today might have been brilliant sunshine, but the air was rivalling the frigid east-coast temperatures and had me pulling my hood up my neck, and the rim of my beanie down past my ears as I stepped off the bus.

The assistant coaches were already passing out the

thick black trash bags and blue protective gloves, along with the rest of the cleaning equipment we'd had. Looking around, I still couldn't see Oz. Two of the guys I'd noticed him standing with at the heist meeting were over by the bus, with a couple more huddled in a circle nearer to the boathouse, but he was nowhere to be seen.

'Quiet. Listen up,' shouted Coach Lassiter, 'you know what you have to do. Same partners as last week, different stretch of the river. Presidents have the lists. Presidents? Where are they? Norris? Cloud?'

He looked around, calling over to a couple of the assistant coaches who shrugged back at him. Naturally everyone else lost interest as he continued searching for the two missing presidents, and the volume levels of the crews standing around in the cold increased. Someone started doing jumping jacks, and I heard several shouts for a coffee trip. Imogen had run back to the bus where she'd left her headphones, and I was just about to follow her to grab a packet of gum when there he was, jogging out of the shadows of the boathouse, Will Norris by his side.

Time could have stood still if I didn't know better, or maybe I didn't. All I knew was my mouth dried up, and my tongue would have fallen out if it hadn't been stuck to the roof of it. He appeared in slow motion like every Hollywood movie I'd ever seen, dressed entirely in navy blue. His short black curls bounced so smoothly with each stride it could have been choreographed, and even from this distance his eyes gleamed bright blue as though he'd woken up and decided to coordinate with the cloudless sky. For the first time I noticed the reaction of every other woman present; for a split second they all stopped what they were doing and looked at him before resuming their conversations or stretches or whatever they'd been engaged in before Oz had appeared.

'Shit, even if he isn't Captain Perfect, you are one fucking lucky lady. How does anyone look that good? It's obscene. It's like a Disney prince was brought to life.'

I startled as Imogen reappeared at my side, the sensation of her whispering so close to me sending shivers down my spine.

I pulled a face, trying to stop the ringing now circling my ear. 'Does that mean I'm the one who needs saving?'

'Hell, no! You save yourself, Asters.'

Our eyes were still glued onto Oz and Will Norris walking over to where the coaches were standing.

'We're here. Just discussing tactics with my fellow pres,' grinned Will, making Coach Lassiter frown. 'We're ready.'

'Good. Everyone get on with it.'

I stayed where I was. It could have been that I was glued to the spot, or maybe it was that I was seeing him for the first time with my new Oz-tinted glasses, and wanted a second to myself where people were too preoccupied to look at him. I was also capable of admitting I wanted him to find me, that a teeny-tiny, insecure piece of me wanted to know he was as excited to see me as I was to see him.

It took him less than ten seconds, and when he did a slow grin spread across his face. Every inch of my body curled under his gaze until I was on the verge of combustion, while he collected our supplies on his march over to me.

'Stop being so obvious,' hissed Imogen in my ear again. 'You need to stop salivating every time you see him if you're going to be sneaking around.'

I looked at the ground, because I was finding it too hard to hold in the smile and the girl had a point. I needed to keep my shit together.

'Mr President,' Imogen drawled at Oz, announcing his arrival.

'Hello,' he replied, his eyes flicking between the two of us, before finally sticking on me. 'Ready, Yanks?'

'What did you call her?' Hannah's head tilted with a slight frown.

'Yanks. Short for Yankee Doodle. Because she's American.'

He grinned at the girls standing either side of him, but they were now staring at me like Christmas had come early. Hannah was definitely wearing heart eyes, while Imogen was gawping like a goldfish.

'Come on. Let's get cleaning.' I pulled him away, turning back to my two friends before we were out of sight, to find them still staring at our retreating backs. Imogen had joined her fingers together in a little heart. 'See you back here for lunch.'

'Alone at last. It felt like the journey here took forever.' He bent closer to me, so close that his lips almost brushed against the top of my head, 'Your friends seem nice. Which one is which?'

'Imogen is the taller one with auburn hair. Hannah is the blonde.'

He chuckled, 'Ahh, Imogen is the one Brooks was asking about.'

One topic of discussion during the week had been our friends, where he'd let slip that one of his roommates had a crush, though he couldn't remember on whom.

'He'll have to get in line, all the guys have the hots for her,' I smirked up at him.

'Not all the guys, Kate Astley,' he replied, a smile curling up his lip, 'I'll let him down gently, don't worry.'

'Actually, there's something else I should have told you this week.' I stopped walking, forcing him to stop with me, his brow already tensed in anticipation of what I was going to say, 'I know we're keeping this a secret, but . . .. well, they asked about you. They saw me shouting at you after the heist meeting, and I told them we were friends . . .' My smile turned into a grimace. 'I'm sorry. I promise they won't say anything.'

'God, I thought you were going to tell me you'd changed your mind about us.' His hand shot to his chest, but his mouth spread wide, showing off straight white teeth. 'Hey, you can tell whomever you'd like, I have nothing to hide. Kate, I don't care who knows.'

I sighed, because I didn't want to care either. But I did, and not because of his reputation, it was because I felt like I was letting down my crew, except I'd only have to look into his eyes and I'd forget why.

'Hey,' he peered down at me, 'we're doing nothing wrong. But I won't say anything, don't worry. Brooks and Charlie won't either.'

'Do they know?'

He nodded, 'Yeah, but in fairness I told them about you the day after we first met, because I was totally smitten and couldn't stop thinking about you.'

'Oh. Okay,' I replied mindlessly, not really hearing the rest of his sentence.

The only thing going round in my mind was that this was easier for him; he was already an accomplished and decorated rower, not to mention a third year. He was leaving school in six months, I had six years to go before I finished.

'Kate,' he shook my shoulders gently, 'it'll be fine, you'll see. In fact, I have something I want to show you, and something I want to ask you.'

'Oh?' I perked up. 'What is it?'

'Surprise, come on.' He picked up his bucket, filled with all our cleaning products, and took my hand in the other.

I followed him along the route we'd taken last time, except instead of going left down to the riverbed, we turned right into a little clearing I hadn't noticed before, filled with evergreen bushes which ran along the side of the path hiding us from the view of anyone passing by. On the far end of the clearing was a wall, which I realized was the other side of what we'd been cleaning last week.

'What are we doing? I don't think this is where we're supposed to be. There's nothing to clean.' I looked around, not noticing how Oz had put the bucket on the ground and was walking me backward until I'd hit the wall and his massive body bracketed me in. 'What's going on?'

His fingers hooked under my chin, tilting it until my entire vision was filled with him. His eyes, the soft stubble coating his jaw, the way his thick lashes fanned out at the edges while he stayed gazing at me, unblinking. His irises were so clear I could almost see my reflection in them, and if I *had* been able, all that would have stared back was a girl utterly mesmerized, blatantly wanton, and totally unrecognizable.

'We're going to the river in a minute, but first, I'm going do what I should have done in September. Unless you have any objection.' His eyes narrowed, as if almost daring me to stop him.

My top lip twitched as his head dipped closer to mine. A freight train could've been bearing down on me, and I still wouldn't have moved a muscle.

The air around me stilled until I could hear nothing but the deafening silence echoed by my own thudding heart. Every sensation magnified itself a thousand times; my chest heaved until the point of hyperventilation as the pads of his fingertips ran across my brow, pushing under the wool of my beanie and into my hair.

I'd woken up late this morning, tired from a long week and an even longer call with my mom last night, where she'd told me at length about a pie she'd baked with this fall's blackberries, so I'd only had time to braid my hair in two while we travelled to London. As always, it was never neat enough or together enough, and all the pieces which had come loose he gently pushed behind my ear. Lifting the end of one braid, he brought it to his nose and inhaled deeply.

'I've been smelling this citrus scent wherever I go, like it's been buried in my memory since the day we met. Even when you've not been around, I could sense it almost. It's become my new favourite smell.'

His smile had my belly doing a little flip thing, tilting back and forth like when you're cresting the top of a rollercoaster and it's going to tip any second. That point where you don't know if your stomach is going to cave in.

The way his eyes were twinkling at me, made me feel I should probably give him an admission too.

'Funny you should say that . . .'

'Oh?'

'That sweater of yours.' I stopped talking, biting down on my top lip instead as I decided maybe my admission wasn't such a good idea, because remembering my shampoo was one thing, sleeping with a sweater under your pillow was quite another.

'I hope you've been looking after it. That's my favourite sweater. I've missed it.'

'I have,' I nodded slowly, crumbling under the weight of his stare as he waited for me to finish. 'It's been under my pillow.'

His eyebrows shot up, and he stepped back slightly as if to look at me properly, but his hands stayed holding the ends of my braids as he flicked the strands between his finger and thumb.

'Really?'

I nodded.

'You've been sleeping with it?'

I nodded again, trying to divert any attention away from the trembling making its way through my body, knowing my face was now pink. Or purple like my mom's blackberry pie.

'You have no idea how hot that is to me.' His voice had dropped an octave; his eyes had turned a cloudy grey, the exact colour of the storm swirling around my bones. He moved in a fraction, closing the final vestiges of space between us, and when he spoke next, I could almost taste the cinnamon gum on his breath. 'Kate Astley, since the second we got interrupted, all I've been able to think about is finishing our kiss. It's become quite the problem for my professors, when I can't get through a simple Greek tragedy.'

I crooked a brow at him, trying to lighten the tension with humour. Lighten something at least, because I felt like I was about to burst from whatever was thundering through me. 'What? I thought you only had an hour a week of study?'

'I do,' he grinned, devilishly. 'So now you know how much time I've had on my hands to think about you, and our first kiss.'

That did it. I stopped breathing. But it didn't deter him, and gone was the light-hearted, fun Oz I'd come to know over the past week. Even the guy I'd first met. He'd been replaced by someone who oozed confidence. Someone who'd never been told no. The guy everyone talked about: ruthless, merciless in his pursuit of victory, didn't just take what he wanted; he *snatched* it.

I was on the verge of screaming for him to snatch me, though I'd go willingly.

'Want to know what I think about?'

My heartbeat was pounding in every cell of my body; its epicentre right in the apex of my thighs; hot and sticky, and so very wet.

'Yes,' I whispered, incapable of any volume.

His hands cupped my cheeks, scalding to the touch of my near frozen skin.

'This.'

Finally, *finally*, his mouth surrounded mine, claiming, owning. There was no permission seeking. Just a desperate need to know what I tasted of after seven weeks of wondering. I knew because I was the same. Seven weeks I'd been resisting this kiss, and for the life of me couldn't remember why.

I couldn't remember anything. My mind was empty of all but him.

He tasted like everything I shouldn't be doing but was going to anyway. Like the sweetness of fresh waffles. Like winters in Vermont. Like decadence.

His tongue moved softly over mine, stroking, searching, discovering me. It was the type of kiss that makes you lose all sense of time and space. The type of kiss you emerge from and four hours have passed. The type of kiss you know you'll remember for the rest of your life.

Moans so soft I never imagined he'd be capable of making echoed around my mouth as my hands pushed into his hair. Even with me reaching as high as possible on my tiptoes and him bent down so low, all I could manage was to thread my fingers through his curls, and before I realized what was happening his palms had left my face and were scooping me up. One big hand on each of my ass cheeks; the perfect fit. Just like his mouth on mine.

'Much better,' he mumbled against my lips, and resumed his exploration.

Except now I was between a rock and a hard place; the wall and what was a very sizable protrusion in his trackpants.

I tried to pull back, but my lips were trapped in his. 'Oz.'

'Yes?' It was almost a purr, and almost had me forgetting why I wanted his attention.

'Oz,' I mumbled into his mouth again.

He released my lip, his head craning back a fraction though his gaze never strayed from my mouth. He stared for a second, and the look on his face could only be described as smug. Maybe satisfied, but mostly smug.

'Yes, Kate?' His head bent into the crook of my neck, his lips ghosting over the stretch of skin at the base of my ear, where my pulse was pounding under the surface as he travelled back up and along my jaw.

'Umm,' I hummed, wracking my brains while I tried to remember. Then I felt it, *him*, right where my thighs were gripping his waist. 'Need ... need to stop. Mustn't get caught.'

When his mouth stopped somewhere between my cheek and my jaw, I wanted to take back all the words I'd uttered, to tell him that I'd been wrong. But he released me before I could, his lips pressing to my temple before he looked at me.

'You're right.' Reluctantly he moved his hands from my ass, and put me on the ground.

All this time he had been holding my beanie, and he gently placed it back on my head, taking care to tuck all the strands out of the way.

'Come on, let's go and make our contribution to cleaning the river. Won't be winning any wagers this week though. In fact, it's probably almost time to go home.' He held his hand out and I took it, long fingers laced through mine and wrapped around my hand, and he pulled me into him, 'Actually, Kate Astley, do you have plans later? Please tell me you're not going home to your cadaver.'

'Why? Are you going to offer up your body for me instead?' My words came out before I could stop myself, even my hand was too late to cover them, but I only had him to blame because now I'd felt him through his track-pants I wouldn't be able to think about anything else.

He was seared into my brain.

But when I looked up at Oz's eyes, all that satisfaction had returned ten-fold, sparkling with amusement.

'No, I wasn't. But now I am. My body is available to you for any study time you might need, consider me your own private anatomy 101.'

I shoved him away with a laugh; after that kiss it was an offer I would take up without a second thought. 'Why were you asking about my plans? I do have to study this afternoon, thanks to you and your heist compadres.'

'Hey! Thanks to me and my compadres, this is now happening.' He pointed his finger between us.

'Anyway, what I'm trying to do is ask you on a date, something I've been meaning to ask all week. Tonight, if you don't have plans, I'll drive over and take you to dinner. Please don't have plans.'

I blinked, once. Twice. I didn't know why I was finding it so hard to understand what he was saying, especially as I'd spent the last half hour with his mouth wrapped around mine, not to mention the last week dreaming about this exact moment.

'Well?'

'Yes,' I replied. 'I'd love to. But don't you have training in the morning?'

'Not until ten. Get excited for our first date, Yankee Doodle.'

He smacked a final kiss to my lips and led me off, and I let him because after that I was mentally planning my first date outfit with the hottest guy I've ever met in my life.

And that was how cleaning the river became the most romantic situation of my life to date.

13. Arthur

(Pies, pies and more pies)

Not to brag, but I brought my A-game to that kiss today.

A plus.

Five stars.

Two thumbs up.

It was fucking excellent, and I'd come to the conclusion that her mouth was made for mine. I'd hypothesized it for the entire afternoon since I watched her step up into the Cambridge bus, for the two hours we travelled back to Oxford, during my very quick shower and for most of the journey to where I was currently sitting in my car, waiting. There was no way that a mouth could fit so perfectly to mine without some kind of higher power being at play, therefore the only answer had to be 'yes'. Which led to the theory that if her mouth was made for me, then so was the rest of her.

Mind. Body. Soul.

I peered out of the window into the rainy evening; the day's brutal cold and sunshine had disappeared into a wet mist the further east I'd driven. It was the type of rain that soaked you quicker than a downpour, sticking to you like a second skin, but not hard enough to have the wipers turning on automatically.

I was debating on whether to move the car and drive down the route I knew she'd be taking to get here, so I didn't see her at first as she came around the corner, dressed all in black, wearing a heavy raincoat with her hood pulled up.

A loud snort of amusement escaped me; even if it hadn't been raining, I could imagine her picking out this outfit for maximum inconspicuousness, because I knew this was her attempt to attract as little attention as possible. It was amusing, even if I also thought it was stupid and unnecessary.

As per her instructions, I'd found a spot to wait far enough away from Downing so that no one would see me, or us. I'd almost suggested meeting her at the boathouse, just for her reaction, but then thought better of it. Plus, she looked smoking hot in black, so I wasn't about to complain she was the hottest double agent in existence.

I jumped out of the car, sprinting over to her with an umbrella in hand. Her green eyes flashed bright, briefly reminding me of an emerald necklace my mother owned.

'Hey.' Her breath trailed in the cold air, further illuminating the rain caught under the streetlamp we were standing by.

I wiped away the raindrop about to run down her nose. 'Hey, get in the car. Do you want a towel?'

'You have a towel?' she blinked up at me.

'Yes.' I opened the passenger door and she hopped in as quickly as she could. By the time I'd got back into my seat, I was almost as soaked through as her, and I'd barely been exposed to it at all. It was times like this when my mother had a point basing herself in Greece most of the year.

I reached into the backseat and grabbed the towels I had piled up, passing one to her.

'Thank you.' She removed her hood and patted her face, wringing out the ends of her hair.

I turned the heat up, and flicked the switch for her seat to warm. 'I should have come to meet you closer.'

'Someone could have seen us.'

I rolled my eyes. 'Yanks, I'm not sure anyone would be out in this weather. And if they were, they'd only be looking at their feet.'

She peered over at me from under the towel, 'Their feet?'

'Yeah, see,' I pointed outside to a lone man walking past us, 'when you walk in the rain you keep your head down. It's weird. Not like it's going to hit you, but we do it anyway.'

'Oh yeah, I never thought about it.' She let out a soft chuckle, folding the towel up and placing it in her lap. 'But still, someone could have seen us.'

'And if they did, I guarantee you they wouldn't care.'

'Well, I'm not going to risk it,' she snapped.

'You talk about it like we're at war and you're venturing into enemy territory.'

'We are.'

I rolled my eyes, and was about to tell her she was being ridiculous before she snapped again.

'Oz, if you're not going to take me seriously, then this whole thing is pointless.'

Her stare was as hard and determined as her jaw was tense. She almost looked ferocious. *Almost*. The raindrop sliding down her nose was diluting the effect, however.

I picked the towel from her lap and gently wiped it away, then threw it in the backseat before an argument started that had her storming back to Downing.

'I'm taking you seriously, Kate. I just don't like hiding who I am, which is someone who'd come and meet a girl with his umbrella, so she wouldn't get wet.'

Her shoulders softened a little as she sighed. 'Thank you. I just have more to lose than you, and I need you to realize that.'

'Okay. I get it,' I replied, even though I didn't get it, but we'd be here all night if I tried to understand now. 'Anyway, more importantly, feeling drier?'

'Yeah.' She smiled, her annoyance with me vanishing as quickly as it had arrived. 'My ass is getting hot though.'

My eyebrow shot up, suggestively, which had her cheeks flooding pink. Even in the dark of the car I could tell it was the same colour she'd turned this morning right before I kissed her. I flicked the switch to turn it off. 'That'll be better.'

'Thank you.' She sat up straighter, her body twisting as she looked around my Land Rover, stroking her hand along the leather arm rest between us. 'You have a nice car.'

I shrugged a shoulder, like it was no big deal, but I winced a little with self-consciousness. To anyone outside of rowing, it was flashy, unnecessary and expensive, especially for a student, but for me this was the car that could fit two shells on its roof and tow a trailer carrying even more. Plus, transport six of my crewmates when we needed to get to the boathouse every morning.

'Practical,' she continued, 'great for the boats. Bet you could fit two or three on the roof.'

'Oh, Yankee Doodle, thank you.' I laughed, the loud whirring in my brain had immediately silenced. Then even more so at her rightly confused expression, 'I like you, a lot.

Yes. Yes, I can and most of the boys back there.' I thumbed to the back seats.

'So what you're telling me is that you're the soccer mom of rowing?'

I grinned wide at her teasing smile. 'No, that's definitely Charlie. Once he's been fed enough coffee, that is.'

Her brow shot up. 'Oh? He's a fellow hater of the mornings, or does he just need a lot of sleep?'

'Both,' I nodded, 'wait, are you telling me you don't like the mornings either?'

She winced, her hands held out in front of her as she weighed her answer. 'I like sleep, therefore I like mornings if I've had enough sleep.'

'I'll remember that, then.'

She blushed again, and now I wanted to find out how far that blush travelled. The other thing about our kiss was having her wrapped around me. She might have been vertically challenged, but she definitely made up for it in all other ways. All the ways that counted.

And that arse. Fuck I'd be dreaming of that for eternity.

'Okay, seatbelt on please. Ready to go?'

The latch clicked into place. 'Yes, where are we going?'

'Well, to accommodate your need for secrecy,' I rolled my eyes, this time in the over-the-top dramatic manner I'd learned from my sister, making Kate laugh, 'we're going to a little place on the outskirts of Cambridge called the Red Fox. It's in a tiny village called Pickford, frequented by locals only as it's virtually impossible to get to unless you have a car. It's highly unlikely we'll see anyone I know, and if we do you can pretend we don't know each other, while I'll attempt to hold my ego together at the rejection.'

She laced her hands together and placed them in her lap, though I could see a sly grin peaking her lip. 'Sounds perfect.'

I put the car into drive and eased off, almost immediately slamming on the brakes and the car back into park. 'Fuck!'

'What? What's wrong?' Her face shot to mine in panic.

Twisting around to her, I cupped the back of her head, and pulled her in. 'I forgot this.'

Her perfect mouth melted into mine with a soft sigh which travelled straight to my dick as quickly as if it had been fired from an arrow. The faint taste of cherries from the balm coating her lips hit my tongue as it swiped along the seam of her mouth, desperate to reacquaint itself with its mate. Thrusting my fingers up the nape of her neck, I gripped her thick, damp strands of hair, pulling her in as close as I could get her, needing her closer, though it dawned on me that maybe I'd never get her as close as I wanted her to be.

Definitely not when we were on time constraints, anyway.

One more swipe around her mouth and I pulled away with a soft pop. Her lips were slightly swollen, considerably pinker and now glistening with my saliva instead of her balm. My dick thumped hard, and I found myself battling whether to scoop her up and take her back to her room – something I was sorely tempted to do – or continue with our dinner plans – something I should do.

The angel shouted the loudest and the latter won, but I allowed myself a final brush against her lips.

'Now we can go.'

I might not have had her as close as I wanted, but I kept my hand on her thigh for the entire journey, her fingers laced in mine.

Thirty minutes later we were sitting at a table near to the roaring fire. I'd spent enough time in here to know that the oldish guy with the beard, and a Labrador sitting at the foot of his bar stool, was the local vet named Thomas. I also knew that the seven other people scattered about in one corner, plus the four at the table on the other side of the fire, was about as busy as the Red Fox was going to get for a Saturday evening.

I wasn't kidding when I told her we wouldn't bump into anyone.

The pub was situated on a hill at the top of a steep, unlit road, and unless you knew the path through the adjacent field, then it was unlikely you were going to visit. Which was just fine for the owners, Matthew and Emily. Olly and I had discovered it several years ago when I was trying to escape a random paparazzi who'd followed me from a race, and his scooter hadn't been able to make it through the potholes. We'd stayed all day, and returned again the following weekend.

It was the perfect spot for us to hide.

She shucked off her raincoat and laid it over the spare chair next to her. 'It's so cute in here.'

Kate might have been looking around at the ornate carvings above the fireplace or the collection of eclectic ornaments placed in every nook and cranny, but my eyes were glued to her, and only her.

The rain had smudged her mascara slightly and a grey smear ran under her lower lashes, but all it did was highlight how green and bright her eyes were. Her cheeks were glowing pink from the warmth of the fire, while her damp hair curled over her shoulders and down her back as it dried. My brain was flooded with images of wrapping it around my fist while I buried myself inside her, over and over again. I knew without checking that my heart rate was kicking up as I watched her; her eyes darting over random inscriptions dotted about the room, or smiling at a painting she found interesting.

But as far as I was concerned, she was the most interesting thing in here, and I couldn't look away.

She floored me. I couldn't even explain it because I wasn't sure I understood enough to, but she'd knocked the air from my lungs.

She was the definition of breathtaking.

'What? Why are you looking at me like that? Oh god, I bet I look like a drowned rat. I'll be back.' Before I could stop her she ran off, so quickly I didn't get the chance to properly appreciate her in a pair of jeans which hugged her thighs like they'd been custom made. I knew it was too much to hope she'd have left the smudges or not flattened down her hair.

By the time she'd returned I'd ordered a bottle of sparkling water and poured it into the glasses on our table.

'I had make-up all down my face!' she hissed, sliding onto her chair.

'You looked beautiful to me.'

Her face softened with a smile. 'Thank you.'

I nodded to the glass of water. 'I didn't think you'd want to drink, but the wine list is on the wall if you would like anything. I can order a bottle.'

She ran her fingers around the top of her water glass. 'I thought I might need something to take the edge off, but water is fine. I don't need anything else.'

I studied her as she sipped her water and put the glass back down, 'Are you nervous?'

'A little . . . No. Maybe.' The corner of her lip edged up, 'I wasn't expecting to go on a date today. We've only Face-Timed, and real life is different.'

'What are you talking about? We've had two practice dates on the river.' I winked.

'Yeah, you're right.' She grinned as her shoulders relaxed, 'I've just not been on many dates, and it made me nervous, I guess.'

I reached over and picked up her hand, holding her palm against mine. Partly to give her reassurance, but mostly because I wanted to be touching her whenever I could. 'I haven't either.'

'What? No way!'

I nodded, 'Yes, way. This is kind of new to me too. I've dated, but I've never been on a date where I've thought for more than three seconds about what I'm going to wear, or with anyone I already knew I wanted more dates with. More anything with.'

Her eyes dropped to the shirt I was wearing underneath another one of the cashmere sweaters my mother bought in abundance and begged me to wear, because *'the English winters are so cold, Artie, darling'*. While Kate still had one of my navy-blue ones, the sweater I'd chosen to wear tonight was green.

'What made you decide on that?' She waggled her finger at me.

'It's the colour of your eyes.'

I held her gaze, and the tiny catch of air and the flare of her irises had my chest puffing, and my heart beating that little bit faster.

'Kate, I'm serious. This is new to me. I'd go as far as saying this is my first proper first date. So, we're both going through the same thing.'

She chewed on her lip, the way I'd noticed she always did when she was thinking deeply. 'What's the food like? I'm starving.'

'Well, it's no lobster roll restaurant,' I began, which had her eyes rolling. I laughed and nodded to the massive blackboard above the fireplace. 'It's good. Best pies in England, I reckon.'

Her eyes widened. 'Pie? Like cherry pie?'

'No, my little American, like steak pie with heaps of mashed potatoes and green vegetables.'

'Sounds awesome. I'll have that. As long as there's cherry pie too,' she called after me as I stood up and went to order at the bar, walking as slowly as I could in the hope she might have been staring at my arse.

'How's Tideway training going?' I asked, when I sat back down.

'Oof.' She puffed out her cheeks, making her dimple completely disappear. 'I don't know. Our second session is tomorrow, but it's hard. I'm not sure I'd have done so well if you hadn't given me a crash course in it. It's different for sure. The Cam is much more like the type of river I'm used to.'

'The Thames is one of the most challenging rivers to row on. If you managed to get your crew safely through the first time, then you did an amazing job.' I sipped my water, 'I've known coxswains to completely fall apart. My first time going out with the Oxford crew our cox managed to sink our boat.'

'Oh wow, okay. I wasn't that bad.' She winced, but her wide eyes said it all. 'Oz, do you think it's cheating that you gave me all that advice? I've never known rivalry like Cambridge and Oxford.'

'No, of course not. I'm not rowing for you, I'm just telling you something you could probably research yourself,' I reasoned. 'Yes the rivalry is deep, but some of my British rowing mates are on the Cambridge crew, so we do have to be reasonable about it. They're not accused of cheating, are they?'

She looked like she was weighing up the pros and cons, so I changed the subject.

'Who else are you up against for the seat?'

'Becka Jones is Blue Boat cox, she was Blondie last year, but I'm not up against her. She'll stay on Blue Boat. There's a girl called Morgan Wright, she seems pretty experienced, she's second year. She's from Scotland, I think.'

'Never heard of her,' I shrugged.

'She's the one I think will get picked for Blondie. The rest aren't experienced enough . . .' her voice trailed off with her train of thought as two of the biggest steak pies known to man were placed in front of us.

I knew I wouldn't have a problem demolishing mine,

but I'd be seriously impressed if Kate managed hers. I wasn't even sure where it would all go. All coxswains were small, they needed to be in order to keep the weight of the boat down and fit into their seat, but Kate was particularly so.

I could probably put her in my pocket.

Picking up my fork with a grin, I pierced through the pastry and started eating.

'How many books do you have to read this week?' she asked, scooping peas into her mashed potatoes and mixing them together.

'No books, but I actually have a couple of essays to hand in. One on the comparisons of architecture between the Greeks and the Romans, the other on the themes of justice within *Prometheus Bound*.'

She forked a piece of steak into her mouth. 'Sounds intense.'

'Coming from the girl who's handling human entrails most days.'

'Sometimes I write essays.' She grinned back, 'I'm just jealous you get to spend most of your day lying in bed reading. That's where I'd rather be.'

I rested my knife and fork down, and slowly leaned forward, 'You'd rather be in bed with me, Katey girl?'

To her credit, she didn't even try to hide her blush this time. Just wore it like a badge of pride and continued eating in silence. Every time she looked up at me I'd raise my eyebrow waiting for her answer and she'd blush even more, which only made me laugh harder.

'How else am I going to become Britain's best-known classicist?'

She put her fork down and leaned back. 'Is that your plan, then?'

'I dunno. I haven't figured it out yet. I'll probably do a PhD to buy me some time, then decide.'

'A PhD at Oxford?'

'Yep, then I can still row,' I nodded. 'What are you laughing at?'

'I've never met anyone who decided to do a PhD just to buy them time.'

I grinned back at her. 'Well I'm not going into politics, that's for sure.'

She didn't reply, just smiled at me and picked up her fork again, and we continued eating in silence, occasionally catching each other's gaze as we did.

I nudged her leg as the waiter removed our plates once we'd finally finished. My plate was clean while all that was left on hers was a small crust of pastry. 'Now, pies . . . I think there's only apple, unless you want to try a blackberry crumble and custard?'

'Ugh,' she groaned loudly, her hands pressing against her waist, 'I can't. If I eat any more I'll be sick. How about next time we start with dessert?'

'That sounds good to me, Yankee Doodle. You have yourself a deal.' I didn't add that anything which included a next time with her would always sound good to me. Instead, I asked for the bill.

It was placed on the table, and she reached for it before I could stop her.

'What are you doing?'

'Checking it.'

'Why?'

'To see if it's correct, and to see what the split is.'

If I looked down my jaw would have been on the floor. Never, in all my time dating, had anyone tried to pay for themselves. Didn't matter whether it was lunch or dinner or just drinks. It was always assumed I'd pay because I had the money.

I knew how fortunate I was. I was fully aware I had enough in a trust for me to never have to work a day in my life, and it was one of the reasons I trained so hard. I never wanted anyone to be able to say I'd bought my way in life, or fallen back on my parents.

Every time I crossed the finish line, every medal I earned was done through blood, sweat and too many shed tears to count. It was one thing money couldn't buy.

But I couldn't hide my money, and while my friends didn't treat me any differently because of it, a girl had never offered to pay. Now Kate had I wasn't sure how to feel about it, and I wasn't entirely sure what it meant.

Maybe I hadn't been clear enough that this was a date. Maybe that kiss hadn't been good enough.

No, not possible. I stood by that kiss.

Maybe it was an American thing.

As far as I was concerned, we were coming to the end of the first date I'd ever really looked forward to, and over my dead body were we going to split the bill like colleagues on a business lunch.

I whipped it out of her fingers. 'Absolutely not.'

Her neck craned back and her arms crossed over her chest like I'd dared challenge the rules of America or feminism or whatever slight I'd made towards something.

But I wasn't budging, and I knew for a fact I could be as stubborn as her.

'I'm not arguing with you about the bill. And before you try to lecture me on equality, one day you'll out-earn me as a doctor when I'm still a classics student, so if you really want to pay, you can do it then. But today, this is mine.'

She breathed in deeply, her lips pursed slightly as she did. 'Then I get to plan our next date.'

I grinned, I should have known I wouldn't get away with this so easily. But I could concede, especially as I wanted to know what she'd come up with.

'Deal.'

'Thank you, Oz. This was really kind of you, I've loved it.'

'You're welcome. Me too. Now I need to get you home before you turn into a pumpkin.'

Her expression saddened as she stood up. 'I'm going to miss the pumpkin pie this year. It's nearly Thanksgiving.'

'Probably for the best if you're spending it with a cadaver all day,' I whispered in her ear as she put her arms through the sleeves of her raincoat I was holding. 'Can you not go home for it?'

She dropped her head with a little shake. 'No, it's a Thursday, and I have classes. Man, I'll miss the pie.'

'You'll have to get some when you go home at Christmas. Ask your mother to save you a slice.'

'Uhhuh,' she nodded quietly, 'yeah, you're right.'

As we reached the car, and I held the door open for her, she stopped with her hand on the frame.

'Oz?'

'Yes, Kate.'

'Are you driving back to Oxford?'

I shook my head, 'No, I'm staying at Olly's. He's away. But don't worry, I'll make sure that no one sees us together and I'll drop you in the same spot I met you.'

She looked down, I could just make out her lips rolling. 'Do you want to stay with me? I could sneak you into my dorm.'

My heart sputtered, and I closed my eyes praying for all the strength I needed. I'd tried so hard not to think about what she would be like naked, what it would be like to run my tongue along the curve of her spine or watch her fall apart under me; and since I'd had my hands on her arse while her legs wrapped around me it had been near impossible. But I also knew it couldn't be rushed.

She deserved better.

She was still looking away, and I caught her chin in my fingers to bring her back to me.

'Yes, Kate, I do, more than anything. But I'm not going to. If I stay we won't be getting any sleep, and we both have practice tomorrow. When I stay it'll be when our weekend is free, because we are never leaving the bedroom. I can promise you that. You and I will be spending an entire weekend in bed.'

She tried not to show it, but I could see the disappointment dulling the sparkle that had been present when we left the pub. I also tried not to be happy about it, because while I was dancing inside that she'd asked me, I also wasn't going to publicize it.

'Kate, I like you, a lot. *A lot* a lot. You're at the point of consuming me, when I'm not rowing I'm thinking about you. So believe me when I say, going to bed alone tonight will be one of the hardest things I've done, but I promise you we'll be staying together soon and when we do I'll make the wait worth your while. You can count on it.' I held her eyes until she finally smiled at me. 'That's better. Now get in, please.'

As I drove us away down the bumpy hill, my hand resumed its position on her thigh, and the goodnight kiss when I dropped her by Downing might have been my best yet.

*

Oz: *Sleep tight, Yankee Doodle. Get planning date two. And make it a good one. X*

Kate: *Don't you worry about that. I'm an A star student. X*

Kate: *Thank you again for tonight. X*

I grinned into the darkness, dropping my phone on the floor as I lay there. I closed my eyes, opened them, then closed them again. Sleep was going to be impossible when all I could think about was Kate two buildings over from me across the Downing quadrangle. I was right. She was made for me. It had taken all my strength to leave her on the steps, when my body screamed and my dick ached for me to follow her.

I'd never wanted to do anything more, or the right thing less.

I wanted to bury myself so deep inside her that I wouldn't have known where I ended and she began. I wanted to claim her heart and her mind, like she had claimed mine.

Picking up my phone again, I scrolled through Google until I found what I was looking for: the recipe for the perfect pumpkin pie. If Kate was missing out on Thanksgiving, then I would bring it to her, except I would need a little assistance.

I sent the recipe to Charlie.

Oz: *Charles, I need to commandeer your culinary skills. Can you help me make this please?*
Charlie: *You mean you want me to make it?*
Oz: *No. I want to make it, but I need your help*
Charlie: *Does not compute*
Oz: *FFS. It's for Kate. She's missing Thanksgiving and I want to make a pumpkin pie and send it to her so she's not homesick*
Charlie: *Okay, I'll make a back-up one just in case*

The man had a point.

14. Kate

(Thanksgiving firsts)

Oz: *What did you subject Leo to this morning?*

Kate: *Nothing, we had labs. Though I did have to write a detailed step by step guide to an autopsy, if that counts*

Oz: *That counts*

Kate: *What did you do? How was training?*

Oz: *Training was good, I hate to say it but your boys are in for a shocking loss*

Kate: *We'll see*

Oz: *We will. I also started reading The Odyssey again*

Kate: *Again? How many times have you read it?*

Oz: *Three. Clearly hasn't sunk in*

I zipped up my backpack and threw it over my shoulder, letting out a little chuckle. Over the past few weeks, I'd realized just quite how intelligent Oz was. I mean, he was at Oxford, so he wasn't going to be a dumbass, but I sometimes had the impression he could waltz into my classes on molecular biology and ace them without breaking a sweat, or a brain cell, and he'd come away with a higher grade than me.

He was the total package.

Brains and brawn all wrapped up in a six-feet-three mouth-wateringly handsome Englishman.

Whereas I'd just been called to stay behind after class

because my professor was worried my grades had slipped from the beginning of term, and I was taking on too much.

I wasn't even sure how the grades question was warranted. They might have dropped a tad, but I was still in the top ten per cent for my last clinical test, I'd provided the correct answer to the question about the seven functions of the liver when I was called upon because I'd spent the evening before cramming, and I'd correctly identified the bile duct on Leo when Professor Hull walked past me in anatomy at the beginning of the week.

I was the only one who'd already decided on a topic for their next essay.

The way I saw it, I was managing the balance pretty damn well. Just like everyone else. Just as I did every other week. The only thing different this week was that it had sucked big time.

Today was Thanksgiving.

I missed my family, and I *really* missed Jake.

Thanksgiving had been his favourite holiday. The day would start with my dad and Jake going out on the boat, just the two of them. They'd net a small catch of oysters, then take the haul around to his guys who worked for him, who all had the day off. It was their thing. When they got home, my mom would make them shower while she cleaned up the catch he'd brought in for us, and we'd all be forced into matching pyjamas for the rest of the day to eat oysters and turkey, and watch the Patriots beat whomever they were playing. The boys would arrive at the house right before the football, and the entire neighbourhood of friends and family would be able to hear them shouting at the TV until bedtime.

Since Jake died, Vinny had started going out with my dad. They'd crack a beer at six a.m., pour one for Jake, then get to work. But it wasn't the same, and everyone knew it.

Even if I'd had the option, I wouldn't have gone back.

I was still in my deep funk as I trudged up the steps to my dorm, where I had to make a lightning change of clothes – no thanks to Professor Osmonay – and run to meet Imogen before our lab classes that afternoon, from where we had to head straight to land training at the boathouse.

Except when I got to my door, one of the Downing College orderlies was standing outside with his hand up in a knock.

'Hello?'

He spun around to me, 'Kate Astley?'

'Yes?'

'I have a package for you.' A large cardboard box was thrust into my arms, one with an English postmark on.

I'd not ordered anything. I wasn't expecting anything. My mom wouldn't have ordered anything without telling me it was en route, mostly because she was the total worst at keeping a secret, but also because she'd already sent my pyjamas for today. Don't ask me if she thought I'd be wearing them to class, I didn't want to know the answer.

'Are you sure this is for me?'

He tapped the box with the electronic pen. 'That's your name, isn't it?'

I looked at it again, then nodded to confirm that yes, it was indeed my name. Didn't clear a single thing up in my confused brain though.

'Then it's for you.' He held out his pad. 'Sign here, please.'

I did as I was asked, still wondering what this mystery box was as the guy walked off. Kicking the door shut behind me, I put the box on my bed and went in search of scissors, which I found in my bathroom after remembering I'd used them to trim the dead ends off my hair last night.

It was like one of those Russian nesting dolls because inside the main box, was another smaller, polystyrene box, with a thick cream envelope on the top.

Ripping it open, I pulled out a piece of matching cardstock.

Yankee Doodle,

Happy Thanksgiving, I didn't want you to miss out on your pie.
I baked it, but I promise I was under adult supervision, and tested it first.

Love, Oz x
Ps. This year I'm thankful for you.

I read it once more, just to double check. My brows shot into my hairline as I gently removed the polystyrene lid and breathed in the scent of cinnamon and nutmeg. Inside, a little crooked around the edges where the crust had broken off, was a pumpkin pie.

No one had ever sent me a pie before.

No one had ever baked me a pie before.

This was the very first pumpkin pie I'd ever had all of my own.

218

I lifted it out of its box with all the care and dexterity of an archaeologist with a newly discovered ancient relic and carried it over to my desk, then stood back. I stared. I stared until my throat thickened, and the weight in my chest built and built until the pressure burst out into a flood of tears, cascading down my cheeks.

Oz. Sweet, kind Oz cared enough about me to make sure I wasn't missing out on pie. He knew how much I loved pie, and he'd made this one for me even though I knew he didn't cook, and I quote, 'I burn water given half the chance.' But this pie didn't look burnt, it looked perfect and – after wiping my sleeve under my nose – smelt perfect, almost like the one my mom made.

Another fat tear slid down my cheek and dropped on the floor.

I don't recommend crying and eating. It's kind of messy, hard to breathe and even harder to swallow, but the pie couldn't sit untouched like that while I went off to my afternoon of labs – it wouldn't be fair. The ruler sticking out from the middle of two piles of coursework made for an excellent knife substitute, and I sank it deep into the dark orange filling until I'd cut a perfect slice.

Turns out, the more perfect a pie, the harder you cry; I cried until I wasn't even sure what I was crying for. I missed home, and Jake, for sure. But it also occurred to me that the past few weeks I'd also had this pressure building up, right between my temples, right in the middle of my frontal lobe, where all my emotions were currently pushing and shoving against each other trying to get first in line, all tied together with a neat Oz-coloured thread.

Oz.

Since our first date, we'd stolen time together on the Saturday river clean-ups – where we consistently made the smallest contribution to the group due to the minimum of fifteen minutes' kissing in the bushes before any cleaning was done – and, on two lucky occasions, we'd sneaked a second and third date. I'd discovered that not only was he the best kisser I'd met, he was the best at hugs too, and as long as no one was around he was always touching me somewhere. But we still hadn't had our weekend in bed, which was something that occupied my brain more and more every day.

Two weeks ago, I'd hopped on the train to Oxford, and taken him to a pie shop I'd read about in a guide book. We tried almost everything on the menu before deciding my favourite was the classic cherry, his was the banana, chocolate and pecan, and it was all washed down with hot chocolate. I got back on the train in dire need of an insulin shot, and with a belly ache I wasn't certain had come from the sugar intake, but from leaving him on the platform.

We spoke every day, and as our schedules were almost identical, FaceTimed most nights before bed. Neither of us was out partying like normal students, because normal students weren't getting up to train on a freezing river at five a.m.

On the surface it was easy.

What wasn't easy was the distance, because ironically we'd become closer. I'd confided more in Oz than I had my therapist, and I listened while he worried about finishing school and what he was going to do next; about his siblings, and his mother, and hating his dad more with every news cycle which mentioned him.

I'm not sure I'd have believed you if you'd told me two months into term I'd be missing a boy I'd met from the rival university so much I could almost *see* my chest aching. One night when I'd not been able to sleep I'd stood in front of the mirror for what seemed like hours while I searched my body for the cracks I swear appeared when I'd left him earlier that day.

All I'd seen was someone I didn't recognize staring back, and I'd nearly fallen asleep in my chemistry class the next morning.

Now, standing here, half a slice of the pie he'd baked in one hand, while I mopped up my tears with the other, it was no surprise he was the only person I wanted to see; to speak to; to touch.

It was true.

I missed Oz.

And because he had a wicked sixth sense for when I missed him, my cell began vibrating with a FaceTime request.

'Hey, Yanks.' He grinned, except the second he saw me his face dropped. I probably shouldn't have answered. 'What's wrong? Why are you crying?'

I did what anyone does when faced with the question he'd asked, I cried more while simultaneously protesting that I wasn't, in fact, crying.

'Kate, Katey. Babe. What's happened?'

'No . . . nothing,' I hiccupped. 'Nothing. I'm fine.'

'You obviously aren't fine.'

'I got . . . the . . . the pie.'

Through my tears I could see his face crease up in confusion, 'Was it that bad? I'm so sorry, don't eat it. I'm going to kill Charlie,' he added with a mumble, which only made me wail louder.

'It's the best pie I've ever had.'

'I don't understand.'

He waited in silence until I managed to catch my breath, and sip at the glass of water on my desk.

'Thank you. It really is the best pie. I can't believe you did this for me. No one has ever sent me pie before.' I sniffed hard before the waterworks started up again.

'Babe, why are you crying?'

I let the shudder run through my chest before I answered, 'I miss home today. I miss Jake, and then when I got back to my dorm, this pie was waiting. It's honestly the best present I've ever had. Thank you, Ozzy.'

A soft, concerned smile etched on his face. 'I don't want you to be sad, is there anything I can do?'

I shook my head with a sigh, 'No, I have to go to class, then I'm going to come back and get in my Thanksgiving pyjamas, and have an early night.'

'Okaaay . . .' he frowned.

I didn't hear the rest of his words as I caught sight of the clock. I'd wasted so much time crying, I only had fifteen minutes to make a twenty-minute journey. However I spun this I was going to be dramatically late to class.

I shouldn't have bothered getting out of bed this morning.

'Shit. I have to go. I'm so late. I'll call you later.'

'You'd better.' He smiled, and I finally smiled too.

The laptop was teetering on the pile of books I'd propped on my chair, positioned at the side of my bed. I had a bucket of freshly popped popcorn thanks to the campus grocery store, and a steaming cup of herbal tea. Sadly this could probably go down as one of the more rock and roll Thursday nights I'd spent here. Two thirds of the pumpkin pie had been eaten, the remainder wrapped carefully in the fridge. I'd have eaten it all, but I was already dicing with the likelihood I'd sink the boat at tomorrow morning's training as it was.

Tap.

Tap.

Hunkering down under the comforter, I pressed 'go' on Netflix, then stopped it again and sat up.

Tap.

Tap.

That noise.

Tap.

I was so cosy in bed, but that noise was so annoying. And there it was again. I threw back the covers and stormed to the middle of my room.

Tap.

The window. It was coming from the window. I threw open the drapes only to be met with mostly darkness, save for the lamps lighting the pathway below.

Tap.

Peering down, I needed a double take. That's right, I was here in my dorm, in my pyjamas, and outside, a baseball cap shielding his perfect face, with a hoodie pulled over the top, was the unmistakable shape of Oz throwing tiny pieces of gravel up to my window.

I glanced around. There didn't appear to be anyone else outside who could see him, and I tugged the heavy sash open, only for the freezing air to blast me in the face, and promptly pushed it back down.

My cell was already vibrating before I reached for it.

'Hey, Yankee Doodle.'

I peered into the darkness. 'Is that really you outside my window?'

'It really is. Now let me up.'

I typed out the code to the security doors and sent it to him before I could blink, or think. I didn't even have time to run a brush through my hair when there was a thud at the door, and I yanked it open for him to rush inside and lock behind him.

I stared, open-mouthed, still not quite believing it, as he rubbed his hands together, then blew into them for warmth.

'Did anyone see you?'

'No, of course not.'

'But wh . . . what are you doing here?'

'I came to check up on my favourite sweater.' He grinned, dropping his head with a smile. 'I came to see you, of course.'

'Why . . . how?'

'You were crying, and I didn't like it,' he replied, like it was the most obvious answer, and I found myself leaning into his big warm hand, cupping my cheek as his thumb swiped along my lip. He bent down, brushing his lips so tenderly over mine it almost set me off crying again. But then he added, 'Nice PJs.'

My head tilted downwards at the little burgers, hot dogs, bottles of ketchup and mustard, slices of tomatoes, pickles and lettuce scattered all over the soft, thick fleece.

When I looked back up, he was grinning wide, wider when I gave a little curtsy.

'Thank you.'

'So this is your room?' He peered around, walking slowly to my desk, running his finger along photos of my family, one of Jake and me, a little plastic lobster keying from my dad's boat, and a clean paper napkin from the pie shop we'd visited. He picked up my bottle of perfume from the dresser and lifted it to his nose, then spied the makeshift movie night I'd set up for myself. 'What are we watching?'

'Just a cheesy romcom. I haven't started it yet.'

'Sounds good to me.' He puckered his lips against mine for the quickest of kisses and turned away.

He first kicked off his shoes, then his cap landed on the desk where he threw it, and he flopped down onto the bed, running his fingers through his hair. The mattress dipped low beneath him, and his body was so long his feet were tipped over the end until he shifted up the bed, propping a couple of pillows behind his head, and lay back.

'Ooh, bouncy.' He patted the space next to him and stretched his arms out wide. 'Come on, babe, get in and give me a cuddle. Do as you're told.'

The second I sank into the mattress next to him the heaviness vanished from my chest, even more so when I got myself comfy in the crook of his arm.

'Thank you for coming,' I leaned up to kiss his cheek, 'this is an awesome surprise.'

'You're welcome.' He reached for the bowl of popcorn, balanced it on his flat stomach and threw a handful into his mouth. 'Let's start the movie, shall we?'

His eyes sparkled so much as he grinned that I almost forgot what we were doing until he dropped a piece of popcorn in my mouth and reached over to start up the movie. But it was too late. His spare arm had wrapped around my side, and the second his palm pushed under my pyjama shirt and brushed against my belly, I lost all interest in watching anything at all.

That one singular, tiny movement was like dropping a match on a pyre. A pyre would have burnt less hot. In a second my body went from cosy in his arms to a fully charged electricity field. I was wide awake, buzzing with latent energy, and he was the source.

Soon every inch of me ached for release.

I removed the bowl of popcorn from its current resting place, and put it on the nightstand.

'What are you doing?'

I opened my mouth to speak, then realized that telling him I was about to seduce him would sound like the dumbest thing in the world. Plus, I was pretty sure you didn't tell someone you were seducing them, you just did it.

He was still propped against the pillows as I straddled him. His thighs were so wide I almost toppled off and his expression transformed from curious to bemused, though given the undisguised twitch in his pants hitting directly in the spot I was aching the most, maybe I wasn't so dumb. He opened his mouth to say something but stopped as I began unbuttoning my pyjamas, and his eyes widened.

Perhaps they weren't as unsexy as I originally thought, though there were a lot of fucking buttons.

'Kate?' he paused, his eyes glued to where my fingers were working. 'Kate, what are you doing?'

'What does it look like?' Another button slipped out of its hold.

He grabbed my hands and stilled them. 'Babe, I didn't come here for sex. I came here so you weren't alone when you were sad.'

'I know that, and you're here and I'm not sad any more. And this is an opportunity we might not get for a while.' I frowned, 'Don't you want to have sex?'

I rolled my hips, feeling his dick thicken underneath me, and he let out a groan that coated my nerve endings in fire.

His hands dropped from mine and found a new home on my hips, which he gripped tightly. 'Is that even a real question? Of course I want to, I've wanted to since I first laid eyes on you, but I don't want you to think . . .'

'I thought you didn't care what people think,' I interrupted.

His fingertips dug into my skin as he slowly rocked me over his lap. 'I don't care what *people* think. I care what *you* think.'

'Well, I think . . . no, I *know* I want us to have sex. Tonight. Now.'

My pyjama shirt fell away and his eyes were no longer on my face. I ran my fingers through his hair, 'Ozzy, you look like your brain is about to explode.'

His hands inched slowly, too slowly, up my skin, grazing across my ribs, and he sat up enough that I could feel his hot breath against my chest, pushing his face between my breasts to inhale deeply.

'I think it might be. Have I ever told you I love it when you call me Ozzy?'

His nose brushed across my left nipple, tightening it

almost to the point of pain, and it was my turn for my brain to break, and my voice.

'No,' I croaked.

'I do. No one has ever called me Ozzy, it makes me feel like I'm yours.'

My heart would have squeezed tight at his admission if it wasn't thumping so hard from desperation, and when his tongue stretched out and flicked the top of my nipple I was convinced I'd pass out, especially when he moved away. A tiny cry of protest fell from my lips.

His pupils had flared so much there was only a faint ring of turquoise around the edges.

'Babe, I need to go get some condoms before I can't stop. I didn't bring any.'

His stubble tickled my palm as I cupped his cheek and smiled at him.

'I have some,' I nodded over to my bedside drawers, 'in the bottom one.'

He reached over, rummaging for a second, then turned back to me with a raised eyebrow and the jumbo box of extra-large Trojans I'd found when I unpacked my case.

I shrugged. 'My mom.'

'And this too?' He held up the golden wand vibrator I'd been using on the regular for the past month; the only thing keeping my sanity in check. He pressed down on the button and it quietly buzzed in his palm.

I shook my head, 'No, that's all me.'

His pink tongue darted out, wetting his lips, and I stopped breathing, waiting to see what he'd do with it. I wasn't sure if I was disappointed when he switched it off and threw it back into the drawer.

'Another time. Tonight is about us.'

Any disappointment I felt disappeared as soon as he reached behind him and removed his sweater and t-shirt at the same time. Since the first day we'd FaceTimed I'd dreamed of reliving that moment, and I stayed mesmerized in his lap while he lay back down with a grin that said he knew exactly what he was doing to me.

Muscles. Perfect muscles. Thick shoulders and heavy biceps which looked every inch worthy of an Olympic medal. Even relaxed they stood to attention, and my core convulsed, sending a flood of hot arousal running down my thigh. With my legs spread open and straddling him, my pyjama pants would soon be soaked through, that's if he didn't remove them in the next five seconds.

But Oz had other ideas.

He took my hand and placed it along his side, over his Excalibur. 'I've wanted your hands on me since the day we met. Since I first turned my head and looked up at you.'

'Even though you were writhing around in pain?'

'The pain went away.' His eyes never left mine as his palms trailed up my hot bare skin again, the gold of his signet ring barely providing any type of cool relief. 'You're perfect, Kate. Perfect.'

My nipples were craving his attention so much my body had arched in his face of its own volition, and I was a second away from begging. Then his face turned serious.

'Are you sure you want to do this tonight? Because once we do . . .'

I nodded, 'I want this, Oz. I need it.'

Even though it was near freezing outside, and the central heating left a lot to be desired, the leaded panes of glass on my windows were dripping with condensation as he flipped me off him and onto my back in one seamless movement.

Only when he stood at the end of my bed, his massive thick cock springing against his stomach as he dropped his pants, did the nerves set in. This was really real, and really happening.

'Holy crap,' I voiced louder than I meant to. I didn't mean to voice it at all.

'We'll take it slow,' he said, completely misreading my expression, but the timbre of his tone had my entire body constricting, nonetheless. 'Lift your hips.'

He tugged on the end of my pants until they found themselves joining the pile of our discarded clothes. Then it was his turn for the nerves to set in, and the next time he spoke his voice shook.

'Fuck, babe, you look incredible.' He began slowly stroking the length of his cock as he stared down at me, studying my body. His gaze may as well have been flames licking along my skin. 'I don't know how long I'm going to last.'

Another heavy throb between my legs told me the same. 'I don't know how long I'm going to last either, but we'll never find out if you stay standing there.'

I hadn't expected my Thanksgiving to end like this, with me watching the most beautiful man I'd ever seen roll on a condom in the sexiest way imaginable, then crawl slowly up the bed until he hovered over me, and dipped his perfect lips until they touched mine.

His mouth stayed there, distracting me while his long fingers slipped over my swollen clit and eased inside me, in and out, keeping rhythm with his tongue until I could feel my eyes falling back in my head, and there was nothing I could do to stop them.

I was so gone I barely heard him whisper, 'Don't stop kissing me,' a second before I was so full, and stretched and tight that I thought I might pass out. A whimper was all I could manage.

'Oh, fuck, babe . . . Jesus . . . fuck, that's so good,' he mumbled against my lips and his fingertips gripped into my thighs as he spread them another inch. 'Nearly, Yanks. Nearly there.'

Was it actually possible to burst? Because I thought I might, right then. I was so full of him I could barely move, yet I so desperately wanted to. Needed to.

And then his dick hit my cervix and he stilled.

'Katey, open your eyes. I want to see you.'

I did, and was met with the bluest eyes imaginable: sincere, genuine, lust-filled, and staring down at me like I was the last slice of chocolate pie.

'Hi.'

'Hi.'

'Is this okay? Do you feel okay?' he asked, his voice trembling like it was taking every shred of concentration not to lose control.

I could barely manage a nod, because every movement I made dialled up the pressure building inside me. Crescent moons from my fingernails marked his biceps where I gripped them, and dug deeper still when his hips began to roll. Soon, each slow pass of his pelvis was grinding against my clit like stone on a flint, shooting sparks across my body and twisting my spine until it was fighting to unravel.

'You feel . . . amazing . . . god, Katey,' Oz sputtered, his voice more of a growl, as his lips moved along my jaw. 'Why did we wait so long?'

I didn't have an answer, my brain had turned to mush, especially when he pulled his entire length out of me and plunged back in.

'Ohhh, oh! Fuck. Ozzy.'

'I know. I fucking know.' And he did it again.

Somewhere between thrusts his hands gathered mine up in his, holding them tight above my head, and then he really lost it. Deeper, harder, each drive of his cock turned up the heat on the pressure cooker inside me, and every single one of my nerve endings was screaming at me to stop.

And then he shifted back and scooped my hips for one final charge forward. It was all I needed; my body shredded itself from the inside out. I came all over his cock to the muffled sound of him crying my name with his head buried in my neck.

I'd turned to jello; it was the only explanation I had for not being suffocated by a two-hundred-pound man as he collapsed on top of me. Even if I could have moved, I wouldn't with a gun to my head, and the rush of air as he slipped to my side felt colder than it should have done.

His arm moved underneath me and tugged me into him, until I was settled on his chest and could hear his heartbeat syncing with mine.

'I missed you today,' he whispered, his hands stroking through my hair.

'I missed you too.'

'How did I manage to find you on your very first night?'

I shifted slightly so my hand rested on his flat stomach. 'I kneed you in the nuts, remember?'

A rumble of amusement echoed through his chest. 'I think we can safely say there wasn't any permanent damage. But you can check them again if you'd like to, doctor.'

I crooked a brow, 'You're ready to go again?'

'We're definitely going again, but right now we have to rest.' He pressed a kiss to my lips, then reached out to switch off the bedside light, his arms wrapping around me tightly.

I fell into a sleep so deep that when I woke I was convinced I'd dreamed the entire evening, dreamed an orgasm that nearly ripped me in two, dreamed falling asleep in his arms and again as he kissed me on the head before slipping out of bed and leaving at some point during the night.

Then I found a note on my pillow.

I'm thankful for movie nights.
  O x

I had to agree.

15. Arthur

(No one looks good in a Christmas sweater)

'Fine work, Mr Osbourne-Cloud. Though do try to hand it in on time in future.'

My three-hour lecture on Reimagining Ancient Greece and Rome had finally finished – *finally* – and Professor Barrow, the head of the classics department, was passing out the essays we'd submitted last week.

'Thank you, sir.' I took it, throwing him a wry smile before we got into a conversation about why it was late because I definitely couldn't remember the reason, and folded it up to stick in my backpack, 'I'll certainly try.'

I didn't miss his eye roll as I passed by, and jogged along the corridor of the first floor of the classics building. Taking the steps two at a time, I burst through the entrance doors and out into the cold air, startling a couple of passing girls who screeched loudly, before realizing it was me and not a lunatic escaped from the nearest asylum.

'Oh, hey Oz,' one of them tittered as I jogged past, pulling up my hood so I couldn't hear the rest of what she was saying.

I waved a hand behind me, which was the limit of any response I was prepared to give. I carried on for another minute, jogging down the cobbled path and breathing in the fresh air, hoping my brain would reboot from the injection of oxygen. Training this week, and especially this morning, had taken on a more sadistic feel, and my muscles were paying the price.

I continued along the road until I spied a familiar figure standing in line at the cash machine. I waited until the girl in front took her money, and he stepped forward.

He was just keying in his pin when I reached him.

'Gimme all your money,' I growled in Charlie's ear.

In his defence, I might have screamed too, and I definitely would have punched anyone trying to steal my money. I'd have also knocked them out. Lucky for me, I was expecting the left hook coming my way.

Therefore, I ducked.

'You dick,' he grumbled, snatching his cash from the dispenser and storming off.

I was laughing so hard it took me a second to catch up with him, especially at the pace he was walking, but I did eventually. Throwing my arm around him, I smacked a kiss on his cheek though it didn't hide the fact I was still laughing hard.

'Christ, you're annoying this week.' He shoved me away, though I could see the beginnings of a smile creeping up his lip. 'What's got into you?'

I shrugged, like I didn't know what he was talking about. 'Nothing. Just happy it's nearly Christmas.'

Only it wasn't nothing, and it wasn't Christmas. It was Kate. Kate had got into me, she was under my skin, seeping into my bones and burying herself so deep in my chest that I almost couldn't imagine how I'd managed to get through my days without her texts, or hearing her voice, seeing her face. And since last week holding her, tasting her, and hearing my name fall off her lips as her tight pussy convulsed around me . . .

It was becoming an addiction.

I'd snuck over to her dorm once more since our first time, cutting it as fine as I could to creep out at four and make it to my six a.m. water session on the Isis. I'd powered through my training that morning as though I'd had a twelve-hour sleep, even Coach Lassiter had commented on how fresh I was looking.

I couldn't take the credit. It was all Kate. Kate had invigorated me.

It wasn't just in training either; I'd bashed out an essay on the Fall of Rome, handed it in on time and received a First for my effort, and when my dad left another voice-mail, I'd simply deleted it, then forgotten about it. I hadn't raged or descended into my usual black mood for the rest of the afternoon, infecting everyone around me.

I was happier than I'd been in a long time.

'Whatever,' Charlie muttered, 'we're late now because of you, so stop dawdling.'

I glanced up at the clock on top of the church spire. It was five minutes past two, and that didn't immediately jog any memory for an appointment I may have had. 'Late for what?'

'Meeting Brooks at the pub, remember?' His head tilted, while his eyes narrowed so much I wondered briefly if he could still see where he was going. 'You forgot, didn't you?'

'I'm not sure. Tell me what it's for then I'll tell you if I forgot. We can't all have photographic memories.'

'We're meeting Brooks to decide whether we're having a Christmas party at the house again this year.'

I stopped walking for a second. I definitely knew we'd been talking about throwing a Christmas party again, and I definitely knew about meeting Brooks. However, I did *not* know about the date or time. 'Are you sure that's now?'

'Yes, Arthur. It's now.' He started walking again, and I followed. 'Seriously, what's up with you? Did you fall out of bed and hit your head or something?'

'My head's fine,' I grumbled, stepping off the path for a moment to let a group of girls pass us. Charlie was still pulling a face at me when I moved next to him, though it was now more knowing and less confused. 'What?'

'Nothing, just realized what's going on.'

'What?'

He moved to cross the road, dodging a cyclist as he did. 'With you.'

Charlie was an inch shorter than me, yet with the speed he was walking I needed to jog to keep up, especially as it seemed to be the same moment everyone else in Oxford had decided to also walk along the road, in the opposite direction to where we were going.

This is how salmon must feel.

I fell into step next to him again. 'Would you like to enlighten me?'

'If you don't know, I think you should figure it out for yourself.'

'Now who's being annoying,' I grumbled.

'Aww little Ozzy, all sensitive now he's fallen in love.'

I smacked Charlie's hand away as he reached to rub my head. 'Shut up.'

Whatever I'd said had Charlie stopping so suddenly a girl behind us narrowly avoided crashing into him, something she wasn't pleased about given her scowl and loud tut as she passed. Except Charlie didn't notice as he was staring at me like I'd suddenly grown another head.

'What, you're not going to deny it? I was joking.'

'Deny what?'

'Being in love!'

'Um . . .' I thought about it. I knew I'd never been in love before, just like I knew I'd never felt the way I felt about Kate, so being in love wasn't totally out of the realm of possibility. On the other hand I'd kind've been put on the spot, and I didn't want to fuck up my answer even if it was only to Charlie's question. 'I mean, I don't know. What did it feel like when you fell in love with Evie? How did you know?'

He scrubbed a hand down his face, scratching through his beard like I'd just asked him to solve quantum mechanics, though he could probably do that. Either way, his face had taken on a distinctly grave expression.

'When you wake up, is everything . . .' he waved his hands, searching for whatever word he needed, '. . . do you feel happy without knowing why? You're in a good mood from the second you open your eyes? Like you have been the past few weeks, annoyingly so,' he added with an eye roll.

I nodded a few times, my head bobbing as I gave it serious consideration. 'I guess. I mean, we're up pretty early and it's dark outside. I still have to hit snooze twice, but after that I'm in a good mood.'

I didn't add that Kate was now the first thing I thought

about when I woke up, or the first person I messaged before I got out of bed. She was the first person I wanted to speak to.

'How soon after she messages you do you reply?'

I shrugged, like I didn't know the answer, but I jumped on those bad boys the second they came in. 'When I see it.'

'And when you speak to her or see her, what does it feel like right here?'

I groaned as he smacked me in the stomach, much harder than he needed and clearly a retaliation for the stunt I pulled at the cash machine. Least I didn't scream like a girl, though.

'I dunno? What answer are you looking for? I like her a lot, not denying that.'

'Like we're standing on the podium about to be awarded gold.'

'Oh. Kind of. That's a good way of describing it, it's not as intense, like with all the cheering, but yeah, I guess I have something similar. It makes me feel like I've drunk hot chocolate and riding the sugar rush, but warm.'

A heavy hand fell onto my shoulder, and he squeezed hard. If I didn't know better I'd assume he was about to deliver a death sentence. 'Hate to say it, Oz, but you're probably falling in love with her. Sorry, mate.'

'Why are you sorry?'

'Because it fucking sucks,' he snapped, walking off again. 'Suddenly your mind isn't your own. You completely lose the ability to think for yourself. Someone else is controlling your every waking hour. There's a reason I've decided to stay single for the rest of my life.'

I held my mouth in a straight line and refrained from

telling him *again* how ridiculous he was. 'Charles, you're twenty-one. It's not that bad.'

His shoulders lifted; the pity on his face said he knew better. 'Just wait.'

I was still frowning at the back of his head when we arrived at the Blue Oar, and pushed through the heavy wooden doors to find the place heaving with revellers. By the looks of some they'd been in here a while, especially the guy with Christmas tinsel wrapped around his head, swaying in the corner.

'Christ, why's it so busy? It's Tuesday lunchtime.'

'It's the last Tuesday lunchtime before term ends. Half the people in here have already finished. The other half are probably first years.'

It took a good five minutes of pushing through the throng of students, the ones wanting to say hello, ask how training was going or to wish us luck, as well as the person who thought I was someone else, before we found Brooks sitting at our table building a tower out of cardboard coasters.

'Nice jumper. Where's mine?'

He looked down at his blue cable-knit jumper decorated with little rowers wearing Santa hats. Brooks' Granny knitted them for him every year, and since we'd been living together the past few years, she'd knitted them for Charlie and me too. We wore them with pride, even if we did look like idiots.

'They arrived this morning. Yours are at home.'

I dropped my backpack on one of the empty seats, then sat down in another and stretched out. 'Nice tower.'

I picked up a coaster to add to the top, only for it to be

snatched away by Brooks who didn't want his structure destroyed. Whatever, it was going to topple soon, especially as it was still wobbling from the last one he'd added.

'What's going on?'

'Oz is falling in love with his American.'

'Oh congrats, mate. Good for you.' He grinned, and the next coaster was deftly placed on the top. 'Is this you officially off the market?'

I thought about it. Could you be officially off something you'd never been on? I wasn't interested in anyone else, so if that made me off the market, then so be it.

My chest puffed a little, 'Yes. Yes, I am.'

'Great.' He picked up another coaster. 'Now can we decide about this party? Because last year there was so much shit to clean up the next morning, and I'm not sure I want to do that again. Plus we're cutting it fine, we've nearly run out of weekends before Christmas.'

'I'll vote for the party if I can bring Kate.'

Charlie had just stood up on his way to the bar, but paused. Brooks stopped building his coaster tower. I didn't miss them briefly glance at each other, then at me.

'Oz, mate, you can't invite her. People will wonder what she's doing there.'

My neck craned back so quickly I heard it crack. 'What? Since when do I give a shit what people think? Of course I can.'

'No, Arthur, you can't. Why won't you get it into your head? It'll get back to Coach and he won't be happy. And I thought you said Kate was worried about being kicked off the Cambridge crew. You know how badly this will look on her. She can't be seen dating one of us.'

I could feel my shoulders squaring off from the way they were both staring at me intensely, challenging me to argue, but instead I huffed out a breath. I'd been trying to ignore the little voice in the back of my head – her voice telling me we needed to keep things secret, and the sneaking around would be going on for a while, because as much as I didn't want to hide, we'd been staying under the radar enough that the press hadn't caught wind of it, and that was the best thing ever. Nor had there been any rumblings about me dating recently, and having silence on that subject was like Christmas had come early. But having spent the last six weeks seeing her on a weekly, if not twice weekly, basis I was also aware that the holidays were starting, and I wouldn't see her for at least a month as she'd be back in America. After that, training would become more intense than it had been already, and if I was lucky, I might scrape a day with her in January before winter training camp.

'Fine. Count me out of the party then. I'm going to the bar.' My chair screeched loudly along the floor as I pushed it back, and I took off before either of them could stop me.

Miraculously, I managed to find the only quiet spot at the bar and ordered three pints. I'd left class breathing in fresh air and feeling I could run ten miles without breaking a sweat, and now my body was coursing with a kind of nervous energy I didn't like. While I took Kate's concerns seriously, hearing the boys voice them too made it feel all too real. They were right. She *was* worried.

I'd never been happy about my life being dictated, and yet it seemed I couldn't escape it. I was finally in a relationship with an incredible, perfect girl – one I was certainly falling in love with – and I had to fucking hide it.

I rubbed my throbbing temples; the Boat Race was in four months. That's all we needed to get through, then I'd be graduating, and no one would care. Three months of sneaking around. I could manage that for something I had no intention of ever giving up.

Handing over the cash, I arrived back at the table to find Brooks scowling at Charlie with his arms crossed firmly over his chest; even when I put the pints down, neither of them paid me the slightest bit of attention.

Weird.

The coaster tower was still intact, so that couldn't be it. I picked up my pint, and waited.

I'd drunk half of it before Brooks turned to me, 'Did you know about this?'

'About what?' I wiped away the foam of beer from my top lip, my head flicking between the pair of them.

'The Evie situation,' Charlie muttered.

I nodded, and turned back to Brooks, 'Oh yeah, Charlie mentioned it a while ago but I've not heard . . .' I turned to Charlie, 'What's the latest? Did you get her moved off?'

His head dropped with a sorrowful shake. 'Nope. I've tried. Really fucking tried.'

'What's the Evie situation?' Brooks snapped, glaring at Charlie again. 'I'm talking about Violet.'

My glass stopped halfway to my lips, once again moving my gaze from Charlie to Brooks, who was looking distinctly less glary and more confused than anything. Hiding my grin with a large sip, I nodded and sat up straighter, suddenly pulled out of my sulk by what was about to unfold. I'd totally forgotten about Charlie's asinine plan to have Brooks' sister, Violet, be his fake girlfriend. Except Charlie had clearly forgotten to fill Brooks in on *why* he wanted Violet.

I put my glass down, taking sudden pity on Charlie. Maybe because I was falling in love with Kate, and now couldn't imagine what it would be like to have to be around her if she'd gone off with some other guy.

Even the thought of her with someone else had my knuckles whitening, and I had to calm myself with a deep breath before I went full-on Hulk. I turned back to the task at hand.

'Do you know about Evie joining his philosophy class?'

Brooks' face dropped just like mine had; the annoyance vanished as his arms uncrossed, and rested on the table. 'No fucking way! You're kidding! How's that happened?'

Charlie picked up his pint and took a long gulp, trying to act like this situation didn't have him tied up in one of the stress balls he kept littered about the house. 'Because my luck sucks.'

'Anyway,' I held my hand up to interrupt, 'obviously no good can come from this. Charlie and I thought that if he had someone pretending to be his girlfriend it would keep Evie away from him. Deter her from being her usual pain in the arse, that kind of thing. Stop Charlie from making a mistake. And we,' I gestured between us, as I tried to implore Brooks' empathy with my nonexistent powers of telepathy, 'were thinking Violet might fit the bill.'

Brooks picked up a coaster and began tapping the corners along the table until they'd all flattened. 'Okay, let me get this straight, you want my sister to pretend to be your girlfriend so that Evie will leave you alone next term?'

'Yes, exactly,' Charlie sighed. It was clear he didn't want to be explaining this situation any more than he wanted to be in it. 'And I need you to give me her number so I can ask her.'

Brooks pushed up his baseball cap and scratched through his hair. Charlie and I waited as he replaced it, then leaned back in his chair.

'Sure, go for it.'

'You don't mind?'

'Course I don't, but I doubt she'll agree to it. But if she does you need to be prepared for what you're letting yourself in for.'

'What? Why?'

'You've met her. She lives to be a pain in the arse, tornados are less destructive. Between her and Evie I'm not sure who's the lesser evil.'

'No one's as evil as Evie,' Charlie grumbled, though his eyes widened in a way that made me wonder if he was having second thoughts.

'I'm telling you, she won't do it.'

'Then you don't mind me asking.' Charlie pushed his phone across the table towards Brooks, who picked it up, and begrudgingly punched in her number.

'Don't come crying to me when it goes tits up.'

My shoulders were still shaking from the laughter I was trying to hide when my phone buzzed with a video call coming through. I left them to their staring contest and ran outside to answer it.

'Hey babe, how's the most beautiful American I've ever met?'

Her gruff giggle rang around my chest. 'I'm good, how was your class?'

'Better when it ended,' I grinned. 'I got a First on my paper, though.'

'Awesome,' she replied, with a smile that was better than any grade, 'Where are you?'

'Just at the pub with Charlie and Brooks for lunch. They're currently arguing over Charlie's love life.'

'Oh yeah? What's going on?'

'It's a long story, I'll tell you when I see you. Which is something I've been trying to figure out; it's been two days and I'm having withdrawals,' I moaned. 'I can't last a whole week.'

'Me too.'

'I have tomorrow night free, I'll drive over after training.'

'No, remember I told you, Imogen invited Hannah and me to her home for a few days so we can study.'

I hit my head against the wall I was standing next to, and tried to keep the whine from my voice, but I failed dramatically, 'Oh man, I thought I had one more chance to snuggle before Christmas, and now I'm not going to get to see you for over a month.'

'A month? Why?'

'Next week is when I'm skiing with my family, then when I get back you'll have gone home, and uni isn't open until January. When are you flying home? Maybe I can figure something else out. If not, I might have to fly over to Connecticut.'

She was silent for so long I thought the call had died, but then – 'I'm not.'

'Not what?'

'I'm not flying home.'

I stood up straighter. What? Had I missed an entire conversation about this? How did I not know she was staying in England? I flashed through every conversation we'd had. We'd talked about Christmas, we'd talked about our holiday traditions. No. I definitely didn't know. I'd have had something to say considering the strong opinions which were forming in my brain right now, along with the little jump of joy that we weren't going to be separated by an ocean for a month.

'You're not going home for Christmas?'

'No.'

'Why didn't you tell me? I didn't know.'

'Because it's not a big deal,' she replied in a way that made it very obvious that it was a big deal. To her, and if I wasn't mistaken, she knew it was a big deal to me too. 'I have a lot of work to catch up on and I'm going to use the quiet time to do it. Plus the flights are really expensive, and I want to get Tideway practice in. I can't miss a month of training or I'll never get selected.'

'But you're not going to see your family.'

'I know.'

'I don't understand why you didn't tell me,' I pushed.

'I didn't know it was a thing.' This time her tone held a little bite. 'It's not a big deal, Christmas is one day. My dad will still be out working, and my mom will still try and drag me around to visit everyone in the neighbourhood. I have too much to do, and I need to train.'

'But . . .'

'Oz, I have to go, Hannah just got here. Speak later,' she interrupted, and the call went dead before I had any chance to respond.

I stood staring at my phone wondering what had just happened, because for the first time ever, speaking to Kate didn't end with me feeling happier.

Quite the opposite.

16. Kate

(It's a Christmas miracle)

'I know, Mom, but I have so much work and training,' I sighed, pushing open the heavy doors of my dorm building. 'It's not long until the Easter break, if you think about it. I've already checked the flights.'

'I'll speak to your dad, maybe if they're not too expensive we can make it over to watch you in the Boat Race. Cheer you from the riverside. Then maybe we can meet this boy who's keeping you busy.'

'That would be awesome, Mom.' I hoped she could hear my smile, though I knew it would take a miracle to get my dad on a plane. *'Humans aren't made to fly, Katey. Or God wouldn't have invented boats,'* had been his reply the one time I'd asked if he'd come and visit me. I didn't bother arguing about it, because it didn't matter how much they missed me, he would never leave his boat. 'I haven't been selected yet though.'

'You'll get selected,' she replied, with all the reassurance of a mother who knows best. 'Okay, sweetheart, I need to get the coffee on.' There was a clattering in the background and I could picture her in the kitchen of our small house looking out to the bay, watching the lights of the fishing boats bobbing on the water. It was five a.m. where they were, and the sun wouldn't be rising for another couple of hours. 'We got your gifts by the way, they're under the tree. You shouldn't have spent your money on us.'

I tutted softly. 'It was nothing expensive, I just thought you'd like them.'

I'd sent them both official C.U.B.C. bobble hats and scarves, because while they might not make it over here, I knew they'd still wear them on race day.

'Thank you, sweetheart. I love you.'

'Bye Mom, I love you too. Have a good day.'

'You too, Katey, my girl. We're all so proud of you,' she added, just like she always did. I couldn't tell whether she'd become so used to saying it that it was now automatic, or she really believed it. Either way, my response was also the same.

'I know.' I let out a small laugh as she hung up, and sat down heavily on the bench by the side of the stone steps, suddenly in less of a hurry to get to the library before it closed for Christmas break.

It was one of the few buildings still open, and I'd been spending six hours a day in amongst the stacks of dusty books since the term ended. I was surprised by how busy it had still been for the first week, but the numbers of students in my midst soon dwindled off once the weekend had passed and we'd ventured into the second week. Yesterday marked three days before Christmas, and I'd only seen two other people working on the far side of the library.

When I'd decided not to fly home for the holidays I'd thought it would be the perfect opportunity to focus on my studies, get ahead of the syllabus for the new year, and cram as much information into my brain as I possibly could.

Professor Osmonay hadn't mentioned my grades slipping again, but I knew it was only a matter of time because since he'd mentioned it, I'd found class harder, and it was taking me longer to learn.

The only short break I'd allowed myself was when term ended two weeks ago, and Imogen had invited Hannah and me home for a couple of days, but even then we'd studied our asses off, outside of eating our body weight in Christmas pies, and training. But they were now cosy with their families – Hannah somewhere in the north of England I could never remember, and Imogen in the Caribbean. And Oz was at home in Oxfordshire; therefore, I'd doubled down on my study time with no distraction.

However, two weeks of my own company was kinda boring. I missed Imogen bursting into my room to divulge her latest piece of gossip, or having her as a study partner, or training with the pair of them. Oz was different – while I was used to him not being around, I hadn't realized how much I'd relied on his messages or calls to brighten up my day and add the needed spring to my step, but now he was hanging out with his family I didn't want to disturb him so I'd tried to keep my messages to a minimum. I'd also gotten used to seeing him every week, and now it was coming up to three weeks since we'd been together.

It wasn't just my body craving him, my heart was too.

I picked up my phone, double checking to see if he'd messaged, but there was nothing since I'd spoken to him after my morning solo training session. I tried not to let my chest cave too much, but it had definitely curled enough that I was tempted to go back upstairs, crawl under my covers and watch Netflix for the whole day – something I'd promised myself for Christmas.

I was still fighting with standing up and heading to the library, or going back to bed, when I caught a movement in my peripheral vision. I had to rub my eyes to check the figure dressed in his uniform of black, ballcap pulled low and striding boldly across the lawns – blatantly ignoring the signs – was not a mirage.

The very audible gasp I let out had his head snap up to where I was sitting. Just like it always did whenever he spotted me for the first time, a grin spread wide across his face making my heart skip in happiness – I didn't have much of an ego, but damn if that didn't give me a boost.

'What are you doing here?' Our voices layered over each other, making us both laugh.

Oz stopped in front of me, pulling me to standing and wrapped his arms around me until I was snuggled up against his thick puffa jacket. His eyes roamed around my face in the way they always did, like he was seeing me for the first time, studying me, committing me to memory or, as he once said, *'trying to figure out how it was possible you've become even more beautiful'*.

His fingers pushed up into my hair, with his arms balanced on my shoulders, and he quickly pressed his lips to mine with a loud smack. 'Why are you sitting on a bench in the cold? It's freezing.'

'I was heading to the library, and I just finished talking to my mom.' I tilted my head, 'Oz, what are you doing here?'

'I came to get you.'

'Get me? For what?'

252

'It's Christmas, and no one should be alone for Christmas. I've left it as long as possible for you to study, but you can do the rest at my home with me.' His finger gently closed my jaw which had dropped open, and he softly pressed his lips to mine once more. 'Come on, we need to pack your things.'

'Oz . . .'

'Kate,' he stepped back, his face as serious and focused as I'd ever seen it, 'it's Christmas. If you can honestly say that you'd rather be alone studying in your cold dorm, or the even colder library, then I'll turn around and drive home once I've had a proper kiss from you. But I'm asking you to come and spend Christmas with me and my family.'

My mouth opened again; panic and adrenaline flooding my brain with a thousand thoughts of why I shouldn't, all of which were silenced when Oz's warm hands held my face, and his lips found mine once more.

I melted into him as his tongue slipped along mine, warm and soft, taking his time to rediscover me like an explorer returning home after months at sea. His hand dropped for the briefest moment to spin his ballcap around, then resumed its position against my cheek, but closer. Deeper. Never once breaking contact with my lips, almost as though he couldn't bear to because Oz knew what was needed to make a kiss good.

And boy did he deliver.

Of all his accomplishments, I could safely say that kissing was probably in the top three of his skill set because in less than a second I'd become a molten, liquefied mess.

'I can see that big brain of yours working overtime,' he mumbled against me as he pulled away, his blue eyes wide and filled with mischief. 'Please come home with me. My mother is expecting you, so you'd only be getting me into trouble if I returned empty handed.'

My shoulders dropped; even though I knew he was teasing, there was a tiny ball of pressure building. I could feel it travelling up from the pit of my stomach.

'I need to study.'

'I need to study too, so we'll do it together.'

'But you're . . .'

He stopped me with another smack of his lips. 'Kate, whatever argument you put forth, I will have a response. And I should warn you that I was president of the debating club, and we never lost. Now please say yes.'

'I don't have any gifts,' I blurted out.

To his credit he didn't laugh as hard as I could tell he wanted to. 'The only gift I want is you. You're all I need.'

I sighed; after two weeks of my own company, the thought of Oz leaving so soon after arriving was enough to bring me to tears. They were already creeping up my throat as it was.

'Okay,' I smiled, 'I would love to come home with you. But only if we can stop to pick something for your mom before we get there. I cannot arrive empty handed.'

'Those are terms I can agree to.' He grinned, grabbing my backpack from the bench and tossing it over his shoulder, 'let's get your things, then we can decide on the way.'

I slipped my hand into his, and we walked back to the dorm building, 'Thank you for coming to get me.'

'I will always come to get you.' His lips brushed against my temple, 'Plus I missed you. I'm not sure I'm cut out for this long-distance shit.'

A little butterfly emerged in my chest at his words.

This was much better than a Netflix marathon.

Wrought-iron gates, the type you'd associate with Jane Austen or *Downton Abbey*, swung open and the car moved slowly along a paved driveway lined with huge oak trees that looked like they'd been present at the dawn of time. Fifty yards in and we passed a small round stone hut, with a large camera bolted to the side which tracked us as we passed, designed to let trespassers know they were being watched.

Oz turned to me, and the hand which had never left my thigh for the entire ride squeezed gently. 'Welcome to my home.'

I knew Oz had money. Vast amounts of money. But now here I was driving along the road and it felt like we could have been entering a small European country for all I knew.

I was just about to ask if I should have brought my passport when the path curved around and opened up; there in front of us, elevated on a slight hilltop, was the most beautiful house I'd ever seen. It was also, quite easily, the largest. I sent out a silent prayer that maybe – hopefully – this was a hotel, and not somewhere my entire hometown could fit into.

'You live here?' was all I managed to say as we drove around an enormous Christmas tree twinkling with white lights, and parked in front of a door easily twice the size of the huge library doors at Cambridge, then, 'Holy shit,' when he nodded gently.

He shifted his body so it faced mine, his expression

holding the exact amount of nervousness that I felt, like he wasn't quite sure how I'd react to all this grandeur. That made two of us. But his nerves did help mine dissolve a little, or enough that I could smile and smooth out his brow.

'I live in Oxford, but this is where I grew up in England. It's my mother's house, and has been in her family for a long time. She spends half the year here and the other half in Greece.'

'Oh right, she doesn't like the cold,' I added, remembering one of many small nuggets of information Oz had given me during our thousands of hours of talking. My brows dropped a little, 'But it's December, and cold.'

'Ah yes,' he winked, 'but she loves English Christmases, and she won't break with our December traditions, otherwise we'd all still be at our place in Morzine.'

'Is that where you went skiing?'

'Yup.' Taking my hands in his he brushed his lips along the tips of my fingers, 'I know this place must seem big, but I promise it's cosy, and you'll soon realize we need the space to escape Phoebe, Hector and Al, who can only be tolerated in very small amounts.'

I wasn't sure I'd ever seen him look nervous, or look *this* nervous, and this time I could laugh away my anxiety. 'Come on, let's go and meet everyone. How bad's it gonna be?'

I was still laughing as I opened the car door, and a flash of pink caught my eye. The handle was yanked from my grip and I found myself being pulled into a near-suffocating embrace, coupled with a deafening shriek, by someone tall and kind of soft, who turned out to be wearing a very fluffy sweater.

Adding to the commotion was a pack of excitedly barking dogs – a Great Dane the size of a small horse, three Labradors and a couple of Jack Russells – the smallest one now in Oz's arms.

'Jesus, Phoebe, put Kate down. Chill the fuck out, will you?'

'I will not,' came a voice as clipped and stern as Oz's, except with a gentler undertone and not as deep. 'I wasn't allowed to come and collect her, and as you wouldn't give me her number when we were skiing, what do you expect? This is entirely your own fault.'

I was released from the embrace, and found myself face to face with the culprit; someone who was unmistakably Oz's sister. Even if I hadn't known it was Phoebe from Oz's shouting, I could have picked her out of a line-up without looking at the other four. The same slanting pale-blue eyes, wide Roman nose, full lips and high cheekbones where the pink of her sweater highlighted her rosiness and bronzed face from their week skiing.

They could have been twins.

Phoebe tossed her thick dark hair over her shoulders until it tumbled down her back like a glossy midnight waterfall, and I stood there gaping, wondering if it was appropriate to have a girl crush on Oz's sister.

'OMG, I can't believe Artie has finally brought someone home. Honestly, you've no idea how excited we've been about this since he told us about you. I've never met any of his girlfriends, not that he's had any,' she leaned in with a conspiratorial whisper, though her volume barely dropped, 'between you and me, I did wonder if he was gay.'

The casual use of 'girlfriend' made me jolt; it was yet to be discussed. Over my shoulder Oz mumbled something I didn't catch over the noise of the dogs. She was just like Imogen – no inhibitions, said whatever was going through her head at the time, completely oblivious to anyone around her, fierce and yet utterly likeable.

'Not everyone wants a revolving door of lovers like you, or has time for them,' he snapped, snatching me from under her arm and wrapping me in his.

'What? I just like seeing you happy.' Even with the way she towered over me, she still needed to reach on her tip-toes to kiss Oz on the cheek.

Oz rolled his eyes at her, except she was winking at me as a soft curve crept up her lip, and I just about stopped myself from laughing again. I'd also been too engrossed in their squabbling to notice the suave middle-aged gentleman dressed in a button-down shirt and dark slacks now standing by the car and holding my small suitcase. I'd seen a picture of Arthur's dad, and this wasn't him, nor was he a member of the family given his blondish-greying hair.

'Arthur, I'll place all the bags in your room.'

'Thanks, James.'

'Miss Kate, may I fetch you a drink after your journey before you sit for lunch?'

My eyes flicked from him to Oz to Phoebe, who were both waiting for my answer like it was perfectly normal to have a strange man taking your things and offering to fetch you a drink, 'Oh . . . I . . . um. Water would be good, thanks.'

'Very well. Let me know if you need anything else.'

'James, please may I have a Coke?' Phoebe called after him as he walked back into the house. 'Diet. Diet Coke.'

'Who's that guy?' I asked quietly.

'James is the estate manager for my mother's properties. He travels with her, makes sure everything is how she likes it, gets the houses ready before she arrives, manages the staff. That sort of thing. He's been with us forever, not sure what she'd do without him.'

'Staff?' I mouthed.

I was not in Kansas any more, nor the Connecticut coastline, it seemed.

'Come on,' he smiled, his hand curling around mine as he tugged me along, 'Phoebe, where's Mama?'

'She's coming, she got a call just as you got here.' The wide grin she'd been sporting since we'd arrived morphed into a hard line, and it made me wonder if her entire greeting wasn't for show and a little distraction from whatever their mom was doing, especially when Oz tensed next to me.

The dogs ran ahead as I followed him mutely into the house, through an incredibly ornate entranceway and under a wide stone arch carved with forest animals and birds, until I found myself standing in an enormous entrance room, with a Christmas tree in one corner by a blazing fireplace. It felt like the type of entranceway where a quartet of violins would greet you upon arrival; instead we were deafened by Mariah Carey blasting out of hidden speakers.

'Phoebe, turn it down! For God's sake, I'm not going to spend the entire Christmas holidays telling you!'

I spun to the left at the voice bellowing from along a

259

hallway to see Oz's mom appear, and it became clear where Oz and Phoebe had inherited their bone structure, along with their height and all-round glamour. Phoebe pulled out her phone with a wicked grin, but did as she was asked and the volume lowered. Her mom took a deep breath, rolled her eyes and turned to me with a smile.

'Hi, I apologize in advance for my chaotic children.'

I held my trembling hand out to shake, because I honestly wasn't sure if I should curtsy in front of this incredible, regal woman, or whether I actually knew how to curtsy, but I was pulled into another enormous hug. A proper mom hug.

'Kate, let me introduce my mother, Daphne.'

She stepped back a little, but held onto my shoulders and I found myself gazing into a set of the warmest brown eyes I'd ever seen. Ones that immediately put me at ease. 'It's wonderful to meet you, Arthur talked non-stop about you last week.'

I knew my cheeks had turned pink. I could feel them heating from her compliment, especially as I also knew Oz was staring right at me with that grin of his. 'Oh, thank you. I've heard so much about you too. Thank you for inviting me, it's very kind, I brought . . .' my head snapped up to Oz, 'I left them in the car.'

'No, they're here.' He held his spare hand up, holding two large pie boxes. The condition I had to bring something for his mom took us to the pie shop in Oxford where we'd been on our second date. I bought two whole ones – my favourite and Oz's favourite – and given where I was standing I was thankful it was too late to have second thoughts about pie being lame. 'Kate loves pie more than life itself.'

'Pie? I knew I was going to like you. Thank you, my dear, this is very thoughtful.' His mom took them like she'd been handed a chest of treasure, smiling again, except this time I noticed a little redness ringing her eyes, 'Now, come on. You must all be famished. Phoebe, go and find your brothers please; they won't be far seeing as they've been complaining about being hungry since breakfast finished.'

Phoebe flung her arm around her mother's shoulder, and sweetly kissed her cheek. She then threw her head back and bellowed the boys' names, something I'd bet my life savings on wasn't what her mother wanted. The three of us winced, before collapsing into a fit of giggles, especially when Daphne attempted to cover Phoebe's mouth with a hand slap but she jumped out of the way before she could.

From the way her smile stretched across her face as she watched her mother laugh, it was clear that had been her goal. Because no one likes seeing their mom cry.

Oz wrapped his hand around mine and we followed in the direction everyone had gone. His head tilted as we locked eyes. 'What? Why are you looking at me like that?'

I lifted one shoulder in a shrug as Phoebe's words came back to me, 'No reason. Have you really never brought anyone here?'

'The boys.'

'No one else?'

He shook his head, 'No, I've never met anyone I wanted to bring here. Until you.'

'Oh,' I smiled at him as my chest squeezed, thinking about the words he'd left unsaid.

It wasn't the first time I'd thought Oz and I were similar, even though I was currently standing in a home bigger than most palaces. Our bank accounts might be different, but even from this brief glimpse into his wider world I could see his life wasn't as gilded as people assumed, that we were much more similar than even I'd thought. His brother might not have died, but he was living with the same grief and anger I did. He didn't just have his mom to protect, he'd taken on the role of protecting his siblings too. No one had come here because he'd never trusted anyone to come here.

The trust he'd put in me wrapped around me better than his sweater still under my pillow.

17. Arthur

(Dead or asleep?)

'Happy Christmas Eve.'

I'd whispered it, but still figured it was loud enough to create some kind of stirring movement. It didn't.

As a person whose internal alarm clock went off at five thirty a.m. every day whether they wanted it to or not, it was incredibly annoying to be lying next to someone who slept like the dead. If she wasn't visibly breathing, I'd have checked her pulse. Especially when I wanted that someone to be awake, so I could take full advantage of the first morning we'd had waking up together, with the sole aim of staying in bed most of the day.

I'd tried to go back to sleep but it had been an impossible task, especially when my body was on full alert with the knowledge that its other half was naked and snoring softly less than a foot away. She'd become a magnet for my dick, and it wanted attention.

Instead, I'd picked up a book, but found my eyes wandering over to her every thirty seconds until I became wholly distracted by the way her long hair fanned across the pillow, how her lips parted with every slow exhale and her thick lashes fluttered against her cheeks as she dreamed. If I was an artist I'd have grabbed a pencil and drawn her, because I'd never seen anything so perfect.

After collecting her from Downing, and bringing her

home, I'd fully expected her to cry off for the afternoon to study, but instead we all curled up with one of Phoebe's movies and ate popcorn. We'd walked the dogs around the estate, played Scrabble – I'd won; played Uno – Kate had won; played poker and no one had won because we'd then sat down for dinner and returned to find Hector's cat had jumped on the cards after being chased through the house by one of the dogs, and they'd scattered all over the floor. So, then we played Monopoly until I was on the verge of yawning and dragged us off to bed to the cries of protest from Phoebe who'd decided Kate was her new best friend.

It fell on deaf ears. After three weeks apart, I'd had plans for Kate before we fell asleep, so I should probably take part responsibility for why she hadn't yet woken up. Yesterday had been a long day, and I hadn't wanted it to end.

It had been a whole day of firsts, and I planned to make many *many* more before we had to go back to the realities of uni and the distance.

Dropping a kiss on her shoulder, I eased out of bed and padded along the floor to the bathroom to brush my teeth, pulling on my pyjama pants and a hoodie as I did. I also added a pair of thick woollen socks, because this house was old and the stone tiles on the ground floor in the middle of December were no joke. Taking a final look over my shoulder to check she was still asleep, I opened the door and made my way downstairs.

The Christmas tree lights around the house and the entrance hall had all been switched on, and the music playing softly down the corridors made it clear Phoebe was yet to wake up. In fact, I'd be surprised if anyone was awake yet beyond the housekeepers, given it was only seven thirty. I followed the smell of coffee into the kitchen to find Biscuit and Cheese, the two fox-red Labradors, barely glancing up from their basket, and my youngest brother, Alexander, over by the kitchen sink trying to shove something into it.

'What are you doing?' He'd been making so much noise, he didn't notice me behind him until I peered around his shoulder, 'Al?'

'Jesus, fuck, Artie,' he snapped.

I glanced down to find half of a newspaper screwed up in his hand, the other half of which was sticking out of the kitchen sink waste disposal from where he'd been shoving it like evidence he needed to destroy.

'You can't put paper down there, you idiot. You break it and James will be on the warpath.' I tugged out the remains and removed the newspaper from his hand, and opened it.

It became clear why exactly he was trying to reduce it to the pulp it once was.

Even though it was incredibly mangled, my dad's eyes could be recognized anywhere because they were the same as mine; the same as all of ours. From the looks of it, and half of his bare chest, he was on a beach. I hadn't even known he was going away, though that was everything to do with the calls I'd refused to answer.

'Where is this?'

'He's in St Barts with that woman from the summer,' Alex sniffed, and for the first time I noticed he'd been crying.

'Al,' I pulled him into a hug, 'oh buddy, I'm so sorry you saw that. Did you know he was away?'

He shook his head and stepped back. 'No, I haven't spoken to him. But I think this is why Mama was mad yesterday when her lawyer called, so I wanted to get rid of it before she woke up.'

I squeezed his shoulder; Alex liked to pretend he was tough, but he was probably the most sensitive one of all of us, and the most thoughtful. Being the youngest, he had taken the news of our father's behaviour the hardest.

While the rest of us were aware of what my dad got up to, and tried to ignore it, at fifteen years old, Alex had always been shielded from the worst of it.

Unfortunately, my father's antics at the beginning of the summer were too big for any of us to hide, and Alex had been accosted by a journalist shouting questions at him as he walked out of school. He'd tried to act like it hadn't bothered him, but when I'd jumped into my car and raced over to see him it was clear he was in shock.

It had been that incident which had set off my mother to issue divorce proceedings; because while my parents might not have liked each other very much, they'd agreed to keep things civil until Alex was old enough and got through his exams, but it had all been fast tracked when the front pages started their reporting. My mother had promptly whisked the four of us off to Greece for the summer, where I would have stayed had I not been training and racing. Since then, Alex had made it his mission to protect our mother, like he was making up for lost time.

If I hadn't already hated my dad before, I would have now.

'Why didn't you just put it on the fire?' I glanced over at the kitchen hearth, neatly laid and ready to be lit.

He shrugged, wiping a hand under his nose. 'I didn't want anyone to see it. I was worried it would take too long to burn.'

'What's it doing in the house, anyway?'

The morning papers were delivered to the house every day and placed on the table in the entrance hall, but it was always the international ones, the broadsheets; we did not order ones best used for lining a rabbit hutch.

'It was inside the *New York Times*, I don't think it was supposed to be there.'

'Well done for catching it, then.' I ruffled his hair, and slung my arm over his shoulder just as Marco, our chef, walked into the kitchen.

'Arthur, can I get you some breakfast? Or a coffee?'

The smell of coffee reminded me why I'd come downstairs in the first place, and I nodded at him with a smile.

'Coffee would be great, thanks, Marco. Two, actually, I'll take one up to Kate.'

'Very good. Alexander, would you like another?'

'No, thanks,' Alex shook his head, then paused with his hand on his stomach. 'Actually yes, I will. Don't suppose there's any bacon to go with it?'

Marco raised one thick eyebrow, accompanying his almost permanently pursed lip. He liked to look annoyed, but it was rarely to be taken seriously. Having been with our family for fifteen years, he was well used to the appetites of three growing boys, and his store cupboard was never empty. He was also prepared for any and all food requests outside of the family mealtimes my mother insisted we kept like clockwork. We'd have been quite happy to cook anything for ourselves if we'd been allowed in his kitchen, but after Phoebe nearly burned the place down a few years ago all four of us had been banished — the one occasion it would be foolish not to take him seriously. We'd never make anything as well as Marco and his team did, anyway.

'I'm sure I can find something, I have some fresh croissants and the morning bread baking, too.'

My belly grumbled and saliva pooled in my mouth. I don't know what Marco put in his croissants but it rivalled crack for how addictive they were. A croissant also might be the solution to waking up Kate.

'You're the best, Marco,' Alex called after him as he walked off to his own kitchen, a grin returning to his face. 'Is Kate still asleep?'

I threw the paper on top of the logs sitting in the grate and tossed a lit match into it. I watched my father go up in flames, and turned back to Alex with a nod.

'I like her, she's fun. Pheebs was so mad when you went to bed. She was convinced she'd be the one to finally beat you,' he snorted.

'No one beats me at Monopoly. She knows that.' I pulled out one of the stools at the kitchen island and sat down.

'Is Kate going to join in for the Santa run?'

I shrugged, 'I haven't asked her, but I'm sure she will. Phoebe will have something she can wear.'

'Are you doing it?'

I scoffed, 'Of course! And I'm going to be beating your arse this year.'

'Don't hold your breath, big brother.'

The newspaper was momentarily forgotten, and we both started laughing as we caught each other's eye, shouting, 'As long as we beat Phoebe.'

Marco returned with a tray of coffee, toast and jams, a plate piled high with warm croissants, and a bacon sandwich.

The tray had barely touched the table before Alex was stuffing an enormous bite of the sandwich into his mouth, and mumbling thanks. He was still chewing as I poured out two coffees and grabbed some croissants, and headed back upstairs to Kate, where she was unsurprisingly still asleep. Thankfully.

Now it meant I got to see her wake up.

I stripped off and snuck under the duvet, covering up her creamy thigh wrapped around the edge, and snuggled in next to her. She stirred the second I wrapped my arms around her.

'Good morning, sleepy head.' I kissed her nose as she peered up at me.

'What time is it?'

'About nine, I think,' I replied, laughing as her eyes bulged and she shot up to a sitting position.

'Nine. Oh my god. We have to get dressed. Your mom . . .'

'Katey babe,' I tugged her back under the covers, and pushed my fingers through her hair, 'take a breath. We don't have to be up for anything, my mother is probably still asleep. I think most of them are.'

She turned around, her face less panicky. 'Really? How have I slept so late?'

'I wore you out. And now we can enjoy our first morning in bed, we can spend all day in here if you'd like.'

'I could cope with that.' She sighed and shifted up until her lips pressed against mine, but before I could deepen our kiss any further she moved back. 'Have you been up already? Is that coffee? And croissants?'

I nodded.

'Wow, breakfast in bed. You're a keeper.' Her hand shot up to cover her mouth as she yawned wide, 'I can't remember the last time I slept this late.'

'You needed it. That big brain of yours has been working overtime.'

'It's gonna need to do some more working today,' she grimaced, 'is that okay?'

'You can do whatever you'd like. I have work to do this holiday, so do Alex and Hector. They both have exams when school returns, but today is Christmas Eve and if you're up to it we have some fun planned this afternoon.'

'Oh yeah? I like fun. What kind of fun?'

'Every year in our village, everyone in the neighbourhood dresses up as Santa and runs around the fields and lanes. It's kind of silly, but it's become a long tradition and at the end of the race we all head to the Lamb and Lamppost – the local pub.'

'Is there a winner?'

I nodded, 'Yeah, they win a medal and a bottle of cream from Farmer Murphy, the guy whose fields we run through.'

'A bottle of cream?'

'Yeah, it's a whole thing. I can't remember why,' I held her gaze, mindlessly looping strands of her hair around my fingers, 'but the only thing we have to do is beat Phoebe.'

'Beat Phoebe?'

'Yeah, it makes her so mad. She's probably been training all year for it, but she can't outrun Alex, or me.'

'What time does it begin?'

'Not for hours . . .' I hummed as my lips found the sensitive spot on her neck, the one I'd quickly learned made her mew softly. My dick knew it too.

She inched closer, the heat of her body almost scalding mine. 'So you're saying we have some time?'

'Oh, we have time.'

In a flash I pulled her on top of me, and the sight of her boobs bouncing from the movement set my heart hurtling against my ribcage. I was so fucking lucky.

I lay there, mesmerized as she smiled down at me; a smile brighter and more beautiful than any sunrise. My fingers ghosted over her thighs, her stomach quivering as my thumb brushed the sensitive spot underneath her pelvis, drawing my eyes right to her glistening, delicate centre.

I slipped a finger inside her. 'Are you sore?'

She should be fucking sore after last night, and most of the wee hours of the morning. Yet I'd never felt sated, not after the first time I came inside her, or the fifth. It was hard to believe we hadn't had enough, but I couldn't ever imagine having enough of her.

'Not when you do that,' she rasped softly, her arousal dripping into my palm and my dick jutting hard in annoyance at being ignored.

Spreading her lips apart with my thumb, I swiped against the pink bud of her clit, 'How about now?'

Her loud moan told me no.

Fuck me, she was something else. I could watch her body forever, I wanted to. I wanted to learn what she needed before she knew; I wanted to witness the way it reacted to every touch I made, every curl of my finger or swipe of my tongue. I wanted to know her body as well as I knew my own. I was captivated by her in a way I'd never been with anyone before. It had never occurred to me to be.

If this is what love was, sign me the fuck up.

'Ozzy, fuck . . .' My name falling off her lips swelled my dick further, and from the way her muscles were clenching around my fingers as they pumped inside her I knew she was close to coming.

Call me selfish, but I wanted that orgasm happening with mine. I wanted to experience that first strangling grip of her pussy around my cock.

'Wait, Katey babe.' I whipped my hand free and reached for the condoms, rolling one on as quickly as I could. I'd lifted her hips and impaled her on my dick before she had a real chance to notice. 'Ohhh, shhiit. How good does that feel?'

Her eyes were so glazed over when I grinned up at her that I nearly came, and again when she arched her back so tightly I could only see the curve of her tits. Gripping onto her hips I rolled her gently, feeling my dick hit right at that point which made her thighs shake. I might still be learning what her body liked but the groan that came next had me thrusting hard inside her just so I could hear it again. And again.

This was going to be quick.

She burst on my cock, pulling me with her a split second after. I exploded inside her with enough force to knock me on my arse if I hadn't already been lying down.

I licked up her chest as a lone bead of sweat rolled between her tits and I wondered how long until we could go again.

I would quite happily stay here forever.

If not forever, at the very least I wondered if anyone would miss us from the run.

I had other plans.

18. Kate

(How long do the holidays last in this country?)

'Kate . . . Katey . . .' warm breath curled around my ear, 'Kate, wake up. It's Christmas.'

I stretched under the comforter as the voice kept whispering, tugging me from my dream of snowmen and sailboats, fields and sunshine, fishing and Jake.

'Yankee Doodle . . .'

Fingers brushed along my arm, my collarbone, my jaw, until consciousness took hold and I opened my eyes to find the most stunning boy looking at me like Christmas had come early. Or right on time.

Maybe I was still in my dream.

Christmas. Shit.

The beautiful boy staring at me was Oz, and I was in his bed, in his home, and it was Christmas.

'Good morning.' His soft lips pressed against mine and I could almost taste his happiness. It was enough that I couldn't help but smile back, even though I was still half asleep and my dream of home was lingering in my brain.

And as always when I dreamed about Jake I never wanted to wake up. I wanted to see him again.

But this boy in front of me was too excited for me not to get swept up in it too.

'Good morning to you,' I mumbled into his lips. 'Happy Christmas.'

His hands inched up under my tank top and rubbed along my back as he pulled me in close. 'How are you feeling this morning?'

I lengthened my arms over my head and pointed out my toes; recognizing the familiar ache of used muscles from the Santa run yesterday. Although run was entirely misleading.

Santa obstacle course was more accurate. Running over hay bales in muddy trench-filled fields, jumping through giant tractor tyres, through the forest and around trees until we reached the finish line where we were handed a cold pint of fresh apple cider.

It was the best thing I'd ever tasted. And the best afternoon I'd ever had.

But no, it was not a run.

I scratched the side of my head, 'I think I still have mud in my ear.'

Oz gently rubbed along my lobe. 'Not possible, I cleaned you up exceptionally well. But I can do it again if you want me to make sure.'

The familiar throb kicked up between my legs, though I wasn't entirely sure it ever really stopped because when Oz was around my body hummed with a low, steady state of electricity; a voltage flowing through my blood which only he could charge.

Like nothing I'd ever experienced before.

I inched up to kiss him again, 'Mmmm, sounds good. Maybe you should.'

'Oh, I definitely will, but first . . .' he smacked his lips against mine, 'we have stockings to open.'

A far-too-cold gust of air hit my body as he whipped

back the covers, and I curled back up to preserve some warmth.

'What? Right now? It's still dark outside.'

He passed me one of his thick hoodies and a pair of pyjama pants. 'The sun is about to rise, but everyone will be downstairs. Come on.'

I groaned, but pulled on my clothes while Oz hurried me along. He begrudgingly allowed me to clean my teeth before dragging me downstairs.

The smell of coffee and pastries hit me as soon as we left his bedroom. From the music playing, it was clear Phoebe was awake, though it hadn't yet hit its usual volume, and we followed the noise of loud chattering through to the great hall, where the biggest Christmas tree stood laden with presents, to the side of the biggest fireplace already blazing.

Phoebe, Hector and Alex were all sitting on the giant couches, and Alex's head was thrown back in laughter — something I hadn't seen much of. He was quieter than his sister and brothers, more pensive, but sitting there like that it would be almost impossible to tell the three boys apart if they were the same age; identical smiles painted their faces, dark curls flopped to the side, and blue eyes sparkling bright.

The dogs all woofed in greeting, Biscuit rushing forward to lick my hand. Of all the dogs, Biscuit was the one who always stayed with me; he was becoming a bit of a comfort blanket to curl up with.

Oz scooped up one of the cats and placed it on the back of the couch, where it promptly jumped off and moved nearer the fire. Stockings adorned the mantel;

there were so many, one for each of the animals plus the kids, that it took me a second to realize there was one with my name embroidered on it too, exactly like the rest.

'I got a stocking?' I whispered, my throat constricting at the unexpected thoughtfulness and kindness.

I'd turned up at the last minute, and they'd already been prepared for me. At least I'd contributed something to the mountain of presents, as luckily Phoebe had dragged me into the nearby village for some last-minute shopping yesterday, so I'd been able to pick up a few things. I could see mine poking out in the bright green wrapping paper, ignoring the meagre contribution they made to the mountain.

'Of course, Father Christmas knows you're staying here. He wasn't going to leave my girlfriend out,' Oz replied in the same way you would to a five-year-old, but the only bit of that sentence I heard was girlfriend.

'Girlfriend?' I whispered.

Oz nodded. 'Yeah, I kind of like the sound of it. What do you think?'

He searched my face, hopefully, looking for my answer.

'I like it too.' I leaned in and kissed his cheek, 'Thank you for my stocking.'

'Told you, it's not me, it's Santa,' he whispered back to me, then turned to his siblings, 'Where's Mama?'

'She's coming, she went to find a notepad.'

Tugging me onto the couch and his lap, I startled slightly when Martha the housekeeper arrived, seemingly from nowhere. I might have gotten used to the size of this house, but I was still working on the fact that anything I wanted was fetched for me within minutes. Even things I didn't realize I wanted, like this steaming cup of coffee and bacon sandwich. I was trying hard not to get used to it. But I was definitely going to need to take a batch of the croissants back with me.

'Thank you,' I smiled.

'Thanks Martha, Happy Christmas.'

'You're welcome, and Happy Christmas to you.' She returned Oz's smile, 'Can I get anything else?'

'No, we're good thanks,' he replied, and she walked out.

Oz's arms wrapped around me and he nodded outside to the petrol-blue skies streaked with the orange of the sunrise. It was so pretty. 'Sorry we couldn't bring any snow for you.'

'Are you kidding, with all this?' I waved my hands around, 'I think I'll manage.'

'What's it like back in America?'

'When I spoke to my mom yesterday, she said it's snowing, but we don't get the thick snow like they do in Vermont, we're too close to the salty ocean air so it never sticks. It sludges.'

'What do you normally do for Christmas?' asked Hector, glancing up from his phone for the first time since I'd walked in.

'Um . . . well, my dad is a fisherman, and every morning he's out on the boat with a small crew, and they're usually finished by mid-morning. So our Christmas Day tends to start a little later, and we see friends.'

'Do you have a big turkey?'

I shook my head, 'No, we do turkey on Thanksgiving, so we usually have lobster or steak, something like that.'

'Nice.' Hector's eyes lit up.

'Yeah, it is. It's been quieter the past few years though, since my brother died.'

Oz's arms tightened around me.

Hector's eyes flashed from mine, to Oz behind me, then back again. 'Your brother died?'

I nodded, 'Yeah, his name was Jake. One morning he just didn't wake up. He'd had an underlying heart condition we didn't know about, and his heart stopped in the night.'

'I'm so sorry.'

'Thank you.'

'Our Christmas is different this year too,' Alex started quietly, 'our dad's normally here.'

I smiled softly as Oz tensed, even Hector and Phoebe had gone quiet, and were paying more attention to Alex than they had been previously.

'I'm sure you miss him.'

'Actually,' Alex bit his lip and I could see his fists balling at his sides as he considered his answer, 'I don't. I thought I would, and I didn't realize at first but there's no tension in the house now he's not here. It's way more chilled, even with Phoebe's shit music.'

'Hey!' Phoebe prodded him hard in the ribs with her toes, making him squeal. 'Take that back, my music is classic.'

'It's shit!' he reinstated loudly, which only caused Phoebe to launch herself at him and pin him to the ground. She tickled him until he cried for a yield, banging his hand on the floor, but by this point me, Hector and Oz were all howling with laughter, tears pouring down our faces, especially when the dogs joined in.

It was right when Oz's mom made an appearance, shaking her head with a wry smile at two of her kids wrestling on the floor.

'What's going on?'

Phoebe turned to find her mom walking across the hall and jumped off Alex. 'Oh good, you're back. Present time!'

'I'm so happy you're here,' Oz whispered in my ear.

'Me too,' I replied truthfully and I wondered if maybe I wasn't just here for him, or me. That my being here helped to distract them all from the person who was missing because, again, Oz was doing what he could to protect his family. 'Me too.'

'What's Boxing Day? Is this the same as the Santa run but we wear boxes?' I lifted my leg from under the warmth of the comforter, and pulled down the edge of my pyjama pants – my new dark-red pyjama pants, which had been a gift from Phoebe – to reveal a large bruise spreading across my thigh. 'I'm not sure I can do another one of those.'

Oz chuckled, brushing his palm against the purple/blueish marbling, and dropped a soft kiss to it, 'No, it's just the day after Christmas.'

'Why's it called Boxing Day?'

'It was traditionally a day when gifts were collected for those in need. They were boxed up and handed out.' His shoulder jerked in a shrug.

'Oh. So what are we doing today then?'

'Whatever you'd like, Yankee Doodle. Probably more eating, Phoebe will have another movie for us to watch, we can take the dogs for a walk across the fields. I should probably do a work-out.'

'I'm never going to get any studying done, am I?'

'Of course you are, and if I'm not mistaken you've been acing your anatomy coursework.'

His grin was so devilish, along with the devious glint in his eye peeking out from under the flop of dark curls, that I couldn't help but laugh at him, or stare, especially when he jumped out of bed and stood at the end. I watched as he slowly moved his palm across his heavily stacked abs, brushing against the tip of Excalibur until his hand dipped under the obscenely low-slung band of his pyjama pants and disappeared.

A barely-there sigh fell from my lips. I've said it before and I'll say it again, rowers have the finest bodies.

'See? You can name all these muscles already . . .' he grinned with a flex of his bicep, stretching the Olympic rings.

It should be cheesy, it *was* cheesy. I should *find it* cheesy. But all it did was remind me of exactly what he could do. What those muscles were capable of.

I wasn't sure how much I'd learned during his anatomy lessons, not anything that could be used in my exams anyway. I'd learned plenty about how my body reacted when his mouth inched up the inside of my thigh, or how he'd discovered a spot to the left of my ribcage that hardened my nipples until they were twisted to the point of painful, or how I knew he loved when I fisted through his hair and gripped onto the strands by the way his kisses deepened and his thrusts intensified until it was me screaming out for release.

But actual studying? No.

However, I was learning about the differences between the US and England and the length of time Christmas seemed to stretch over here. It felt like every day there was another thing to celebrate or take part in, whereas back home life would have returned to normal by the day after Christmas, if not the afternoon of.

I had friends who'd drive into the city to exchange their presents the second the stores reopened; a fact which had shocked Phoebe to her core. My cousins would be back working. My mom always took the tree down the day after Christmas because *'I've had enough of it getting in the way,'* and nothing would stop my dad from being out on the fishing boat.

It was helping me understand why Oz had made such a big deal about me not going home, because Christmas in England was centred around spending time together, family and love. And he'd brought me back to experience his, because here Christmas went on forever.

Right now, I wasn't even sure what day of the week it was.

What's more? I kind of liked it.

But I did need to study, and the dull panic that I hadn't done anything for days was getting louder.

'Come on, let's go and work out. You can explain the process of my muscles working correctly, then I'll show you exactly how my muscles can work for you.' His thick eyebrows wiggled at me, making me roll my eyes in response because he still hadn't run out of innuendos between my medical degree and his dick.

If studying was my top priority, sex was his.

After Oz had dragged me off yesterday on the pretence of taking the dogs for a walk but instead taken me to a pretty awesome tree house in the woods on the far side of the estate, it had become clear he was on a mission to have sex in every square inch possible.

It was something I was only too happy to help with.

While my mind might belong to me, I no longer owned my body. It was the property of one Arthur Osbourne-Cloud.

I'd never experienced anything like it. The way he could control every sensation I felt, reaction I gave, every breathless response to the questions he'd ask – do you like that? Does that feel good? You wanna see how deep I can get?

My entire body quivered in desperation for him. The way things were going, my heart would be following.

On second thought, maybe studying wasn't my top priority.

I threw back the covers and scrambled after him into his dressing room to fetch my workout clothes.

'I'm never going to get this right,' huffed Alex, almost to himself, as he dropped his text book on the floor, 'there's too many. Too many!'

I looked over to see him stretching out in the armchair on the other side of the living room. Phoebe was on the floor by the fire writing notes as she read *Othello*, Oz and Hector were huddled together at the opposite end of the enormous couch I was sitting on, going over Latin verbs, and none of them paid the slightest bit of attention to their youngest brother who appeared to be on the verge of a nervous breakdown.

I put down the book I was reading about rowing the Tideway – something else I had to master. When term broke I still hadn't been selected as coxswain for Blondie, so I needed all the help I could get.

'What's up, Alex?'

Sitting back up with a loud groan, he turned his head toward me, 'I have to memorize the periodic table and I can't remember them. It's boring and pointless.'

My nose wrinkled in agreement. It *was* boring, though I did need to use in it medicine so couldn't totally agree on the pointlessness, but for him it kind of was seeing as he'd decided he only wanted to study languages, but was still at the age where sciences were compulsory learning.

'I learned it using mnemonics, have you tried that? It helps a lot.'

'No,' Alex shook his head, 'I don't think so. What does that mean?'

'Like when you make up a little poem with the first letters of each word. It helps you remember.' His face remained blank as he looked at me. 'You know, so the first two lines of the periodic table would be Happy Henry Likes Beer But Can Not Obtain Food . . . that's the one I was taught, but you can make up your own.'

He followed along with the elements I was reading out, his eyes widening as understanding set in. 'Oh, yeah. I get it. I'll try that, thanks, Kate.'

'You're welcome,' I smiled, 'let me know if you want help with them.'

'Did you know the word mnemonic comes from the Ancient Greek word meaning memory?'

'No one cares, brainiac,' Alex shot back at Oz with an eye roll, and went back to muttering under his breath.

'*You* should, you're half Greek.'

Alex ignored him.

Instead, Oz winked at me, just managing to hold in his laugh, and continued where he had left off helping Hector with his verbs. I'd been watching him almost as much as I'd been trying to study, and even though he'd sworn he also had studying to do I was yet to see him open any book, not even the one by his lap. Instead, he'd been working through Hector's coursework, helping him with the exams he had when he returned to school in the new year. I was fascinated by his patience and understanding, the way he went over and over explaining the same point until he knew Hector understood completely on his own.

I stretched out and nudged his ass with the tip of my toe, 'Hey, wanna come and find some of that leftover pie with me?'

Phoebe glanced up from the floor. 'I want pie.'

'Me too,' came Alex.

'And can you get me a Diet Coke?' added Phoebe.

'I'll have regular.'

Oz's eyes widened at me, 'Jeez. Look at what you started now.'

I grinned, even more so when Oz shook the end of my foot and stood up holding out his hand to me, 'Come on then.'

The second we were out of sight I wrapped my arms around his waist, 'I don't care about pie, I just wanted to get you alone.'

He stopped and pushed me up against the dark wooden panelling of the corridor, 'Oh, really?'

'Yep.' I popped out the 'p'.

'Well, that's a coincidence because I've been thinking about how to get you alone.'

'Oh yeah?'

'Yeah. So tell me, what did you want me alone for?'

Reaching up, I twisted a curl of his hair around my index finger, 'I just wanted to kiss you, and hug you and tell you that I think you're an awesome brother.'

The smug grin mask he'd been wearing for the last minute dropped, and he stilled in my arms. 'What d'you mean?'

'You're an awesome brother to those three. You act like they're a pain in the ass, but even in the few days of being here I've seen how fiercely you protect them and love them. You've spent most of today helping Hector with his Latin when you have your finals coming up this year, and Alex told me yesterday about the newspaper he'd found and how you helped him get rid of it.'

He looked at me, really held my gaze until I could see the gratitude in his eyes, the relief at being seen for something other than the tabloid version of him. Because no matter how much you tried to avoid the gossip, there would always be a tiny part of you that wondered if it were true. Or if perhaps you really were the person people said you were.

'Thank you.' His head dipped until his lips brushed mine, pressing harder until I opened up and allowed him access.

Softly, slowly, his tongue moved against mine as his hands cupped my cheeks, but he didn't deepen it. The kiss stayed as wholesome as a kiss could be, because this wasn't a kiss which was leading anywhere. It was almost a kiss of relief, and when he stepped back and held my gaze I knew I was right.

'Thank you.'

'For what?'

'For being here. For being you. I'm so happy I found you, Kate Astley. You've no idea.'

'I think I do, thank you for inviting me.' I brushed my thumb against the soft stubble on his cheek. 'You're a great teacher, you know. You really should think about pursuing it. You should be teaching. Why don't you talk to your mom while you're here?'

His mouth held in a straight line, but he didn't reply and when his stomach rumbled, he grabbed it. 'Come on, you might have got me out here on a pretext, but I'm hungry and we have a tray full of snacks to take back to those beasts now.'

We walked toward the chef's kitchen where the pie was, but I didn't ask what he was thinking as we continued in silence because I was too busy answering the question I'd asked myself when I'd first arrived here.

If he was busy protecting everyone else, who was protecting him?

Me, I decided.

'Oz,' his name stretched out on my wide yawn as I watched him rush around. 'Why are we awake so early? The sun hasn't even risen yet.'

'You'll see. We have a busy day,' he called from his dressing room.

'What are we doing?'

'Surprise. Now do as you're told, and get dressed.'

My curiosity got the better of me and I threw back the covers. I always expected it to be cold first thing in the mornings, just like the winters were back home before the stove was lit, but for an old house it was surprisingly well insulated.

'What am I wearing?'

'Something warm.' He kissed my head as he walked past. 'I'll see you downstairs in five minutes.'

I frowned after him as he closed the door, wondering if I'd ever seen him so focused or distracted. He hadn't even used the opportunity to squeeze my ass, which might be a first, but seeing as I was on a time constraint I snapped into action and pulled on the warmest leggings I could find, along with a long-sleeve t-shirt, thick hoodie and woolly hat.

'Four minutes and forty-three seconds,' Oz announced as I reached the bottom of the stairs.

'Were you timing me?'

'No, I'm timing Phoebe, but you happened to arrive first.' He grinned, picking up a steaming to-go cup of coffee and handed it to me. 'Here you go.'

'Phoebe?'

'Yes, she's bound to take longer than five minutes, but I'm giving her the benefit of the doubt.'

I was still trying to figure out what we were doing when Alex slid down the banister, clearly racing Hector who was sprinting down the stairs, both jumping off at the bottom and landing square on the floor.

'I won.' Hector threw his hands into the air.

'No, I did. I hit the ground first.'

'You did not.'

'I did. Kate? Who won?' demanded Alex.

'I didn't see.' I rubbed my eyes. 'What are we doing up so early?'

Hector and Alex both turned to Oz, who answered with a swipe of his fingers zipping across his lips.

'Sorry, we can't tell you,' Hector replied with a shrug and a yawn.

'You three get in the car, and I'll find Pheebs,' Oz ordered, running back up the stairs two at a time.

I trundled outside, not understanding why Hector and Alex had sprinted out of the front door, nor why they were so chipper, only to find small tubs of steaming porridge and a tray of wrapped, hot bacon sandwiches had been left for us on the passenger seat. Hector had already taken such an enormous bite of one sandwich that there was almost none left in his hand.

I slid into the seat next to him and picked one up. My mouth was already pooling with saliva as I unwrapped the foil.

Alex mumbled something I didn't understand.

'What?'

He swallowed his bite, 'Oz will want you in the front seat.'

'Oh, I don't care. You're all much taller, I'm fine here.' I bit into my sandwich. 'Where are we going?'

'You'll see,' was all the reply I got.

'Is your mom coming?'

'No, just us.'

I went back to my bacon sandwich.

As Alex predicted, the second Oz walked out with Phoebe, who looked even sleepier than me, I was promoted to sitting in the front passenger seat because '*I can't hold your hand if you're in the back*'.

I didn't argue.

An hour and a half later, along a surprisingly busy motorway for the time of morning, the sun was rising bright in the distance ahead of us. Phoebe and I had gone back to sleep almost as soon as Oz had driven through the estate's gates, and waking up now I glanced around at the vaguely familiar surroundings. In front of where we'd stopped was a slightly ramshackle arch-roofed wooden building, which could do with a fresh coat of paint. I was having the strangest sensation of déjà-vu until I noticed the flag flying on top. One I recognized immediately.

I turned to Oz, while the others were piling out of the back seats into the cold London air. 'Are we by the rowing club?'

He nodded, 'Yes, the one across the river.'

I looked back up at the flag. It had been one of the first things I'd noticed the first day we'd had river-cleaning duties. That day when all I could think about was how mad I was at Oz, especially because all I'd wanted was for him to kiss me.

The week after, he'd done exactly that.

And every week since I'd made a wish of some kind, in case it was a lucky flag and perhaps a genie lived in the flag pole. It was the first thing I looked at whenever I'd come out to the river for Tideway practice, asking for it to bring me and my crew safely home.

'What are we doing here?'

'Tideway practice.'

My neck snapped around to him, hard enough that I needed to rub the sharp pain away. 'What d'you mean?'

He picked up my left hand and sandwiched it between both of his. 'You need the practice time on the river. You deserve a fair shot at coxing Blondie, and I want to give it to you because when we both win our races, we both get to celebrate.'

I stared, unblinking, as his words sunk in. We – not just him and me, but Phoebe, Hector and Alex too – had got up at the crack of dawn and driven to London so I could get Tideway practice in during the holidays, for a rival team. Something he'd arranged.

'You did this for me?' I whispered, too shocked to compute the magnitude of his gesture.

'Of course.' His lips smacked against mine before he turned and opened his car door, 'Come on, let's get going. We've got a full day of training.'

I got out to find the other three waiting for us. 'You guys, thank you. I can't believe he persuaded you to get up for this.'

'It beats revision,' replied Alex.

Phoebe looped her arm through mine and dragged me to the boathouse. 'We're a rowing family, the four of us grew up on this river. We can help you through the steers and tough turns. It's not coxed eights, but it'll help you.'

I turned back to Oz, 'This is beyond anything. Thank you.'

'You're welcome.' He passed me a coxbox and headset, 'Now tell me I'm cute.'

I grinned, 'There will never be anyone as cute.'

'Good. Now what are you waiting for? Guide us out of the boathouse.'

Every day over the past week Oz had surprised me. Being with him had surprised me, the ease with which we spent our days together felt like I'd known him my entire life, and the past week had been the first time in a long time I'd felt truly happy and content.

Which is why the dread I felt about going back to Cambridge sucked big time.

Being separated from Oz again sucked even more.

But the worst bit – I wasn't sure I wanted to go back at all.

19. Arthur

(Happy New Year)

'Where's Kate?' Alex threw the dice across the board and moved his little dog three spaces, looking up at me when I didn't answer, like he hadn't already asked the same question five minutes ago, and five minutes before that.

'Still in the kitchen, stop complaining. She won't be long.'

'I'm hungry!'

'You're always hungry.'

'That's not true. Sometimes he's asleep.' My mother winked at him.

I picked the dice off the board and shook them. 'And remember she's been working all morning on this, so even if you don't like her cooking, you're going to like it. Understand?'

I hoped I'd made myself clear, but it only garnered an eye roll from my two idiot brothers.

'Chill, Oz. We all know how to act,' piped up Olly, who'd arrived about an hour ago because we always spent New Year's Eve together, and this year was no different. 'She's probably just making burgers or hot dogs.'

'Arthur, darling, I'm sure whatever it is will be great,' my mother added, still wearing the same slightly baffled expression she'd had for most of the morning.

It had been a while since anyone but Marco had cooked for us, so no one really knew what to make of it. Phoebe was initially excited but now looked indifferent, the boys were clearly becoming impatient and hungry, even with the bottomless snacking they'd partaken in and Olly was, well, just being Olly.

I'd barely seen Kate since after breakfast when she announced she'd like to cook lunch, and we were to spend the rest of the day sitting outside by the roaring firepit, relaxing and enjoying each other's company, because it was a beautiful, bright and very cold New Year's Eve. She then promptly disappeared.

I'd managed to surmise it had required a trip into the village, but nothing more. The second I'd heard her return, I'd gone hunting and found her in the kitchen but was barred from entry and shooed off to hang out with my family.

She'd barely given me a kiss goodbye.

For the past three hours we'd been on the patio, which we'd found set up with thick cosy blankets and cushions, board games, plenty of snacks and an ice bucket filled with soft drinks, fresh juice, beer and a bottle of champagne, along with a scattering of New Year's party poppers and hats. Olly was already wearing his hat.

We didn't normally spend much time out here in the winter, but looking around at everyone snuggled up, including the dogs, I wondered why.

Throwing another log on the fire, I turned back to the house to see if Kate was on her way, but only saw Mister Gingerbreadman, Phoebe's black lab, trotting towards us. It was a good sign though; he had a sixth sense for knowing when food was about to arrive.

'That's a grand you owe me, now. Cough up.' Hector held his hand out to Alex, whose throw of the dice had taken him to Park Lane and the little green houses Hector owned.

'Fuck's sake,' Alex snapped, his panicked eyes darting to our mother who was deep in conversation with Phoebe, and sighed in relief when she didn't react to his swearing. 'That's all my money you've taken now. You're cheating. Banker! I object.'

Olly peered over the board. 'Looks fair to me. You'll have to borrow.'

'I'm not borrowing,' he sulked at Hector, 'I'm not playing any more. It's boring.'

'You're such a shit loser, Al.'

'I'm not a shit loser, it's impossible to beat you! One day I'm going to find out how you consistently cheat in Monopoly. There's no way you can always win without it.'

I sat back, lacing my hands behind my head as Olly and I shared the same grin. It didn't matter how often we played, the game always ended with Alex quitting.

Phoebe sat up from where she'd been lying on our mother's lap, grabbed the bottle of champagne and poured out a glass for herself and another for Mama, topped them both up with grapefruit juice, and settled back against the cushions.

'Oh, here she is.'

I spun around to find Kate carrying another bucket of drinks in one hand, and a tray balanced in the other; James and Marco followed close behind, their arms also full. I jumped up and ran over to help, relieving her of paper napkins and small bowls of ketchup and mayonnaise.

Looking at what the guys were carrying, it all became clear what she'd been doing.

'Holy shit, you made your lobster rolls!'

She grinned up at me, 'I did.'

As I breathed in the scent of dill, butter and fresh lobster, saliva pooled in my mouth. 'I'm such a dumbass, why didn't I guess this?'

'Hey, don't speak about your ass like that,' she snarled playfully, 'it's nothing but cute.'

She leaned into my lips as I kissed her cheek, a move I was quickly becoming obsessed with. 'Come on, I'll walk ahead then you can watch my arse.'

Hector was hurriedly clearing away the Monopoly to make space on the table; Phoebe's contribution was to put on the purple New Year's hat and pull a popper as we arrived back so the streamers floated in the air. Most of them landed in the ketchup, which was swiftly removed and replaced.

'Sorry it took so long,' Kate smiled, placing her tray down next to the huge bowls of fries and rolls the guys had set in front of us. 'I hope you're hungry.'

'Starved,' Alex stole a fry and stuffed it in his mouth.

Kate picked up a plate and handed it to him, 'Help yourself, then.'

He didn't need telling twice, and took the nearest one to him brimming with lobster meat, and dripping in sauce.

There was silence for an excruciating ten seconds, all eyes on Alex before he broke it with a garbled mouthful. He tried again after washing it down with a swig of his Coke and being scolded by our mother for poor table manners.

'Holy shit, this is really good. You seriously made it?' he barely glanced at Kate before reaching for another one.

She nodded, nervously, 'Really? You like them?'

He nodded through another enormous mouthful, looking over at me, 'Yeah, seriously. I'm not even faking it.'

Kate took a deep breath of relief while everyone else reached in and helped themselves. There was another ten seconds of silence as we made our own assessments. Alex was correct. They were excellent.

'Yeah, these are better than that place in Cornwall.'

'These are so good. How've you made them like this?'

'Do you remember those lobster rolls in St Barts? They weren't as good as these.'

Even the renowned hard-to-impress Daphne Drakos was impressed. 'Kate, these are truly excellent. You must give the recipe to Marco, we should have these again.'

'What's in them?' asked Alex, reaching for his third, and I now understood why she'd made so many.

'A secret,' Kate's grin spread, in fact it had yet to drop since Alex took a first bite and his eyes widened until I thought they might burst.

'And you made all this?' he repeated.

'Only the rolls,' she nodded, 'Marco made the fries, I can't do fries, but I made the rolls from scratch; the dough, mayo, and shelled the lobster. I got them from the fishmonger place in town I noticed when we went for a walk the other day, so I pre-ordered them. Thank god, too, there was a line out the door today. Everyone was picking up oysters for New Year.'

I held the plate up before her nervousness got the better of her and she began hyperventilating. 'You haven't had one yet.'

'Oh, yes!' she reached out, then paused, 'Oh, shoot! I'm

a dumbass. I forgot the butter sauce. Hang on, I'll be right back, you have to have it with the butter sauce.'

She took off like a whirlwind before I could stop her.

My mother kept her eyes trained on Kate until she disappeared into the house, and sat back, 'Arthur, these really are excellent.'

'Yeah, I know. When we first met, she said if she wasn't studying medicine she'd want to open a restaurant which sold lobster rolls.'

'Well, if she's as good a doctor as she is at making these, she'll go far in life.'

'I really like her a lot, Artie,' Phoebe added unnecessarily, seeing as we were all well aware of the girl crush she had on Kate, and stuffed a handful of fries in her mouth.

Alex and Hector nodded in agreement.

'Thank you. I'm glad you do because I like her too, *a lot a lot*.'

My mother sat up a little straighter, Olly's grin widened and Phoebe leaned forward, pinning me with a squinted eye. 'More than a lot?'

I hesitated; I hadn't told Kate I loved her yet, so I certainly wasn't going to tell my gossipy sister who'd probably try and beat me to the punch by declaring her love for Kate to her first. I loved Kate, and I wanted everyone to know, but she'd find out before anyone else. Thankfully, my mother interrupted before an interrogation took place, because I would definitely crumble.

'I'm glad you persuaded her to come. It's been a lovely Christmas, and wonderful to have all my babies home with me.' She pulled Phoebe and Hector, sitting on her left, into a hug.

I caught my mother's smile. None of us needed her to add to the sentence; that Christmas would have been a lot different this year without Kate.

One thing I knew for sure, if my dad had been here instead, we'd have been miserable and arguing.

'Here you go, pour this over your rolls.' Kate placed a couple of small sauce-filled jugs on the table when she returned, her eyes flaring as she glanced at the plate. There had been two dozen rolls when she'd left, but it was now half empty. 'If you can fit any more in.'

'Yeah. Course we can,' Alex reached for another – possibly his fifth – free-pouring the creamy sauce over the top, and bit into it, 'ermigawdsogoog.'

'Safe to say he likes it.' I turned my nose up at his disgusting mouthful and passed over the plate to her before he could inhale the rest. 'Are you going to have one?'

'Sure am, thank you.'

'Kate, Arthur told us you want to open a restaurant.'

Kate swallowed her bite, picking up her water with a kind of forlorn nod as she faced my mother, 'Oh, yeah, I did. I mean, I do, it would be cool. But I don't know when I'd have the time, I'm studying for the next six years. So I guess it's a pipe dream.'

'If it's a dream, you must find a way to do it, my dear.'

Kate tensed beside me, 'Yeah, it's a bit complicated.'

'Mama . . .' My voice held a warning tone to stop because I knew she was about to push on the point, but Kate's complication lay in the fact she was studying medicine because of her brother, not because she wanted to. Except Kate waved me off.

'No, it's okay. When my brother died he had been

299

accepted to study medicine at Cambridge on a scholarship. My parents were so proud of him – he would have been the first in our family to go to college, and it was a big deal. So I'm trying to make them proud too.' She picked up her lobster roll and bit into it, ignoring the silence of everyone else at the table which I could hear at full volume.

My mother reached out and took Kate's hand, 'My darling, they would be proud of you, whatever you chose to do. Parents just want to see their children happy.'

'Yeah, maybe,' she replied, though it lacked any conviction.

'And where did you learn to make these?'

Kate's smile returned, 'Oh, my grandma taught me. It was her recipe, and she used to make them for us as kids every weekend. My grandpa would bring in the hauls, and always save the best-looking lobster for her. It was his business, and my dad took over the boats about fifteen years ago.'

'Does she still make them?'

'No, she died a few years ago, before Jake. So I'm sure they're all together with my grandpa laughing down at us.'

'They certainly are. In Greece, we believe happy memories are what keeps the spirits living on, and they're sent to Elysium to continue a new and brilliant existence.'

Kate picked up a fry and fed it to a slobbering Biscuit, who'd been glued to her side since she sat down. 'That's a lovely thought, thank you.'

'Now tell me, what will happen when your father retires? He doesn't want you to take it over?'

This time Kate blushed, 'Oh no . . .'

'. . . because you want to work in medicine?'

'Actually,' Kate's cheeks flared even redder, 'I get sea-sick. Those waves are huge sometimes. It's much safer for me to be on land. Or flat water.'

My mother stared at her, then burst out into loud, *loud* laughter. Louder than we'd heard in a long time. Next to her Phoebe started giggling, so did Hector, then Olly and finally Alex. Suddenly each of the dogs stood up and began jumping around.

'Oh my goodness, that is the funniest thing I've ever heard.' My mother wiped her eyes and picked up a new bottle of champagne, which I took from her to open and poured out three glasses; for her, Kate and Phoebe. 'At least rowing only needs calm waters.'

'Yeah, my dad wasn't too impressed,' Kate chuckled, 'but when he retires, my cousin Vinny is going to take over. He's worked on the boat with my dad since he was a teenager, and he was always much more talented at catching than Jake or me. I'd have probably ended up working in the boatyard office.'

'Family-owned companies are important. Family is important.'

'Yes, ma'am.'

Since we'd been talking Marco's team had cleared away the lunch, replaced all the dirty plates with clean ones, filled the ice bucket with more drinks, and – the best bit – brought an enormous bowl of marshmallows along with chocolate buttons, digestive biscuits and little bowls filled with M&Ms, sprinkles and gummy bears.

Our own personal sweet shop.

Olly, Alex and Hector had started up a new game of

Monopoly, pretending to listen to the rest of our conversation, and Phoebe had gone back to whomever she was texting but chiming in with a comment every now and then.

I threw half of my blanket over Kate's lap and pulled her into me. She softened against my side, and somehow I felt myself relax further as I tried to recall a time when I'd ever felt this content.

I couldn't.

For the first time ever I didn't want to go back to Oxford. I was suddenly desperate to slow the hours, so we'd have more of them. Christmas had passed too quickly.

'You must come out and visit us in Greece this summer; Arthur will usually make some time outside of his rowing commitments. And I promise our yacht won't be sailing in big waves.'

'I'd love to, thank you.'

'Have you two thought about what you're going to do?'

My fingers stilled where my arm was draped over Kate's shoulder. 'What d'you mean?'

'With the Boat Race . . .'

'Mama, we're not racing against each other. Kate will be in Blondie.' I received a nudge to my ribs and peered down to find Kate staring with pursed lips, 'What?'

'I doubt I'll be racing at all, I'm still a first year. Don't jinx it.'

'You'll get selected,' I assured her at the same time as my mother added, 'Arthur said you're a natural.'

'What?' I shrugged at Kate's frown. 'You are. Even Phoebe said so.'

'Huh,' my sister grunted, her fingers moving fast over her phone screen, 'what did I say?'

'That Kate is an excellent coxswain.'

'Oh!' Phoebe put her phone down and turned to us. 'Yeah, you were so good the other day. We nailed the river. I've never made it along the course so quickly.'

Kate smiled softly. 'Thank you. I appreciate you telling me.'

'We'll be there to cheer you both on,' my mother laughed.

'I'll send you a Cambridge jersey.'

'Please do, my dear.'

She was still smiling at my mother when Alex and Hector interrupted. Or rather their constantly growling stomachs did.

'I'm cracking into the marshmallows. Who wants one?'

'Yeah, make me one will you, Al?' asked Phoebe who was back on her phone and didn't bother looking up. Instead, my mother moved to help him before he set fire to something, likely himself.

Kate turned under my arms, her voice quiet, 'Hey, you want to make s'mores with me?'

'I would love to make s'mores with you.' I laced my fingers through her hair until her head tipped back enough so I could kiss her delicately on the nose, and my heart suddenly punched against my ribcage so hard I thought it might have cracked. 'Thank you, Kate Astley.'

She crooked her head as much as she could with me cupping her cheek. 'What for?'

'Just you. Everything. Being here and spending time with my family. I think this has been my favourite Christmas ever.'

'Really?'

I nodded, 'Yeah, I've always loved Christmas, but being home was always hard with my dad. I was worried Hector and Al wouldn't enjoy it, but they've had such a great time too. And it's everything to do with you.'

She reached up and stroked my cheek, 'Oz . . .'

My heart was squeezing so tightly it was almost hard to breathe, 'Can I tell you a secret?'

'Of course.'

'I don't want to go back to Oxford, and have you at Cambridge.'

Her face fell, and her expression mirrored mine. 'I know, me too. It sucks.'

'Let's spend tomorrow figuring out when we're going to see each other? Because I can't go a week without you, even over FaceTime.'

'Yeah, that's a great idea.'

As always the shorter strands of her hair had fallen loose from the tie and I wound them around my fingers 'Can I tell you another secret?'

She nodded. I looked over at my family who were now too busy squabbling over marshmallows to overhear me.

'I've fallen in love with you.'

Her bottom lip stuck onto her teeth, and I pulled it free.

'Can I tell *you* a secret?' she asked.

I nodded slowly.

'I've fallen in love with you too.' Her face lifted up until her lips pressed against mine. 'Happy New Year, Ozzy.'

And that's how the worst year of my life became my best.

20. Kate

(It had to go tits up some time)

'How did it already get to be the fifteenth of January?' Imogen flopped onto my bed with a dramatic sigh, and tugged her long ponytail from where it had gotten stuck underneath her shoulder. 'Not to mention how did it get to be the fifteenth of January and we already have enough work to last us the term?'

I picked up my giant water bottle and glugged it down while I thought about a response, not that she wanted one per se – I had the impression it was more of a rhetorical question – but either way I still wasn't quite sure of the answer. Christmas and New Year seemed far longer ago than two weeks; the bliss of being away from school while spending time with Oz and his family was now a distant memory. Not to mention that since we'd gotten back to school ten days ago, I'd only seen Oz once and I was missing him so much I'd been carrying around a permanent ache in my chest.

The only time I was given temporary reprieve was during Boat Race training. It had now stepped up so intensely that I didn't have any space in my brain during our sessions to do anything other than concentrate on guiding my crew through the river. We barely had the energy to get another few hours of study in before collapsing into bed every night.

Oz was the same, except his coursework had increased given his finals were only a few months away; it had provided a glut of teasing that he now finally seemed to have the same amount of work as I did.

I joked, but in reality I had a fuck ton to do and not enough time to do it. I'd been trying not to panic, but if I couldn't keep on top of my work within the first few weeks, then I had no chance of being able to manage my load, and train at the same time.

I stared down at the piles of flash cards Imogen and I had made ahead of our mock histology exam next week – the one we'd only been told about on Monday.

I dropped down next to her. 'Why did we choose medicine?'

'I don't know,' she groaned, 'think it's too late to switch to a different course?'

'No.'

'Really? Because I'm having serious thoughts about moving to English. At least people's lives won't be at stake if I fail my paper on Shakespearian tragedies.'

'That's very true,' I chuckled quietly.

'That boyfriend of yours has it right. Only an idiot would take medicine and want to be selected for the Boat Race crew. A genius picks classics.'

I grinned next to her, still staring up at the ceiling, 'Yeah, you're right. He has a crap ton of work at the moment, though.'

'How's their training going?'

I shrugged. 'Same as ours, I guess. We don't really talk about it beyond having it twice a day. Sore muscles, that sort of thing.'

'You don't talk about Boat Race training?'

I turned on the mattress, propping my head on my elbow to face her. 'We talk about ourselves as individuals – you know, like the other day when I took us through the stream too late and I lost us the race. Or he'll tell me how much he's lifted in the gym because he loves to brag, that sort of thing. But we've never talked about crew training.'

She nudged me gently, 'That wasn't your fault on Saturday. The weather was shit, and we pulled too early.'

I shook my head, not wanting to relive the disaster and humiliation, 'I should have steered you better. I could have done better, I've totally blown my chances for Blondie.'

I'd been beating myself up for the last five days. Our first race back since the holidays had been against King's College London and had taken place along the stretch of Tideway I'd been practising. The same stretch Oz had taken me over Christmas.

After the starting pistols had been pulled, my crew had raced ahead ready to move into the stream of water running down the centre of the Tideway, as we always did, the bit where the water is the smoothest. It was exactly what the cox for King's had urged his crew to do too, except I hadn't studied the wind speeds carefully enough before the race and turned the boat too hard. Instead of slipping ahead, Imogen in stroke position had clashed oars with King's bow.

It was a stupid mistake, and one I should have never made. I knew better.

Safe to say, Coach was pissed.

I'd called Oz and cried to him for an hour.

'You have not, don't be stupid. You're still miles better than Morgan – she's not aggressive enough. We're so much slower with her than you.'

'She doesn't cause you to clash oars though.'

'Asters, it was an accident.'

I sighed again and fell back. I knew part of the reason I was giving myself such a hard time was because I desperately wanted to be named cox for Blondie, and if I wasn't a hundred per cent certain I'd blown my chance, I was ninety-nine.

So not only was I struggling at medicine, I was struggling at rowing too and at this rate I'd go back to the US and have to tell my parents I'd failed at everything. A situation which was unacceptable to me.

'Come on, cheer up. What did Oz say?'

'Same as you.'

She nudged me again, 'He must be smart then. Perhaps I did misjudge him.'

I laughed into the air.

'I still can't believe you spent Christmas with him. I'm so jealous.'

'Why? You were in the Caribbean.' I turned my head. Her tan had faded from the disgustingly dark golden colour she'd waltzed in wearing when she'd returned, but only slightly. She'd looked so healthy and glowy, I'd have booked a seat on the return flight if I'd had the money.

'Because it's Arthur Osbourne-Cloud's house. My cousins went to a party there once, it's supposed to be fabulous.'

Sometimes I'd forget what Imogen said because I was too busy listening to her accent and how she pronounced words like faaaa-bu-lus. You'd have thought I'd have gotten used to it by now.

'Yeah, it was awesome. Like something from *Downton Abbey* or whatever shows you guys have. I sent my mom a picture, and she thought it was Buckingham Palace. It wasn't stuffy though, it felt super cute and cosy.'

'What was his mother like?'

'The nicest. I was so nervous to meet her, but she's a hugger.'

'God, I'd have been so nervous too.'

I propped myself up on my elbow again. 'The thing is, my life on the east coast is so far removed from his that to compare would be pointless. Like, you could have fitted my parents' whole house in the front hallway.'

'Was his dad there?'

I shook my head, and that was about as much as Imogen was going to get out of me on the subject of Oz's father. I wasn't about to add to the gossip train.

'So you guys are super serious now then?'

I nodded, 'Yeah, we are.'

'Fuck,' she giggled, and soon she couldn't stop, 'I can't believe you're dating A.O.-C. What are the chances of that happening?'

I shrugged again, joining in with a little giggle because the whole thing was still surreal to me; not the dating Oz part, or that he seemed to be tarred with this celebrity-type status, just the fact that we'd found each other.

'At least you only have a few more months of hiding, then you won't need to keep it a secret any longer as both he and Mary Heston will have graduated.'

I nodded, taking a deep breath as I did. 'Yeah. She's

been so intense, did you see her shouting at the Blue Boat crew this morning? I'm kind of glad she's leaving this summer, then we'll never have to train under her. She scares the crap out of me.'

'Totally, she's just desperate to win, but she wants a clean sweep. She wants Cambridge to take them all.'

'It's only because she's dating Will Norris. She wants to be crowned winner with him.'

'Ha, yeah! He's so laid back, I don't know what he sees in her. Bet she makes him do burpees and crunches before they have sex.' Imogen dissolved into a fit of giggles, setting me off too.

'Yeah, or ten press-ups per thrust when he's on top.'

I missed Imogen's response as a knock sounded at the door, and I rolled off my bed still giggling.

'Good afternoon,' I greeted dramatically, throwing the door open wide but my laughter died with the creak of the door hinges, and Imogen gasped behind me. 'Mary?'

Mary Heston peered around the door frame to see Imogen now on the floor, surrounded by flash cards. 'Working hard, I see.'

The way she said it made it sound like she didn't think we'd been working hard at all, but all I was worried about was how long she'd been standing outside and whether she'd heard everything Imogen and I had said. The walls weren't that thick, and she was exactly the type of person to be listening outside.

'We were on a break,' I replied meekly, then wondered why. I didn't have to justify myself to her. I stood up straighter, and forced a smile. 'What's up, Mary? Want to come in?'

'It's not a social visit.' She stepped in anyway.

'Okay.' I was about to close the door behind her when a hand gripped the edge.

'Knock knock.' The owner of the voice pushed the door wide again. 'Mare, for fuck's sake, why are you here?'

I looked over to Imogen, who was staring up at Will Norris and Mary Heston; the widening of her eyes was in direct correlation to how defiant Mary continued to look as Will's frown deepened.

'I told you I was coming,' she replied eventually.

'Fine, I'm not staying, and it should be noted that I want no part of this.'

I bit down on my smirk as Imogen grabbed a pen and one of the spare flash cards, and scribbled something across it. 'I've noted it. Now would you mind explaining what you're both doing here.'

I assumed Will would go first as he didn't plan to stay but he merely stared at Mary and gestured her forward.

Mary cleared her throat, a quiet little noise that evoked a sense of dread out of nowhere. 'I have a friend whose family lives in Chewton-under the-Wold, and she was there for Christmas . . .'

The sense of dread intensified immediately, especially with the way Mary was slowly blinking while she waited for me to catch on. For the whole of Christmas I'd planned to ask Oz what 'under-the-Wold' meant, seeing as it was his village, but it had slipped my mind every single time.

Out of the corner of my eye I caught Imogen sitting up straighter. She knew it was his village too. Neither of us said anything.

'Anyway,' continued Mary, 'she loves to post on

Instagram. It's hard to keep up with how much she posts, but last weekend I happened to have been scrolling through, and caught one from Christmas Eve. She'd taken part in the annual Santa run they hold in the village – you know the one, right, Kate?'

Mary stared at me, but I stayed silent. Imogen was less patient than me, however.

'Mary, spit it out. Enough with the dramatic reveal. Ask what you came to ask.'

I glanced over to Will Norris leaning against the door frame and looking at his feet.

'Are you in a relationship with Arthur Osbourne-Cloud? And did you spend Christmas with him?'

'Mary, I've told you, it's none of your business who Kate spends Christmas with,' snapped Will.

'It is when it's direct competition to us. How do we know she's not sharing training secrets?'

Will tutted loudly and shook his head. He'd clearly been over Mary's arguments more than once, especially when he muttered, 'You're ridiculous.'

'I'm not!' she snapped, turning back to me. 'You're here on a rowing scholarship, aren't you, Kate?'

I didn't need a translator to understand her very arched eyebrow was the not-so-subtle threat that by dating Oz I was putting my scholarship in jeopardy.

'You are being ridiculous,' Will argued back, and looked at me. 'You don't have to answer her.'

I smiled gratefully, though my insides were spinning like a tornado, 'Why are you here, Will?'

'Coach wants to see you. I was heading over here anyway, and I told him I'd give you the message.'

I frowned in surprise, 'Oh, did he say what for? Or when?'

Will shook his head, but from the look on his face he knew exactly why I'd been summoned, and my stomach plunged another few inches.

'Is it . . .' I pointed at Mary whose head was flicking between me with pursed lips and Will in confusion, 'Is it to do with this . . .'

'No, though it's probably not something you should mention to him right now. You're not doing anything wrong, Kate, and it's got nothing to do with your scholarship, but it'd be best to keep it on the downlow anyway. Just go to the boathouse and see them as soon as you can. Now if you have time.'

'Them?'

'Yeah, Westcott and Stephens.'

'Both coaches?' shrieked Imogen, making my stomach clench. If it wasn't about Oz then it was about the weekend race against King's College. It had to be.

'I know nothing about this,' snapped Mary. 'Why do I not know what this is about? I'm women's president.'

Will reached out and tugged her jacket, 'Come on, Mare, let's go.'

'No, I want to know what's going on.'

I crossed my arms over my chest, and popped my hip, 'You and me both.'

'It's nothing bad, Kate, I promise. Your Christmas is no one's business anyway.' He glared at Mary just as she was about to speak, and pulled her out of my room. 'I'm sorry about all this.'

I closed the door behind them. 'That was so weird.'

Imogen jumped to her feet. 'Yes, but let's get down to the boathouse now or we'll be wondering all afternoon.'

'I was going to go before training. We've still got an hour of study time allotted.'

'You'll not be able to concentrate,' she argued back, though she had a point. 'Let's pack up the cards and finish our revision in the break room, then we're saving time.'

'Yeah, okay, good idea.'

In what must have been record time for Imogen, she packed up the cards and her training bag, and was ready to leave a full thirty seconds before me. Gossip was a strong motivator.

'Come and find me when you're done,' she said, heading to the boathouse break room as soon as we opened the doors. 'Good luck.'

It was hard to ignore the nerves as I knocked on Coach Westcott's door. Every worry I'd had about Oz and every comment from my professors about a slipped grade was twisting itself into a giant ball of knots in my stomach.

'Come in,' Coach Westcott boomed, and I gingerly opened the door, trying my hardest to put on my most genuine looking smile, 'ah, Kate. Come in. Sit down.'

I did as I was told, and slunk into the chair facing his huge desk piled high with papers. I'd not been in here before; I'd not even been in Coach Stephens' office in its entirety, just peered over the threshold to speak to him. Roan Westcott had been a world-class rower in his day; the medals and photographs adorning the walls proved it. Five Olympic golds, World Championship golds, and photos of him on the podium at Henley, the Boat Races he won, including as president of Cambridge.

He'd been one of the best rowers, now he was one of the best coaches.

The door opened, and I turned to see Coach Stephens. I thought he was about to close the door, but he was followed by Coach Godwin and Coach Thistleton, my coxing coach and the coxing coach for the boys.

I was officially confused.

Godwin closed the door behind him, and smiled. 'Hi Kate, thanks for coming.'

'No problem. Happy to.'

Again, I called up Will's words that this was nothing bad, before I spiralled into another panic assuming I was about to get reamed out for clashing oars and losing our race last weekend.

That would definitely class as bad.

Coach Stephens sat on the edge of the desk. 'We've been very impressed with you, Kate. Very impressed. For a first-year coxswain who's never been along the Tideway before you're as competent as anyone who's spent years rowing there.'

I swallowed, thickly, 'Thank you, Coach.'

'Even last weekend showed a level of guts I've not seen in a while, and with some intensive training and discipline you'll make a world-class coxswain.'

I ran my palms along my leggings, but it wasn't helping the churning in my gut, and muttered my thanks again.

'Okay, you're probably wondering what you're doing here,' started Coach Westcott.

I chuckled lightly, 'You could say that.'

'Well, we've run into a slight issue. Do you know Mike Short?'

I nodded as my brows knotted, 'Blue Boat cox? Yeah, sure.'

'Good, well you might not have heard but he contracted mumps over Christmas, and he's still in hospital.'

I gasped, 'Oh, I hadn't. That sucks, I hope he's better soon.'

'He's out of the woods and they're saying he'll make a speedy recovery. But he won't be fit enough by March for the Boat Race.'

My eyes widened as I realized why they'd called me and I breathed a sigh of relief; I felt kind of honoured about it. I wasn't sure I was qualified to advise on the boys' cox seeing as I hadn't spent much time with them, but I'd still watched some of their training sessions and been impressed by a couple.

'What about Rich Blackley? I saw him compete last week and his boat won by a length; they were behind until the last hundred meters. It was an awesome finish.'

Westcott nodded, 'Yes, we've considered Blackley, but he's not ready for Blue Boat.'

'Could he take Goldie and you move up James Deyton to Blue Boat cox?'

Westcott leaned forward, steepling his fingers as he did so. 'It was a possibility, but James has got the Goldie crew to an amazing place, they're syncing perfectly in training and in races. We don't want to risk the upset of two boats if we move him to start over when we'll certainly win with Goldie if we leave him where he is.'

I sighed, sinking a little in my chair as I did, 'I can have a think for you, and let you know if anyone comes to mind.'

'Oh, we don't need that.' Coach Stephens shifted where his ass was sitting on the desk. 'We've already got a solution.'

'Oh,' I replied, 'well, let me know what I can help with.'

Coach Westcott smiled, and it occurred to me that I hadn't ever really seen him smile. It was kind of nice, beat him shouting anyway.

'You can help by coxing Blue Boat.'

He sat back and stared at me. I blinked, my head moving from Stephens, to Godwin and then to Thistleton. They were all wearing the same expressions of mild amusement while they waited for Westcott's words to sink in.

'Excuse me, could you repeat that?'

'Yes, you've been promoted to Blue Boat coxswain. You'll be training under me and Coach Thistleton moving forward.'

'But . . . but . . .' I stopped, unsure what I was trying to say. Or whether it was appropriate to refuse. But also, what the holy crap was going on? 'Sorry, I don't understand. How can I cox the men's boat?'

'The same way you cox the women's boat, I'd hope.'

'But Coach . . .'

'There's nothing in the rule book to say women can't cox the men's boat, or vice versa. I've checked with the rowing federation, and we're good to go.'

'Sir . . .' I began again, but stopped because I really wasn't sure what to say.

'Kate, I'm announcing in today's session that you'll be

training as the new coxswain for Blue Boat. We're impressed by your skill and motivation, and we want you on the blue team.'

'But James Deyton, and what about Becka Jones or Morgan Wright?'

'Morgan's going to take Blondie. As I said, James is already settled well with Goldie and the same goes for Becka Jones in the women's Blue Boat. It's been discussed, and you in the men's Blue Boat gives us the best chance at winning in a clean sweep.'

My mouth opened, then closed. Blue Boat. I was a first-year coxswain with no experience of rowing the Tideway, and I'd been put in charge of securing a victory for Cambridge in the Boat Race.

And it didn't seem like I had a choice in the matter.

'Wait behind after training tonight and we'll go through your new schedule. I've already spoken to Will Norris about additional Tideway sessions so you can get up to speed with the boys. We think we've selected the final eight, so we should be good to go.'

'Okay,' I replied numbly, while actively concentrating on not being sick.

'Congratulations, Kate,' Coach Stephens smiled, 'this is a good thing. You'll win for us this year, I can feel it.'

I got up and walked to the door on autopilot, and headed straight for Imogen in the break room.

'Well, what happened?' she asked as I walked through the door. 'Why do you look like you've seen a ghost?'

I sat there, trying to figure out the words.

'Kate. What's happened?'

I stared at her, 'I've been made coxswain for Blue Boat.'

She blinked several times before her face broke with a wide grin, 'Wow, that's awesome! I'm bummed we won't be racing together, but so happy for you. What happened to Becka Jones?'

I shook my head as I slowly repeated Westcott's words, 'No, not the women's boat. The men's. I'm racing the men's boat. Mike Short is out for the season. They want me to take his place.'

Imogen stood up, then sat down again and stared hard at me. 'Blue Boat? Men's Blue Boat?'

I nodded, 'Yep.'

In fairness to her it took less time for her to register what I'd said than it had for me to hear it, but it came eventually.

'Holy shit, Asters. Blue Boat!' she screeched, then her face fell with a loud gasp and she dropped into the chair. 'You're going against Oz.'

'I know.' I nodded slowly, my voice barely above a whisper, and doing my best to hold my nerve when my insides were thickening with a tornado of anxiety. 'Will said the news wasn't bad. But this is way worse than bad.'

Imogen stared at me, for the first time struggling to find words.

The bubble I'd been living in since Christmas had well and truly burst, letting the January blues rush right in.

Except they were the Cambridge Blues.

And I had no idea how to beat them.

21. Arthur

(A not-so-knight in dark-blue armour)

'Marshy . . .' I called out, spotting Pete a hundred paces ahead up the path as we all left the boathouse following a gruelling training session. We were ten weeks out from the Boat Race and my muscles were feeling it. 'MARSH. WAIT UP.'

He spun around, and even from this distance I could see the frown lines which had become permanent over the last few months. In fact, he hadn't been his usual buoyant self for a while.

Every morning we'd trained together, I'd taken his instruction, listened to him and watched him, but something had been off. He'd been short tempered more than usual, and since term had restarted I'd caught him slamming his locker on more than one occasion, *and* he'd opted out of drinks last Saturday night – something almost unheard of.

'Hey,' he removed one of his ear buds, 'what do you want?'

I shifted my backpack onto my opposite shoulder, and ignored the annoyance in his tone. 'Hey mate, just checking in on you. Haven't spoken to you properly in a while, so I wanted to see if you were okay.'

'I'm fine.' Pete frowned and began walking again, but

with our height difference it didn't take me any effort to keep up with him.

'Really? Because you don't seem fine. You seem like you're pissed off with the world, and have been for a while.'

His eyes narrowed at me, but he didn't slow his pace. 'Oz, I'm fine. You don't need to follow me home. I'm not a kid.'

'You're not fucking fine, so I'll keep walking next to you until you spill, because something is eating you and it's not going to do you any good to keep it bottled up.'

He stopped dead and dropped his bag on the ground with a heavy sigh. We were next to a bench, so I took the opportunity to sit.

I stayed there, looking at him and waiting. A couple of the guys from training walked past us, but they must have sensed we were in the middle of a conversation because they simply nodded and left us to it. When Pete finally looked at me, it was like someone had carved deep sorrow into his features. Grief, almost. As he took a seat next to me, his face fell into his hands.

'My parents are getting a divorce,' he began, almost whispering. 'They told me a couple of months ago, but they only told my younger sister at Christmas, because she's been travelling, and they didn't want her to fly home early. She came home, excited to be spending Christmas together, and they told her the morning after she landed. It was the only day my dad was in the house, because then he fucked off skiing.'

I waited to see if he had anything else to add, but he remained silent. I put my hand on his shoulder.

'Oh, mate, I'm so sorry. That fucking sucks, I know. You should have told me sooner, especially as I know exactly what you're going through.'

'Yeah, thanks. I'm sorry I didn't. I thought you've had enough on your plate and I didn't want to add to it. At least my parents' divorce hasn't been documented in the international media,' he laughed dryly.

'You should count yourself lucky then.' I smirked, making him laugh again, though we both knew there was nothing funny about it. 'Seriously though, it's shit. I get it and I'm so sorry. Did you know it was going to happen?'

He shook his head, 'No, that's the thing. I always thought they were totally in love with each other. But turns out they've been faking it since Sophie went to boarding school and they realized they had nothing in common but us. Fucking award-winning acting, I'm telling you.'

I put my arm around his shoulder and pulled him in for a hug. 'This was the first Christmas without my dickhead father too. Not that it's the same situation, but it will get easier, I know that.'

'Yeah. I'm just so pissed at them both. I can see the logic in them waiting, but they should have just fucking told us when it happened. Instead of years of lies. I've spent the past couple of months trying to figure out what was true and what wasn't.' He leaned forward, resting his elbows on his knees. 'I'm sorry I've been a moody fucker recently, I didn't realize how bad it was.'

'If it helps, I don't think many of the guys have noticed. But I get to see your pretty face up close every morning, and it's definitely not been as smiley.' I nudged him hard, but at least I got a genuine laugh out of him. 'You've also not been taking the piss out of Charlie quite as much. That's what really made it obvious.'

'Yeah. Thanks, mate.'

'Any time, Marshy. Any time.' I followed him to standing and grabbed my backpack, only to feel it vibrating.

Pulling out my phone it was the one person I never wanted to miss a chance to speak to. I looked at Pete, 'Hey, I've got to take this. I'll come and find you later though, I can bring some steaks over, and you can cook them.'

'I appreciate that,' he grinned. 'But I can't tonight, I need to finish my chem paper.'

'Another time. I mean it, I'm here to talk about divorcing parents whenever you want it, I'm the expert right now. You can call me twenty-four seven.'

He offered me up a nod and a sad smile, and took off while I sat down on the bench again.

'Hey! How's my favourite girl?' I asked as her face came into view, except she wasn't smiling like I'd expected her to be. Wasn't smiling at all. Her face was blotchy and red from what looked like a fuck ton of crying. 'Katey, baby, babe! What's wrong? What's happened? Who's made you cry?'

I could feel my heart pounding like I was back on the rowing machines, especially when the tears started up again after she gave a loud sniff.

'Everything,' was all she wailed.

'I'll call you back.' I stood up and took off at a full sprint for home, more specifically my car.

*

I pulled the rim of my cap farther down and yanked the door open just as the girl on the other side swiped her pass to exit.

'Thanks,' she muttered, staring up at me, but by that point I was already running down the corridor for the stairs to the first floor.

Kate wasn't much better than when I'd put the phone down two hours ago, though the surprise of me bursting through the doors did dry her eyes for a second. The eyes of the girl on the floor next to her – the one Brooks had a massive crush on, and I could never remember the name of – bulged wide, and her hand flew to her chest.

'Christ. Make an entrance why don't you?'

'Sorry,' I mumbled, compensating by closing the door as quietly as possible behind me.

'Don't worry,' the girl stood up, collecting a pile of tissues next to her and throwing them in the bin, 'I'll be across the hall if you need anything.'

She bent and gave Kate a kiss on the cheek, whispering something as she did so.

'Thanks,' I nodded to her as she left, and I turned the lock behind her.

Kate's tears started up again as soon as I pulled her onto my lap.

'Hey . . .' I wrapped my arms around her as tightly as I could without cutting off her air supply, 'hey, tell me what's wrong.'

'You don't . . . always . . . have to come over . . . when I'm crying.' She sobbed through each word.

'It's only the second time,' I smoothed my hands over her hair, 'and when you call me and you're crying I'm coming over. I haven't seen you in five days as it is, and I've missed you.'

The sobs got louder, so I wasn't sure if that had been the wrong or right thing to say.

'Now are you going to tell me, or do I have to guess?'

She moved back from my chest, though didn't shift off my lap entirely, and I used the sleeve of my sweater to wipe her tear-stained face.

'I had to go and see Coach Westcott today, you know, the men's coach?' She hiccupped. I glanced around until I spied a glass of water on her desk and reached for it.

'Yes, I know him,' I nodded, while she took a sip.

'Coach Stephens was there with both the coxing coaches.'

'Okay . . .' I wasn't quite sure where this was going, but it was either that she hadn't made the Boat Race crew – which is what she'd been thinking anyway – or she had. But neither of those options seemed like it would garner this waterfall level of tears. 'What did they want?'

'They've . . . they've . . .' hiccup '. . . named me cox . . .' hiccup '. . . of Blue . . .' hiccup '. . . Boat.'

Another wail of tears barrelled up from inside her and she heaved them out while I was trying to understand what exactly there was to be sad about, because these were definitely sad tears. I was positive.

'You've been made cox for Blue Boat?'

She nodded with a loud sniff, and a long swipe of her sleeve under her nose.

'Wow. Yankee, baby. That's incredible, congratu-fucking-lations. I'm so fucking proud of you!' The kiss I planted on her cheek was loud and I came away with the taste of salt on my lips, 'Holy shit, that's fantastic. Babe, why are you upset about it?'

The hiccups continued, 'Because I . . . don't want . . . to race against you.'

'Why would you be racing against . . .' I frowned, and then her words sank in, 'wait, you're coxing the men's Blue Boat? Is that what you're saying?'

She nodded, and dissolved into another fit of tears.

Blue Boat. Holy shit. That was huge, and a massive honour.

I knew she was good, better than good, I'd seen it that day on the river. But, Blue Boat; it was *the* boat. It was everything. However, I still couldn't see what would warrant this much crying, and if she continued any longer she'd need electrolytes to stop her getting dehydrated.

'Babe, take a breath,' I kissed her temple, resting my lips there until I felt her pulse slowing, 'tell me what happened.'

'There wasn't anyone else suitable for the men's and the coaches have been impressed with me. I have to do a week of training with the boys, but they already named me in tonight's meeting, so I don't think I have a choice.'

'Why would you want a choice? This is huge.'

'I know!' she almost shouted, sniffing hard again. 'What if I fuck up?'

'Why would you fuck up?' I asked, but she only sniffed her response. 'They're not going to have given this to you if they thought you'd fuck up. It's too important. If they've given it to you it's because they think you're the best chance at winning. Westcott's an amazing coach, he knows what he's talking about.'

She dropped her head, while mumbling something I didn't catch, and I tilted her chin back up until she was looking at me.

'I don't want to race against you.'

'Why? It'll be so fun. And this way one of us will win, so we'll definitely have a reason to celebrate.'

'But you've told me all about your tactics and what Marshy does to be aggressive . . .'

'Katey, babe, it's fine. It's better than fine, now I'll get to see your face when I'm in my seat and it'll power me forward.' I grinned, though only fifty per cent of how much I really wanted to grin. I thought the full hundred might tip her over the edge again and she'd only just stopped crying. She wasn't seeing the funny side of this situation the same way I was. 'Has something else upset you? There are a lot of tears for something you should be happy about.'

'There's something else.' She took a deep breath, and another big gulp of her water. 'You know Mary Heston, the women's president?'

I nodded. As much as I liked Will, Mary Heston was one of those type-A, overly ambitious pains in the arse who needed to control every minute of every day. It was exhausting just being around her, which unfortunately due to Will being part of the British Rowing squad, I'd had to endure too much for my liking over the summer.

'Yeah, Will Norris' girlfriend. Why?'

'She came to see me today, she had pictures of us together from Christmas and accused me of telling you all our training secrets. She kind of threatened me with my scholarship, and this was before she found out I'd been moved to Blue Boat. I'm scared she'll tell someone, then I'll get kicked out of Cambridge.'

If Kate hadn't been sitting on my lap I'd have jumped up in outrage; as it was my blood hit a steady simmer, and it took me a second to control the anger in my voice and the grind in my jaw.

'You're not going to get kicked out of Cambridge because I'm your boyfriend.' My hands were slowly running up and down her leg, initially to calm her, but it was working to calm me too. 'For one thing, the Boat Race and your degree are totally separate. For another, she doesn't have the power. It's also completely allowed, people from Oxbridge date all the time.'

'Mary doesn't like me, she's made it clear she wants me off the crew because of us, and what if she tells someone, and they agree that I've been discussing our tactics? Then what if you win? Then it'll really look like I have. It's different when you're on the rowing crews.'

'We are capable of winning without your help, you know,' I teased, running my nose along her jawline. She smelt like the rose garden at home after a heavy rainstorm, and I wanted to wrap myself around her and never let go. I also wanted to remove the panic that had her heart racing like she'd sprinted five miles.

'It's not funny. I'm on a rowing scholarship. If they kick me off the squad for this then I can't stay at Cambridge. I'll lose my visa. I'll have to go home,' she sniffed.

With that sobering thought I made a mental note to move Mary Heston to the top of my list of things I needed to deal with. Whatever box she'd jumped out from, I would ensure she got back in.

'Babe, I promise us dating is not going to cause issues for your visa, or uni work. Please stop stressing.' I hugged her tighter. 'We have two months until the race is over, and then we can stop sneaking around. I can't fucking wait, either.'

Kate looked up at me. The tears had turned her green eyes a deep shade of emerald, set off by how bloodshot they were. 'Oz, I don't think we can stop sneaking around straight after. Everyone's going to be talking, and they'll think one of us will have cheated.'

'Let them talk.'

'I don't want to let them talk.' She shook her head so hard a tear flew out and hit my shirt. 'I can't let anything jeopardize my scholarship. I have six years here. And you'll still be at Oxford.'

I did not want to start this argument again, nor did I want to have us sneaking around for a second longer than necessary. The entire situation was giving me a headache as it was.

'Babe, I love you. It'll be okay, I promise. I'll speak to Will.'

But she shook her head. 'No, please don't. It'll make it worse. I don't need my boyfriend fighting my battles.'

'Kate . . .'

'No,' she snapped. 'No. I don't want to think about it any more. We can talk about it later, please just stay and kiss me.'

'Okay. That I can do.' I brushed a strand of hair away from her eyes, wishing I could also brush away the worry and sadness from them too, and surrounded her mouth with mine until she softened against me.

I might not have been able to reassure her that this wasn't as big a problem as she thought, but as I pulled her sweater over her head I was about to have a damn good try at making her forget about it instead.

22. Kate

(From bad to worse)

'On my command. Hands on the boat.'

All eight boys followed my directions; they were so in sync with each other you'd think we'd been working together for years, instead of less than two weeks.

'Up to the waist. Ready . . . Up.'

I watched another seamless transition, and the boat was lifted high above their shoulders. Wrapping up my coxbox and headset, I followed them away from the water, shouting further instructions until the Blue Boat was rested safely in the trailer and ready to head back to Cambridge.

'Nice one, Asters,' Will Norris called over to me from the bench where he was lacing up a dry pair of sneakers. 'What was our final time?'

'I'll reveal all once we're on the bus,' I replied. 'How did it feel?'

'Quick. The second time around I think was the quickest.' He grinned, 'Was it? It was, wasn't it?'

I held my mouth in a straight line, not wanting to give anything away, and walked past him and a couple of the other guys pulling on dry clothes, and made my way to the changing room to do the same. It was so tempting to get underneath a steaming-hot shower, but we'd been given a five-minute turnaround to get our things together and be on the bus, and I wanted more than five minutes in a shower. I needed more than five minutes.

It was so cold this morning it would take me a few hours to thaw out. I thought I'd easily survive a winter in England, given the ones on the east coast were enough to freeze the breath from your lungs, but I'd been wrong. I'd taken to sleeping in the clothes I would wear to training so I could get out of bed and not have to bare a single unnecessary inch of skin to the frigid air. And while I tugged on more thermals I'd question my sanity, as I looked longingly at my warm, cosy bed.

The only thing that had kept me going the past two weeks was our results from the Tideway training. Since I'd taken over as cox for the men's Blue Boat, our mornings had begun earlier – leaving at five a.m. (yes, puke) – for the drive to London, so we could practise. It had taken me a week not to feel guilty about dragging them all out of bed, but they hadn't complained once.

Every morning we'd take to the River Thames in the dark, and row the Boat Race course over and over, and Will Norris had been correct; they were getting faster.

Much faster.

We'd knocked off a minute and thirty seconds from their time set at the beginning of last week – my first day out on the water with them. This morning, they completed the Boat Race course in their second-fastest time yet.

Most of the boys were still sitting on the benches by the time I made it out to the bus, even though Coach Westcott was still shouting for everyone to hurry up and get on it. Something else I'd learned in the past two weeks: the boys set their own schedule.

'Asters, give us the time,' called James Potting, the Cambridge number three, who was yet to put his sneakers on.

'Get on the bus and I will,' I shouted back, jogging out of the boathouse and into the warmth of the Cambridge bus.

I settled into my seat halfway down, pulling my thick dryrobe over me like a comforter. If I was lucky I'd get another hour's sleep before we arrived back, maybe longer. Even though we had all been told to hurry up, and we all had to get back for morning class, it was still another five minutes before we were ready to set off.

'Finally,' barked Coach Westcott, jerking me awake. 'Everyone here?'

Will Norris stood up, taking a quick roll call, 'All present and correct.'

I groaned quietly as the bus lurched forward and set off down the narrow path away from the river, and out of London. As I had every morning when we'd trained here, I watched the big flag flying on top of the boathouse opposite – the one Oz had taken me to – and made a small wish the second before it disappeared out of sight.

My wish this morning was the same as all my wishes had been recently.

To make it through the race. To succeed. To win.

To try not to think about the fact that me winning meant Oz losing.

Or if Oz won, it meant I'd lost. And if I lost, there was a good chance I'd lose more than a race.

I'd also tried not to think about Mary Heston, but since her performance in my dorm room and her not-so-veiled threat about my scholarship, it was nearly all I'd been

333

thinking about, even if Oz did keep telling me how ridiculous I was being. In fact, the more I tried not to think about it, the more I did.

I'd done my best to avoid her as much as possible. While my training timetable had been flipped because I now trained with the boys, we still had weekend sessions together, and after it had been announced I'd be coxing for the men's crew she had very strongly voiced her opinion that I wasn't good enough for the role. Thankfully, it was something none of the coaches agreed with, though it didn't stop the small voice in my head from wondering if perhaps she was right.

I'd given up trying to figure out whether I was more determined for us to win to prove her wrong, than I was to *win* win because it was my first-ever Boat Race. It was something I'd questioned every morning after a hard ninety minutes on the river. Thankfully, I was wrenched from today's impending doom spiral by Coach Westcott's not-so-dulcet tones.

'Excellent work this morning,' he barked. 'We're still eight weeks out from the race, so I don't want to get any hopes up, but I think we can be quietly confident in a victory again this year.'

Several whoops sounded out from the boys sitting on the back seat.

'Where's Kate?' Coach asked, and I raised my hand, sitting up straighter.

'Here.'

'Want to share the times this morning, let the boys out of their misery?'

Eight more sets of eyes turned to me, along with Coach Westcott's two assistant coaches, Thistleton and his assistant, plus Barker the team physio who'd been joining our early mornings on the river.

I grinned, flipping my notepad open.

'The first go around we took the course in eighteen minutes dead.' I glanced around and waited to see if anyone would react, but nothing. I'm not sure I even saw a blink. 'The fourth and final session was raced in seventeen minutes and forty-three seconds.' I paused again, nothing. 'The third go around we did it in sixteen minutes and thirty-eight seconds, but the second time we raced our time was sixteen minutes and thirty-two seconds.'

There was a sharp inhale of silence right before a deafening cheer which echoed around the steamed-up windows as the boys high-fived. Even the rarely seen smile of Coach Westcott stayed put.

'Holy shit,' cried Ben Roache, the number five seat, 'that's only thirteen seconds slower than the fastest time ever set in the history of the Boat Race – by Cambridge, of course!'

'Everybody quiet and sit down,' yelled Westcott again, even though no one was out of their seats. Everyone stopped talking. 'As I was saying, you can be quietly confident but no more. There are sixty-eight days between now and the race, and we all know that's plenty of time for things to go wrong. We must stay tight and vigilant.'

We all knew Coach was right, but it didn't stop several of the boys rolling their eyes as they settled back into their seats for a quick nap. I was about to do the same except my legs were knocked off the seat next to me by Will Norris, who sat down.

'How're you doing?' he asked.

'Good, thanks,' I nodded. 'How 'bout you?'

'Same.' He tilted his chin up to where Coach was. 'Nothing like a Westcott pep talk, right?'

'Yeah, right. Must be effective though; he's been here forever.'

I rested my head on the seat and waited for Will to say whatever it was he'd come over here to say. Although he was president of the men's club we hadn't talked much since I'd been brought onto the crew, and while I hadn't gone out of my way to talk to him, I'd had the impression that perhaps he'd been doing the same.

Understandable given what had happened in my dorm room.

'How are you finding the training?'

I turned my head with a broad smile. 'Even with my alarm going off at four fifteen, I'm loving it. It's so awesome to be working with you guys, you really know how to power through the water. I love having a front row seat for it.'

'We're glad you could come,' he smiled back. 'I don't want to speak ill of the ill, but the results you've got from us have been amazing. Westcott might want us to stay quietly confident, but I have full confidence we're going to smash Oxford.'

I rolled my mouth into a hard line, 'I think I agree with you.'

In my periphery I could see him nodding to himself, before he spoke again, quieter this time, 'How's Oz getting on?'

I took a deep breath, filling my lungs with much needed fresh oxygen while I thought about my answer.

'We don't talk about training, we like to keep it to ourselves. Can't be trading secrets now, can we?'

I didn't even have to lie. We really didn't talk about it any more. It was something I'd found harder than I thought I would, and Oz was the same. Neither of us had realized how much we relied on our daily conversations around training and preparation. The reassurances we were both doing a good job, or the advice we doled out following a shit day. I missed his stories about Charlie, Brooks and Marshy, and I had none to swap because I hadn't trained with Imogen and Hannah for two weeks.

Our conversations now revolved around school, him getting another First, and me falling asleep in my neurobiology lecture and being sent out.

But not talking about rowing was nothing compared to how much I missed him. I thought after the first week it would become easier, but it was quite the opposite. Ten seconds of silence stretched out between us before Will spoke again, 'I'm sorry about the other week. I'm sorry about Mary . . .' he trailed off.

I smiled softly. 'Don't worry about it, it's not your fault. And you shouldn't be apologizing for your girlfriend.'

'Well, actually, she's not my girlfriend any more. We broke up.'

I spun around to face him properly, 'What? When did that happen?'

'Last week.'

'I'm really sorry, Will. I hope that wasn't because of . . . you know . . . this.'

He shook his head. 'No, it wasn't. It's been on the cards for a while, I just hadn't found the right moment. I should be thanking you for helping with that.'

'Is she okay?'

He shrugged. 'I'm sure she's fine. Probably too distracted with how to win the race.'

'Yeah,' I chuckled, 'she's very determined.'

'Got that right. Anyway, I just wanted to say I'm sorry, and I'm glad you're on our crew.' He stood up to go back to his seat, then paused. 'Oz is a decent guy. I enjoy rowing with him.'

'I agree.' I smiled up at him.

Since I'd been sitting down, my hands had stayed warm clasped around my phone in the little pouch on the front of my hoodie, and I pulled it free.

Kate: *Hey handsome <3*

Oz: *Hello my little American, how was training? (just simply asking after your welfare not for insider intel)*

Kate: *It was good. I miss you*

Oz: *Only one more sleep until we're together. I'll drive over as soon as training is done*

Kate: *You better hurry that cute ass over*

Kate: *ps. I have a biology test the next day, can you quiz me?*

Oz: *I'll quiz you on my biology . . .*

Oz: *I've got a special bonus question for you*

Kate: *Is the answer 'your dick?'*

Oz: *Might be*

Kate: *See . . . you're an excellent teacher*

I shut my phone off with a quiet chuckle, and peered out of the window. By my calculation I had forty-five minutes before we arrived back, which was just enough time for a power nap.

I was towel-drying my hair when Imogen and Hannah flung my door open and flopped down on the bed and desk chair respectively.

'How did you make it back before us when you were so much further away?'

'Not sure,' I replied, picking up my brush in an attempt to rid myself of the tangled mass on top of my head. 'You're late back though.'

'No thanks to Mary Heston,' Hannah grumbled, biting into an energy bar. 'Her mood's been getting worse and worse, she was positively foul this morning. Urgh, I wish you were still in practice with us. It sucks without you.'

'Say that again?' I asked, yanking my brush through a particularly knotty knot.

'She screamed at Ivy, then got called into Coach's office and we all had to stay behind.'

'Who screamed at Ivy?'

'Mary Heston.'

'She's probably upset about Will.' I yanked again.

'Why?' asked Imogen, who was now under my comforter and looked ready to fall back asleep. She couldn't though, we had Professor Hecherty's chemistry class at ten a.m. and we always stopped for second breakfast on the way.

I stopped brushing. Was I about to deliver some news that Imogen was yet to hear? 'Will told me that they'd broken up. Happened last week.'

'What?!' she screeched. 'No way!'

'Wow,' added Hannah, 'no wonder she's been on the rampage, and before the Boat Race as well. That's really ruined her plans to be crowned winning president with him.'

'Yeah, poor Will. I feel like she'd make his life a misery.'

'Yeah, he didn't seem that cut up about it.'

'Still, I would not want to be on her bad side. She's certainly been making our lives hard enough and we didn't even do anything. What else did he say?'

'Nothing really.' I shrugged and picked up the blow dryer, shutting it off almost immediately when Hannah started waving her hands around, and pointing to my cell.

'Hello, Kate's phone,' she answered, 'and who may I say is calling?'

She passed it to me with a shrug, holding her hand over the speaker. 'Professor Hull? Weird.'

Imogen bolted upright. 'What? Why would she be calling?'

'She? That's not a female voice,' frowned Hannah.

I looked at the screen as I took it, but it was a private number. And no one ever called me, except the two girls in front of me, Oz and now Phoebe. Plus my mom, and it was too early for her to be awake.

'Hello?'

'Is this Kate Astley?' said a voice that wasn't Professor Hull's. Hannah was correct, it was a man. A man whose tone immediately froze my bones.

'Who is this?'

'I'm calling about your boyfriend, Arthur Osbourne-Cloud, and how you feel about racing against him in this year's Boat Race. He's president of Oxford, and you're cox for the Cambridge men's. It'll be quite the rivalry this year. Do you think you're going to beat him?'

'Who is this?' I repeated.

'How did you meet?'

'Who is this?'

'Is it true you've been training together? Swapping tips in bed, have you?'

I hit call end and my cell thudded as it dropped to the floor.

'Asters, why's Professor Hull calling you?' asked Imogen again, now sitting upright. 'What did she want?'

'I told you, that wasn't a woman on the phone, unless she's got a deep voice,' repeated Hannah. 'Kate . . . who was that?'

But I was still staring at my cell by my feet, and trying to figure out what had just happened.

'Kate? Are you okay?'

'Kate, who was on the phone?'

I looked up at the girls, then back down at the cell like it might suddenly grow tentacles and attack me. 'I . . . I don't know.'

'What did he want?'

'Um . . .' I stepped away from the offending hardware, 'he was asking about Oz and how I felt about racing against him.'

I glanced up again to find Imogen and Hannah staring at me with their mouths open.

'What the fuck?' spat Imogen.

I wrapped my arms tightly around myself; it was a poor

attempt to stem the chill seeping under my skin and leaving a cascade of goosebumps. 'Who would call to ask that? He asked if we'd been swapping training tips in bed.'

'Ew. What? That's gross.'

Hannah picked the cell off the floor. 'It was a private number. We can't call it back.'

I stood staring, trying to figure out what was going on, but the swirls of anxiety ricocheting around my belly were too distracting for me to figure out anything. I think my chest had started caving in.

'This isn't good. He knew about me and Oz. He called him my boyfriend. How would he know?'

Neither of the girls had the answer I was looking for, or any answer at all. Then my cell started buzzing again and we all jumped.

'Kate, it's Oz.' Hannah held it on her palm, and I took it with a shaking hand.

'Hello?'

'Kate? Katey, babe?'

'Oz?'

'Babe, are you okay?'

I took a deep breath, 'I don't know, someone just called me.'

'I know, I got called too.'

'Oz, who was it?'

He took a second to answer, and I wasn't sure I wanted to know. 'It was one of the tabloid newspapers.'

'What? How . . . how'd they get my number?'

'I don't know.'

'Oz, he asked about how I felt racing against you as my boyfriend. People know we're dating.'

'I know, but it was bound to happen some time, right?' he replied, but from the sharp intake of air he heard me take he knew it wasn't what I'd wanted to hear. 'Katey, I promise it'll be okay. I'll fix this, babe.'

On any other occasion Oz's unwavering reassurance would have calmed me, but even he couldn't disguise the panic or the volcanic levels of anger shaking his tone.

23. Arthur

(At this rate, I should just hand over my credit card)

Not only had I not fixed it, it had got worse. Much worse.

'Come in.'

I pushed open the door and slipped into Coach Lassiter's office where I'd been summoned straight from training. He threw his reading glasses onto the desk and gestured to the empty chair in front of it.

'Oz. Sit down.'

I did as I was told. I knew why he'd called this meeting, but from the bordering-on-furious look he was staring at me with I had zero clue what he was about to say. I removed my baseball cap and ran my fingers through my hair, trying hard not to tug the ends out as I did.

'Coach?'

He leaned across his desk and laced his fingers together, but his face softened. 'How're you doing?'

How was I doing? It seemed to be a simple enough question, though the answer was anything but. I could see today's newspaper neatly folded in the wastepaper basket, and knew he was expecting more than a 'fine', because today's edition contained another story about Kate and me, alongside pictures of us training with our teams, older photos of me with other women I'd rowed with, and rumoured relationships I'd had, and predictably these had

344

all been linked back to my father and his predilection for a workplace relationship.

Therefore, 'fine' would be the answer I'd have given a week ago.

A huffed, dismissive 'fine' after I'd spoken to Kate as she'd sobbed down the phone to me, after the picture of us in the Lamb and Lamppost, following the Santa run, had been blown up from the background of someone's Instagram and printed in the tabloid papers. If it had been a different time, I would have claimed it was a great picture, maybe even framed it – a candid shot of her in my arms, while I was kissing her cheek and wearing a broad grin, as we both laughed loudly at something Alex had said – but instead it was spoiled forever.

A week ago I'd have said 'fine' but I have shit to deal with now, shit I don't want to deal with, nor have the time for. But shit nonetheless. Shit tied up in a neat little parcel of baggage, which inevitably followed behind wherever I went.

Except, over the past week, since the newspapers had reported their story about the President of the Oxford University Boat Club not only dating the American-born coxswain for the Cambridge Blue Boat but going head-to-head against her in the Boat Race at the end of March, 'fine' had sunk quicker than a lead weight dropped from London Bridge.

Instead, a slow news week had been blown apart by a new spin on a centuries' old-rivalry.

'I've been better, sir,' I replied truthfully.

'Yes, I've no doubt you have, and we've all had better weeks. But I wouldn't be doing my job properly if I didn't ask whether your head is still in the game. If you're still capable of leading the crew and representing this university.'

I took a deep breath, reading between the lines of unspoken words.

Was I distracted?

Could I still win the race?

Where did my allegiance lie?

The answers were yes, yes and with Kate. But that didn't mean I was about to give up my presidency. My seat on the boat was the only place I felt calm, the only place my head cleared enough for me to think about the task at hand. The only place I was free from distraction.

'I am, Coach. I'm not going anywhere.'

'Because after what happened on Wednesday . . .'

He left his sentence hanging in the air, but we both knew what the rest of it was and he was testing to see if my anger was still raging enough that I'd take a cricket bat to something else.

On Wednesday, Will Norris had called to tell me about the guy who'd followed their Tideway training in a speedboat, and driven so close to them that an oar became mangled. The wake from the propeller had been powerful enough that most of the crew were tipped into the water.

Kate had been so distraught she couldn't speak, and thus my anger – the one I'd inherited from my father – had made its presence well known. Not only had I not been there to protect her, I wasn't there to comfort her either. I had a lot of property to replace, including a section of the locker rooms where the doors were now so dented they wouldn't close properly.

My fists clenched. 'Coach, that guy nearly capsized the Cambridge boat during practice. He had no business being out on the water. He put everyone in danger to get a picture of Kate, which wouldn't have happened were it not for me. This entire situation is my fault, so yes, I was angry . . .' I stopped, taking another deep breath. It was deep enough for my heart rate to slow so that I didn't feel the need to smash something else. 'I'm still angry. But as long as the Cambridge crew and Kate are safe, then I'll be okay. Neither of us is giving up our spot in the race. We've both earned them fair and square.'

He stared at me, and I used the time to calm my heart by several more beats. My resting heart rate usually sat at forty-seven bpm, and to get it to the point where it felt like my chest was about to cave in took a lot of effort. Or the tabloid media, evidently.

'Coach Westcott and I had a call with the Thames Coastguard this morning, and it's been decided that from now up to race day all training for Cambridge and Oxford will be supervised by the Marine Police Unit.'

My eyes widened at his words and my surprise from his announcement also had me sitting up straighter, 'Oh, that's good to hear. Thank you. Thanks Coach, I appreciate it.'

'We also have campus security on the boathouse and stationed here at Fleming,' he added, and if he'd still been wearing his glasses, he'd be peering over them at me. 'It should deter any unwanted visitors, but try and keep a low profile over the next few weeks, will you?'

'Yes, Coach,' I nodded. 'I'm only at the house, lectures

or at training anyway. It's other people who think my life is way more interesting than it is.'

I noticed a small twitch at the corner of his mouth, but it disappeared before it turned into a full smile at my weak joke. 'Very well.'

'Was there anything else?'

'No, you can go.'

'Thank you, Coach. I'm truly sorry about all this. If there's anything I can do to help, please let me know.'

'It's not your doing, Osbourne. This is not your fault, nor your responsibility. You're a good kid, you work harder than most I've seen come through these doors, and you don't deserve it. We needed some new lockers anyway,' he added with a wide grin, picking up a stack of papers, which had been thrown into one of the trays on his desk. 'I have to say, it's a first for me. The Boat Race doesn't normally make it off the sports pages, especially seven weeks out.'

'Glad I could be of service,' I replied, making sure my tone was as droll as possible, and stood up.

Coach was already sifting through more of his in-tray by the time I left to find Brooks and Charlie waiting for me outside the door. I should have known they'd be there. Even though we were all going home together, and I was driving, over the last week they'd turned into my shadows.

Their presence had helped me keep a semblance of calm while my anger slowly bubbled under the surface and ran through my veins. They'd also been the ones to hold me back before I smashed up the entire boathouse.

'How did that go?' asked Charlie, turning to walk down

the corridor, sticking closer to me than Biscuit, my Labrador.

I shrugged, moving an inch nearer to Brooks on the other side of me. 'Good, I guess. He spoke to Westcott this morning and the coastguard police – or someone – will be supervising all the Tideway training moving forward, for Cambridge and us.'

'Wow,' replied Brooks.

'Yeah, I know. Such a bullshit waste of resources though. They'd be doing something worthwhile if it weren't for me.'

'Nah, they're probably happy you're not smuggling drugs down the river. Nice change of pace for them.'

I scoffed out a small laugh at their attempt to make me feel better.

'Hey,' Charlie nudged me, 'it's not a race without a touch of added drama.'

'Yeah, maybe.' I pushed open the doors to the car park. Aside from Coach's car, plus a couple of the other trainers, the place was empty. Good job none of us had morning lectures today. I threw my keys to Brooks as we got to my car, 'Here, you drive.'

Charlie's face screwed up. 'Why can't I drive? I'm never allowed to drive.'

'Because we're on country lanes not a race track, and you already have six points because you don't seem to know how to use the brake.'

'They were bogus points, and you know it,' he grumbled, opening the back door.

I dialled Kate as soon as Brooks started the engine. The screen cleared and my heart clenched in equal parts happiness and guilt as she came into view. Every time I'd seen her over the past week, the stress of what she was going through because of me had my throat tightening, and for a split second I needed to remind myself how to breathe.

'Hey,' she smiled down the lens, though the sparkle usually present when she saw me had disappeared into the dark circles under her eyes.

'Hey, Yanks.'

Charlie's head appeared between the front seats, 'Hey, Kate.'

She pushed a strand of hair under her beanie, 'Hey, Charlie, how're you doing?'

'Can't complain, can't complain,' he replied, 'how are you? Any more early swimming sessions in the Thames recently?'

If she hadn't smiled at his teasing I'd have turned around and thumped him; instead the tension running along my jaw eased slightly at her light giggles.

'No. Thankfully.'

'Good to hear,' he nodded, and sat back.

I turned the phone back to face me, 'How are you really doing? Are you okay?'

'Yeah, I'm okay,' she shrugged, 'I could live without everyone staring all the time.'

'Has anyone tried to speak to you?'

She shook her head, 'Not really. Imogen scares most people off, so I'm thankful we have all our classes together. She also yells at anyone who looks at us, breathes near us or even attempts to walk in our direction, so in hindsight

350

they might be staring at her. But it feels like I'm always being watched.'

I sighed heavily. I knew that feeling. I hated that feeling. Even after years of eyes following me everywhere, I was yet to get used to it.

It was one thing having to deal with it by myself, but quite another to know I was the cause of someone else going through it, especially someone I loved.

'I'm so sorry, babe. I really am. I'm so sorry I brought this all on you.'

The sadness in her smile was enough to crack my heart open. I desperately wanted to see the dimple reappear, along with the cheeky glint usually present in her eyes. 'It's not your fault. You didn't ask for this either. I didn't realize it would be such a big deal outside of us rowing, that's all. I don't understand why people care so much.'

'It's because you're dating England's number-one heart-throb, and number-two rower. Everyone wants to be you,' called Charlie from the back seat, and once again I wanted to thump him until Kate grinned.

Maybe I should pay him to follow her around and tell jokes. Even his shit ones.

'How was your training this morning?'

'Good, and I spoke to Lassiter after. He told me about the coastguard on the Tideway for all teams.'

'Yeah, they were there this morning. It was helpful,' she started laughing again, though it wasn't her usual loud guffawing I'd become used to, the one where she let out a little snort at the end, 'at least I wasn't the one who nearly sank the boat. Not directly anyway.'

But I laughed with her, even if I was only giving twenty per cent. 'That's true.'

I was about to speak again when her focus drifted to the left of her screen, then back to me. 'I need to go, Imogen's here and we're late for class.'

'Okay babe, I love you. I'm going to drive over after training later, I haven't seen you since last week.'

It was brief, but she hesitated before she answered. I wasn't one to read into things, but that hesitation did not make me feel good. Quite the opposite, in fact.

'Okay, see you later.'

The screen went black before I could tell her to have a good day, and before she could say she loved me too, and I found myself scowling into the silence of the car ride analyzing every word she'd just spoken.

'She seems okay, considering,' said Brooks, turning off the lane and onto the main road leading into Oxford.

'I guess.' I scratched through my hair and tugged hard on the ends, as I really thought about it. Maybe 'considering' was all it was that had caused her hesitation. It didn't make me feel any better however. 'Yeah, I guess. She's had a baptism of fire into my life and it's exhausting enough for me to deal with, let alone someone who isn't used to press attention. I should have prepped her for this.'

It dawned on me that on top of her mountain of coursework she was also training for the Boat Race harder than anyone else, because she was so determined not to let the crew down. And now this shit storm had hit because of me. What was the point of being her boyfriend if I was the one she needed protection from?

I didn't want to voice aloud that if I was her, I'd run as far away from me as possible.

I'd never felt so helpless in my life, and the entire situation had me reaching for the Pepto Bismol before my stomach lining dissolved from all the anxiety swirling around.

'Sorry mate, it fucking sucks. You kinda need to be in two places at once right now, really. Just to make sure she's okay.'

'Tell me about it,' I grumbled. 'If only time travel was a real thing.'

Charlie's head popped back through the centre console, 'It is real.'

'Not today it's not, Charles.' Brooks pushed Charlie's head back and quickly glanced at me, then snapped his fingers. 'What about Olly?'

'What about him?'

'He could keep an eye on her.'

I turned to face Brooks. He was still focused on the road, but the eager expression on his face was directed to me.

'Yes. You're fucking right. He could.' I hit the voice activation on the car's speakers, and it only rang once before Olly answered.

'Hey, mate. How're you holding up?'

'Same bullshit, different day. I'm in the car with Charlie and Brooks, and have a favour to ask.'

'Oh yes?'

'Are you busy this week?'

There was a muffle of noise in the background followed by the sound of a door closing. 'I guess it depends on your definition of busy, some of us have less free time than others.'

'Can you keep an eye on Kate?'

'How exactly am I supposed to do that?' he laughed loudly.

'Aren't you used to following women around, Ol?'

'No, Charles. They follow me.'

I held my hand up to silence Charlie before he could snap back; they could banter all they wanted once I'd dealt with my much more urgent issue.

'I don't know, but if she needs to go somewhere outside of her classes can you go with her? She says everyone's staring and right now it's only her and her friend, Imogen . . .'

'Is that the hot one?'

'Yeah, she's smoking,' interrupted Brooks, unnecessarily loudly, before I could answer.

'Then consider me their own personal bodyguard.'

I rolled my eyes. 'Really? You'll do it?'

'Yeah, I know what it's like to be part of your entourage, remember.' He laughed. 'I saw her yesterday as I was leaving Downing, and she didn't look too happy to be outside. Send her my number, and send me the hot one's number too.'

'Thanks Ol. I'll message Kate, but you'll need to do your own dirty work for Imogen.'

'Jeez,' he tutted. 'Do a favour for your best friend and get nothing in return.'

'I'll put in a good word for you. It's the best I can do.'

'You got yourself a deal then,' he chuckled. 'Seriously though, Oz, are you okay?'

'I will be once this fucking race is over, and everyone's got bored with reading about it.'

'Hey Katey, babe. I'll be a couple of hours, I'm just coming out of training and need to shower.'

There was silence on the end of the line when I should have heard some kind of *'yay, can't wait'* or *'get your cute butt over here'* like I usually did.

'Kate?'

'Oz, I don't think you should come tonight.'

I stopped walking; she'd said it so quietly I wasn't sure I'd heard correctly. I hoped I hadn't. 'What?'

'I don't think you should come, it's not a good idea right now.'

'What's happened? Did something else happen?' I blurted. 'Tell me.'

'No, not something else, just a continuation of the same thing, and if someone spots you it will only make things worse.'

I sighed deeply and yanked off my beanie hat. I was suddenly too hot, too tense, too agitated at this whole fucking mess. 'I know, I'm sorry, I'm so sorry. But we haven't seen each other in a week, I miss you.'

'I . . .' the way she paused again made my stomach churn more than it had been, 'I can't tonight. I need some space to wrap my head around what's happening. I know you're used to it, but I'm not and I'm here by myself. If anyone saw you coming to visit it would only create another wave of drama.'

'But Olly's going to look out for you.'

'I don't need Olly looking out for me, I need for people

not to care that we're dating,' she bit out in a tone I'd never heard her use before.

'Kate . . .'

'No, Oz, it's too much right now on top of everything else. The press went to my parents' house today. They knocked on the door. They've been asking around our town about me.' Her voice was getting more and more shrill, in direct contrast to my stomach sinking further and further down. 'My dad . . .'

'I'm sorry,' I whispered again. 'I didn't know.'

'Of course you didn't, and this isn't your fault, it's just . . .'

'A consequence of being with me,' I snapped more harshly than I meant to, but at least she didn't hear the loud crack as my heart started to break.

She took a deep breath. 'Oz, I love you, but . . .'

There was another fucking pause, like I was supposed to fill in the blanks. But I couldn't. Even the thought of what I thought she was saying had my gut churning until I was ready to puke.

'But what, Kate? What are you saying?'

'I just need some space. *We* need some space until the race is over.'

'What's space? What does that mean, you're breaking up with me? Please, Kate.' My voice had taken on her panic. 'Please, please don't. This isn't the answer, I promise you. It'll blow over.'

'It won't blow over!' she shouted so loudly I was convinced the guy walking on the other side of the street could have heard. 'I have six years of studying here, and you're never going to leave Oxford, so, no, it won't fucking blow over. It'll be the same story every Boat Race for the next six years!'

'So it *is* my fault?' I snapped back. 'My fault because I don't want to go into politics? But what about you? It's your six years we're talking about, yet it's obvious to anyone that you don't want to be a doctor.'

'Oz . . .'

Her tone was laced with a warning that I was stepping over the invisible line we'd built around us where we avoided talking about the future, but I was on a roll; the week of helplessness and frustration at putting us in this situation had boiled over. I would take the blame for getting us here, but not for stopping us moving forward. That was on both of us.

'No, Kate. You don't get to say to me that the next six years of our future is in jeopardy because I won't stand up to my father, when you won't tell your parents that you have your own dreams to pursue, instead of Jake's,' I hissed, trying my best to make sure no one could overhear. 'You're keeping your future on hold as much as I am.'

'It's not the same thing, and you know it.'

My teeth gritted at her tone. 'That's the problem though, it is. And I seem to be the only one of us who realizes it.'

'Jake died.' She let out a loud sniff, which hit me straight in the gut.

I swallowed down the lump in my throat. 'Yes, I know. But that doesn't mean you get to put your life on hold in order to live his. You're still alive.'

All I could hear down the phone was her muffled sobs,

each one slicing into my chest like a tiny paper cut. But I could see things clearer now. The call might have started with her breaking up with me, but now I couldn't be certain if perhaps I wasn't breaking up with her. If she didn't want people to be interested in us dating, then we wouldn't date. Simple. And my messy life wouldn't interfere with hers; breaking up was the only solution until I could figure out a more permanent one.

'Kate . . .' I moaned, or maybe sighed. Whatever it was, it felt like her name dragged through my bones. I pressed my palms into my eyes to stem the burning, and wipe away the tears already falling. 'If we can't get through this together, we aren't going to work long term. So, let's call it quits now rather than prolong the inevitable.'

Her shocked gasp did nothing to help repair the shattering in my chest, 'Oz, no.'

'I'm sorry, Katey. I'm sorry for everything.'

'No,' she sobbed; great rasping sobs that made me want to reach down the phone and pull her through it so I could hold her as close as I could get her.

'I have to go.' I hung up before she said another word, and I was spotted crying my eyes out on the cobbled street I was still standing on. The papers would fucking love that.

'I thought you were off to Cambridge,' said Charlie, mashing potatoes, as I stormed into the kitchen ten minutes later heading straight into the pantry to find what I was looking for.

I uncorked the bottle of Glenfiddich single malt with a loud squeak and lifted it to my lips. 'Change of plan.'

The whisky burned all the way down.

It had been a long time since I was so drunk I'd forgotten my name, and I'd just been handed the perfect opportunity to do it again.

Maybe if I drank enough I'd forget Kate's too, but I didn't think there was enough alcohol in the world for that to be possible.

24. Kate

(There's strength in failure. Right? And stepping on
a Lego is painful)

'I got a Third. Another goddamn third grade,' I grumbled
to Imogen as we walked out of the science school. 'I
busted my ass on that paper. I put in extra lab time with
Leo and I still get a goddamn Third.'

'I know you did, I'm sorry.' She put her arm around my
shoulder and hugged me into her. Sometimes I wondered
if this was what it would be like to hug a giraffe.

'What did you get?'

'A First, but only just.' She grimaced. 'You could ask
Professor Vestin for a regrade.'

I shook my head, dropping it as I did, 'No, it's not her,
it's me. This is the third one I've had in a row, and they
weren't all from her. I'm not clever enough, it shouldn't
take me so long to grasp first-year biology, and we're not
even through the year. I don't know if I can cope with
another five. I don't know if I can cope with the rest of
the term, I can't see any way through the coursework.'

'Give yourself a break. You've had a lot going on the past
few weeks, I'm amazed you have any space left in your
brain. You've been training twice as hard as me, you're
clocking more water time and with everything you've been
through with Oz . . .' she added quietly then paused, waiting to see if I'd start crying again, like I had been doing for

the past two weeks whenever his name was mentioned, but I managed to hold it in. 'It's a wonder you haven't imploded, I would have. At least the media has quietened down for the moment.'

'Yeah, for the moment.'

'And I was just getting used to his funny little friend following us around. We won't need him any more. Shame.'

I managed a dry chuckle as we continued walking back to Downing, along the path of trees still waiting for the blossom shoots to appear. Imogen had not taken well to Olly checking up on us, and they'd had more than one very loud, very public argument about it too. But after a guy jumped out of the bushes in front of us as we were heading to class last week, and Olly had promptly thrown him back in, they'd come to a truce.

Thankfully that was the last time anything happened. No one had dialled my cell, no one had been around my parents' house again, no one had interrupted training, and beyond a few small gossip articles, any news about the Boat Race had focused solely on the race itself. I would have asked Oz if he'd had anything to do with it, but he wasn't speaking to me, and I had started to feel foolish for the fuss I'd kicked up. He said it would be fine, and I should have believed him.

I was trying hard not to think about Oz when Imogen mumbled something, and I looked up to find Mary Heston walking toward us. Her head was down so she hadn't spotted us yet, but that only stoked the rage burning in Imogen.

'Hey, Mary, sold any more stories?' Imogen yelled almost in her face as she reached us.

To her credit, Mary didn't even startle. She peered up

361

from her phone, her snub nose crinkled with derision, and simply raised an eyebrow. 'You need to watch who you're talking to.'

'Looks like I'm talking to a back-stabbing witch. Am I wrong?'

Instead of responding to Imogen, Mary glanced over at me. 'You really spend time with the worst people.'

'I'll disagree on that point.' I leaned in closer, no longer intimidated by this girl who used to have me trembling with nerves. Instead, I saw her as the girl who'd brought my current life as I knew it to a crashing halt, the one who'd caused me three weeks of headaches from too much crying, and to lose the first boy I'd ever loved. 'I know it was you.'

'You know nothing. And anything that may or may not have happened was done for the good of the Boat Race. Cambridge is the superior team, and we deserve to be crowned winners. If Oxford wins, it will only cast doubt on how they've won, and I'll report you to the racing federation for cheating.'

I was about to laugh in Mary's face, but Imogen got there first. 'You're insane, Mary. If Oxford wins it's because they rowed better on the day. Training tips aren't going to make any difference if their crew isn't prepared.'

Her eyes narrowed defiantly, but she didn't argue, just scoffed and continued walking.

'I hope you step on a Lego,' I shouted after her.

Imogen threw her head back with a loud snort and a laugh. 'A Lego?'

'Yeah, it would hurt.'

'Brilliant,' she laughed again, 'brilliant. I'm using that next time someone pisses me off.'

'Do you really think she did it?'

'Yes! Or got her friend to sell that picture. She's the worst. No idea what Will Norris ever saw in her,' she added, before quietly asking, 'Have you heard from Oz today?'

I shook my head.

The amusement I'd felt a moment ago had vanished, allowing the sadness to sink back in, not that it ever disappeared; it was always there and I knew full well if I started talking or even thinking about Oz my tears would reappear, but I didn't have time for that today. I had to study, then train again, then study *again*. Instead, I bit down hard on my cheeks to distract me from the heavy tightening in my chest.

It had been gradually getting worse over the past weeks, like a dense fog dragging itself through my body and sticking to my bones. I'd almost gotten used to it, or forgotten it was there, but then it would remind me at the most inopportune times – like the beginning of Tideway practice when I peered up to see my magic flag flying, or when I'd be studying and have to look up a Greek or Latin word instead of messaging Oz for the meaning, and he'd invariably give me the entire origin, and usages. Or like right now.

I rubbed down my throat hoping to loosen the tension.

'I'm sure you will.'

'No, I won't. We've broken up, I haven't heard from

him in two weeks. There's no reason why I would hear from him today.'

'Because it's Valentine's Day, silly.'

'Yeah,' I huffed, 'how could I forget the obstacle course of cards and flowers I needed to step through in order to get to your door this morning?'

'You're welcome to them. They'll mean as much to you as they do to me, which is to say not a lot.' She put her arm around me again, 'We can be each other's Valentine's today.'

'That sounds like the best idea I've heard all day.' I smiled at her, 'Come on, let's go and find Hannah. She normally finishes about now, we can all go for lunch.'

'Oh Katey, you look skinny. Are you eating? Have you lost weight from all this training? Do you need some food? I'll send you some pie. I just made apple, I'll send it to you. It'll stop you looking so tired.'

'Thanks Mom, sounds good.' I tried to smile at the barrage of questions, but I was too busy wishing I hadn't answered the call in the first place.

'Anyway, Happy Valentine's Day, sweetheart.'

'Thanks, Mom. You too. Thanks for my card.' It was the only card I'd gotten.

'And what about the sweater? Are you wearing it?' She put down the sheet of pastry she was rolling and peered closer to the camera.

Like the Thanksgiving pyjamas, and the Christmas pyjamas, my mom also went all out for Valentine's. The one she'd sent for me this year had a cartoon bear on the front, sitting inside a heart. Around the outside read 'I

Love You Beary Much'. Even if people hadn't been trying to snap a picture of me as I walked around campus, there was still no way it was being worn in public.

I groaned, with a shake of my head. 'No, Valentine's isn't such a big thing here.'

'What? How is that possible? It's everywhere.'

'The Brits don't buy into Hallmark like we do.'

Given the expression on her face, I expected her to burst into tears any second, and it made me laugh so much I forgot that my own tears had been forming at the sound of her voice. It didn't last long.

'And what did Oz send you? Please tell me he sent you flowers after everything that's been going on.'

I shook my head as fat droplets rolled down my cheek. I wasn't sure why I hadn't told my mom about breaking up with Oz when I shared everything else, but perhaps if I didn't voice it out loud to her, I could fix what had happened. Though I still hadn't figured out how.

'No,' my breath stuttered, as I tried to keep my shit together, 'we broke up.'

Her rolling pin clattered on the counter, 'What? Oh honey, why? Why didn't you tell me?'

'I dunno, because I panicked, I guess. It was all too much, and I needed some time to process it all, but he took it to mean a break-up. I've been so stupid recently.'

'Oh, Katey, you're not stupid, the boys are the idiots. You'll fix it and it'll all blow over.'

She started rolling out her pastry again, because everything was *that* simple. Except it wasn't and it only made me sob harder, because I realized my stupidity wasn't exclusive to Oz. I was sitting at my desk, and the last two papers I'd been handed back were in front of me, both with a big red number three scrawled on the front; the third was burning a hole in my backpack. To the left was a pile of material I hadn't attempted to start reading yet, and my laptop was open showing a blank document which I'd been staring at for the past hour, typing and deleting words I couldn't seem to get right.

It was the story of my life. I was getting nothing right.

Not Oz, not my coursework, and barely even rowing.

The pressure inside my chest suddenly became so overwhelming that I couldn't stop the onslaught of tears now pouring down my cheeks.

'Sweetheart, don't cry. You're doing such a good job, and you have your race soon. You'll be fine.'

'I'm not doing a good job. I'm failing at everything,' I wailed.

'Rubbish,' she scoffed, and pointed the rolling pin at me. 'You're at Cambridge, studying to be a doctor. A doctor. That's not failing, Katey. I was telling Mrs Rogers how well you're doing there, and you have yourself a handsome boyfriend. It's all great. Jake would have loved it, he'd be so proud of you.'

Whatever pep talk she thought she was giving me didn't have the desired effect, quite the opposite in fact, and my palm slammed on my desk loud enough that she stopped rolling her pastry.

'Mom. Enough!' I shouted. 'Stop bringing Jake into this. He wouldn't be proud, he'd wonder what the fuck I was doing. *I'm* wondering what the fuck I'm doing!'

'Katherine Astley . . .'

'No, Mom. I'm not doing a good job, stop telling me I am.

I've messed up my course, I've messed up with Oz, and at this rate I'm going to lose the race. I'm failing, Mom.' I sobbed again, snatching away the tears streaming down my face. 'I'm a failure. Jake wouldn't be proud, and you shouldn't be either.'

She stayed silent, letting me sob and sob until there were no tears left to cry, but she wasn't going to stay silent forever.

'Kate, I know you're not telling me how I should feel about my kids.'

'Mom . . .'

'No, it's my turn. If I want to be proud of you, I'm going to be damn well proud of you. I *am* proud of you,' she paused, taking a deep breath, 'but it sounds like you're not proud of yourself.'

I picked up a paperclip from my desk and began uncurling it, 'Mom . . .'

'Katey, if you don't know what you're doing, then take some time to figure out what you do want to do. And figure how to make yourself proud, whatever that may be.' She looked hard at me again, 'Maybe get some sleep while you're at it.'

Yeah. Sleep. I definitely needed sleep.

I picked up a tissue and blew my nose loudly, 'Thanks, Mom.'

'That's what I'm here for. Now go and sleep, while I get this pie filled.'

'Okay, I love you.'

'Love you, too.'

Throwing my phone to the side I scooched down onto my pillow. I'd allotted myself two hours for studying before I had to leave again for training but only had twenty minutes left. It was pointless studying now anyway, when the time could be used more effectively for a power nap. My eyelids were tugged down by an invisible string.

They'd barely closed when a heavy thumping on my door had me sitting back up. It wasn't Imogen or Hannah; we'd gotten to the point where we walked straight in without knocking. The Downing College orderlies didn't bang quite so hard. The only other people who'd ever been in here were Will Norris and Mary Heston, and after this morning it wasn't going to be her.

My heart pounded as I ran through the list of people it could possibly be – a very short list – before panic set in. I wasn't about to answer the door to a stranger, especially one who'd quiz me about Oz or snap a photo before I could stop it.

I was still deliberating on whether to open the door, when the thumps started up again. On second thought they sounded more like hard kicks.

'I know you're in there, Kate.'

I frowned; the voice was vaguely familiar, but not familiar enough to instil the confidence I needed.

'Who is it?'

'Olly. Open the door, or I'm going to drop this.'

I flung it open, 'Drop wh . . . whoa.'

I assumed it was Olly, though I couldn't see him for the giant vase of roses he was holding in his arms, just his legs. It was enormous. I'd never seen so many in my life outside of a garden; there were easily several rose bushes' worth of stems. I wondered if there were any roses left in Cambridge.

And the scent . . . like a summer's day on Nantucket, a trip to the beach, cold beers and lobster rolls.

'Kate, move out of the way!'

'Sorry.' I jumped into action, and guided him in as he wobbled through, rushing to clear space on my desktop, though I wasn't sure it was big enough. Olly must have decided the same, because in the next moment he'd placed the vase on the floor.

'How . . . where? Um.'

He stood up, stretching out his back, and pulled a thick envelope from his pocket which he handed to me. 'Here.'

I took it, but was too busy staring at the roses. Even with the vase on the floor they were nearly as tall as I was. 'How did you carry these?'

'I convinced the florist to drive them close to the steps, then I carried them up.' He grunted as his spine let out a loud crack. 'Last time I do any favours without checking the fine print. He owes me, I'm telling you.'

But I was still staring open-mouthed at the display. I tried counting the stems but lost my spot when I got to thirty. It had to be a hundred, all big fluffy heads and deep red petals. I'd never been given so much as a card before from anyone who wasn't my mom, and now I had enough Valentine's roses to last me a lifetime.

I bit down on my lip. I didn't know how I had tears left, but they were there. Olly reached one long arm out and patted me on the shoulder, which was exactly the amount of comforting I needed.

'They're not from me, obviously, they're all Osbourne. You know that, right?' He looked so panicked that I'd

369

think they were from him, that it dried up my tears enough to laugh.

'Yeah, I got that.'

'Good,' he nodded, his mouth straightening into a hard line as he glanced to the door, then back at me. 'He's miserable, by the way. Really fucking miserable. I saw him yesterday and he was revising. *Revising*!'

My heart skipped a little, scratch that, it skipped a lot. Every night since we'd broken up, I'd lie awake and my mind would race thinking about the last things Oz had said to me, about putting my life on hold. Then I'd wonder what he was doing, how he felt, whether he was okay and living his life again, or maybe – as I did during the darkest stretches of the night – if he'd forgotten about me.

But hearing he'd been miserable? That made me feel a little better.

'Oz's life isn't a piece of cake, you know? But since he met you, he's been different. More relaxed, happier.'

I peered up at Olly, 'Really?'

'Yeah,' he nodded, 'and I get it, I do. I've seen how it's been for you the past few weeks, but if you want Oz in your life you need to learn how to tune it out. And speaking from experience, having Oz in your life is so much better than not having him, and he's loyal to his fucking core.' He drew in a breath, but held in whatever he was going to say next. 'He's my best friend, Kate. I don't like seeing him like this. He can't help his life, he can't help his shitty father, don't make it more of a problem.'

'What am I supposed to do?'

'You asked for time, and you wanted people to stop

showing an interest in your dating life.' He shrugged. 'He's given you what you want.'

'What does that mean?'

'Dunno.' He lifted one shoulder dismissively, like it was my problem to figure out. 'Anyway, I've said what I came to say. You have the race coming, maybe concentrate on winning that. I've got a lot of money on Cambridge crossing the finish line first.'

As he opened the door, I realized the flowers were still on the floor.

'Hey,' I cried out, 'you can't leave them there. I won't be able to lift them.'

He marched over and picked them back up, placing them on my desk, and we stood back waiting to see if it was going to fall.

I didn't wait for him to close the door behind him before I ripped open the envelope.

Yankee Doodle,

We might not be together right now, but you'll always be my Valentine.

I'll see you at the finish line. I love you.

Oz xxx

The finish line. It seemed so far away in more ways than one.

My mom had said I needed to figure out what I wanted, but I already knew what I wanted.

I wanted Oz.

I wanted to win the Boat Race.

And, as I looked at the textbooks I'd tossed on the floor to make room for the giant display of flowers, I wanted to do something for me; something I loved. Something that wasn't medicine. Something that gave me my life back, and Oz in the process.

What I *needed* was to figure out how to get all three, and I had a month to do it.

25. Arthur

(I'm no Michael J. Fox but it's time to go Back to the Future)

'Another excellent piece of work, Mr Osbourne-Cloud. Well done, very well done. Your interpretations of Prometheus and Pandora are very interesting, I applaud you for your originality.'

I took the essay Professor McRothy was holding out to me and dropped my head, 'Thank you, sir. I appreciate that.'

Annoyingly, because he clearly sensed that I really didn't want to stand here talking, he held onto the end of the essay when I tried to take it. This is why you should never be last in the queue to get out.

'Tell me where the visualization of Hope as a young lady came from.'

I was *not* about to tell him, under any circumstances; instead I shrugged and said, 'Just came to me, sir.'

He narrowed his beady eyes at me, 'Hmm, well it was excellent.'

'Thank you.' I tugged on the essay and once again was thwarted from taking it by the firm grip of a septuagenarian.

'Have you decided on a path for when you graduate this summer?'

I waited a beat, but then shook my head, 'Not yet, sir.'

'Oh good, good,' he chuckled. 'For a second I thought you were going to say politics and follow after your father.'

I blinked in surprise. In the past three years I'd spent a minimum of five hours a week with Professor McRothy, and during that time he'd not once expressed an opinion on my, or any of my coursemates', futures. I'd almost go as far as to say that he forgot about us the second we walked out the door. Like Professor Barrow, he was one of those teachers who seemed to live in his world of Ancient Greeks with very little awareness of what was happening in real time, but it appeared I was wrong.

'You don't think I should go into politics?'

Instead of answering he leaned back against his desk and crossed his arms. 'Did you know I taught your father?'

For the second time in as many minutes I was both surprised and very wrong about Professor McRothy's attention to detail.

'No. I didn't. He studied politics though, didn't he?'

'He did, eventually, but his first year here he took my class on Ancient Greek literature. It soon became clear the classics weren't for him, they're too delicate and nuanced, whereas your father is more like one of those bulls hurtling down the streets in Pamplona.'

I snorted loudly, more out of surprise than amusement at my professor describing my father more accurately and succinctly than I'd ever heard anyone else.

'He used to sit in class and argue black was blue. It didn't matter what the truth was, he saw what he wanted to see and tried to convince you to join his argument.'

I nodded. 'Yes, sir, that sounds about right.'

'Now, your father, he *was* a politician. He couldn't have been anything else. But you, Mr Osbourne-Cloud, you can be anything you want to be. You're one of the most gifted students to walk through my door. It would be a shame to waste such talent; the world has too many politicians as it is.'

I realized that all the time he'd been talking he was still holding my essay, and he finally let it go.

'Thank you. I appreciate the support,' I smiled, and nodded, then gradually made a step towards the door.

I'd almost reached it when he called me again, 'And Arthur?'

'Yes?'

'Whoever that girl is you've painted as Hope, she'll get you there.'

This time I didn't reply, just offered up another smile and made my way slowly out of the classics building, sticking my headphones on as I did.

Stepping out into the cold March air, I pulled off my backpack to stuff my essay inside, taking a final glance at it as I did.

Hope. The only good thing remaining in the Pandora's Box that was my life.

Kate. Kate was my hope. Except right now everything seemed hope*less*.

I'd written that essay the day after we'd broken up, almost one month ago. Twenty-nine days to be precise. I'd sat down at my desk with the worst hangover I could have ever imagined and typed until my fingers cramped. Four hours and 6,000 words later, and I'd painted the picture of my life as told through the Ancient Greeks.

And today I was awarded a high First for the effort. I chuckled to myself, maybe I should get drunk more often. Now I just needed to finish sorting the rest of my shit out; something I'd been trying to do since it blew up in my face.

Twenty minutes later I flung open the front door and took the stairs two at a time until I reached my bedroom, only to find Brooks, and Charlie sitting on my bed. Or Charlie was on the bed, and Brooks was in my rocking chair.

'Hello,' I said, throwing my backpack on the floor and peeling off my hoodie, which also landed on the floor. 'What are you two doing in here?'

'Waiting for you,' replied Charlie, like it should have been obvious.

'Okay, why?'

'Oz, where are you going?'

I swapped out my jeans for a pair of long running skins, followed by shorts. 'The gym. Have you seen my t-shirt?'

Brooks tipped the end of his protein shaker and hit the bottom where a big clump of chocolate had stuck, until it fell in his mouth. 'Didn't you already go after water training earlier?'

'Yes.'

'Then we can wait until later, when we have scheduled land training.'

'I'm going now, too. I did legs this morning, I'll do back and shoulders this afternoon.' I shrugged one of said shoulders, and looked around my room again. 'Have either of you seen my t-shirt?'

Charlie stood up, stepping in front of me with crossed arms and a deep scowl. 'Oz, all you've done is train and eat for the past month.'

I stopped looking for the t-shirt I wanted to wear; a

white one with the Wizard of Oz embroidered on the left breast, standing on his Yellow Brick Road.

I'd been walking through Oxford with Kate, trying to find the pie shop she'd heard about. As we'd ventured down one of the narrow cobbled streets, she'd spotted the shirt in the window of a weird little bric-a-brac charity shop. By the time I figured out what she'd been laughing so hard at, I'd already been dragged inside where she promptly removed it from the headless mannequin and handed it over to the cashier.

She paid £3, folded it up into her bag, and took it back to Cambridge with her. A week later I arrived home to a parcel containing the shirt, freshly washed.

It became the most precious thing I owned, and the one thing that made me feel close to her.

Except now I couldn't fucking find it.

I glanced over at Brooks, then back at Charlie. From his tone it was clear he wasn't happy, and from the way he was looking at me, I could surmise I was the reason, though I had no idea why.

'That's what we're supposed to do, Charles. Train.'

He slowly but firmly shook his head, 'Not at the rate you're going. You'll collapse. You're doing double the training than everyone else.'

'We have a race to win at the end of the month, if you haven't forgotten.' I opened up another drawer, but the t-shirt wasn't in there either. 'Where is my fucking shirt?'

Charlie's hand stopped me from opening the next drawer. 'We will win, Oz, but you need to chill out. You're not going to do us any good with fatigued muscles. Have a KitKat and go take a fucking nap, will you?'

I was beginning to find Charlie very annoying, and my patience was becoming so thin it was nearly see-through.

'I don't need to take a nap.'

Brooks got up from the rocking chair and stopped Charlie from arguing back, 'Oz, mate, you're exhausted.'

'Who are you, my mother?' I snapped, marching over to my closet to see if my t-shirt was in there. It wasn't.

'No, I'm fucking not. We're your best friends and we're worried about you.'

'I'm fine. I just want to find my t-shirt so I can go to the gym.'

'Your shirt's in the fucking wash!' Charlie erupted, slamming the closet door so hard it nearly took the tips of my fingers off. 'You've barely taken it off for a month, so I've washed it because it was disgusting. I should have burned it, instead.'

My head snapped round to where he was standing with flaring nostrils. I was about to ask him what the fuck he thought he was doing, but found myself taken aback by the expression on his face. I wasn't sure I'd ever seen him so angry; Charlie's mood usually limited itself to staying anywhere north of annoyed, and rarely did he descend into anything resembling a temper.

'You want to punch me, Osbourne? Is that what's about to happen? Because I will put you back on your arse if you try.'

Charlie was a big guy, a rower, with dense, powerful muscles, just like me, and to any outsider he would certainly come across as intimidating. But I'd known Charlie half my life and had never once seen him punch anything, or anyone. He wouldn't even kill a spider. I was almost tempted to be the first victim, but as my eyes flicked over to Brooks, whose eyes were also wide, I couldn't hold in my laugh, and at the same time his own burst out loudly.

And just like that, the exhaustion they'd been banging on about overwhelmed me and I slumped back against the closet door and slid to the floor.

'I'm not going to punch you, dickhead,' I told him, resting my elbows on my knees, 'and thank you for washing my shirt. Kate gave it to me.'

'Yeah, no shit,' he grumbled, sitting on my bed again. 'I'm sorry, mate. I know breaking up sucks balls. I totally get it, I've been there, remember? But running yourself into the ground isn't going to help anyone.'

I closed my eyes, trying to will away the headache knocking on my skull. 'I don't know what to do.'

'About what?'

'About Kate, about everything,' I sighed, 'about my fucking messy life. I need to sort it out if I want to be with her.'

Brooks perched back on the edge of the rocking chair, 'Oz, your life isn't messy. Not all of it, anyway. Rowing, school, this house . . . that's all clear. The only thing you won't do anything about . . .'

'I know,' I interrupted him, 'my father.'

'I was going to say graduating, but I guess it's all the same thing.'

'Yeah. All roads lead to my father.' I shook my head in defeat, because I'd finally reached the point of no return. 'Fuck.'

Charlie stood up, put his hand on my shoulder and squeezed. 'Don't worry, mate, it'll all be fine. It can't get any worse than it has been. Speaking from experience.'

'I guess,' I nodded, just as his words registered and it occurred to me that in my fog of Kate I hadn't checked in on Charlie for the past month, nor had I heard an update on his Evie situation since Brooks had given him Violet's number. And now I came to think about it, he'd been unusually quiet since the start of term. 'Hey, hang on. How are things with you? Did your fake girlfriend plan work?'

Even Brooks stopped mid-stride and turned to Charlie, waiting for his response.

Charlie looked like he was about to say something, but then thought better of it. Instead, he offered up a shrug and a 'Yeah', then walked out offering nothing more.

Brooks raised a single brow at me indicating he knew as much as I did, which is to say nothing, and followed Charlie out, leaving me sitting on the floor.

I rested my head back on the wall. They were right, it couldn't get any worse.

If the last month of being without Kate had taught me anything, it's that I didn't want to be without her any longer. When I told her I would see her at the finish line, I'd set myself that deadline to figure out how to get her back. If I wanted to be with Kate, I needed to address the issue of my future, and for that to happen I needed to do the one thing I usually avoided at all costs.

May as well get it over with.

I picked up my phone and hit dial. He picked up almost immediately.

'Dad, we need to have a chat.'

26.

(One Day. One Race.
One Winner. There's no second place)

Kate

'Oh my god,' I whispered, as the bus pulled into Crabtree Boathouse. 'I think I'm going to be sick.'

'If you need to be sick at least wait until you're out of the bus,' said Will, stuffing a cereal bar into his mouth as everyone else stood up and began collecting their things to get out.

I knew he was trying to be helpful, but I didn't find it helpful, and if I was honest, I didn't think I wanted to get out of the bus. Not if it meant I'd be out in *that*.

That *noise*.

I'd become aware of a low rumbling approximately thirty minutes ago. Twenty-five minutes ago, I'd realized it had gotten louder and had glanced out of the window to see three large black helicopters circling overhead. I'd shrugged and was about to ask Will what he reckoned they were doing there, when the bus had turned the corner I always used as a marker point on our training mornings. It was the first time the river came into view, and it always brought a smile to my face.

Except today, there appeared to be an event of some kind drawing the crowds, because there were hundreds of people. As the bus continued, the three helicopters became six, and the hundreds of people turned into thousands of people, then tens of thousands of people all spread out along both sides of the riverbank, pushing and shoving to get a spot on the edge.

Then it dawned on me that the event they'd come to watch was *my* event. My stomach immediately bottomed out, and my ears hadn't stopped ringing since.

I peered out at the boathouse I'd spent hours training from every week, except it didn't look like the boathouse I knew any more. Its cute, slightly run down, black and white painted front was now covered in light- and dark-blue flags, hanging from the railings and plastered to the awnings outside. In fact, all I could see was a sea of Cambridge and Oxford flags billowing in the wind.

Up and down the river, the colours alternated like a patchwork quilt of blue. People were waving them, dressed in them; hundreds of thousands of people lining the banks of the Thames, and the millions more watching at home – my parents and their neighbourhood included – to watch this one race I'd been training for for the past eight months.

The Oxford and Cambridge University Boat Race.

Yep. I was definitely going to be sick.

Will hitched his backpack over his shoulder and moved to follow the rest of the boys off the bus, 'Come on, Asters. Get up. Let's go and meet our public.'

'What?' I screeched, another wave of panic crashing through me as I looked back out of the window at the hordes and hordes of people. 'No one said anything about meeting them. I don't have to meet them, do I?'

All I heard in response was Will's chuckle.

'That's not funny,' I hissed, and stood up. 'I've not been here before. Don't do that to me!'

'We're here every week,' he grinned, clearly enjoying my misery.

'Not like this, we're not.'

He spun around and gripped onto my shoulder, 'Kate, you're going to be fine. You'll see. All you have to do is go out there and absorb the noise like it's your life source. It'll be the energy you need to power us through to the finish line. They're cheering for you.'

I listened again. It was hard to decipher anything at all from the cacophony, and certainly not my name. 'They're cheering for Cambridge.'

'You're part of Cambridge. A key part. The most important part, I'd say. You're our eyes and ears. You're in charge of us.' He squeezed my shoulder, but his smile dropped. 'Now, take a deep breath, and calm the fuck down, before any of the boys see you falling apart. Coach will be looking for you, so you need to get your shit together. You can do this, Kate. You've got it.'

I looked up into his warm brown eyes. I could probably have done with a slap to the face too, but his pep talk would need to do. I opened my lungs and drew in as much air as I could, instantly feeling myself calm.

'Okay, I got it.' I offered up a nervous smile, but definitely felt better than I had five minutes ago. 'Yeah, thanks Will. First time nerves, I guess.'

'We've all had them.' He took my sunglasses from my head and slipped them onto my nose. 'Now, let's get off this bloody bus.'

I followed closely behind, concentrating on keeping my anxiety in check enough to put one foot in front of the other until I reached the safety of the boathouse. I nearly faltered as I took my first step into the outdoors. I don't know how but the windows had muffled the volume of the crowds, and I realized why most of the boys had been wearing their headphones as they left the bus. As for me, I was certain my ears were bleeding from the thunderous combination of helicopters and cheering.

Then the deafening noise was silenced as I was sucked into a vacuum of my own creation. For there, in the doorway of his own bus a hundred yards away, was Oz.

Arthur

I jerked forward, almost tripping down the bus steps as Charlie knocked into me.

'Ouch, fuck,' he grumbled, rubbing the bridge of his nose where it had made contact with my shoulder. 'Why d'you stop?'

I glanced back to where Kate had been standing, but she'd already disappeared, swept away in the light blue of the Cambridge boys. I hadn't expected to see her so early. I thought it was unlikely I'd even lay eyes on her before we stepped into our boats for warming up before the race.

But fate had a different plan.

'Oz! Move!'

'Sorry,' I mumbled, marching forward and keeping my head down as we passed the crowds of Oxford supporters dressed in their dark blues lining the entranceway to the Westminster School Boat Club, all cheering our arrival.

I barely had time to unpack my bag and sit down before my name was called.

'Will the Oxford President please make his way outside to the bank?' a voice barked over the tannoys positioned around the boathouse, 'Oxford President outside, please.'

I stood up and looked over to Pete, who was pulling on his boots. Over the past month, the crew had been in deep discussion over which side of the river we wanted if we won the coin toss. Even though Pete preferred Surrey, we'd lost on that side last year and in the vote we'd taken yesterday the results were unanimous for Middlesex, but I still wanted to double check because Pete was the one who'd be driving us through the slipstream.

'Middlesex?'

He nodded, 'Yeah. Let's do it.'

I zipped up my Oxford rowing jacket and made my way outside to the podium where the coin toss would take place. The cheering from the crowds surrounding the boathouse, which had been on a constant but low rumble, boomed louder as they spied me walking. Their excitement was palpable. Addictive, almost. I'd rowed in the Henley Regatta, the World Championships, the Olympics, and nothing, *nothing* rivalled the crowds at the Boat Race where it was just Oxford and Cambridge, two sides always against each other.

Television cameras followed my path as I stepped up onto the dark-blue carpet laid out on the Oxford side of the podium to find Will Norris standing on the other in his Cambridge blue colours.

'Hi mate, how're you doing?' Will winked, as he shook my hand. 'Ready to lose again?'

'You wish, sunshine. You bloody wish.'

'We'll see.' He leaned in closer. 'What station are you picking?'

I tapped my finger against my nose, 'You'll find out when I win the toss.'

He laughed, 'It won't help you.'

I glanced up to the flag flapping high above us. There was a strong gust in the air today and it was making the water look very choppy. It didn't mean anything to me though; there were advantages and disadvantages to whichever side of the river you rowed on, and the weather wouldn't make a difference.

I held in the chuckle as he looked up too. 'Don't be so sure about that.'

'I'm sure. We have your girlfriend, and she's probably the best coxswain I've ever rowed with.'

The banter was over. My fist balled as I tried not to get distracted from the race with thoughts of Kate, which is likely what Will had planned.

Well, mission accomplished.

She'd been wearing her sunglasses when she stepped off the bus, so I hadn't been able see that beautiful shade of green I'd been dreaming about every night, or tell what she'd been thinking, or whether her heart had stopped like mine had the second I'd looked over and spotted her. But distraction ended there.

I had an hour to go before we crossed the finish line, and once that happened my entire focus would revolve around getting her back.

But I didn't have the discipline to stop myself asking about her. 'How's Kate doing?'

'Great, the crew will be sad to lose her.'

My eyes flicked to Will's. 'Lose her? What does that mean?'

But it was then that the president of the rowing federation decided to make his appearance on the podium with us, and I remembered we weren't alone. No. We were standing in front of the live camera feed of the BBC, and the long camera lenses belonging to the world's sports press who'd been given a front row seat.

'Sorry for the delay, chaps.' He positioned himself between us and smiled ahead, for our official Presidents' photo, clapping his hands together when it was over. 'Great, time to choose your stations. Mr Norris, as president of last year's winning crew, it's your call on the coin toss.'

The president reached into his pocket, and pulled out the same sovereign coin used every year to decide which side of the river we rowed, and threw it in the air.

'Tails,' Will called as it spun in the air, before it landed tails up.

'Well done, Cambridge.' The president shook our hands and stepped down off the podium. My mind immediately went back to Kate and I wasn't paying attention to anything else. 'Good luck to both of you. Please head back to your boathouses, and let's have a good race.'

I grabbed Will before he could follow. 'Norris. What did you mean?'

'About what?'

'Kate. Why have you lost her?'

'Because she's leaving.'

'She's what?!' I shouted, far too loudly.

'Presidents? Back to your boathouses,' called the president again, only to be ignored, *again*.

Will looked over to where the cameras were still pointed our way, then back at me. 'Didn't she tell you?'

'We broke up.'

His eyes widened in surprise. 'Shit, I didn't know that. I'm sorry, mate, when did that happen?'

'Last month.' My brows shot up, 'She didn't tell you?'

He frowned with one shake of his head. 'No. Not a word. And the other day I asked her how you were getting on, and she said you were good.'

'Really? Are you sure?'

'Positive.' Though from the way he was scratching his chin, it didn't look like he was *that* positive.

'Presidents! Make your way to your boathouses. I won't tell you again.'

'Hang on!' I snapped back, forgetting for a second who I was addressing, and swiftly followed up with a very apologetic 'I'm so sorry, sir. We're almost done.'

'No, Mr Osbourne-Cloud. You *are* done.'

I turned to give Will one last silent plea, but he'd already disappeared into the Cambridge crowds.

'What did you get?' called Pete, the second I stepped over the threshold of our boathouse, and everyone else glanced up with the same question in their eager gazes.

'What?'

'Which station are we rowing?'

Fuck.

I realized I'd been so distracted with thoughts of Kate

and where she was going that I'd completely blanked on what side of the river we'd been awarded.

Not a good start.

Not a good start at all.

Kate

'Boats. Five minutes,' the umpire's voice echoed through the megaphone.

I gripped onto the rowboat holding us in place. The water was choppier than it looked from the land, and the boat rocked viciously as we moved into our starting position; lined up exactly with the stone marker seventy metres to the right of me. It was the marker Oz had pointed out the first day we'd cleaned up the river, when he told me about coxing on the Tideway and taking part in this race. I swallowed my smile; our stretch looked no cleaner. We didn't get much cleaning done.

It was the same day he'd begged me to give him a chance, to see him for who he really was.

That had been five months ago, and I was not the same person I'd been five months ago.

'Crews. Get ready,' came the order from the umpire, and my hand immediately shot up to signal we weren't.

'Boys? How we doing?' I peered down the boat to see most of them nod to me as I adjusted my headset. 'Take your time, take your time.'

A quick glance to my right and Pete's hand was also in the air, so I took the opportunity for a second glance at

Oz directly in front of him – because when opportunity strikes and all that.

I could barely see him under his cap, pulled down so low on his face that the shadow almost merged with the thick stubble coating his cheeks, and dark strands of hair curling up the rim.

But even from this distance he still had the ability to render my heart to a near stop.

Just like in all the YouTube videos I'd been obsessively watching, Oz's jaw was working overtime as he channelled the adrenaline coursing through his body, making his nostrils flare with every deep inhale. His muscles looked bigger than I remembered; deep crevasses appearing along his triceps as they flexed while he made the final checks to his oar, clenching and unclenching his fists around the rubber grip. My eyes stayed glued as I watched him settle.

He was power personified. He was devastatingly handsome. And a beat before his head tipped up to let Pete know he was ready, he glanced over to me.

The earth may have stopped spinning as we locked into each other.

His pale blue eyes shone bright against the gloomy grey of the sky, and I could almost feel his breath against my neck, sense his heartbeat next to mine as it slowed, and I found myself able to take a lungful of air for the first time in a month.

Just like when I'd stepped off the bus, it was the balm I needed, because Oz had this way of calming the storm around me, quieting the noises buzzing in my head, and I remembered exactly why I was here, and what I was doing.

What I planned to do.

A month ago I'd given myself three things to accomplish. I was already one down. There were twenty minutes between me and the next two items on my list to check off.

Win the Boat Race. Win Oz back.

I zoned in, muting the sound of the helicopters and drones high above, the loud judder of the dozen speedboats behind us where the umpires were watching with eagle eyes, along with the support boats of first-aid crews and rescue teams, all battling with the roar of the fans stretched either side of the river.

My eyes snapped to the flag on top of the pole; my lucky flag. 'Bring Oz back to me,' I whispered, 'and give us a win.'

I looked straight ahead, to my crew of eight; the boys I'd spent more time with in the past couple of months than anyone else. They'd welcomed me onto their crew, they trusted me to lead them to victory.

That's exactly what I planned to do.

'Okay, boys. We're here. We're finally here. We're at the starting line we've trained eight months to get to, and we're going to prove to all of them that we're the best, because we are the best. For the next twenty minutes you're going to power harder than you've ever done before, you're going to fight harder than you've ever done before, and we're going to fucking win this race. We are going to win.'

Murmurs of 'Yes boss,' sounded out.

'Okay. Call out when you're ready.'

'Ready . . . ready . . . ready . . .' the boys' shouts moved down the boat until only Tubbs was left in the stroke seat directly in front of me. I pulled my sunglasses down to meet his eyes.

'Tubbs?'

A grin split his face. 'Ready, Asters. We're going to fucking cream those dark-blue motherfuckers.'

I smirked, moving my sunglasses back into place, and brought my hand down.

Pete's hand came down too.

We were ready.

'Attention,' called the umpire, and we all held our breath. My fingers gripped around the steering mechanisms by my side. 'Go.'

The red flag dropped.

Eight oars made the catch.

As planned, we went out fast. Tubbs set a punishing rhythm and I could feel the crew thundering us down the first stretch of the river towards the Fulham bend. The water smashed against the blades and waves rocked the boat, but we powered on. Fifty yards ahead I could see a calmer stretch of water and pressed down on the rudder to steer us towards it, which earned me a warning from the umpire behind us for being too close to the Oxford boat.

'Ignore him,' I shouted down my headset to the boys, 'we're not close. We have clear water.'

Twenty yards to my left, the Oxford boat was pushing just as hard, and from the pace of Oz's rowing I could tell Pete had asked them to up their stroke rate. But we'd been expecting it, and I had no intention of letting them slip past.

'Okay boys. Pressure's on. Keep to my beat. One and one and one and one,' I shouted out, watching as they hit each call. 'Nice. Nice. Stay with me. Good.'

I glanced over, and from the way I was now lined up nearer to Oz's seat than Pete's, I could tell we'd inched ahead.

'We're hitting the mile marker, boys. Remember what we practised. Give me ten per cent more until Hammersmith Bridge.' The waves crashed against the side of boat. 'Ready? On my marks . . . Push. Push. Push.' Each of my orders set the tempo I needed them to keep, and we burst forward. 'Hips and knees. Hips and knees. Hips and knees. We have to get through it first.'

I might not have an oar in my hand, but my heart was racing as hard as if I had. In front of me Tubbs had turned a healthy shade of pink. Sweat dripped down his face as he exploded from his seat for each giant push on his thighs.

I glanced down at my stopwatch as we passed under Hammersmith Bridge. It wasn't the fastest time we'd ever done it, and we weren't going to set any records, but it was fast enough, and as we came away and moved around the bend it was clear we'd gained another foot length against Oxford. I could no longer see Oz.

The crowds screamed, flags, banners and scarves were all waving in the air as we passed the second mile marker, followed by the Chiswick Eyot on our right and Chiswick Steps on our left. The wind blew past us.

'Ten minutes in, boys. We're past the halfway point. You're doing great. Keep it up. Keep it up. Keep it up.'

Glancing over at Oxford, I was now level with Brooks

in six seat. We were still half a length ahead, but there was every possibility Oxford would step on the gas coming into the third mile, and we couldn't afford to be complacent.

'Another burst. Let's dig deep, in three, two, one. Row. Row. Row.'

Tubbs looked like his jaw was going to break from the tension, and let out an ear splitting bellow with each stroke he blasted through his oar.

'Come on, boys. That's it. It's working. We're nearly a full length in front. Let's go. Let's go. Let's go.'

Cheering crowds took us under Barnes Bridge, the final bridge before the finish line, and along past the pubs lining the river, their customers leaning over the railings waving pints of beer in the air as they saw us approaching. Whistles and shrieks provided our soundtrack as we powered on.

The end was in sight.

'Final stretch, boys. Give me twelve more. Keep together. Keep together. Keep it together.'

This wasn't a race. This was a gladiatorial fight to the death.

I channelled every drop of sweat I'd lost over the past eight months, every tear I'd shed, every ounce of stress which had balled me up in knots, every news story, every dropped grade and lost night of sleep to get us to this point. I channelled Jake and my family.

But most of all, I channelled Oz.

I looked to my left. I couldn't even see the Oxford boat.

One last cry of 'Legs. Legs. Legs.'

And over the finish line we went.

Arthur

I collapsed back onto Charlie, sucking in as much oxygen as I could to quench the burning in my lungs, but it wasn't enough. My entire body felt like it had been dipped in gasoline and gone up in flames. Every inch of skin, every cell, every nerve ending screamed in pain as my muscles shuddered from the lactic acid pumping through them.

'Fuck! Fuck! FUCK!' sobbed Charlie behind me as the boat drifted underneath Chiswick Bridge. 'We fucking lost. I can't believe it. I thought we had them. I can't believe it. I cannot fucking believe it.'

I yanked off my cap, still not getting enough air to my body, and peered up at Pete who seemed to be in a similar state. Anguish was etched over his face.

Eight months of hard training for nothing.

That was the brutality of the Boat Race.

'Oz, I'm sorry,' he gasped out.

I sat up, grabbing him by his despondent shoulders. 'You coxed a fucking good race. Nothing to be sorry about.'

'I should have pushed the pace harder.'

'I think I'd have died if you'd pushed harder.' I managed a grin, though even my face was hurting.

'I wanted you to win.'

I cupped my hand around the back of his neck, pulling him in closer. 'I haven't lost yet.'

He turned to the left where the Cambridge boat was being pulled into the dock. Three of the crew had jumped out in victory as soon as they'd passed over the finish line, and were now kicking about in the water. But there was only one person I had eyes for, and she was currently being hoisted onto the shoulders of Tubbs as her body shook with laughter, except the laughter died when he threw her into the river, instead. Kate's scream rang through the air and she landed with an enormous splash.

I shouldn't have found it so funny, given the rest of my crew were still in a state of near collapse, but I knew the look on her face when she finally emerged from the water, and Tubbs should probably run for safety.

As was tradition, the presidents were supposed to shake hands at the end of the race, but Will Norris would have to wait, because as luck would have it, Kate stepped onto the dock at the same time as I did, her feet sloshing underneath her. From the left I could see Imogen and Hannah sprinting over to congratulate her, but they'd also have to wait until I was done. She was so focused on wringing out her jacket she didn't notice immediately that I was in front of her, but then she finally peered up, and my heart beat so loud it could have been heard over the helicopters, the cheering, the deafening megaphones – all of it.

Except when she glanced up at me, her green eyes wide in surprise, everything else silenced and I forgot we were standing in the middle of chaos, surrounded by hundreds of people.

'Hello.'

'Hey,' she breathed out.

'Congratulations.'

'Thank you. I'm sorry you lost.'

I shrugged. 'That's okay. You deserved that win. I'm so fucking proud of you, Katey.'

'You can try again next year.'

I was about to tell her that there were other things I now wanted to win more than next year's Boat Race, when Will's words shot back into my brain. In the commotion of the race, and seeing her again, I'd almost forgotten them.

'Will told me you're leaving,' I blurted out. 'Tell me that's not true. Please.'

She opened her mouth, then closed it. 'Um . . .'

All the adrenaline I'd burned through the race once more coursed through my body, coupled with a heavy dose of panic that I'd blown everything and she was going to slip through my fingers before I could stop her. For the last month I'd been working through a plan for our future, one which would keep us together, but her leaving Cambridge was throwing a very large spanner in it.

Good job I could think on my feet.

'Okay, okay. You're leaving. Well, okay. That's fine but bottom line is wherever you're going, I'll come too. I can come. I can travel. Wherever you go,' I announced, my words shooting out in rapid succession, while I attempted to mentally plot out a hundred solutions to my problem. 'You can leave, but I'm done with being apart. So, yes. That's what I'll do. Where are we going?'

She waited in silence, making sure I'd finished with the firing line of words I'd shot her way, then her brows dropped, and a sly curl edged up her lip. 'Oxford.'

'What?'

'Oxford. We're going to Oxford.'

'I don't understand.'

'I thought I'd come to Oxford to study, while you're becoming Britain's best-known classicist.'

397

I scratched my head, trying to make sense of what she was saying. Her coming to Oxford was not one of the scenarios I had plotted.

'Are you telling me you've transferred your course to Oxford?'

She shook her head slowly. 'No. I've quit my course. I'm going to do something else instead.'

'You're not studying medicine?'

Her shoulders sagged as she smiled up at me, and let out a long, heavy sigh. 'You were right. I didn't love it, I've never loved it. It wasn't my dream to pursue, it was Jake's.'

I blinked, not really believing what I was hearing. Not daring to hope what I was hoping. 'So, what are you going to do instead?'

She grinned wide, almost blinding me with how beautiful she was, and let out one of her giggles I loved so much, and had missed even more. 'I'm going to business school in Oxford. Now we'll be in the same place. We can be together.'

I heaved a sigh of relief that could have been heard over the still cheering crowds and my grin turned into a laugh. A loud laugh. 'Oh man . . .'

Confusion fell across Kate's face. 'What's so funny? Aren't you pleased? I thought you'd be pleased.'

'I am,' I grabbed her shoulders, 'I am. I'm so pleased for you, but the thing is . . . I'm not going to be in Oxford.'

She stepped back, her arms crossed over her chest. 'What? Where are you going to be?'

'Well . . . um, actually . . . I thought I'd come and join a winning team instead.'

'What . . . what does that mean?'

'I've been accepted onto the teacher training course at Cambridge. And I was planning to try out for the Cambridge crew, seeing as my girlfriend is the winning coxswain.'

Her mouth dropped open again, though this time it didn't fill me with the panic I'd experienced before.

'But . . . what about your father? What about your future as a classicist so you don't have to leave Oxford and go into politics?'

'Well, I realized something.' A droplet of water ran down the side of her face, and I brushed it away. 'I realized that you're my future, if you'll have me. If it's not too late.'

'I don't understand.'

'Katey, babe, I'm so sorry for everything. I'm so sorry for all the stress I caused you and for acting like a brat, and for not listening to you when you said us being together would cause you problems. I didn't want to believe it, because you're the first perfect thing I've ever had in my life and I didn't want to hide you.' I pressed a finger to her lips as she opened them to speak, 'No, let me finish. I'm so sorry, and I'm planning to spend as long as I need to make it up to you. Which is why I called my father and told him I wasn't going into politics. That I wanted to be a teacher. Oh, and I was going to Cambridge.'

'Oh my god,' she gasped, her hand flying to her mouth. 'What did he say?'

'He hung up, and hasn't spoken to me since,' I shrugged.

'Oh Oz,' her face dropped, 'I'm so sorry.'

'I'm not. It's totally worth it. You taught me how to follow my dreams, not the dreams of my family.' Her face was warm against my hand as I cupped her cheek.

'I guess it's something we taught each other. I'm sorry too. I'm sorry for not trusting you more. If I had, maybe we wouldn't have had this time apart.'

I shook my head. 'No, we needed it. We wouldn't be here now without it. But how about, from this point on, we stop dwelling on the past and focus on the future. Starting with where we want to live.'

'I don't care, as long as it's with you.' She smiled, her perfect smile, and tugged my shirt down until my mouth was close enough to brush against hers.

'I'm going to hold you to that.'

It took me a second amongst the cacophony of everything else, but the familiar click of camera lenses brought me back to the present. 'Um, babe. Let's go somewhere quieter. People are watching us.'

She stepped back a little, enough that I could see her cheeks were more flushed from our almost kiss than the cold air still blowing around, and smiled. My heart lurched again, I'd really fucking missed that smile.

'I don't care. Let them watch. It's worth it if it means I get to have you.'

'You have me. You've always had me. And this time I'm not going anywhere, except maybe into the changing room to get in some dry clothes.'

And with that, I took her hand in mine again and led us back to the boathouse.

A light blue and a dark blue, step by step.

Epilogue

Arthur

'Babe, where am I putting this?' I held up the lobster-shaped chopping board – a present from my sister.

Kate peered around the kitchen door and shrugged unhelpfully. 'Wherever you want.'

I shook my head and reached out to pull her back in, wrapping my spare hand around her waist, and dropped a kiss on her nose.

'Nah uh. The kitchen's your domain. You know I can't cook for shit, and seeing as you wouldn't let me bring James to come and help organize it, you need to help me with where you want stuff. It's your new career after all.'

She wriggled out of my grip and marched over to an open cabinet on the kitchen island. 'Put it in here.'

'Okay,' I replied, stealing another quick kiss as she walked out to continue unpacking the rest of the living room.

We'd been here five days, and were yet to make a dent in half of the boxes. I wasn't even sure they were all ours, because for the life of me I couldn't figure out how we had so much stuff. But this morning Kate had woken up and, to my dismay, shot out of bed without so much as a cuddle, announcing the rest had to be done *today*. Then promptly invited our family and friends over for dinner as incentive to get it all cleared up in time.

I ripped open the tape on the next box I had to unpack,

pulling out the bottle of champagne she'd been presented as winning coxswain for the Boat Race. It was hard to believe four months had passed since then, or how much we'd managed to cram into the time.

As predicted, I'd graduated with a First in classics.

Kate had opted not to finish her year, and we spent the one weekend England decided to have an early 'record-breaking' heatwave packing up her room and moving her into my house for the summer, much to the delight of Charlie and Brooks, who'd fallen in love with her almost as deeply as I had.

Though I think in Charlie's case, it was that he finally had someone to share the cooking with, and in Brooks' case it was the regular visitor in the form of Imogen, who'd frequently arrive unannounced, and stay for the night.

It had taken me less than a week of living together to realize I never wanted to be apart from Kate again, and a week after that I realized how hopelessly I'd fallen in love with her. Without our demanding schedules we actually had time to sit, and plan out what we wanted to do.

Plan our future.

It didn't take us long to decide on Cambridge as our new base. Kate moved her course to the Cambridge Business School, which meant her visa could transfer more easily than moving to the one in Oxford, and I got to pursue my dream of a Cambridge education in teacher training.

Plus, it was where we'd met and fallen in love.

So, I tapped into my trust fund and bought us a little cottage in the city centre, equidistant from the University, Kate's school and the river; because we were both still rowing, obviously.

'Babe,' she called out from the living room, 'do you think it's cheating to buy the fries tonight instead of making them?'

I headed in the direction of her voice to find her sitting on the floor surrounded with the food charts she'd been writing when she had time. Because Kate's days now revolved around cooking and testing new recipes; the successful ones of which would be sold in the Lobster Roll restaurant she planned to open next summer.

That's right, I wasn't the only one following my dream.

The only downside for her was that she still missed her family, even though my mother had practically adopted her as a fifth child. But, as a surprise, I was flying her parents over next week. Or her mum, because her dad refused to get on a plane, so her cousin Vinny was coming in his place *'to check me out'*. I'd already enlisted Olly's help to ensure the experience would go as smoothly as possible.

'No, babe. It's not cheating. No one will know.' I peered down at the card she was holding, the one with the recipe for the lobster rolls she'd made at Christmas. 'You're making these tonight?'

'Yeah, among other things.'

'Best make double if Hector and Al are coming.'

'I'd planned to.' She chuckled, tipping her chin up to mine for a kiss, and I willingly obliged.

She went back to the cards, and I stood there staring down at her as she flicked through them, wondering how I'd got so lucky.

I might not have won the Boat Race, but I'd definitely come away with the biggest prize.

Her.

Acknowledgements

The conversation went like this . . .

'Hey, Valentine, is your mom around? I need to ask her something.'

The question wasn't about her being my agent, but somehow two days later Georgana *was* my agent, and I wouldn't be writing this today nor would you, lovely readers, have ~~read~~ devoured and loved this book without her. I'm so indebted to her for this opportunity, along with my wonderful editor at Penguin Michael Joseph, Hannah Smith, who is almost as obsessed with these characters as I am.

It was a busy year, and I wouldn't have managed half of what I did without my lovely assistant, Taylor, who runs my online life far smoother and with much more capability than I'd ever be able to. She also owns a wonderful little romance bookstore in Wilmington, North Carolina, so if you're ever in the area please pop in and give her a hug (and buy some romance books).

My wonderful readers, there's not a chance I'd be here today doing a job I utterly adore without you and all the belief you had in me. You make such a difference to my days with your posts, outpourings of love and messages about the Luluverse, and everyone who hangs out in the Jupiter Reeves Fan Club. I am so grateful to all of you whether you're new or you're a ride or die. I appreciate all the support and will never take it for granted.

Becka, for listening to my 17,891 hours of voice notes, generally talking me through all the panic about rowing being way too niche and how no one will like it. Thank you for being the first to read *Oar With Friends*, and loving it.

To my puppy, I know you love the walks and the hours of swimming in the Thames, but honestly, we could have probably done a few different routes if I hadn't wanted to watch all the rowers pass by every morning.

Charlie, for all the wine.

And finally, to my sister, Sarah, I'm so happy you read this and loved it. I love you.

**READ ON FOR A SNEAK
PEEK OF THE NEXT BOOK
IN THE OXBRIDGE SERIES:**
YOU FLOAT MY BOAT

WHICH BOOK WILL YOU READ NEXT?

1. Charlie

Violet Brooks was officially late.

I'd already been warned by her brother that she would be, which is why I'd arrived a quarter of an hour after the time I'd given her, but that was forty-five minutes ago.

I checked my watch again; it didn't make the hands move any quicker. Neither had drumming my fingers against the table, or tapping my foot, or glancing at the door every two seconds.

The condensation slid down my pint of soda water. Even though it was freezing outside, and snow was beginning to fall thickly, the fire I was sitting beside made the Blue Oar seem positively tropical. It was also quieter in here than usual seeing as it was technically still the Christmas holidays, but by the weekend the place would once again be heaving with students gearing up for the new term.

I glanced out of the window, where there was still no sign of Violet, so I picked my phone up and typed out some formulas I'd been thinking about for my physics paper – may as well not completely waste my time sitting here.

I was deep in thought about all possible solutions of $F = -kX$, when a flurry of white snowflakes whooshed through the air as the doors flung open. The Christmas decorations, yet to be taken down from the ceiling, blew around and barely hung on by their single silvery threads. The air cleared to reveal a girl standing on the threshold of the pub, and the doors slammed shut behind her. Her bright blue eyes scanned around the pub, widening as they landed on me.

'Chazzle!'

The fluffy emerald-green coat, which a poor Muppet had been skinned for, had already been shucked off her shoulders by the time she arrived at the table.

The scarf came next, metres and metres of multicoloured cashmere, that looked more like a blanket sufficient enough to keep a family of five warm. I stood as she yanked off her large, navy knitted hat with a giant pink bobble on the end of it and dropped into the chair opposite.

'Sorry, sorry, overslept.'

Overslept?

I certainly wasn't a fan of early mornings, but it was two in the afternoon.

'God, it's bloody boiling in here,' Violet exclaimed, and proceeded to remove more layers of clothing; this time a black polo neck to reveal a tight white vest, and I briefly wondered if maybe she'd been wearing it in bed and thrown on the nearest items of clothing she could find before running here. I pushed that thought away only for her tits to squash together as her arms crossed and she pulled the neck of the jumper over her head, finally freeing herself from the confines of cashmere.

Staring at a girl's breasts was a big no-no, staring at my best friend's sister's tits currently snuggled into a green lace bra was absolutely forbidden under any circumstance.

Long caramel curls, the colour of my golden retriever, Magic, tumbled over her shoulders. Except the bottom inch looked like it had been dipped in purple paint – violet paint – contrasting with the deep azure of her eyes, ringed in navy, and the rosy flush of her cheeks.

Finally, she sat back and looked at me and the whirlwind she'd walked in with calmed, but in less than a second she sprang up from her chair.

'Sorry, I didn't hug you hello.'

I was still yet to say a word and found myself pulled into a hot embrace, as she pressed hard against me. She was raised on her tiptoes as her arms wrapped around my neck. Her lips brushed against my cheek and the scent of dark violets and woody amber invaded my nasal passages, making my chest tighten.

'Well, Chazzle, long time no see.' She grinned, picking up my pint of soda and taking a massive gulp. 'Can't wait to hear what you summoned me for. Huey, wouldn't tell me. Have you been working out, you look bigger. How's training?'

I blinked, staring as I tried to make sense of the staccato firing of words before a broad grin spread across my face.

'Violet?'

'Yes.' She finally paused her ramble.

'Would you like a drink?'

'Yes, please,' she replied, picking up mine again and downing the rest of the soda. 'Maybe something a little more alcoholic than water this time.'

I stood up and went to the bar, ordering a glass of Pinot for her and a pint for me. I had planned to cut alcohol out until after the Boat Race, but in hindsight this conversation would probably need it. While I waited to pay, my eyes found themselves wandering over in her direction.

The last time I saw Violet Brooks she'd been a gangly seventeen-year-old. It was the summer after our first year had ended – Brooks, Oz and I had been at Brooks' parents' house in Somerset, where we all chilled out after the Henley Regatta, sleeping, swimming and eating for a week before we'd left for Greece with Oz.

Violet had been packing for a year abroad – she'd been a tornado spinning through the rooms, leaving chaos and piles of books in her wake.

Now, sat here, her long legs were crossed underneath her, and I peered down at her shoes – Nike high-tops. At six foot four, it was unusual to meet a girl where a hug didn't result in neck strain from them clinging on to me, but Violet had clearly inherited the Brooks' family height.

Eighteen months and she'd both completely changed and hardly changed at all. The chaos was still there, but the softness in her features had hardened a little, turning her from a pretty teenager to a beautiful woman.

Tapping my bank card, I walked back to the table and placed the drinks on it before settling into my seat.

Violet's eyes reminded me of a twilight sky as she spied the wine. 'Mmm, thank you.'

'You're welcome.'

'So.' She sipped, put her glass down and leaned back in her chair. I forced my eyes straight ahead instead of her chest where her arms were now crossed, 'what's the emergency?'

Ah, yes, the reason we were here, and the reason I'd sent Violet not one but four messages, and another two to Brooks begging him to get her to reply, before she *finally* replied.

'Didn't Brooks tell you anything?'

She shook her head. 'No, Hugo is incredibly annoying that way.'

I sighed.

I'd kind of hoped he would have done, then I'd have to explain as little as possible because Violet just *got it* and would agree to my request without further need for clarification. It would also save me from reliving the worst moment of my life; the day my heart had shattered so violently it couldn't be mended or glued back together over time.

It had imploded into dust.

The day I vowed never to love again.

'You haven't been over to the house,' I started, hoping a little small talk would ease the anxiety ball in the pit of my stomach, the way it did whenever I thought about Evie Waters.

Violet leaned forward, the movement forcing a thick lock of hair to fall over her eye, which she pushed away. Her slender wrists rested on the table and I noticed a tiny, hand-drawn stack of books on the inside of her left arm, directly above her pulse.

'I have, only you've not been there. It was very handy that the three of you were on river duty every Saturday morning. Huey's bath is wasted on him.' She smirked.

The pint glass stopped halfway to my lips, and I put it back down. 'Have you been breaking into our house when we're not there so you can have a bath?'

'No, of course not.' Violet shook her head. 'I have a key.'

I stared at her, my frown deepening. I knew that Oz would never have given anyone a key to the house we shared with Brooks, just like I knew that Brooks would never have given his sister a key without asking us.

I was also struggling to understand how the comprehensive security system I'd set up hadn't been triggered, because there was a hidden camera angled on the front door and it was supposed to alert us of anyone who approached. Not to mention the alarm we set every time we left, along with motion sensors in the garden.

Was it overkill for three students? Probably, even if one was Oz and his billions. But I'd been bored, and it had only taken me a couple of hours on a Tuesday morning after we'd moved in and finished unpacking. Master of security systems was another skill to stick on my resume, at the very least. Or maybe not, it seemed.

'But how did you get the key?'

'I borrowed Huey's,' she shrugged. 'And copied it.'

I barked out a loud laugh. I wasn't sure what I was laughing at more – the look on Brooks' face when he discovered his sister had stolen his house key, or the idea of Violet having a bath in our house every Saturday when we were in London . . . no . . . nope . . . absolutely not. My brain ground to a halt for the second time; the image of Violet naked and wet in our house was not something that belonged in my head.

'You could just ask.'

'Where's the fun in that?' She winked. 'It wouldn't annoy Huey nearly as much. I don't have a bath in my room, not sure what I'm going to do for one this term now you three have finished your punishments.'

'Which college are you in?'

'St Anne's.' She picked up her wine and sipped, the burgundy liquid matching the glossy paint on her fingernails. 'Come on, Charlie. Don't keep a girl waiting, why have I been summoned?'

I drummed my fingers against my pint glass again. Thinking about it, maybe I was being stupid. Overreacting.

I could handle seeing my ex-girlfriend; I was a grown man and it had been four years, give or take. But then I remembered the anger that had ripped through me when I found out she'd been assigned to my philosophy tutorials and decided otherwise.

'I need you to be my fake girlfriend for the rest of the term.'

Violet held my stare. To her credit she didn't flinch, nor did she burst out laughing; the only indication she'd heard was the tiny crease in the centre of her forehead. She stared until it dawned on me she wanted further explanation.

'My ex-girlfriend is joining my philosophy class, and I don't want her to think I'm interested in her again.'

Out loud, to someone who didn't know the history of Evie Waters, this plan sounded so stupid. I couldn't blame Violet when the tiny crease on her forehead deepened.

'Why can't you just tell her you're not? And why do you assume that she's interested in you?'

Both very good and valid questions. If only the answer was as simple. The answer was more than I cared to admit, because Evie had been the love of my life and I knew it wouldn't take long for her to wrap me around her finger again. She would pull me back.

She was the drug of choice for my addict heart.

She was equally as toxic.

'Evie and I were together during sixth form. She cheated on me and we broke up. When I started at Oxford, she was here too and we briefly got back together, but then she met someone else.' My fist clenched so tightly cramp shot along my arm. 'I've managed to avoid her for three years, but for some reason she always seems to think she can get me back. And this term she's joining my philosophy class. I figured if she knew I had a girlfriend then she wouldn't talk to me.'

There, that was enough explanation without revealing the sheer panic I felt at the thought of being in the same room as Evie again. I might be strong enough to bench press 180kgs, but I was no match for Evie Waters, no matter how hard I tried.

I'd never told anyone that the reason I changed my number in first year was because she wouldn't stop texting me.

Violet sat back, pulling the stem of her glass to the edge of the table and shifted it side to side between her fingers as she looked at me.

'Charlie, do you want to make her jealous?'

I shook my head so hard my neck cracked. 'No.'

'You don't want her back?'

'Fuck, no. Never.'

'So you want me to be your bodyguard,' Violet began, a smirk cresting the corner of her plump lip, 'I'm Kevin Costner and you're my Whitney Houston?'

I wasn't sure how I felt about being called someone's Whitney Houston, but I shrugged anyway.

'Why can't you say no to her?'

'Because . . .' I sighed again, 'because she has this way of making me do what she wants. It's like I'm under her spell, against my will.'

Violet's head tilted slightly; I couldn't tell if she was curious or looking at me with pity. Either way, the silence stretched on for far longer than I was comfortable with, made worse by the thoughts I knew were playing out in her head, even if I didn't know exactly what those thoughts were.

I could probably guess.

'Violet, I'll pay you. Name your price.'

She grinned wide, her smile lighting up her face. The heat of the fire had deepened the flush in her cheeks, and the reflection of the flames danced in her eyes.

'I'm not going to take your money, silly. I'll do it for free. It'll be perfect experience for the Dramatic Society, we're doing *Twelfth Night* this year. I'm hoping to get the lead.'

'Oh,' I replied, wondering why her response felt so anti-climactic, and what the Drama Society had to do with anything. 'What were you thinking about then?'

'What a girlfriend of yours would look like. I need to fit the part.'

I laughed, and the ball of anxiety stopped bouncing. 'I think you fit just as you are.'

'We'll see. I like to throw myself all in.'

'Are you studying drama?' I asked, because I realized I didn't know.

'English. But I joined the Dramatic Society.' Her eyes widened, *dramatically*. 'And you're studying philosophy? Do you like Nietzsche?'

'I'm studying physics, actually. But I have physics and philosophy this term.'

'Oh, what's that?'

'We try to answer the complexities of the universe.'

'Oh. Good luck with that.'

'Thank you.' I grinned back, picking up my pint.

'How are we going to do this then?' She waved her hand between the two of us.

I scratched along my jaw. I'd been so fixated on having Violet be my fake girlfriend that I hadn't actually taken any time to consider *how* she'd be my fake girlfriend.

'Um . . . well, I guess you'll have to meet me after class.'

'Yes, obviously. And . . . ?'

'And what?'

'What else?'

'What do you mean?'

'Charlie, if we're in a relationship, it's going to consist of more than me meeting you after class. What about handholding? Kissing? Touching? If we're going to do it, we have to do it properly.'

I coughed up the air which stuck in my throat. 'Kissing?'

Violet leaned forward, her fingers laced together and propped under her chin. 'Yes, Charlie, kissing. You need to be convincing. We're not courting in a Jane Austen novel.'

Shit.

The kissing never occurred to me. Or touching of any kind. I assumed that Evie would see us together and that would be enough. Maybe I needed to think this through more. I'd assured Brooks that nothing would happen between Violet and me, yet kissing didn't quite fall into that category. Maybe I could stipulate I meant no tongues.

No tongues would be acceptable. I hoped.

'Okay.' Violet slapped her palms on the table and pushed herself to standing, 'while you think on that, I'm going to the loo.'

The entire time we'd been talking, the Blue Oar's navy doors had been opening every couple of minutes as new patrons came in from the cold. Every time a small gust of wind had blown past us causing the flames to crackle and spit in annoyance. I'd stopped getting distracted by it after Violet had sat down and commanded my full attention, whether she meant to or not. I'd been sucked into her orbit the second she arrived.

I was still thinking about how I'd explain kissing her to Brooks, when another burst of air flurried past me. The temperature dropped immediately, much more than any other gust before it.

I glanced at the offender. My heart stopped dead. My stomach curled in on itself.

Offender was too kind of a word.

Evie Waters.

If I didn't know better, I'd swear she had a tracker on me. But I had secured my phone enough to know that wasn't possible. She didn't. She just had a sixth sense for where I was going to be and when – like she'd always had.

Like a bad smell following me wherever I went.

No, it was worse than that. It was like being summoned by a demon.

She'd once been the most beautiful girl I'd ever met. She still was.

Aside from a handful of times when I'd seen her outside my tutorials or walking my way in the library, done a swift about-turn and sprinted through the stacks, I hadn't seen her in 562 days. Hadn't seen her up-close, but nothing had changed.

Her hair was so dark and shiny I'd once joked I could see my reflection in it. It still was. Straighter than an arrow, falling in a sharp line to her even sharper jaw; there was not a hair out of place. Even the snow falling outside didn't appear to have touched her.

I wish I didn't know she woke up like that, each strand falling perfectly where it was supposed to be, like it daren't do otherwise. Or the way her apple cheeks were always the same shade of pink as her lips, and her eyelashes as black and thick as her soul. There had been a time when she'd only have to bat them at me and I'd fall over myself to do her bidding.

The thing I hated most of all though was the way my heart was now thumping hard against my sternum and my dick twitched. Like neither of them remembered what she'd done. Or maybe my dick did, and that's why he suddenly wanted to give her his full attention. Even worse was the way she knew what was happening, because the second her eyes landed on mine, I knew she was in here looking for me and from the slow, sly curve of her lip, she knew I knew.

I'd all but forgotten exactly why I was in the Blue Oar on a snowy Wednesday afternoon in January until a large unidentified lump collapsed into my lap. Unless it was the asteroid I'd just been praying for.

Except asteroids didn't kiss.

The taste of the Pinot I'd bought Violet was still fresh on her tongue as it slowly slid against mine, licking me with as much heat as the flames next to us. I was so shocked I did nothing to stop it. I didn't want to stop it, especially when she moaned softly because then all I could think about was how perfectly her arse fitted into my lap, and how I liked the way her fingers were pushing into my hair. My dick definitely liked it.

'Come on, babe. I've had enough of being out of bed, let's go back,' she whispered against my lips, and my brain short circuited.

The diamond-bright twinkle in her eyes didn't explain what had just happened, however, but I found my fingers were twisting around the violet ends of her hair nonetheless, as her lips fell on to mine again.

I was beginning to question my sanity and my memory when a small, deliberate cough to my left reminded me exactly what was happening and why.

Violet's body twisted in my lap as she peered up at our intruder. 'Can I help you?'

Evie replied with a smile that didn't stretch to her eyes, 'No, you can't. I saw Charlie and came to say hello. I'm an old friend.'

Violet turned to me, a genuine smile beaming across her face, in total contrast to the mask my face had frozen into. I couldn't find the words to explain what was happening; I didn't know why Violet was smiling. Maybe she didn't realize she was in the presence of evil. But then her head turned back to Evie.

'Are you sure? He doesn't seem to know *you*.'

Evie ignored Violet, her eyes boring into me like lasers. 'Charlie?'

Violet looked at me again trying to ascertain whether I was in fact going to say hello – I wasn't – then flicked back to Evie. 'Strange, I've known Charlie a very long time, and I've never heard of you.'

But Evie wasn't paying the slightest bit of attention to anything Violet said. 'Charlie . . . are you really going to ignore me?'

Violet shifted on my lap, and I felt her draw in a breath.

'It would seem that way, wouldn't it? Old friend or not, you should try and frown less, it won't help that line you have right there.' She reached out and prodded Evie's impeccably smooth forehead. 'I can recommend some good cream if you'd like,' Violet continued sweetly, 'but you probably need to get Botox on that before it gets worse.'

My eyes widened so much they burned. For the first time ever, Evie Waters was speechless.

Violet eased off my lap, and the air cooled along my thighs giving me some respite from her body. I was still too much in a state of shock to find it amusing at how she towered over Evie. In the same haphazard manner as she removed them, Violet pulled on her hat, and scarf. It was the Muppet green coat contrasting with Evie's signature black that jolted me back to myself as I stood, only too happy to follow Violet's lead.

I picked up my pint and drained it, addressing Evie for the first time in over two years. 'Would you like our table? We're going home now.'

My fingers laced with Violet's as we walked out of the pub, leaving Evie in exactly the same spot. The bitter adrenalin coursing through my veins was soon replaced by a level of satisfaction I'd never felt before.

'Fuck.' It was the only word I could manage. It didn't even occur to me to ask how Violet knew who Evie was.

'I think I totally nailed the role of your girlfriend, even if I do say so myself,' Violet giggled, as we walked into the cold and the doors shut behind us, putting back a much-needed barrier between Evie and me. She pushed her hand in the pocket of my jeans like it belonged there and looked at me, 'come on, you can walk me back to St. Anne's, but you need to put your arm around me. We have to make everyone believe this if you want her to.'

I did as instructed, walking side by side with Violet whose head was now resting on my shoulder. I hadn't been entirely sure that using her as my girlfriend would convince anyone, let alone Evie, but all my doubts had been melted away by her award-winning acting skills.

This would work perfectly.

Now I just needed to figure out how to tell Brooks I'd been making out with his sister. With tongues.